ELT Review
General Editor: Chris Kennedy

The Development of ELT: the Dunford Seminars 1978-1993

Editors:

GERRY ABBOTT and MIKE BEAUMONT
University of Manchester

THE UNIVERSITY OF BIRMINGHAM
Centre for English Language Studies
Westmere, Edgbaston
Birmingham B15 2TT
United Kingdom

First published 1997 by
Prentice Hall Europe ELT
Campus 400, Spring Way
Maylands Avenue
Hemel Hempstead
Hertfordshire, HP2 7EZ
A division of Prentice Hall International

Cover by Denis Holland Design

Typeset in 11 on 12 ITC Century
By Microset Graphics Ltd

**Printed and bound in Great Britain by
Redwood Books, Trowbridge, Wiltshire**

A catalogue record for this book is available from
the British Library

ISBN 0-13-741562-1

 5   4   3   2   1
99 98 97

English Language Teaching Review is a series of monographs and thematic collections of
articles in the field of ELT/Applied Linguistics, under the general editorship of Chris Kennedy.

Correspondence on editorial matters and proposals for the series should be addressed to:
Chris Kennedy
Centre for English Language Studies
University of Birmingham
Westmere
Edgbaston Park Road
BIRMINGHAM B15 2TT
UK

(Tel: 0121 414 5695/6; Fax: 0121 414 3298; e-mail cjkennedy@bham.ac.uk)

Contents

Foreword   vii
CHRISTOPHER BRUMFIT

General Introduction: The Meanings of 'Development'   1
MIKE BEAUMONT AND GERRY ABBOTT

PART 1   DEVELOPMENTS IN ELT 1978–84   12
MIKE BEAUMONT

1.0   The Communicative Curriculum   22
MIKE BEAUMONT

1.1   Communicative needs profiles (1979)   23
ROGER HAWKEY

1.2   Materials production (1979)   31
JOHN MOORE

1.3   Approaches to curriculum design (1984)   35
JANET MAW

**1.4   Educational technology and curriculum
        renewal (1984)**   37
MARTIN PHILLIPS

2.0   Communicative Methodology   42
MIKE BEAUMONT

**2.1   The three dualities, or 'new wine in old
        bottles' (1980)**   43
ROBERT O'NEILL

2.2   Communication with traditional materials (1980)   45
BARRIE WATSON

2.3   Why 'communicative'? (1982)   46
MIKE BREEN

2.4   The relationship between teaching and learning (1984)   48
DICK ALLWRIGHT

3.0 Evaluation 52

MIKE BEAUMONT

3.1 Evaluating communicative performance (1979) 53

IAN SEATON

3.2 The project approach: the human dimension (1981) 58

PATRICK EARLY

3.3 Extracts from consultancy reports (1981) 59
   a: Sudan: some key ELT concepts
   b: Somalia: textbook project

ALAN MOUNTFORD

3.4 Evaluation of curricula and syllabuses (1984) 67

CHARLES ALDERSON

4.0 Teacher Training 72

MIKE BEAUMONT

4.1 Some problems (1982) 73

SEMINAR PARTICIPANTS

4.2 Teacher training: nature and choices (1982) 75

PETER STREVENS

4.3 A case study: course design proposals for teacher training at the National Language Institute (INL), Angola (1982) 78

MARGARET TARNER AND ANDREW McNAB

4.4 Teacher training courses: design and implementation (1983) 82

KEITH MORROW

PART 2 ELT IN DEVELOPMENT 1985–92 92

GERRY ABBOTT

5.0 Values and Costs 100

GERRY ABBOTT

5.1 Investing in education (1992) 101

ROGER IREDALE

5.2 Economics and ELT (1992) 106

ALASDAIR MACBEAN

5.3 Evaluating the effects of ELT (1991)   116

DESMOND NUTTALL

5.4a The value of ELT in development projects (1992)   119

JOHN TURNER

5.4b Towards a synthesis of outcomes (1992)   122

ANDY THOMAS

6.0 Administering ELT Aid   125

GERRY ABBOTT

6.1 The English language as aid (1986)   126

ROGER IREDALE

**6.2 ELT in a fisheries training project:
       work in progress (1985)**   128

KATHRYN BOARD, ROBIN CORCOS, JOHN HOLMES, OLIVER HUNT, STUART MATTHEWS,
MIKE SMITH AND ANDREW THOMAS

6.3 Project administration (1989)   131

MYRA HARRISON AND HECTOR MUNRO

**6.4a Managing change in communication skills
       projects (1991)**   134

MAGGIE JO ST JOHN AND DAVID CLARKE

6.4b How a project can break down (1990)   137

PATRICIA AHRENS

7.0 Appropriate Methodology   140

GERRY ABBOTT

7.1 A debate on appropriate methodology (1986)   141

ROGER BOWERS AND HENRY WIDDOWSON

**7.2 Overseas students' views on language learning
       in the UK (1986)**   145

ALAN TONKYN

**7.3 Teaching large classes and training for
       sustainability (1990)**   149

HYWEL COLEMAN

7.4 Sustaining ELT in normal circumstances (1990)   159

GERRY ABBOTT

8.0   ELT, Culture and Development   161
GERRY ABBOTT

8.1   Socio-economic roles and ELT (1991)   162
JOHN BURKE AND ROD BOLITHO

**8.2a Attitudes to language and learning in Britain   164
      and the Arab world (1985)**
CLIVE HOLES

**8.2b Cross-cultural constraints on sustainability: 167
      a view from South India (1989)**
ROBERT BELLARMINE

8.3   Linguistic imperialism (1991)   168
ROBERT PHILLIPSON

8.4   ELT and development: projects and power (1991) 170
ROGER BOWERS

PART 3   LOOKING INTO THE DISTANCE (1993)   180
GERRY ABBOTT AND MIKE BEAUMONT

9.0   Language Issues in Distance Education   185
GERRY ABBOTT AND MIKE BEAUMONT

9.1   The logistics of distance language teaching   186
JOHN TURNER

9.2   Distance learning for non-formal education   193
TONY DODDS

**9.3   Cognitive styles and the design of instructional 198
      materials**
EUGENE SADLER-SMITH

**9.4a The practicalities of running a distance learning 208
      programme**
GILLIAN WALSH

**9.4b Teacher education and empowerment: 213
      a view from a distance**
JULIAN EDGE AND MELANIE ELLIS

9.5   Where do we go from here?   218
RICHARD WEBBER

Bibliography   224

Foreword

Christopher Brumfit
Centre for Language in Education
University of Southampton

In 1978 the British Council inaugurated a series of annual seminars, held initially at Dunford House in Sussex, each of which explored a significant theme in current ELT. I am delighted to be invited to introduce this collection of papers from these seminars, which became significant events in the calendar of British Council ELT professionals. Although I never belonged to an organisation rich enough to pay the fee required of outsiders for participation, I was lucky enough to attend parts of a number of seminars as an outside speaker. Consequently I have been able to 'spot-check' activity in seminars ranging from the first (which coincided with Ian Botham's explosion of runs and wickets as England defeated Pakistan's cricketers) to the Alston Hall, Lancashire seminar in 1992 (which accompanied Pakistan's defeat of England). In this period, as the editors note, the emphasis shifted from concerns with ELT as a vibrant, and apparently unproblematic teaching activity, to concerns with ELT in the development process – as some saw it, from autonomous ELT to ELT as a servant of other agendas.

Any teaching is necessarily the servant of other agendas, for learning is a means to an end (though 'understanding' may be an entirely desirable end in itself). The security of the late 1970s had to be illusory, if only because of the changed economic role of Britain. The shift of economic power to oil-producing states had assisted a major demand for ELT expertise as educational modernisation accompanied economic, political and religious ambitions pursued by increasingly independent countries. Functions and notions, languages for specific purposes, needs analyses, interlanguage, communicative expectations of all kinds enriched and challenged both researchers and teachers. Publishers and writers, critics and adherents alike, were excited by the atmosphere of expansion, creativity and change.

In contrast, the 1980s appeared to be a period of consolidation. Innovation centred on methodologies and materials, task-based learning for teachers, classroom interaction patterns for researchers. Professionally, the generation of ELT specialists who had trained in conventional teacher education programmes and taught in formal state education in developing countries became greatly outnumbered by the newer generation of those who had trained via specialist EFL diplomas, particularly the RSA, and taught in private sector schools for young adults. Academic interest had shifted from schools to higher education during the 1970s, and (as far as ELT was concerned) never really returned to schools. School-level ESL in Britain, let alone in India or Africa, seemed far away from the concerns of the most innovative textbooks and the latest methodological panaceas.

Yet there was something of a paradox, for many of the ideas of communicative language teaching were derived from general pedagogy (use of groupwork for example) or from the second-language experience of school-level practitioners. But the market no longer lay with primary or secondary schooling, and the tertiary pipers called the methodological tune.

One effect of this was that the one worldwide organisation to have a strong remit for ELT, the British Council, had both to keep its feet on the ground, and keep up with the pace of innovation and the ever-increasing expectations of those who wanted effective English for their advanced students, and wanted it now! The Dunford seminars are a record of the Council's efforts to be simultaneously innovative, critical, relevant and practical in a period of shifting professional expectations.

Nor is this all, for it was not just professional expectations that shifted. The governmental context for independent state-funded bodies like the Council, the BBC – and indeed universities – shifted radically as the government redefined its relationship with the welfare state tradition. Enforced concentration on free-market values reduced dedicated funding for activities which would not provide measurable returns on a fairly short timescale. ELT was seen not just as a cultural and political asset, but as a marketable asset, continuing a trend that has been observable since the early 1970s. A much greater split developed than in the past between the ELT market and ELT in development.

Educational values (necessarily long term and difficult to quantify) were in constant competition with consumer choice. Expertise was pulled (some would say distorted) by the need to attract the maximum return from customers. Consumers understandably want rapid success with minimum outlay and effort. Effective language learning need not be nasty, brutish and long, but the temptation to proclaim that it would be enjoyable, British and short confronted many in ELT, in both public and private sectors, whose careers were thrust unexpectedly into a crude, insensitive and recession-dominated market-place. Government funders appeared more suspicious of professionals (whether doctors, lawyers, teachers, civil servants, British Council officers, or academics) than they had been when the economy had been less of a threat. Inevitably, all government-funded bodies steered a delicate path, avoiding as best they could five major temptations. First was short-termism (which might get quick funding but eroded the structures on which their quality work was based). Second was excessive self-promotion (which alienated much-needed collaborators). Third was resentment (which poisoned motivation); fourth, resistance (which might alienate funders, usually government); and fifth, total acquiescence (which denied the hard-gained expertise that *knew* the need for long- and mid-term strategies, for respected and highly motivated staff, and for an honest reputation). Such were the unenviable temptations and pressures, each with its own disadvantage. No organisation could manage this difficult task perfectly, but the Council's interest in English survived as a major element of its activity, and the series of seminars continues.

Thus policy for ELT in the 1980s and 1990s has to be seen in the context of a general insecurity among professionals, whose knowledge and trust-worthiness has been unexpectedly doubted. The commentary provided by these papers has to be seen within this wider background, as a tribute to the maintenance of professional values and a principled and critical commitment to practice.

Such a context enables us to make more sense of the emphases on accountability, evaluation and 'value for money', but also of the concern for human resources, for aid as well as markets, and ultimately for values as well as value. These papers reflect a many-sided argument, partly technical, partly practical, partly philosophical – but it is an ongoing argument with many of the issues of principle as yet unresolved. This collection of papers is an invitation to continue the debate.

Preface

Our remit as editors in this volume was to review the reports on the first sixteen of the annual Dunford seminars (1976–1993) and abstract from the mass of lively material a set of samples illustrative not only of major movements in British ELT but also of issues likely to be of continuing importance to the profession. It seemed to us that by and large the subject-matter of the first fifteen seminars fell into two sets: the first seven focused upon the narrower concerns of ELT (syllabuses, methodology, evaluation, and teacher training), while the following eight switched to a wide-angle lens, as it were, to examine the literally global context of the aid programmes served by ODA funded/British Council administered ELT personnel. This enabled us to divide our labour accordingly. The one remaining seminar in the period under review set the lens at infinity and examined Distance Education. We therefore end this volume with a selection of the proceedings of that 1993 seminar.

For lack of space we have had to omit a large number of useful contributions, in particular many case studies that provided a wealth of detail on ELT work in progress around the world; we have also tried to keep our introductory material brief. In sequencing our selections we have for the sake of coherence sometimes departed from chronological order. For the sake of the record, however, the year is shown after each title.

Throughout this volume, ODA stands for Overseas Development Administration; this is the Government department now known as DFID (Department for International Development).

The Editors

Acknowledgements

The editors would like to acknowledge the assistance given by Dr Richard Webber of the British Council in supervising this project. They also wish to thank the following for their assistance in this publication: Julie Brett, the British Council, Manchester; librarians at the School of Education and John Rylands Library, University of Manchester; and all the staff of Central Typing Services at the British Council, Manchester.

General Introduction: The Meanings of 'Development'

Mike Beaumont
Gerry Abbott

The entry under the headword *development* in the 1944 edition of the Shorter Oxford English Dictionary begins as follows:

1 A gradual unfolding; a fuller working out of the details of anything. . .
2 Evolution, the product of a natural force, energy or new form of matter 1794.
3 The growth of what is in the germ 1844.
4 Growth from within 1836.

The rest of the entry deals with the uses of this noun in mathematics, photography, and music. The entry for the verb does allow for people who develop theories, photographs or themes but does not record that people may develop other people; the only other transitive sense given is: To cause to grow (what exists in the germ) to evolve 1839.

For the SOED at that time the semantic core of the word *development* was the concept 'growth from within': a person or a society might intransitively develop, but neither was considered capable of being developed by anyone else. More recently, however, transitive uses of *develop* have proliferated. The Collins Cobuild English Language Dictionary records a total of ten. As well as developing ideas, photographs and musical themes, people can now develop businesses, land, habits, skills, illnesses, machines and stories. Concepts of 'transitive' social development are found somewhat earlier. The term *development economics*, for example, is largely an outcome of post-war plans for international aid, notably President Truman's undertaking to make 'the benefits of America's scientific and industrial progress available for the improvement and growth of under-developed areas'.

In this paper we shall examine how in recent years the noun *development* has been used within the field of English Language Teaching and its associated disciplines, and within the broader, global context of educational and economic development. For the sake of convenience we shall use the labels *intransitive* and *transitive* to characterise respectively 'growth from within' and 'growth by intervention' as two distinct concepts of linguistic, educational and social development.

'Development' in ELT

It seems true to say that over the last twenty years or so the use of the terms *develop* and *development* in English language teaching, and related fields, has become more frequent and more refined. A scan through the contents and index pages of some key methodological texts of the 1970s reveals few references to the words. Rivers and Temperley (1978: 212) recommend six stages of reading development to help students develop progressively their ability to read more, and more fluently and independently, materials of increasing difficulty and complexity, and they suggest suitable activities for reinforcing the developing reading skill. We have here both a transitive and intransitive use of the verb. In the first case, it is the students who are, in the words of the SOED, 'causing their reading ability to grow'. In the second, it is the reading skill itself that is 'gradually unfolding'. The teacher's role, it seems, is to help the learners to develop their skills or to help those skills to develop. Whether or not these two expressions amount to the same thing, in neither case is the teacher said to be developing the learner. During this period parallel use of the term '*vocabulary development*' can be observed.

Also becoming current were notions of *syllabus development* (see for example Shaw 1977) though the sense here was very much a transitive one, syllabus designers being responsible for replacing, extending or improving existing syllabuses in the light of more functional approaches to language description. Dakin (1973: 5) uses *development* to refer to the third stage of what he calls the 'whole' teaching process. Preceded by *presentation* and *practice* and followed by *testing*, it is the stage: 'when the teacher has to relax control over the pupil's performance. . .(and when) as far as organising and developing his own utterance is concerned, he is largely on his own'.

Dakin's use here is similar to what later came to be known as the production stage in the so-called PPP methodological model. Again, the teacher's role does not seem to be a transitive one.

In the 1980s, concepts of development begin to assume greater prominence and acquire greater precision. The primary influence on this trend was increasing work in the areas of first and second language acquisition. Ellis (1985) has three entries in his index: *developmental errors, developmental principles* and '*development' in language acquisition*. In the first case he is referring to the growing realisation that the longitudinal study of learners' errors could throw considerable light on the process of second language acquisition. References to such notions as the learner's 'developmental sequence' and 'the natural order of development' are frequent (ibid: 52). Ellis's discussion of the second entry refers to Wode's (1980) proposal that:

> language acquisition manifests 'developmental principles' which he (Wode) defines in terms of the linguistic properties of the target language. . .(that is). . . the order of development is determined by the nature of the linguistic rules that have to be acquired (1985: 190).

Here the notion of *development* is discussed within the wider contexts of language universals and development psychology. In much of this early debate on second language acquisition, little distinction is made between language acquisition and language development. However, in his discussion of the third entry, Ellis examines the distinction made by Chomsky between *acquisition* and *development*.

> 'Development' is real-time learning of a language. . .
> 'Acquisition' is language learning unaffected by maturation and is dependent entirely on the learner's language faculty (1985: 197).

Ellis notes that the two terms are closely related to Chomsky's earlier and better-known pair of concepts, *competence* and *performance*.

> 'Acquisition' is the evolving linguistic competence of the child. 'Development' is the product of maturation; as the child's cognitive abilities develop, so does his ability to perform his competence (1985: 197).

Here is not the appropriate place to discuss the distinction in detail. For us, the significance of this refinement of the term *development* lies in the implication that environment plays an important role in the learner's progress in the language. As Berko Gleason (1993: vi) puts it:

> Since development is always the result of the interaction between innate capacities and environmental forces, we take an interactive perspective, one that takes into account both the biological endowment that makes language possible and the environmental factors that foster development.

The index of Ellis's most recent (1994) survey suggests that the use of *development* in second language acquisition is still increasing, since we now have seven references. The distinction between 'development' and 'acquisition' is further discussed, as is the notion of 'developmental errors'. There is no reference to 'developmental principles' but included are the additional terms 'developmental axis', 'developmental factors', 'developmental patterns', and 'developmental sequences'. In essence, this proliferation of terms represents a continuing refinement through research and speculation of the study of second language acquisition.

The impact on English language teaching of research and debate in second language acquisition has been considerable. The realisation that language learning is much more developmental than incremental has stimulated a re-evaluation of approaches to syllabus design, introducing the concepts of *process* (Breen and Candlin 1980) and *procedure* (Prabhu 1983). In terms of methodology we have seen the loosening of the relationship between input and output with arguments for exposing the learner to 'richer', more natural and less linguistically controlled data (e.g. authentic texts), and allowing learners much more freedom to exploit the full range of their linguistic resources in production activities, recognising that errors are inevitable, necessary, and from the teacher's point of view, diagnostically important. Indeed, in the case of some elements of grammar, evidence suggests that the teacher may have very little control over the learner's linguistic development (see Beaumont and Gallaway 1994 for an example). Finally, changing views on syllabus design and methodology have, necessarily but slowly, led to a reassessment of testing procedures. To become more 'communicative', tests have had to recognise the differences that may exist between learners' receptive and productive abilities, and to distinguish between their capacity to display knowledge and demonstrate skills. Consistent with a more learner-centred approach, there have also been significant developments in the area of self-assessment.

The sequence of these changes seems to us to be significant. The Dunford seminars addressed the issues of syllabus design, methodology and assessment in that order, and this is very much the sequence in which educational policy changes during the 1980s tended to be made – a point we will return to in the introduction to Part 1. It was only after these three topics had been debated that Dunford turned its attention to teacher education, which has seen parallel, though not so technical, refinements to the notion of development. Freeman (1989: 37) is one of a number of authorities who since the late 1980s have sought to give more meaning and significance to the idea of teacher *development*, as opposed to teacher training: '. . .within the general process of language teacher education, a valid operational distinction can be made between two functions, which I will call *training* and *development*.' He suggests that training should be seen as 'a strategy for direct intervention by the collaborator, to work on specific aspects of the teacher's teaching' (ibid: 39) while development is 'a strategy of influence and indirect intervention that works on complex integrated aspects of teaching; these aspects are idiosyncratic and individual' (ibid: 40).

Woodward (1991: 147) elaborates the distinction in the columns shown below. It is significant for our argument here how many of the criteria in the 'development' column apply equally well to the more global sense of 'development' we address in the second half of this introduction.

Teacher training	**Teacher development**
Compulsory	Voluntary
Competency based	Holistic
Short term	Long term
One-off	Ongoing
Temporary	Continual
External agenda	Internal agenda
Skill/technique and knowledge based	Awareness-based (personal growth, attitudes/insights)
Compulsory for entry to profession	Non-compulsory
Top down	Bottom up
Product weighted	Process weighted
Means you can get a job	Means you can stay interested
Done with experts	Done with peers

The notion of intervention seems to us significant. In language teaching a deeper understanding of the processes of language development has made us realise that teachers need to be less interventionist in their approach, recognising not only that learners need time and space to develop their language skills, but also that there are significant differences between what teachers teach, or think they are teaching, and what learners learn, or think they are learning. There has been a parallel (but interestingly, much slower) recognition that teacher educators also need to be less interventionist. The education of teachers for successful and continuing career development requires a more trainee-centred approach especially – and some would argue, necessarily – in the field of in-service teacher education, but equally importantly on pre-service courses. Incidentally, it is interesting to note that in a debate which now tends to use 'teacher education' as a superordinate for the combined concepts of 'training' and 'development', no parallel superordinate has emerged for the term 'trainee'.

We have seen, then, a gradual refinement in ELT of our understanding of *language development* on the one hand and *teacher development* on the other. In both cases, the use of the term is consistently intransitive. We have observed the emergence of a less interventionist role for the teacher in the language classroom, and a similar trend in teacher education. This should not be seen as limiting the respective roles of teacher and teacher educator but rather as extending them, indeed rendering them infinitely more complex, subtle and demanding. The function of the teacher/educator is not to develop the learner/trainee but to aid, influence, foster, promote their development – a notion much closer, we would argue, to the true meaning of education.

Global 'development'

Just as the focus had been shifting from the transitive to the intransitive in ELT (that is, from the concerns of teaching to the processes of learning, and even learning-to-learn) so too a similar shift had been taking place in societal development studies, the 'learner-centredness' of the classroom being matched by a growing 'people-centredness' within the wider socio-cultural context.

In the 1960s, designated in the UN as the First Development Decade, the prevailing notions of global development had been, like President Truman's, transitive and fundamentally ethnocentric: development was a process of bringing about a growth in material wealth, of modernisation, of 'catching up' with the advanced west – the assumption being that western goals were the best, and therefore suitable for all. The west would develop the rest. However, the transfer of scientific and technological know-how that had been expected to transform the productivity of the poorest countries and turn the 'have-nots' into 'haves' did little to mitigate the effects of poverty, let alone eradicate its causes. Nor did loans to the developing world produce a desirable outcome. Too often, the huge debts incurred led to a desperate need to pay them off through trade, and the only feasible exports were agricultural produce and raw materials; the growing of crops on a massive scale soon led to monoculture and other undesirable farming practices that left land degraded and rural populations ill-fed and under-employed, and the consequent urban drift led in turn to unemployment, poverty, crime and corruption. Meanwhile, the debts remained undiminished. By the time of the first Dunford seminar in 1978 there were calls for a release from this burden of debt, and some were advocating more intransitive development policies, arguing that true development was a matter not of national economic performance or of material wealth but of the 'empowerment' of the impoverished. The poor should be helped to understand fully the causes and nature of their plight; solidarity should be achieved through discussion and co-operation; and each community should itself identify priorities and be enabled to carry out its own local development plan. In this way, each group would work out a form of 'modernity' in optimum harmony with its own cultural structure. The need to respect cultural diversity has now been cogently expressed in almost all of the countries of the south – see, for instance, the contributions in Sachs (ed. 1992) – and for Verhelst (1990) it constitutes the central theme.

However, since most Third World nations are multicultural and administered largely from their capitals, their governments would probably regard such a decentralising process as at best potentially divisive and at worst positively subversive – a thorny problem indeed for any aid agency tempted to adopt a people-centred philosophy and promote cultural diversity. This fact alone has no doubt helped to perpetuate the 'we-develop-them' attitudes that still prevail.

The very idea that 'we' could or even should develop 'them' had always been questionable, but there are practical reasons why 'them-and-us' attitudes are inappropriate to any consideration of Third World development. For one thing, many of the difficulties experienced by the poorer countries can be understood only by taking into account their political and commercial ties with the richer nations. Again, we now know that some of the environmental problems involved are not just local but transnational: for example, the diminishing birdsong in the southern USA results from the clearance of Amazonian rainforest to make way for cattle ranches to satisfy the USA's own craving for beefburgers. Finally we should recognise that, with the quality of life rapidly deteriorating in the world's richest countries (consider for example the rising levels of work-stress, unemployment and poverty), many of the First World's growing social problems are no different in kind from corresponding ones in the south. For these reasons alone, the subject under discussion must be not 'them' but 'all of us'; but a more fundamental reason has been the growing conviction that true development really is intransitive, and that traditional attempts at development through aid programmes, however well-intentioned, tend only to beget *mal*development – some authorities even regarding much bilateral aid as a cynical exercise in the maintenance of power over the

Third World for the sake of First World economic growth (see for example Hunt and Sherman 1986: 622ff).

The pursuit of growth entailed plundering the south's natural resources in order to create wealth, much of which ended up in the north; but a growing awareness of the links between this policy and phenomena such as environmental damage, social upheaval, unemployment and poverty began to influence economic thought. The Chilean economist Max-Neef (1982:51) has observed that instead of ensuring that in a world of finite resources everyone gets a fair share of the existing cake, we persist in making a larger one. We may intend that everyone should get a larger slice, but in the process 'the poor's share of the cake diminishes'. In catering for basic human needs such as food and shelter, some countries are successful while others are being deprived. Soper (1993: 125) cites Sweden, adjudged as 'average best performer' in catering for its citizens' needs, but with a per capita energy consumption that is one of the world's highest. This imbalance led Max-Neef (op. cit: 53) to invent the concept of the 'ecoson', a hypothetical 'ecological person': a user of few resources, for example a villager in Togo, might register as only a fraction of one 'ecoson' on the imaginary scale while a city-dweller in the United States might represent 50. We are hardly likely to see such a scale put to practical use, but the 'ecoson' concept itself is valid and, along with others such as Lovelock's Gaia theory and the sometimes almost spiritual aspects of the Green movement (see for example Button ed. 1990), would deserve a place in any Development Studies course. Perhaps, in both north and south, formal education should include such a syllabus so as to supplement the growing public awareness created by informal means, by television in particular.

In the south, a great deal of faith had been placed in humanistic education as an agent of lasting change and, where English was the medium of learning, ELT was expected to play an important part. Pattison (1955:7) pointed out that development was not just a matter of learning new techniques but also involved psychological adjustment.

> Development has come to mean learning from a different civilization, and it must bring changes in values and standards and attitudes. If education neglects them, the promised land will turn out to be a disappointment when it is reached. We ought to consider not only the response of English to social demand but the contribution it can make to education in the fullest sense.

In pre-war Britain, education had indeed been largely concerned with improving the minds, morals and manners of the young, but by the 1960s it was also being used as a means of issuing or withholding work-tickets – the higher the qualification, the more prestigious the employment. In the Third World rush for education it was this function that led to what Dore (1976) labelled 'the diploma disease': the masses saw education first and foremost as an escape route from the traditional to the modern, from insecure dirty-handed jobs to safe white-collar posts, and the primary school became 'not the place where one is educated for a useful life, but the place where one competes for an exit visa from rural society.' (Dore 1980:71).

The existing education systems of newly independent nations were viewed by many as inappropriate and even as processes of oppression. Rodney (1972:241) was particularly scathing: 'Colonial schooling was education for subordination, exploitation, the creation of mental confusion, and the development of underdevelopment.'

Since he clearly considered education to be one cause of under-development, he used *underdevelop* as a transitive verb in the title of his book: *How Europe Underdeveloped Africa*. The possible relationship of formal education to 'underdevelopment' will be considered further in the introduction to Part 2.

Freire (1972:42) had insisted early on that in development activities intervention may be necessary but is never sufficient. 'The liberation of the oppressed is a liberation of men, not things. Accordingly, while no one liberates himself by his own efforts alone, neither is he liberated by others'.

The fact that self-help is vital has fundamental implications for aid agencies, as Max-Neef (1991:8) points out below, and since British ELT is involved in development aid programmes, the implications extend to the teaching of English. Note that where we have used the grammatical terms *transitive* and *intransitive*, Max-Neef uses *object* and *subject* for similar reasons:

> Attaining the transformation of an object-person into a subject-person in the process of development is, among other things, a problem of scale. There is no possibility for the active participation of people in gigantic systems which are hierarchically organized and where decisions flow from the top down to the bottom.

At international level, too, the usual flow of initiative could be reversed. A recent Swedish report (Serageldin ed. 1993:143) neatly combines the concepts 'bottom-up' and 'growth from within' in specifying the desirable features of the development process. It advocates a partnership between rich and poor countries designed so as to produce:

> development that is people-centred and gender-conscious, that is environmentally and economically sound, and that promotes empowerment of the weak and marginalized. The lead role in this partnership must come from the developing countries. Development is like a tree: it can be assisted in its growth only by feeding its roots. . .

To sum up, we see a historical shift in the use of the term *development* in both the ELT and global contexts. It seems that in both contexts movement can be observed from one polarity to the other on a number of parameters: from the transitive to the intransitive, from top down to bottom up, from intervention to autonomy, from authority centred to participant centred, in effect from imposition to empowerment. Reference to *paradigm shifts* is now commonplace in ELT. (See Woodward 1996 for an example.) However, there are dangers in viewing this shift as simply from one pole to the other. The movement needs to be more subtle than these polarities imply and centres on the negotiation of an appropriate role for the agent of intervention: the teacher, the trainer, the volunteer, the aid agency, the consultant, the government department. The continuum may be partially illustrated by the following diagram:

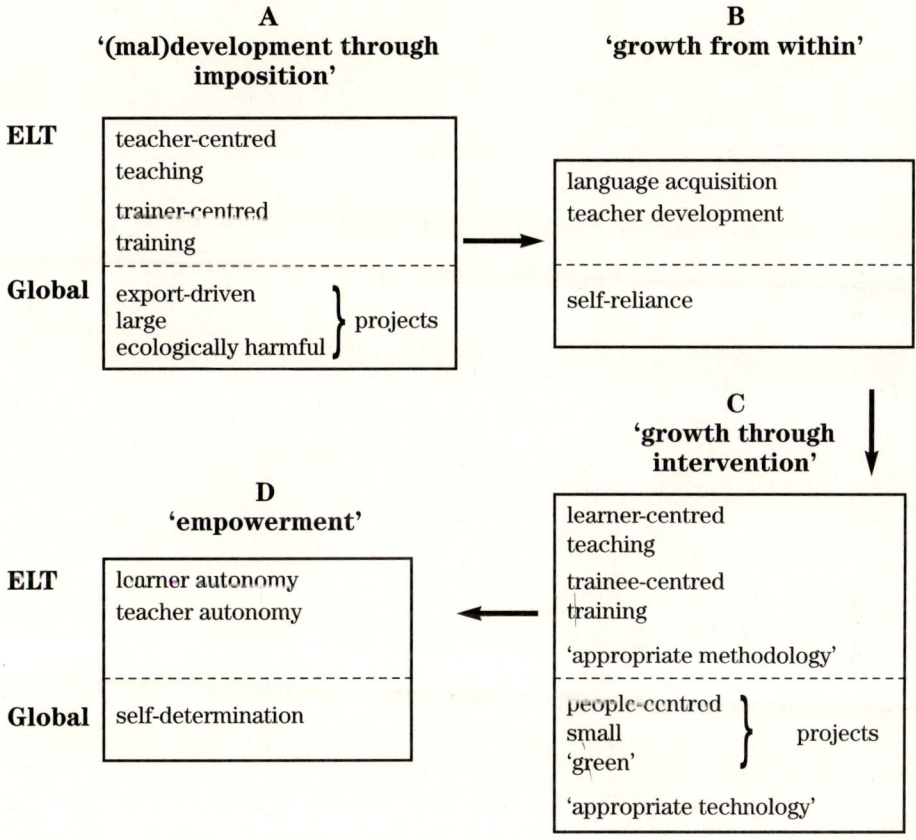

The potential dangers can be highlighted by relating the cells to Underhill's (1989:254) four uses of power. Development is impossible where power is imposed and therefore not exercised in the interests of the beneficiaries. This is authoritarianism. Nor is autonomous development achieved by relying simply on 'growth from within', by letting things sort themselves out 'naturally'. This is the philosophy of market forces and represents an abdication of power by those in a position of influence. Empowerment (autonomy, self-determination) results from the authoritative, responsible, and above all appropriate use of power by the agents of intervention. The art, as in all walks of life, is to judge when and how to intervene, and when and how to withdraw. We hope the collection of insights offered by the contributors to this volume will usefully amplify such issues.

As explained in the Preface, Part 1 of this book will cover the earlier Dunford seminars, which dealt with such topics as those labelled 'ELT' in the above table; Part 2 will deal with the later years, when Dunford participants debated matters concerning ELT in global aid programmes; and the final part will consider how ELT in the global context may be shaped and furthered particularly by means of Distance Education.

PART 1

Developments in ELT
1978–84

Part 1: Developments in ELT 1978–84

Mike Beaumont

Introduction

The topics chosen for the seven Dunford seminars that spanned the period 1978 to 1984 can be seen in retrospect to form a cycle: from syllabus / course design, to methodology, to assessment, to teacher training, and back to syllabus design. I shall attempt to set these early Dunford seminars within a wider situational and historical perspective, arguing that the cycle itself is significant. I suggest a possible explanation for the reservations that have been expressed about the appropriacy of the 'Communicative Approach' to certain language teaching contexts; and I venture to hope that what follows may have implications for the way in which curriculum innovations are carried out in the future.

The concern of the 1978 seminar was quite specific: ESP Course Design. According to the Dunford Seminar Report for that year (DSR 1978:9), this ten-day seminar was seen at the time as forming part of a series of seminars devoted to ESP and was in fact the second to be held on this topic. (The first, of five days' duration, had taken place the previous year at the British Council's London headquarters.) Dunford 1979, further extended to two weeks, continued to concern itself with ESP and Course Design, but widened the perspective to include more general purposes for ELT. The report's conclusion summarised the emerging philosophy:

> the series of seminars as a whole offers the opportunity to test a 'theory of practice' against the accumulated experience of specialists working, in a wide range of contexts, on many aspects of the teaching of English. (DSR 1979: 128)

It also concluded that Dunford 1979 had completed the focus on the syllabus specification component of the course design/implementation process and that:

> if, as many of the practitioners on the seminar would wish to argue, linguistic specification is only one element in course preparation, the justification of a particular learning approach implying distinctive materials and teaching strategies must merit study. (DSR 1979: 132)

In expanding the theme to teaching English for more general purposes, doubts had also risen about the validity of applying to these contexts the particular syllabus design model (Munby 1978) which had provided the theoretical framework for the first two seminars.

> For the school student learning English for 'no apparent reason', where a needs analysis may produce no restricted specification of EAP requirements and where EOP requirements may be either heterogeneous or non-existent. . . a fresh and valid approach to school syllabus design. . . is likely to rest upon the recognition of motivations of an individual nature and upon the findings of child language acquisition – in other words, a *process* rather than a *product* orientation. (DSR 1979: 131)

In consequence, Dunford 1980 turned its attention for the first time to Communicative Methodology, the main aim being to examine current ideas and practice in the development of more communicative and learner-centred approaches to the ELT classroom. Interestingly, the process-product dichotomy, referred to above and one with which the 1980s was to become increasingly familiar, makes an early appearance in the 1980 report, albeit in a different context. 'There was general agreement at the final evaluation session that the most effective part of the seminar had been the process rather than the product.' (DSR 1980: 1)

This is probably accounted for by the introduction in 1980 of a feature that was to become central to future seminars: the case study. In the previous two years, participants had been presented with, and had worked in groups on, particular learner profiles, but the 1979 report had recognised that there was 'scope for expanding the time available for discussion of the selection, adaptation and production of materials *for a given student group*' (my emphasis) (DSR 1979: 133) and that more time was needed to exemplify and test the different strategies implied by varying course objectives and contexts. For the 1980 seminar, therefore, several participants had been asked to provide in advance full documentation for the case studies on which groups were to base their work in the second week and, by the end of the seminar, as Deyes points out (1980: 110), the broad basis of a reading scheme for a Thai university course, a teacher training course for Technical Institute English instructors in Sri Lanka, and a new examination format for a Punjabi secondary school class had been worked out. Although, therefore, the participants had valued the processes involved in designing these programmes, the products had also been significant. This continued to be the case for the remainder of the seminars in this period.

Already, however, a number of dichotomies were emerging that have continued until now to stimulate debate about approaches and priorities both at Dunford seminars and in the wider ELT forum. We have referred, directly or indirectly, to several of them above. The first was that between ESP, that is teaching contexts where learners' needs could be quite specifically defined, and what became increasingly known as 'general' English, where the future needs of the learners were either heterogeneous (English for mixed groups) or were difficult, even impossible, to specify –

situations which Abbott (1981) termed TENOR (Teaching English for No Obvious Reason). Underlying, but not totally analogous with this dichotomy, were at least three others: that between teaching in tertiary education and teaching in the primary or secondary sector, that between teaching in the private sector and teaching in the state sector, and that between teaching in the so-called 'developed' and 'developing' worlds. In terms of the Council's own work, differently emerging priorities and concerns could be observed between staff working in its own income-generating DTE (Direct Teaching of English) institutes, and project-based KELT (Key English Language Teaching) staff, funded by the ODA and attached to ministries or teacher training institutes in the state education sector of the 'Third' World. Both contexts entailed the close co-operation of staff employed on short term contracts and staff appointed to the permanent career service of the Council. Evaluating Dunford 1980, the report recognises such divides but attempts to treat them positively.

> Many people noted that one of the most rewarding aspects of the seminar was the chance to discuss their work with others – not only those in similar situations, but also meeting people working in very different conditions. The DTE/KELT fusion was appreciated on both sides, and it was felt that each group had something valuable to contribute to the other. (DSR 1980: 108)

An emerging cycle

The idea of the Dunford seminars forming some kind of cycle had emerged for the first time in the introduction to the 1980 report (DSR 1980: 1), though without specifying how long the cycle was intended to last nor what topics the future stages of the cycle would address. However, by the time the introduction to the 1981 report was written, a measure of *post hoc* rationalisation had emerged.

> The 1981 Dunford Seminar brought to a conclusion a cycle of four seminars which began in 1978 and covered course design, syllabus construction, communicative methodology and, now, questions associated with evaluation. (DSR 1981: 1)

In the context of seminar planning, the evaluation perspective had developed from a rather narrow interpretation, that of the evaluation of student performance to, subsequently, the evaluation of design work, project planning, materials, and the methodology and training of teachers. In the end, the report admits 'the scope of the seminar widened to take in almost the whole range of ELT philosophy.' (DSR 1981: 1)

Moreover, the report recognised not only the wide dimensions of the topic but also its complexity.

> In a world which has moved away from the comfortable and measurable certainties of behaviourism and structural linguistics to the newer and amorphous realms of cognitive-code learning theory,

generative linguistics and communicative methodology, these
questions have lost any simple answers they might once have had
and become much more vexed. (DSR 1981: 1)

Such scope and complexity, and the dichotomies to which I have referred,
were all represented in the 1981 'product', with case studies focusing on
the construction of a course unit to introduce primary school teachers to
basic testing procedures, the design of the evaluation component of a new
primary school syllabus, an assessment of the evaluation needs and
implementation strategies of a university language centre, an evaluation
system for a Council DTE operation, the evaluation of a secondary level
materials production project, and the working out of a blueprint for setting
up a Business English examination. The *fin de siècle* tone of the 1981
seminar was accentuated when, curiously, the introduction to the 1982
report established no link with, indeed made no explicit reference to,
previous seminars. It merely stated that its purpose was

> to provide an account of the intensive investigation into current
> questions concerning English Language Teacher Training and the
> curriculum . . . (and) . . . a starting point for further work on the
> detailed development of teacher training syllabi. (DSR 1982: 1)

However, in retrospect, the logic of the move to teacher training can be
clearly understood, as indeed can that of the sequence of topics of the
earlier seminars.

From syllabus design to methodology

During the 1970s, the language teaching debate had been dominated by
questions of syllabus design. 1973 had seen the publication of significant
papers by van Ek, Richterich, Trim and Wilkins, all arising out of the
Council of Europe initiative, begun in 1971, to develop a language teaching
system for adult European learners. In 1976 Wilkins published *Notional
Syllabuses*, bringing to a wider audience the concept of a syllabus based
on 'categories of communicative function' rather than on grammatical
structures. Talk of 'functional syllabuses' became common, gradually
replaced towards the end of the decade by the term 'communicative
syllabuses'. Simultaneously, and, at least to begin with, more or less
independently, ESP developed as a major force within ELT. As Howatt
(1984: 222) observes, Swales' *Writing Scientific English* (1971), although
containing features that anticipated the communicative movement, adopted
an essentially linguistic view of course design. The notional/functional and
ESP perspectives began to merge from 1974 with the appearance of the
OUP *English in Focus* series and, from 1976 onwards, the Longman
Nucleus materials. During the same period, the British Council had under-
lined its commitment to contribute to 'state of the art' thinking in ELT by
funding a number of its experienced ELT specialists to undertake doctoral
research. John Munby was one such, and *Communicative Syllabus
Design*, published in 1978, was the public version of his PhD. It was no

coincidence, therefore, that the Council should select ESP Course Design as its theme for the first Dunford, and that Munby's framework was the focus of debate.

With the benefit of hindsight, it is surprising that throughout this period there had been relatively little discussion of the teaching methodology that might accompany such 'communicative' syllabuses. Alexander contributes an appendix, 'Threshold level and methodology', to van Ek (1976), Brumfit and Johnson (1979) include four articles in a section entitled 'Methodological perspectives', and articles on communicative methodology begin to appear in the *English Language Teaching Journal* (for example Olsen and Gosak 1978 and Rixon 1979). However, in the contributions to Dunford 1981, it is possible to see a number of subsequently important influences that had begun to impinge on ELT classroom practice. In general, a shift could be observed away from the *content* and *product* of language *teaching* (structures, notions, functions, text, discourse – all of which contributed to a narrowly linguistic definition of group needs) towards a greater consideration of the *learner* and the *process* of language *learning* (entailing a more holistic view of individual needs). In another sense, the shift from syllabus to methodology represented a move from the sociological to the psychological and psycholinguistic. Among the influences on the 1981 debate were second language acquisition theory and research (with the names of Pit Corder and Krashen appearing for the first time), humanism (Maslow, Rogers, Curran and, within ELT, Stevick), and what might loosely be termed the 'fluency' movement from the language teaching profession itself (Brumfit's accuracy-fluency distinction, Maley's drama techniques, Johnson's 'deep end' strategy). In short, a number of unlikely bedfellows contributed to shaping a communicative methodology which, combined with the concept of a communicative syllabus, began increasingly to be termed the 'communicative approach'. Another significant methodological influence that crept into the 1981 seminar, relatively unnoticed, was the use of video, both as an aid to communication in the classroom and, through the recording of microteaching, as a tool for teacher training. Dunford had to wait until 1984 before the other, more dramatic, technological advance – the computer – began to make its presence felt.

Evaluation

So the new syllabuses began to acquire a methodology to go with them. This had important implications for testing. Tests and examinations are amongst the most conservative, and yet most powerful, features of education systems. Ministries and institutions that had replaced their old structural syllabuses with functional or communicative ones, and had encouraged their teachers to teach more communicatively, found that without making requisite changes to the examination system little would change. Worse still, the inertia born of tradition or complacency could merely be replaced by confused resistance. It was obvious, therefore, that Dunford should turn its attention to evaluation.

As we have seen, the products of the Dunford 1981 case studies, accounting for well over half the pages of the report, focused mainly on devising tests for students in different contexts. Another significant contribution was a report on early developments in the British Council English Language Testing Service (ELTS, later IELTS), a scheme for determining the language adequacy of overseas students for entry into higher education courses in Britain. The scheme now tests thousands of students annually and has played a major part both in rationalising entry requirements and in placing students on appropriate pre-sessional courses. We have also observed, however, that Dunford 1981 eventually cast its evaluative net wider than testing students. In the report we can see an emerging concern for the more systematic evaluation of projects, foreshadowing later Dunford themes relating to values and costs, but also pointing up the need for such systems to be flexible and sensitive to local conditions. Finally, 1981 also saw the first attempt to engage participants in debate with specialists from outside British ELT with invitations to Brian Page of Leeds University to report on the graded objectives initiative in modern language teaching in British secondary schools, and to Mats Oskarsson of Gothenburg University to discuss growing interest in self-assessment. What is surprising, perhaps, with hindsight is that there seems to have been little discussion of what might constitute 'communicative' testing, despite the publication in the previous year of Carroll's *Testing Communicative Performance* (1980).

Teacher training

So ended the cycle as the seminar organisers saw it. However, it is obvious that innovations in syllabus design, methodology and evaluation, particularly if they are instituted as a matter of public policy, have deep implications for teacher training, both pre-service and in-service. In fact, the case study element of the first four seminars had necessarily engaged participants in the issue, as many of them occupied posts in the teacher training sector. It was perhaps inevitable, therefore, that Dunford 1982 should pick up the teacher training theme, a topic carried over into 1983. In the introduction to the 1983 report, we see a renewed awareness of the way in which continuity had been developing through the early seminars.

> Continuity in this context means continuity of theme, of organising principles and (to a lesser degree) of personnel. Continuity of *theme* is important because it is simply no longer possible in a single 10-day seminar to give adequate coverage of any area of ELT at both the macro and micro levels. The tendency, therefore, has been to see the Dunford Seminar moving in roughly two-year thematic cycles. Continuity of *organising principles* ensures that the implementational factors associated with success in one year can be built on in the next. And continuity of *personnel*, at both the course organiser and participant level, ensures this thematic and organisational linkage from one year to the next. (DSR 1983: 1)

So, as well as the overall thematic development that we have observed, there was also a sense in which the early Dunfords were seen as being paired. The first two were devoted to syllabus and course design. The 1982 and 1983 seminars concentrated on teacher training. It is a little harder to see the same kind of link between 1980 and 1981, particularly in the plenary presentations. However, in the case studies, or at what was now being termed the 'micro' level, projects on materials production were necessarily requiring the integration of the methodologies of (communicative) teaching and testing.

Because of the intense concentration of the 1970s on syllabus design, teacher training was another area, like methodology, which had received little attention in the literature, despite its crucial role in the effective implementation of a communicative approach. The October 1974 issue of the *English Language Teaching Journal* had devoted itself almost exclusively to the topic, but in subsequent issues teacher training received only occasional attention. It was not until 1979 that the first book on teacher training for ELT appeared, when Susan Holden of Modern English Publications edited an excellent collection of papers, some of which remain seminal. By the time of the two Dunford teacher training seminars, little else had emerged except the British Council's own ELT Documents 110 *Focus on the Teacher*, the initial work for some of which had been done at Dunford House. O'Brien's EROTI model, for example, appears in DSR 1980 as *The Cobden Model*.

A number of significant themes emerged from Dunford 1982 and 1983. One was the key role of teacher training in curriculum innovation. Such issues, labelled 'macro' by the 1983 report, were the primary concern of the 1982 seminar, during which participants were asked to engage in complex simulation tasks or syndicate exercises, exploring the interface between the agendas and priorities of the host country or institution and those, on the one hand, of funding agencies such as the British Council and the ODA, and on the other, of the individuals involved in the day-to-day professional contact. A second theme, in many ways connected to the first, surfaced under a variety of headings, typically 'problems' or 'constraints'. There appears to have been a growing concern, particularly amongst participants working in developing countries, that considerations of the local in-country context were in danger of being swamped by an implicit assumption that application of the newly coherent communicative approach was the principal aim of all projects. A third theme was the growing refinement of the notion of process in teacher training, a recognition perhaps that training methodologies needed to match the communicative methodology of the language classroom, that the *process* of teacher training needed to reflect and be consistent with its *content*, that is the communicative approach or aspects of it. This concern to examine process is directly exemplified by the reports on the 1983 case studies, which include 'process diaries', where an individual member of each case study group was asked to observe, and publicly reflect on, how the group members carried out the assigned tasks. Other subsidiary themes were classroom observation, both from the research point of view, through discourse analysis, and from the point of view of trainee supervision, classroom language, particularly support for the non-native speaking teacher, and teaching styles, that is the observed reluctance of some teachers to abandon a transmission style of teaching in favour of more communicative methods. Finally, the 1982 report details further developments in the use of video in teacher training, charting the progress of one of the major British Council projects of the 1980s, the production of the *Teaching and Learning in Focus* materials, still one of the most significant resources available for the practising teacher trainer.

Widening perspectives

By 1984 we have come full circle, and return to the topic of the first Dunford, though the wider term 'curriculum and syllabus design' replaces the original 'course design'. This widening of perspective encapsulates the developments that had been taking place over the course of the first seven Dunford seminars. We no longer have a concentration on a particular aspect of ELT (as the first and second seminars had on ESP), nor on a particular framework for examining it (the Munby model). Rather we see an attempt to define an educational philosophy that might apply to both teaching and teacher training and to all teaching and learning contexts.

> The title of this year's seminar reflects the broader concerns of practitioners in the English Language Teaching profession. Teachers and academics alike are becoming increasingly interested in trying to grasp the teaching/learning situation as a whole. This means looking beyond the narrow confines of one approach or one method and trying to include the practice and context of language learning, as well as the evaluation of these, in one coherent whole. (DSR 1984: 5)

As a result, the papers presented to the seminar covered methodology and evaluation as well as curriculum and syllabus design. The key concept emerging from the seminar and indeed from the whole of the period under consideration was 'process'. We have already observed how research into the process of learning had begun to influence teaching methodology and how this was having a washback effect on the methodology of training. In his keynote address to the seminar Brumfit summarises this trend.

> A concern for 'process' implies certain views on teaching methods, for 'process' classrooms tend to be more learner centred, to have more group work and co-operative procedures, and to be more concerned with development than knowledge. (Brumfit 1984: 10)

However, the 1984 seminar was also invited to address the (to ELT) relatively new notion of a process syllabus. Reference was made to the views of Breen and Candlin (1980) and to the growing interest in Prabhu's innovative work in India with procedural syllabuses (Prabhu 1983). Both

Brumfit, in the paper referred to above, and Maw, in her contribution to the seminar (reprinted in this volume), show how the roots of this thinking can be found in much earlier work in curriculum development, notably that of Peters (1959) and Stenhouse (1975):

> the idea of designing a curriculum around a statement of what is to *happen* is not new, but in contemporary writing the common factor uniting a cluster of writers has been a rejection of the tyranny of objectives . . . where specification of precise outcomes is seen as impossible or unethical.
> Stenhouse developed his argument from an early paper by Peters, who was then arguing that a liberal education is defined by its mode of acquisition rather than by content or aims. Stenhouse adopted Peters' concept of 'principles of procedure' as a means of structuring an appropriate classroom process by asking the question 'What classroom procedures are implicit in our aim?' (Maw 1984: 14)

Conclusion

By 1984, then, the conceptualisation of what Howatt (1984: 279) called the 'strong' version of the communicative approach was almost complete, and it might be claimed that the Dunford seminars had played a significant part in that process. Dunford had provided an important and perhaps unique forum for theorists, administrators and influential fieldworkers to confront and debate the latest and most challenging issues. It might be no exaggeration to say that during this time the deliberations at Dunford were as close as any to the cutting edge of British ELT. However, we can also detect in the Dunford reports a number of concerns and caveats about the communicative approach, largely but not exclusively to do with its implementation. First of all, reservations were being expressed, largely by practitioners, about the *extent* to which the communicative approach could be put into practice in certain teaching contexts, principally those which were characterised by particular constraints. These constraints comprised such factors as lack of resources, large classes, poorly trained and motivated teachers, and the restraining effect of local educational cultures. There seems, however, to have been an unquestioned assumption that the problems lay in overcoming these constraints and not in the approach itself. This issue of the validity of the communicative approach was to be taken up in 1985 with a public debate in the pages of the *English Language Teaching Journal* between Michael Swan and Henry Widdowson.

Secondly, it was becoming increasingly possible to observe the results of policies which had attempted to put the communicative approach into practice on a large scale and it was clear that many such attempts were meeting with only qualified success. In retrospect, it is possible to argue that such disappointments could be explained by the way in which these innovations tended to be carried out. We have drawn attention throughout this paper to the underlying cycle of topics in the first seven Dunfords. This sequence is significant. The development of the communicative approach was stimulated by new thinking in the design of syllabuses. It was only after considerable work in this area that attention turned to a methodology through which the new syllabuses could be taught and tested. As a final step, thinking had been applied to training teachers to teach and test in the new way. In many contexts which had kept in touch with this theorising, curriculum innovation had been implemented in much the same sequence with syllabus changes preceding attempts to reform teaching methods and testing procedures, followed only then by the development of effective pre- and in-service teaching training. Rather later than the questioning of the communicative approach, the profession began to see the management of innovation and change as a crucial question and recognise that it was the practising teacher that should be at the heart of such change if it was to be effective. Kennedy (1987) was one of the first to address this issue. He observes how top down, non-consultative innovation, whether instigated by 'insiders' (for example Ministries of Education) or 'outsiders' (for example a foreign agency like the British Council), invariably fails because the agents ultimately responsible for the implementation of change, the teachers, have not been engaged with the *need* for change or with the theoretical principles underlying the *nature* of the change. He argues, therefore, that the process of innovation should *begin* with teacher development, implying a cycle of change which is the complete reverse of that observed above, a cycle which does not start from, but results in, syllabus, materials, and methodological development.

The end of this first cycle of Dunford seminars, then, represents an intriguing watershed in the development of British ELT. On the one hand, it brings to a close a period of intense and often exciting theorising, theorising which resulted in the emergence of the communicative approach as a coherent framework for the teaching and learning of second languages. On the other hand, it heralds an era of what might best be termed 'reflection and application'. As we see in Part 2 of this volume, the next decade essentially addressed itself to a critical examination of the concept of 'communicative' (both theoretically through research and practically through the development of materials and techniques) and to the social, cultural, political, economic and educational consequences of applying the approach to numerous and varying teaching and learning contexts.

1.0   The Communicative Curriculum

MIKE BEAUMONT

During the 1970s, the British Council maintained strong links with the academic wing of ELT, not only encouraging its ELT specialists to engage in debate with teachers and teacher trainers in higher education but also funding a number of them to undertake research and to complete doctorates. The result of one of these studies was Munby (1978). Munby's work on syllabus design was immensely influential in the late 1970s and early 1980s and played a key role in the development of increasingly sophisticated models of needs analysis. As West comments (1994: 2):

> The size and scope of Munby's work have meant that needs analysis is now crucial to any consideration of ESP course design and almost every modern survey of ESP . . . accords it a central place.

Despite this scope, West outlines two areas which Munby's work did not address. The first, the constraints affecting the learning situation, was deliberately ignored by Munby and other early approaches to needs analysis. The second, described by West as the 'big and often political questions that were originally deemed outside the scope of needs analysis' (1994: 4), relates to larger scale factors which contribute to what is now termed a *language audit*, and which determine the longer-term language-training requirements of a company, country or other professional sector. In the first extract below, Hawkey explicitly points out that the Munby model did not take account of 'implementational constraints' and he can already be seen to be reacting to the kind of criticism that was current at the time, noting that the model should not be criticised for failing to perform tasks which it did not set out to perform and that it had been used with success on a number of projects. The extract, apart from providing a useful summary of the approach, also includes the product of a case study in which one of the working groups at the 1979 seminar applied the model to an imaginary participant on a pre-university course in Bangladesh.

In the next extract, Moore argues that it is the materials designer's task to effect the compromise between needs and constraints and he outlines three sets of factors to be taken into account in translating a Munby-type needs analysis into materials. Design factors involve consideration of the functions the materials are intended to fulfil and the structure and layout of course units; exploitation factors enable students and teachers to make the best use of materials according to their interests and needs; and production factors include specific issues affecting the process of materials production and broader questions relating to the professional, academic, political and cultural context in which the materials are being produced.

Maw's paper was one of the first Dunford contributions to come from outside the specific field of ELT. Such perspectives are extremely valuable for at least two reasons. First, they help to restrain the kind of creeping parochialism that can affect all professional sectors, particularly those with the size, independence and energy of ELT. Second, they can serve to reassure ELT practitioners that current thinking is consistent with developments in the wider educational world. In this case Maw enabled Dunford participants, five years on from the first seminar, to see the dangers inherent in an essentially *a priori* model of syllabus design such as Munby's, and to relate developing ideas on *process* and *procedural* syllabuses to longer-term and more general thinking on curriculum design.

Finally, Phillips signals the arrival of the computer on the educational scene and poses a number of fundamental questions to which we still do not have definitive answers. He concludes by assessing the relevance of such advanced educational technologies for the 'teacher working in the African bush', wisely observing that at both the superficial level of increasing availability and the deeper level of their impact on curriculum change, no teacher is likely to be untouched by such developments. The danger lies in the long term effects of rash and unthinking investment in the new technology.

1.1   Communicative needs profiles (1979)

ROGER HAWKEY

Time would be spent studying and using a needs analysis model which would provide a set of Communicative Needs Profiles (CNP) and Syllabus Content Specifications (SCS). Discussion suggested that 'needs' could be both linguistic and non-linguistic, and that these were interdependent; that 'analysis' implied more than mere description; that a 'model' implied a dynamic process rather than a static framework. Effective use of the Munby model of needs analysis undoubtedly depended on the skills and intuitions of the operator, and this could be interpreted by some as a weakness of the system. The model was particularly concerned with 'ESP' contexts, but a simple dichotomy between 'specific' and 'general' needs and courses should be avoided and contexts seen rather in terms of a cline from ESG (English for specific groups) to EMG (English for mixed groups), as indicated in Fig. 1.

Degree of specificity of target communication

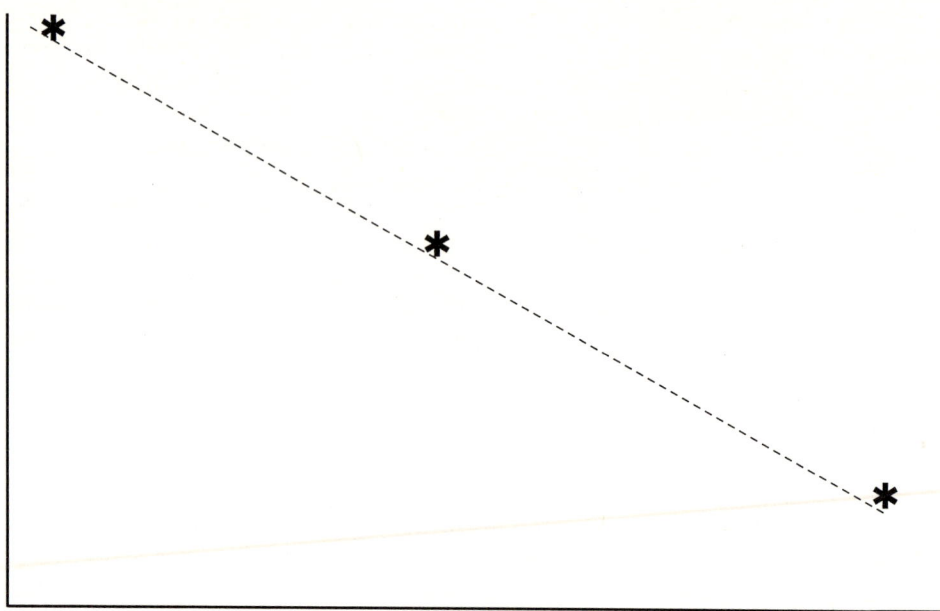

Types of learner group

Homogeneous groups with narrowly specific and predictable needs/ wants – probably quite clearly perceived by learners and sponsors e.g. air traffic controllers.	Mixed groups within same general field (e.g. 'business') but a variety of specific purposes within this field; needs/ wants not so clearly perceived by learners or sponsors.	Mixed groups with broad and varied needs and wants; some needs/ wants in common but not all clearly perceived by learners or sponsors.

Figure 1

It should nevertheless be remembered that the Munby procedures were oriented towards ESG contexts, informed by functional views of language and biased towards a sociolinguistic interpretation of competent language use. Hymesian notions of contextualised language use and Hallidayan views on the functions of language were thus reflected in a systematically organised, sequential, cumulative and comprehensive set of procedures for defining the communicative needs of a particular potential language user. It was important to recognise what the model (presented in Fig. 2, taken from Munby 1978) did and did not claim to do.

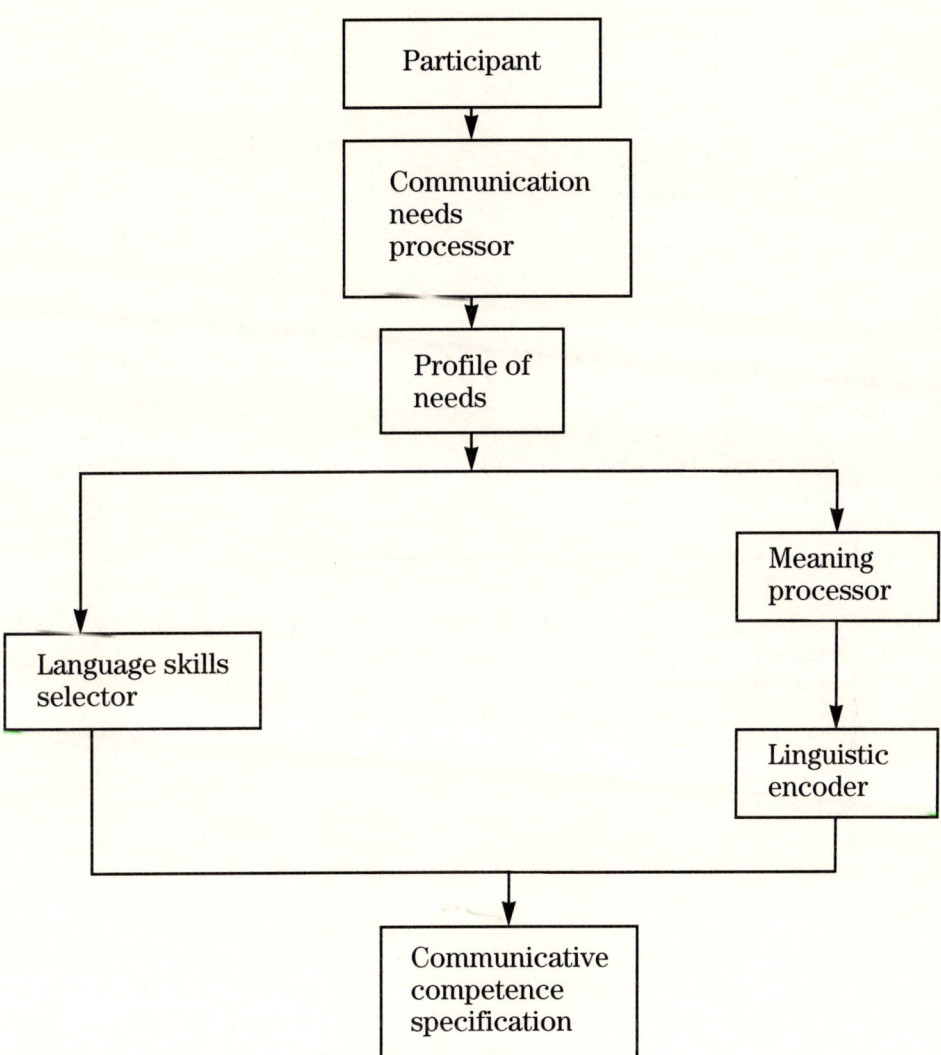

Figure 2

In broad terms it took only two steps – needs profile and target syllabus – towards course design (see Fig. 3).

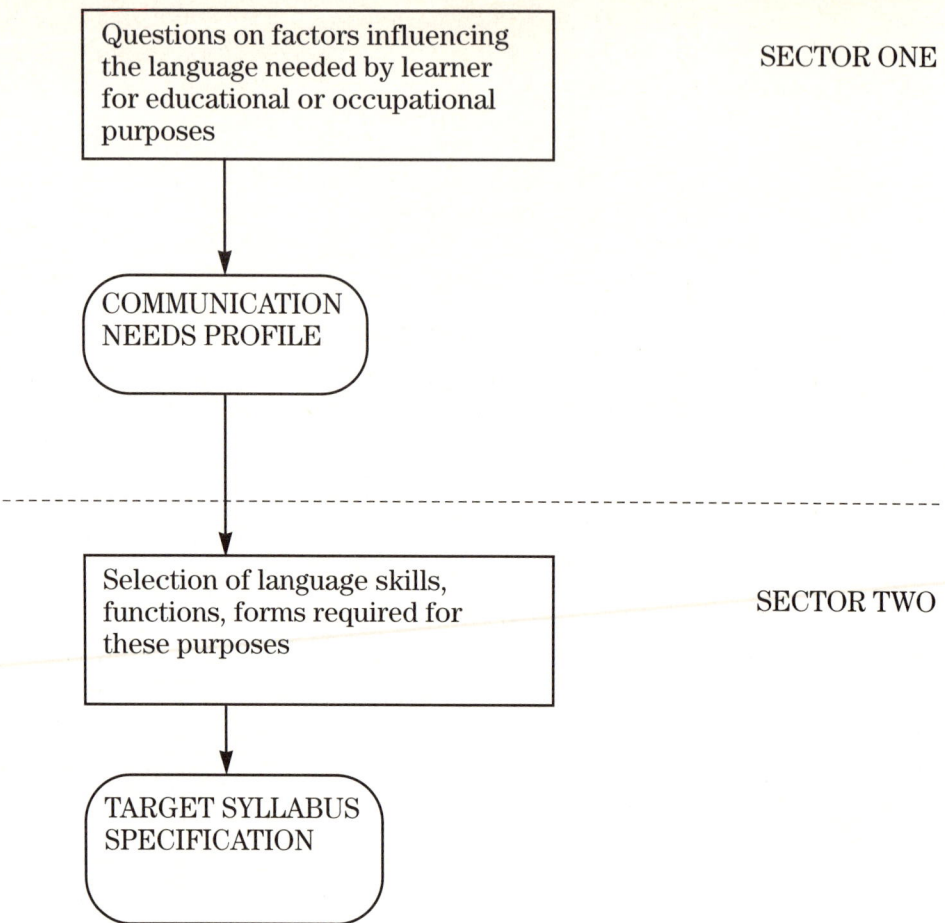

Figure 3

It did not take account of implementational constraints: the syllabus specification could be adjusted later. A distinction was therefore drawn between target syllabus and pedagogic syllabus. It did not specify how data should be collected and analysed. It did not claim to generate directly language realisations. The first step was to define: who would be using English, for what purpose, where, with whom, in which media, using which dialects, at what level, to perform what activities, to convey which tones. The second step was to identify the skills, notions, functions (and possibly forms) which were required in order to satisfy the user's requirements. Critics should beware of accusing the model of not performing tasks which it did not purport to do.

A brief extract on video of John Munby warned against embarking on course design on the basis of the constraints involved; the syllabus content specification should reflect the learner's needs and only later be modified to take account of actual constraints.

The model had been used with success in the course of various consultancy projects. Needs analysis data had to be collected quickly through discussions with students, teachers and administrators. In Venezuela, a course had been developed following the production of a blueprint. John Moore had used the model in project design at vocational training centres in Jeddah, and also in Bahrain where the task analysis approach was already used in teaching at the College of Health Sciences. Roger Bowers had used it in Damascus University to define the programme of a Key English Language Teaching-assisted Service English Department and also in the Singapore DTEO for the development of conversion courses for Chinese-medium teachers of geography and history. The CNP/SCS statement was not only of intrinsic value but also a useful statement to clients of what was offered. Overall evaluation of Munby's procedures was part of the output expected from the work of the English Language Testing Services Unit. Participants were then introduced to Chapter 2 of Munby (1978), which described the processes involved in designing the model, and Chapter 9, which took the reader through the operational instrument stage by stage. Chapter 10 offered examples. Particular attention was drawn to the possible choice between a skills-based and a functions-based specification.

Detailed discussion of the CNP stage, step by step, then led into the establishment of workgroup tasks. Each group (A–E) produced the needs profile of an imaginary participant, selected by the group as being relevant to their own teaching experience, past and potential. The CNP produced by one group follows.

Group A   *P = Bangladeshi pre-university student*

General discussion points

a) Should purposive domain be considered purely in the short term, which would be restricted to EAP, or should post-university EOP considerations also be allowed?

b) Should target level be specified in terms of the ideal or of a realistic anticipation of eventual performance?

c) Could the authors of books to be read be considered as a role-set with whom the P, in a sense, interacted?

Profile

0.0   PARTICIPANT

0.1   **Identity**

     0.1.1   18–19 years old

     0.1.2   Male

     0.1.3   Bangladeshi

     0.1.4   Living in Sylhet, Bangladesh

0.2   **Language**

     0.2.1   Mother tongue Bengali

     0.2.2   Target language English

     0.2.3   Present level 'lower intermediate'

     0.2.4/5 Also knows 'a little' Urdu

1.0   PURPOSIVE DOMAIN

     1.1/2   English is needed for discipline-based educational purposes, and will be learned in-study.

     1.3/4   The discipline is civil engineering, in areas defined by faculty courses, within the general field of engineering.

2.0   SETTING

     2.1   In Dacca, Bangladesh: en route on buses, and in lecture rooms/theatres, laboratories/workshops, library and private study areas at Bangladesh University of Engineering and Technology, a 'small' institution.

     2.2   English is used regularly and often, for 30–50 hours per week, mornings and afternoons.

     2.3   Psychosocial settings involved are:

         culturally similar
         age discriminating
         sex non-discriminating
         educationally developed
         technologically sophisticated
         familiar and unfamiliar physical
         familiar human
         demanding
         formal
         hierarchic
         authoritarian and non-authoritarian
         serious

3.0 **INTERACTION**

    3.1   In the position of university student with:

    3.2   lecturers
             other students
             (authors)

    3.3   with male adults, mostly Bangladeshi and a few British and Americans; mostly as individuals, sometimes in small groups.

    3.4   Social relationships involved are:
             subordinate to senior
             junior to senior
             contestant to judge
             learner to instructor
             younger to older generation
             equal to equal
             adult to adult
             own sex to own sex

4.0 **INSTRUMENTALITY**

    4.1   Medium: spoken receptive, written receptive, written productive, and (minimal) spoken productive

    4.2   Mode: monologue spoken to be heard, monologue spoken to be written, monologue written to be read, and (occasionally) dialogue spoken to be heard

    4.3   Channel: face to face unilateral, print unilateral, print bilateral and (occasionally) face to face bilateral

    4.4   Non-verbal medium: pictorial, mathematical and scientific (in both cases receptive and productive)

5.0 **DIALECT**

    5.1   Needs to understand and produce 'sub-continent' English, spoken and written, and to understand standard British English.

6.0   **TARGET LEVEL**

6.1   **Dimensions**

	Spoken		Written	
	Receptive	Productive	Receptive	Productive
Size	7	1	7	5
Complexity	7	4	7	5
Range	7	4	7	5
Delicacy	4	2	4	2
Speed	5	2	5	3
Flexibility	2	2	2	2

6.2   **Conditions**

Tolerance of:	Spoken		Written	
	Receptive	Productive	Receptive	Productive
Error	2	4	2	2
Stylistic failure	4	4	4	3
Reference	4	4	3	4
Repetition	4	4	3	4
Hesitation	2	4	2	4

7.0   **COMMUNICATIVE EVENT**

Main

7.1   Attending lectures

7.2   Laboratory/workshop practice

7.3   Private study

Other

7.4   Seeking information, advice and clarification

Activities

1   Listening: note-taking: asking questions

2   Listening: carrying out instructions: asking questions: writing

3   Private study: reading: note-taking: report writing

4   Asking questions: reference skills

1.2   Materials production (1979)

JOHN MOORE

A course plan covering the factors taken into account in selecting or adapting materials was clearly a necessary preliminary to the production of materials. The Munby model, by establishing parameters for relating language to communication – both in real life and as simulated in the classroom – enables the materials writer to ensure the relevance of his materials, to focus on the components of communicative uses of language, to manipulate authentic language and to construct examples of language use. The model does not make the decision on what materials should be written: it is for the designer to resolve the usual potential conflict between *needs* and *wants* and *constraints*. Munby's view of syllabus design might be tempered by Mick Jagger's view: 'You can't always get what you want but sometimes you get what you need'.

The 'CRESP' materials (developed to Roger Hawkey's initial design by the Instituto Universitario Politécnico Experimental de Guyana, Venezuela) were an example of straightforward application to course design of a needs analysis approach.

Design factors

Having defined language learning objectives, it was then necessary to consider design factors – first, the functions that the materials were intended to fulfil, for example:

- select/sequence/present examples of language use and practice activities;
- set tasks, provide stimuli or models, confirm responses, provide branches and options;
- convey meanings;
- give information (cultural, linguistic);
- promote attitudes;
- evaluate progress;
- manage activities;
- guide learning.

Having established the text functions, it was then necessary to examine ways in which parts of the unit related to each other, and the unit related to the whole, in realising a particular sequence or complex of functions. The development of a unit might, for example, appear as follows:

Example of unit development

1   Introduction

State   a) focus points
               b) behavioural objectives

2   Present, practise focus points

    Texts 1–3:   a) informal statements of focus points
                     b) text
                     c) explanation/exemplification of focus points by reference to text
                     d) practice exercises
                         1   related to text
                         2   extended to other contexts.

    Text 4   Text followed by further practice of all focus points.

3   'Getting the meaning' strategies
    a) explanation with examples drawn from lesson texts
    b) extension practice

4   Conclusion
Restate behavioural objectives for self-evaluation.

Such a summary shows the effect that such considerations may have on materials layout, which will reflect the way the learning task is viewed. Compare, for example, these two structures:

Form ⟶ Function

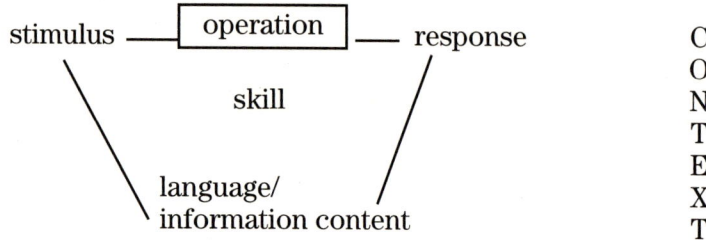

Function ⟶ Form

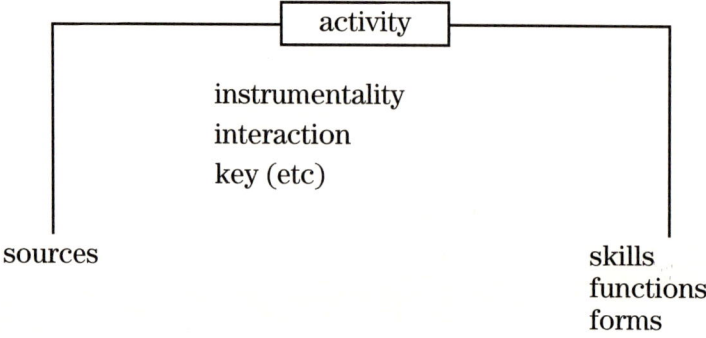

Layout is important in that it should assist the learner:
- to predict the content of a passage;
- to see the passage as realising a particular body of information;
- to interact with the passage;
- to combine extensive reading and product questions with intensive reading and process questions;
- by providing glosses.

The different ways of assisting, and exploiting, the text can be made quite explicit in layout. For example, in *Reading and Thinking in English* (OUP 1979) the layout of a unit is

Exercise to manipulate information from text which follows. Questions to establish purpose in reading text which follows.

	PASSAGE	Micro
Questions to aid reading of passage		questions on passage
	Macro questions within passage	

Exploitation factors
Materials are designed for purposes of exploitation, both performing specific functions and enabling others to be performed. While writers should make explicit the intended exploitation of their materials, it is doubtful how far they can be prescriptive as materials are interpreted very differently by both students and teachers. Do the materials enable students and teachers to co-operate in the learning process, to do what they can do already, or to do what they cannot do alone but would like to do?

Working from Earl Stevick ('Adapting Existing Materials to Other Specialised Uses', in *Materials Production for the Seldom-taught Languages*), three criteria are particularly important in materials production:

lightness	that is, not burdensome, including variety and some light relief;
transparency	that is, the relationship between their actual form and their purpose should be clear;
strength	that is, they must engage the student's interest and bring to bear his full resources.

Bringing light relief and thought-provoking, imaginative tasks into course design can sometimes hinder the achievement of the task in question. The learning tasks must be assessed in terms of whether they accomplish effectively the stated aims and whether they are derived from needs or wants.

A page from the *Daily Mirror* was used to illustrate the range of exercises which a single text could initiate.

Production factors

One can take a product view of materials, that where appropriate ones are not available they must be developed; or a process view of materials, that their production is a valuable promotional and professional activity in any situation. The materials writer must therefore consider:

> process vs. product;
>
> relationship of producer to users;
>
> participation in production;
>
> job specifications in group production context;
>
> feedback mechanisms within project;
>
> the need for prototype lessons;
>
> general production schedules.

In broader terms, he needs to be aware of:

> curriculum development models and insights;
>
> procedures in research, design and development, dissemination and adoption; and interaction between these phases;
>
> political and cultural perspectives.

The problem is to balance the real and the ideal worlds, to innovate and improve with recognition of what is constant.

Discussion
Among the issues arising were:

> *the divergence between research culture, classroom culture, and commercial culture;*
>
> *the problem of marketing materials to satisfy a range of customers;*
>
> *the length of time for which materials are designed to remain in use;*
>
> *the need for negotiation between writers and teachers to ensure appropriacy.*

1.3   Approaches to curriculum design (1984)

JANET MAW

In recent years writing on curriculum design has tended to move away from the dogmatic certainties of the early 1970s, when the 'rational curriculum planning model' was equated with the strict use of behavioural objectives as the only permissible structuring device in curriculum design. The crusading nature of the movement's devotees, at least in the United States, was acknowledged by a car-sticker exhorting the reader to 'Help Stamp out Non-Behavioural Objectives'! An early twinge of doubt is shown by the modification of this sticker to read 'Help Stamp out *Some* Non-Behavioural Objectives'!

Since then writing on curriculum design has become more diverse, reflective and exploratory, less strident and assertive. It is recognised that curriculum design cannot be treated as a purely technical problem, that it is inescapably value-saturated, and the absence of theories and laws equivalent to those of the physical sciences is not simply the result of a perverse failure on the part of curriculum theorists and designers to be adequately and properly 'scientific', but derives from the nature of the problems we face in curriculum design. Reid includes these problems in the category of 'uncertain practical problems', which are characterised by their need for action, their dependence on context (which nevertheless cannot be exhaustively analysed), their inevitable selectivity of values and interests, and the impossibility of fully predicting the outcomes of any course of action decided upon. In such a situation the curriculum designer needs to use theory flexibly and imaginatively, to be both eclectic and heuristic. A curriculum is not to be judged on how closely it approximates to an *a priori* model of design but on how appropriate it is to a particular context of implementation, and on the extent to which it respects the integrity of the subject matter presented.

In practice, we find three main approaches to curriculum design, that is, structuring by:

a)   specification of outcomes or objectives;

b)   specification of content; and

c)   specification of process.

However, these approaches should not be seen as unitary 'models' as there is a variety of writing in each design focus, and they are certainly not mutually exclusive, indicating emphasis rather than completeness. In part, the appropriateness of structuring focus depends upon whether the rationale and purpose of the curriculum concentrates on skills, performance or product, on induction to a knowledge area, or on the development of values, attitudes and dispositions.

Objectives have been used in various ways in curriculum design, and for teachers there have been problems in the confusion of terminology. At times 'objectives' have been qualified by the descriptions 'educational', 'instructional', 'behavioural', and 'operational' – the description becoming increasingly precise and prescriptive over time. Other writers simply *assume* that 'objectives' means behavioural or even operational objectives, even when this is neither clear nor obvious. What is meant by 'behaviour' also varies. One of the most influential writers on curriculum design, Tyler, insisted that objectives should be specified in terms of both content and behaviour, but not necessarily in precise form, largely because such precision is a practical impossibility in teaching. This patently obvious fact was ignored by later writers. In practice, the use of objectives in curriculum design has been overwhelmingly in the middle range of precision, clearly specifying the nature of behaviour, but not its precise form. The move towards greater precision was dictated by the needs of evaluation rather than design, and it is against the precisely specified objectives that the arguments of reductionism, trivialisation, mechanistic manipulation and materialism have their greatest force. In this country, the Schools Council Project 'Science 5–13' used objectives flexibly and imaginatively, and in spite of the various arguments against them objectives are alive and well and living in the Assessment of Performance Unit, Local Authority testing and graded tests, *inter alia*!

Specification of content is, of course, the traditional focus of curriculum 'design' in this country – the 'syllabus' as a list of 'topics to be covered'. Such an approach is characterised by its assumption of a common educational background, and a common set of values and morals. It communicates to an 'in-group' and relates to a conception of the school or college as a set of semi-autonomous units – Bernstein's 'collection code' in operation! It is highly conservative and resistant to change because its value base is largely tacit and unquestioned. In practice, all curriculum theories incorporate content in some form, but where content approaches have an explicit rationale, it is fundamentally epistemological, based on an analysis of the nature and structure of knowledge. A key international writer here is Jerome Bruner, who in the early 1960s argued that every discipline has an internal structure of interrelated concepts, ideas, generalisations and laws which allow the organisation and generation of a great deal of specific information, and hence allow both an economy and a transfer of learning. The curriculum design task is to delineate these 'key concepts' and keep returning to them in increasingly complex and challenging form (the 'spiral curriculum') through an appropriate mode of representation. In spite of such issues as whether all disciplines do, in fact, conform to Bruner's model of structure, and to what extent we can agree on which ideas of a discipline are structural, Bruner's ideas have been very influential. The most powerful exemplar of the structural approach to course design was 'Man, a Course of Study' (MACOS) for which Bruner himself was consultant.

Again, the idea of designing a curriculum around a statement of what is to happen is not new, but in contemporary writing the common factor uniting a cluster of writers has been a rejection of the tyranny of objectives, a rejection based in their experience of curriculum design in the arts, humanities and social sciences, where specification of precise outcomes is seen as impossible or unethical. The most fully worked out model in contemporary research is that of Stenhouse, derived from his work on the Humanities Curriculum Project. Because of the team's adopted values of autonomy, diversity, controversy and understanding, structuring by objectives was seen as inappropriate; structuring by content was inadequate to the non-disciplinary nature of the project. Stenhouse developed his argument from an early paper of Peters, who was then arguing that a liberal education is defined by its mode of acquisition rather than by its content or aims. Stenhouse adopted Peters' concept of 'principles of procedure' as a means of structuring an appropriate classroom process by asking the question 'What classroom procedures are implicit in our aim?'. The Humanities Project is a complex curriculum structured by a central classroom strategy, just as MACOS is a complex project structured around key concepts, themes and generalisations.

In summary, a reading of curriculum design literature would no longer programme the aspirant designer towards a 'correct' design model, but lead him to analyse which approach might be most appropriate, effective and feasible in relation to:

a) the level of sophistication of teachers and learners;
b) the context of implementation; and
c) the nature of the discipline or subject matter.

There are many roads to Rome!

1.4   Educational technology and curriculum renewal (1984)

MARTIN PHILLIPS

In this paper I shall take a broad view of what is meant by curriculum renewal to encompass a wide range of areas in which changes in current practice are possible. I shall take a relatively narrow view of educational technology and focus mainly on the newest technologies, particularly computers, as having the most potential for effecting far-reaching changes. Within this perspective I want to explore the nature of the issues involved and raise some questions. I believe that when we consider the part that educational technology may have to play in curriculum renewal, there are the seeds of an important debate, a debate which is usually assumed as settled. All I can do here is try to stimulate that debate.

The computer is the most sophisticated technology yet to become available to the teacher. It is useful to consider just how it is different from earlier 'sophisticated technology'. An example of the latter which is often compared to the computer is the language laboratory, a notable disappointment for most teachers. The language lab was always a specialised piece of technology restricted to educational institutions. Apart from this relative inaccessibility, the type of learning offered by the language lab was also limited. Based on behaviourist psychology and programmed learning, the learning experiences offered by the language lab were both inflexible and uninspiring. In contrast the computer is both more generally accepted (beyond learning institutions) and more versatile. It has the capacity to store and manipulate large amounts of information, and it can respond to instructions and demands in a very short time, in human terms virtually immediately. These features make the computer an invaluable resource for generating personalised learning experiences.

These possibilities are, however, not neutral: the computer is not, as many seem to think it is, an impartial 'delivery system', simply a medium which does not affect the message. The new technology has profound implications for our activity. It brings into question quite fundamental notions such as the nature of the curriculum, the concept of the classroom itself, the locus of control over the learning process as well as the status of materials, the nature of methodology, the role of the teacher, and of teacher training. Let us briefly look at the sort of issues involved – we will not have time to explore any of them in any detail.

Curriculum
An example is the Logo programming language which allows children to relate geometrical concepts to their own experience. This amounts to the definition of a new kind of geometry, procedural or experiential geometry rather than demonstrative geometry (see Papert 1980). Thus the nature of the task has changed and with it our yardsticks for evaluation.
Question: Is there any reason to suppose that the new technology could not have the same impact on the definition of the language curriculum? Is this what is needed to give muscle to the notion of 'procedural syllabus'? (see Prabhu 1983).

The concept of the classroom
The technology offers the prospect of the distributed classroom – the use of micro bulletin boards, telephone teaching, etc.
Question: With the prospect of direct student-to-student communications unmediated by the teacher (perish the thought!) who then decides whether performance criteria have been achieved? This raises the following issue.

Locus of control over the learning process
One of the conventional justifications trotted out for the computer is the justification for any self-access approach: learner-centred, self-pacing. The proportion of teacher-led to learner-controlled activity can change. More importantly it offers choice: if a student doesn't like one computer assisted language learning (CALL) program, (s)he calls up another

instantaneously; programs can also be sensitive to level and, in the future, self-adjusting in real time in response to what they 'learn' about the student. Students have a tool which allows them to assume mastery of their own learning experience.

Question: Is this a liberation or a new tyranny brought about by a 20th-century *trahison des clercs*, the abandonment to a machine of functions that should be performed by people, teachers?

Status of materials

Hitherto, video has been passive; nothing the student said or did could influence in a deep sense the linear progression of the tape. This is even truer of print materials of course. Now, as I have just suggested, they can be self-modifying to accommodate themselves to the requirements of the individual student. In a sense this is already with us, this is what is meant by interactivity.

Question: What are the implications of having materials that can 'bite back', as it were? Is it desirable that more of the management of learning be embodied in the materials themselves rather than in the way they are exploited?

Nature of methodology

New technologies often bring about changes in the methodologies of the subjects the teaching of which they are designed to facilitate. For example, the introduction of video in ELT applications has stimulated completely novel teaching techniques. The changes are not necessarily for the good. One of the criticisms I would raise against most of the current generation of CALL materials is that they are methodologically retrograde.

Question: Can we be sure that the introduction of a new technology necessarily leads to positive benefits in terms of its impact on methodology?

Role of teacher

If more of the management of learning can be embodied in the materials themselves, how does this affect the role of the teacher? Given the arguable advantages of the new technology for individualising learning, does this mean that it will replace the teacher as some claim and seem to be happy to envisage? I do not believe this either is or should be the case. The more interesting CALL programs, for example, are those that generate a task which involves inter and intra-group negotiation for its solution. It seems to me that helping to ensure that relevant learning takes place in the course of responding to, say, a computer-managed simulation demands skills of a very high order at least commensurate with anything required by the more sophisticated techniques in communicative language teaching.

Question: What might the nature be of the new equilibrium that will be brought about by the new technology in the delicate balance among students, materials and the teacher?

Teacher training

All the above considerations have implications for teacher training programmes which are themselves in a reflexive relationship to the curriculum. Through familiarisation with new educational technologies, teachers develop their perceptions of their role.

Whether the new educational technologies merely reinforce current practice (or, what would be even more sterile, fossilise outmoded methodologies), or in contrast offer fruitful opportunities for curriculum renewal depends in part on our willingness to identify and face issues of the sort I have just outlined, in part on technical advances and in part on theoretical progress. These are not separate problems. To exploit fully the potential of the new technology for language learning, a number of currently distinct applications need to be integrated and the man–machine interface has to become considerably more sophisticated than it is at present. Linguistic databases containing lexical and syntactic information, word processing functions, natural language parsing, knowledge based systems, speech synthesis and ultimately speech recognition, need to be integrated with pedagogic programs and testing routines if the use of interactive technologies in language learning is to transcend its present trivial level of development. At the same time, we should beware of claiming for computer assisted language learning more than we know about language or learning. Our theories of both are not yet adequate to have really powerful, and more importantly, trustworthy technologies based on them. It is crucial, then, that we do not lose sight of the 'assisted' in computer assisted language learning.

What relevance does this have to, say, the teacher working in the African bush? All this talk of advanced technologies and the problems they raise hardly affects that working environment. But I would claim it does in two ways, one relatively short-term and superficial, one longer-term and fundamental. In the short-term we shall all have to get to grips with the new technologies. I have heard of plans by one of the major British manufacturers of home computers to produce a self-assembly version of its most popular model which will run off a twelve-volt car battery. It will soon not be possible to ignore the threat and the potential. This makes it all the more urgent to face up to the issues. To return to the analogy with the language lab, I believe the questions raised by the new technologies are far subtler and the temptations more seductive than they ever were with the language lab. So the deeper relevance is that it behoves us to consider our position, to prepare ourselves for the impact of the new technology and to absorb its implications for curriculum change so that we can channel its force in appropriate directions. Otherwise most of the developing world (and a large part of the developed world too) risks being littered, firstly with the hardware wreckage of ill-conceived CALL and half-baked interactive video and secondly with the aftermath of the curriculum changes that they have brought in their wake. I shall leave you with a final question.

What sort of learning environments do we want to create with the new technology?

There is an even deeper reason why this question demands urgent consideration. This is because it is not merely a technical question, that is a matter of technique, nor yet a political question concerned with ensuring that appropriate technologies are used where they are needed rather than where manufacturers would like to sell them, but ultimately an ethical question. We have to be clear about the nature of the curriculum renewal we want to bring about by the use of educational technology because the answer we give reveals our views of what it means to be human and of what it is proper to delegate to machines.

2.0   Communicative Methodology

MIKE BEAUMONT

We have observed in the Introduction to Part 1 how the term 'communicative' initially became attached to the notion of syllabus design, most noticeably in the title of Munby (1978). In the late 1970s and early 1980s, however, attention began to turn away from needs analysis and syllabus specifications to an exploration of what it might mean to teach 'communicatively' both in the detailed sense of specific classroom techniques and in the broader sense of an overall teaching approach. Both perspectives are represented in this collection of four papers from the Dunford seminars of the period.

The first two papers very much exemplify what Watson terms the 'chalk-face' perspective. O'Neill concentrates on three 'dualities', as he classes them; we might also see them as representing three dilemmas that began to face the 'communicative' teacher. The first relates to the extent to which a functional approach should focus on form. O'Neill concludes that it should, not least because the functional language needs of even a small group of ESP learners *as perceived by the learners themselves*, may be extremely disparate. The second picks up the accuracy-fluency debate, suggesting that successful communication should be the main priority and that an over-emphasis on accuracy could inhibit the learner. The third explores the connection between receptive and productive language skills. O'Neill favours loosening the traditional tight relationship between teaching input and learner output, allowing learners more choice and freedom in their production of language.

Watson tackles the problem of trying to introduce more communicative methods in a context where innovation is constrained by a number of fundamental factors: poor and overcrowded classrooms, lack of books and other resources, and untrained, examination-oriented teachers with little motivation, or reason, to change. Watson's perspective neatly and simultaneously illustrates one dimension of several of the dichotomies we referred to in the Introduction to Part 1. Applying a communicative methodology to secondary level, state sector, TENOR contexts in the developing world is not only difficult but, some commentators were later to argue, questionable in itself.

In an extract from a much longer paper, Breen takes on the broader perspective, outlining three major 'defining features' of a communicative classroom: communicative content, that is the nature and use of communicative competence in the classroom; communicative process, the means by which the learners are engaged with the content; and the communicative context, that is the recognition that the classroom itself is an authentic context for the 'investigation of communication and learning'. He also suggests that curriculum innovation has three sources: practical experience, theory and research.

If O'Neill's and Watson's contributions exemplify the first source, and Breen's the second, then Allwright, in the final paper in this section, explores the potential of the third. Drawing very much on the implications of early research studies in second language acquisition, he proposes six hypotheses to guide possible future research into the relationship between teaching and learning, between 'what gets taught', as he puts it, and 'what gets learnt'. By implication, he makes the case for much more classroom-oriented research – the need to examine more rigorously and extensively the effect of instruction on classroom learning. In this way, we should not only discover more about the processes of teaching and learning, and how they interact, but also be able to test empirically the claims of particular approaches, notably the communicative approach. In this sense, Allwright's paper can be seen to anticipate a decade or more of research into such issues, research which has provided us with much more evidence of what actually happens when language teachers teach and language learners learn.

2.1   The three dualities, or 'new wine in old bottles' (1980)
ROBERT O'NEILL

The speaker began with a resumé of his own career as an English language teacher which started in 1960 when language teaching was almost 'a shameful activity'. Without an academic background he had developed his own style, and he stressed the importance of developing one's own style rather than being stereotyped. As a course writer himself he aims now to provide material that may be used in a variety of personal teaching styles. He defined the three dualities of his title as follows:

(i)   FORM–FUNCTION
(ii)   ACCURACY–FLUENCY
(iii) PRODUCTION–RECEPTION

Form–Function
The traditional view of teaching was that after the learner had absorbed the forms of the language he naturally passed on to *use* of the language.

Functionalism concerns a prediction of the needs of the students, and here the speaker referred to his own experience when teaching six businessmen in Germany. Their functional requirements were not at all those supposed by the native speaker. In what seemed like a perfect teaching environment the functions were totally divergent, or related to one person only (the speaker confessed to having ended up by reading detective stories to his pupils!) It proved impossible to begin with a functional description of their needs.

Accuracy–Fluency

The dualism between accuracy and fluency can be painful. Should one mark all mistakes? How should one treat the learner offering? Insistence on accuracy too early may humiliate or destroy a learner's real powers of language acquisition. The teacher has to decide what levels of accuracy to insist on at any one time, and she needs a wide repertoire of correction strategies. The speaker likened teaching a language to the training of UK artillery observers when the shot must be called immediately; the imposition of a theoretical framework impairs accuracy. Should one worry about the importance of intonation? So long as a non-native speaker can make himself understood, isn't that really the main thing? Insistence on accuracy may well result in 'pathological trauma'.

Production–Reception

Reference was made to those who insist on developing listening fluency before speaking. Language is best acquired through oral practice. Functional schemes still use audio-lingual methodology, and while audio-lingual materials may have been done away with, the method has not disappeared. A method should be created whereby one allows pupils to respond but does not insist. In this fashion, teaching should provide a long chance to listen, acquire and produce. The feedback from the learner is useful and must not be extracted by force.

The speaker's solution (the compromise) to the problems posed by the three dualities were as follows:

1   There can be no function without a certain degree of form. Structural progression cannot be dispensed with.

2   Regular models should be provided, but without insistence on accuracy.

3   Learners should have the opportunity to hear different varieties of language before having to produce it. Information, with its in-built redundancy, can be received at a level way above that of productivity.

In subsequent discussion the speaker was asked whether it was possible for the course writer to provide a teacher's book for all purposes, or was this a search for an El Dorado? O'Neill saw the function of teachers' notes as prompts to an internal methodology and his criteria for satisfactory teaching materials were:

a)   *brevity – presentation should take 3-4 minutes;*
b)   *adaptability – improvisation should be possible; and*
c)   *functional relevance.*

In answer to a question about the place of the new radical methods, as to whether they are mutually exclusive or whether they can be absorbed into present methods, O'Neill thought the teacher needed a repertoire of strategies, taking nothing to the extreme but based on a firm methodological core.

2.2   Communication with traditional materials (1980)

BARRIE WATSON

The speaker gave a full description of his working situation in Chandigarh, India, and he outlined the problems of secondary teachers in his region: poor classrooms, overcrowding, lack of books, aids and other equipment; untrained teachers who are not language specialists and are resistant to change; a textbook produced in the 1960s based on a sketchy list of structures to be covered; and examinations (held static by teachers) containing texts already studied in class and in which success hinges upon accurate reproduction of such texts. The typical result of all these constraints on effective classroom teaching was as follows, all classroom talk (apart from reading of the text) being in the mother-tongue:

TEACHER	PUPILS
1 Reads text.	Follow in textbook.
2 Translates (exam necessity).	Follow, write translation in books.
3 Explains commonly confused items. (Teacher here shows off own knowledge and establishes supremacy.)	Do not challenge or question.
4 Elicits/corrects.	'Make sentences' with specified items.
5 Elicits/corrects.	Translate text orally (exam necessity).
6 Corrects.	Read text aloud.
7 Reads out questions given after text.	Answer by reference to text.
8 Elicits/corrects.	Repeat these answers.

The speaker's main aims in attempting to remedy the situation were as follows:

- to eliminate the boredom of pupils and teacher;
- to produce *users* of the language; and
- to create activities which require participation without disturbing the security of pupils and teachers.

Watson explained that he regularly teaches a local secondary class and is trying out an approach that attempts to achieve these aims. Given that 'some teachers have discovered that there is almost nothing valuable that they know that was told to them by somebody else', he refuses to feed meanings, explanations or 'help' to the pupils. He tries to free them from a 'teacher-bound' learning process whilst still remaining linked to given materials. This is a different approach from that of making draconian changes in the teachers' methods, materials, etc., – which would clearly be impossible in this situation.

The speaker then gave a demonstration of the strategy of pupils guessing the identity of objects using the foreign language with the mother tongue at the beginner stages, so that pupils discover the real meaning of the English words. Analogies with 'memory game' techniques are easy to see. No information is given to the pupil to help him sort or retain but security is there because both teacher and pupils know that they will eventually arrive at the correct responses. The possibility of failure is eliminated.

The main point was that teachers should not offer information to pupils which would 'deaden their acquisition'. The demonstration worked through the stages of vocabulary presentation, reading comprehension and questions and answers at a beginners' level. A great deal of interest was aroused by the demonstration and there was general appreciation of the need for analytical blow-by-blow accounts of what life is really like at the 'chalkface' in many British Council-served countries.

2.3   Why 'communicative'? (1982)

MIKE BREEN

I believe it is fair to say that there is, at present, a shift of focus within the 'communicative approach' to language teaching. Initially, much energy and discussion was devoted to the communicative content of language teaching, with particular reference to needs analysis and – especially – to the construction of syllabuses on the basis of functional or notional categorisation of the target language. More recently, and possibly because of a growing recognition of the limitation of such a content-specific focus, there seems to be an interest in identifying the 'communicative approach' more particularly within methodology. Thus, there is a shift of concern away from content towards the teaching-learning process, perhaps to the point where specifically communicative content may no longer be one of the distinctive hallmarks of the overall 'approach'. In this context, I wish to balance the main methodological orientation of this paper against a brief answer to a large question: Why 'communicative'?

The classroom which I have in mind can be regarded as communicative because of three major defining features: its content, its teaching-learning process, and its own social context.

Communicative content
In the communicative classroom, the learners are directly concerned with communication as the primary content or subject-matter of their learning.

That is, they are not only working upon the language as a formal system but are also working upon – and through – those rules and conventions which govern social behaviour with language and the use of language for the meaningful sharing of ideas and points of view. Learners are also involved in developing communicative abilities and skills; how to exploit and apply knowledge of rules and conventions in actual instances of communication. Therefore, one of the major aspects of the content for the classroom is the nature and use of communicative competence, which entails knowledge of the language as only one of its elements or components.

Communicative process

The most important materials in a communicative classroom from a pedagogic point of view are process materials. These materials provide activities as springboards for much of the work of the class. Also, the defining characteristic of the activities is that they will generate in the learners the need to communicate. Central to the work cycle in the class are the explicit contributions of all the participants. The major motivation for the encouragement of explicit learner contributions is that they can enable the learners to directly engage in and share the learning process within the classroom group. Clearly, such explicit contributions entail a communicative process. The teacher's priorities are to activate these contributions and to facilitate an overt and public interaction between different and changing curricula. In all of these ways, communication is not merely the objective and content of the classroom, it is also a crucial *means* for the actual processes of teaching and learning.

Communicative context

The actual social and interpersonal reality which is special to a classroom can make the classroom itself a genuine and valuable language learning resource. Because it is a context in which a group of people meet to share the common overall problem of coming to terms with a new language, it provides its own inherent communicative potential. The actual need for authentic communication between participants can be optimised if the classroom is exploited as a laboratory – or experimental milieu – for the investigation of communication and learning, as the real location for the creation of the curriculum of the group, and as a place where participants may value and mutually benefit from each other's contributions.

In proposing these three characteristic features of the communicative classroom, I wish to suggest that the contribution of the communicative approach to the teaching and learning of languages should not be perceived as narrowly methodological nor alternatively limited to syllabus design. Communicative language teaching represents a genuine redefinition of the purpose or objectives of language courses. It similarly implies changes in the ways in which we may select and sequence the content of our lessons, and the kinds of content or subject matter appropriate to the language class may now be differently specified. Communicative language teaching certainly offers us an alternative approach to the organisation and management of the teaching-learning process in the classroom – and this alternative has been the particular theme of the present paper. Finally, communicative language teaching implies new directions for evaluation procedures. Not only those procedures which focus upon learner achievement but also evaluation which can have a formative influence during learning and a direct role in the adaptation of our courses so that they can be more sensitive to the particular learning groups for which they were designed. In essence, what I am suggesting is that communicative language teaching offers potential innovation throughout every element of a language teaching curriculum – its purposes, contents, methods, and procedures for evaluation.

However, it would be foolish to assume that communicative language teaching is totally innovative. Perhaps the most valuable innovations are those which have their roots in what has been tried and tested, and particularly within the volatile reality of actual language classrooms. Many teachers may already facilitate those conditions in their classrooms which reflect the kinds of principles which are expressed and described in this paper. Professional experience, developments in theory, and discoveries in research may, at times, jointly lead to particular innovations so that new directions are motivated from all three perspectives. I believe that communicative language teaching, or more particularly, the communicative curriculum for language teaching, represents precisely this kind of push for innovation from practical experience, theory and research. What I have tried to show is that the classroom itself is the place where genuine curriculum innovation is actually worked out and implemented. And the communicative classroom is one in which the learner's contribution to curriculum innovation – an important fourth perspective – can be more directly called upon.

2.4   The relationship between teaching and learning (1984)
DICK ALLWRIGHT

Teachers do not expect their learners to learn everything that they teach them but, if their learners have no other opportunities to learn, then teachers are likely to expect that *what* their learners learn is directly related to what they teach. Research suggests, however, that the teaching-learning relationship is far more indirect. There are two main approaches to the problem of understanding this indirectness.

a)   We can assume that the relationship is itself direct (causal), and then look for some factor or factors that may be intervening to obscure the relationship for the observer; or

b) We can assume that the relationship is in fact indirect and then look for some factor or factors to explain how it is that learners come to learn whatever it is that they do learn.

Some factors have already been suggested in relation to these two approaches. Let us consider six hypotheses.

1 The incubation hypothesis

It has been suggested that whatever one's learners are taught will need an 'incubation period' before it can be expected to appear in their performance. Such an incubation period could account for findings that otherwise appear to point to a lack of causal relationship between teaching and learning, because it would predict that recently taught items would, in performance, appear not to have been learned, and it would also predict that items would appear to have been learned that had not recently been taught. The incubation hypothesis, however, would not predict the appearance of items not yet taught. To account for such findings an alternative hypothesis is needed.

2 The interaction hypothesis

It may be that what learners are taught is not simply the 'syllabus', as planned and implemented in a one-to-one fashion by the teacher, but something potentially much more complex – the product of the classroom interaction process, whereby what gets taught becomes modified, probably enriched. This hypothesis would suggest that the lack of apparent relationship between teaching and learning is an artefact of the failure to observe and take properly into account what actually gets taught in the classroom, as opposed to what has been planned to be taught there, or assumed to have been taught there. The hypothesis could be tested by relating detailed observation of actual teaching to learning performance. An alternative hypothesis would be needed if much appeared in performance that could not be traced back to specific acts of teaching.

3 The input hypothesis

It may be that what learners can learn from is not just what gets specifically 'taught'. They may be able to learn from things that happen in the classroom that are not in themselves specific acts of 'teaching'. Perhaps classroom interaction offers a wide range of inputs to learners' learning processes. Perhaps they can learn from all the classroom management talk, for example, at least if it is conducted in the target language. It may be that in this way 'what is available to be learned from' offers such a variety of learning opportunities that it should come as no surprise if what learners learn is only weakly related to that subset of learning opportunities produced directly by acts of teaching. Perhaps the mere frequency of learning opportunities for a particular item, whether or not 'teaching' is involved, will be enough to facilitate learning.

In principle such a hypothesis could be tested by relating a detailed account of the occurrence of learning opportunities to learner performance. If the hypothesis were not falsified in this way, then we might ask whether 'frequency of occurrence of learning opportunities' is in itself a sufficient explanation for whatever learning takes place. By what processes, we might ask, is something learned when it is frequently encountered? For that we shall need a further hypothesis.

4   The acquisition hypothesis

It may be that, even if frequency itself is not crucial, learners get whatever they get from the classroom input by processes that are importantly different from those the teaching is trying to invoke. If the learners are using some 'natural processes' rather than those assumed to be involved in formal instructional settings, then this might explain why what they get from a lesson is different from what has been taught (and not just 'less than' what has been taught).

We might be able to test this hypothesis by comparing the performance of learners receiving only formal instruction with what is known about the performance of untutored learners (or 'acquirers'). If their performance could be better predicted in this way than by trying to relate it directly to the teaching then the acquisition hypothesis would receive support. We might also, in trying to make sense of the performance data, invoke a further hypothesis.

5   The natural order hypothesis

It may be that teaching and learning are only indirectly related because learners, even in a formal classroom setting, are following a natural order of acquisition which is unrelated either to the teaching syllabus, or to whatever actually does get taught, or even to the frequency of whatever 'becomes available to be learned from' in the classroom. Again one should be able to test this hypothesis (in principle at least) by comparing the performance of classroom learners with that of untutored acquirers. But it would be difficult to maintain the 'natural order' hypothesis if learners' 'orders' turned out to be idiosyncratic. For such results we might turn to the last hypothesis here.

6   The personal agenda hypothesis

It may be that learners follow a 'personal agenda' in their learning (or acquisition), selecting whatever it is that they personally want from all the learning opportunities that classroom interaction engenders, and perhaps doing interactive work on occasion to ensure the occurrence of items on their personal agendas that do not otherwise arise.

Some general comments

a)   These hypothesis are not in themselves novel (except perhaps the 'interaction hypothesis'), but they do not appear to have been related to each other in the above way before, or to the general question of the relationship of teaching and learning.

b) All the hypotheses have already been studied, to a greater or lesser extent, and all seem investigable by relatively familiar research techniques.

c) It nevertheless seems most unlikely that any of them will ever be conclusively falsified, if only because they are likely to be extremely difficult to disentangle from each other.

d) Only settings permitting a clear comparison between 'formal instruction only' and 'informal acquisition only' will allow us to obtain anything like clear results, if any are ever to be obtained at all.

e) It seems most likely that we shall eventually have to accept that all the hypotheses (and probably others as yet unimagined) are needed to help us understand the complexities of classroom language learning. Any apparent incompatibility between them is probably an illusion.

f) None of the six hypotheses is required if further research suggests that what learners learn is simply a subset of what they are taught. There are plenty of other hypotheses to account for what may be straight-forward after all. The first problem is therefore to establish that there really are discrepancies between what teachers teach and what learners learn, discrepancies that cannot be explained merely by drawing attention to the fact that teachers are not perfect, and learners are not perfect. That we know.

3.0 Evaluation

MIKE BEAUMONT

Evaluation, as Alderson is anxious to point out in the last of the extracts in this section, involves a lot more than simply testing students. The four papers have been chosen, therefore, to reflect the multi-dimensional nature of the topic. They also show how, over a period of six years, conceptions of and attitudes to evaluation changed and broadened. In the first, taken from the 1979 Report, Seaton begins to tackle some of the implications for language testing of a communicative approach to teaching. Several important issues emerge here. First, there is the realisation that, if the syllabus and methodology are to be more communicative, and students are to be tested on what has gone on in the classroom, then testing language performance becomes much more difficult than hitherto. Second, if testing is to be carried out in the context of a syllabus specified in terms of target language performance, then criterion-referenced approaches need to replace the traditional norm-referenced approaches. Third, if the approach is criterion-referenced, then detailed specification of performance levels or bands becomes feasible. Many of the subsequent developments in testing for ELT can be seen as related to these questions.

Early argues, as we have elsewhere in this volume, that the 1970s had seen an 'overriding preoccupation' with syllabus design and he argues strongly for a renewed concentration on methodology. In particular, this should take account of the psychological factors that characterise learners and the constraints that affect teachers in various contexts. He wonders whether methods can be designed with the same rigour that had been applied to syllabuses and, in answering this question, introduces a rather wider sense of evaluation. The best we can do, he feels, is to instigate a classroom process that is evaluated in a continuous, sensitive and honest way so that our course design is appropriate and compatible with the needs and wants of the learners. In a postscript which refers to a curriculum innovation project in Germany, we have a tantalising hint of a cycle of change which begins with teacher training, a cycle for which we make the case towards the end of the Introduction to Part 1.

Following Early's paper are two extracts from consultancy reports by Mountford on materials design projects in Sudan and Somalia. They both introduce a different and still wider interpretation of the concept of evaluation. The first observes that the criteria for evaluating such projects are frequently far from clear and that such criteria can only be made clear if projects are designed and structured in a rigorous, systematic and explicit way. The second adds three further points: first, that the constraints that emerge from any evaluation process should be seen as contributing positively to the shaping of a project; second, that the project design itself should be subject to the evaluation process; and third, that the really significant variables in a project can only be evaluated using qualitative rather than quantitative methods.

In the final paper of this section, Alderson overviews the whole field of evaluating curricula and syllabuses. Evaluation is essentially an information gathering process. Information allows for description. What has been described can be judged. Evaluation, therefore, is part of the process of understanding. To be successful, the evaluation process should involve all interested parties and take into account their different perspectives; the process should be continuous and should be built into a project from the beginning; and finally, the process should be responsive to changing circumstances and appropriate to varying audiences and purposes.

3.1   Evaluating communicative performance (1979)

IAN SEATON

Evaluation was a deviation from the main process of turning Communicative Needs Profiles (CNP) into materials.

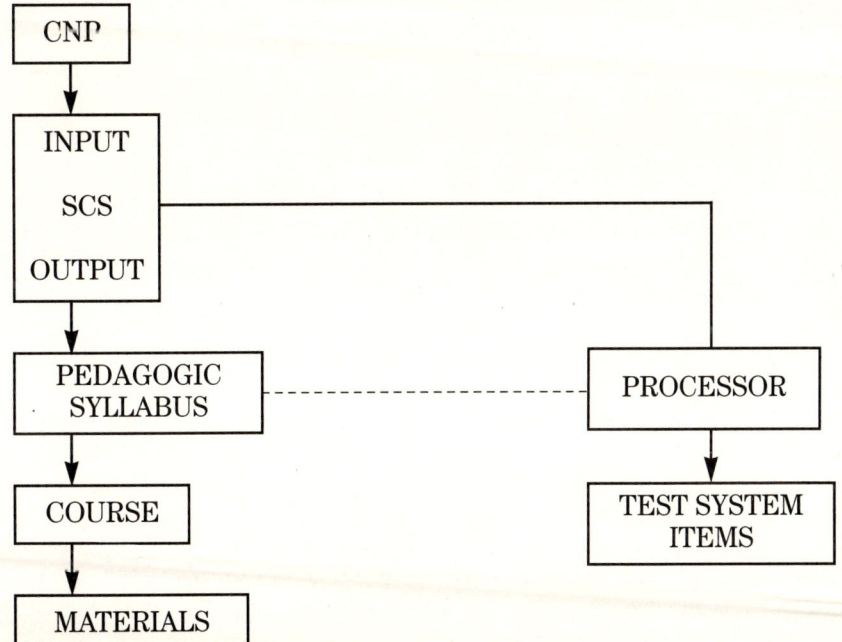

Figure 1

Target performance testing aimed to measure present performance in relation to the syllabus content specifications (SCS) and performance after the learning programme. Two particular problems which emerged in focusing on the evaluation of performance were:

(i) the question of *independence* (from interlocutors, dictionaries, teachers and so on) that is, the means of assessing fully autonomous language use (see Fig. 2); and

(ii) the question of the 'real time' in which language activities usually take place and the 'artificial time' of the examination context, that is, the authenticity of tested performance.

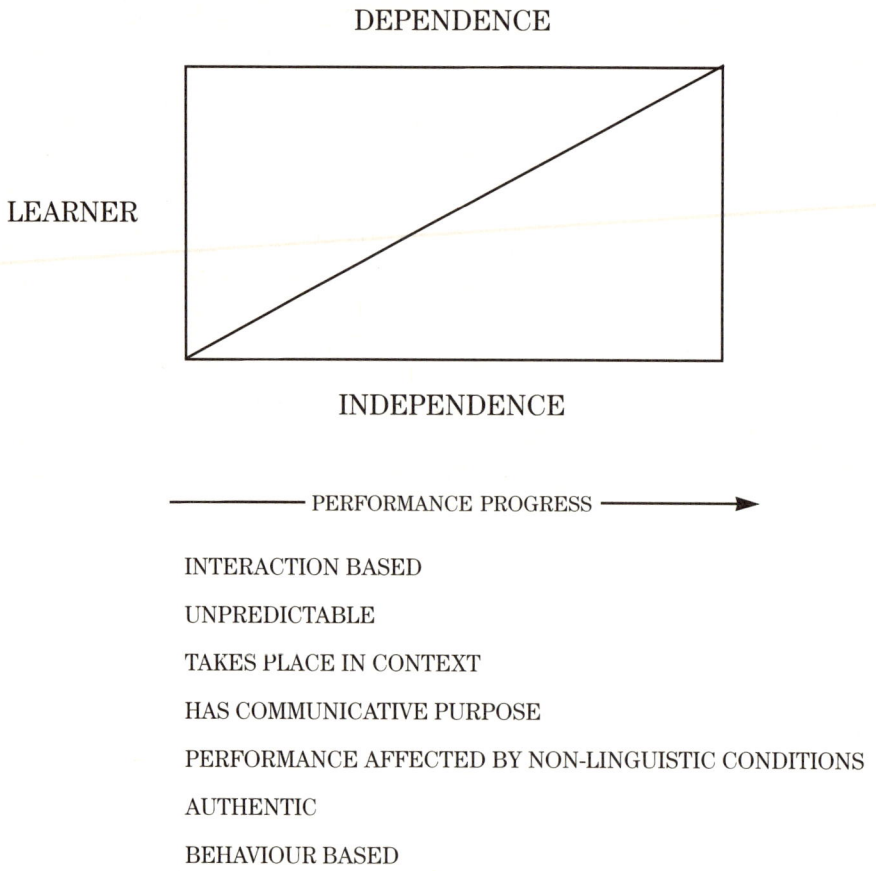

DEPENDENCE

LEARNER

INDEPENDENCE

PERFORMANCE PROGRESS

INTERACTION BASED

UNPREDICTABLE

TAKES PLACE IN CONTEXT

HAS COMMUNICATIVE PURPOSE

PERFORMANCE AFFECTED BY NON-LINGUISTIC CONDITIONS

AUTHENTIC

BEHAVIOUR BASED

Figure 2

In addition, it was necessary to distinguish between *low-level* and *high-level* interaction (see Fig. 3). In both Figs. (2 and 3) particular testing problems arise on the right-hand side.

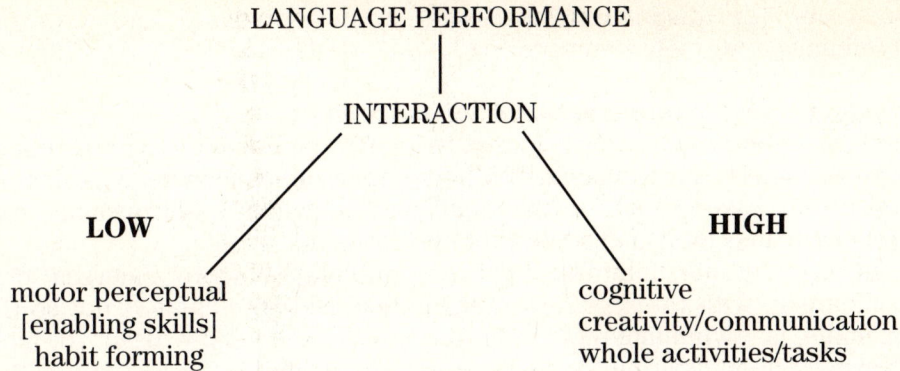

LANGUAGE PERFORMANCE

INTERACTION

LOW

motor perceptual
[enabling skills]
habit forming

HIGH

cognitive
creativity/communication
whole activities/tasks

Figure 3

In general, testing work could be divided into two main schools: the *criterion-referencers*, who claimed *validity* and concentrated on *ends*; and the *norm-referencers*, who claimed *reliability* and concentrated on *means* (see Fig. 4).

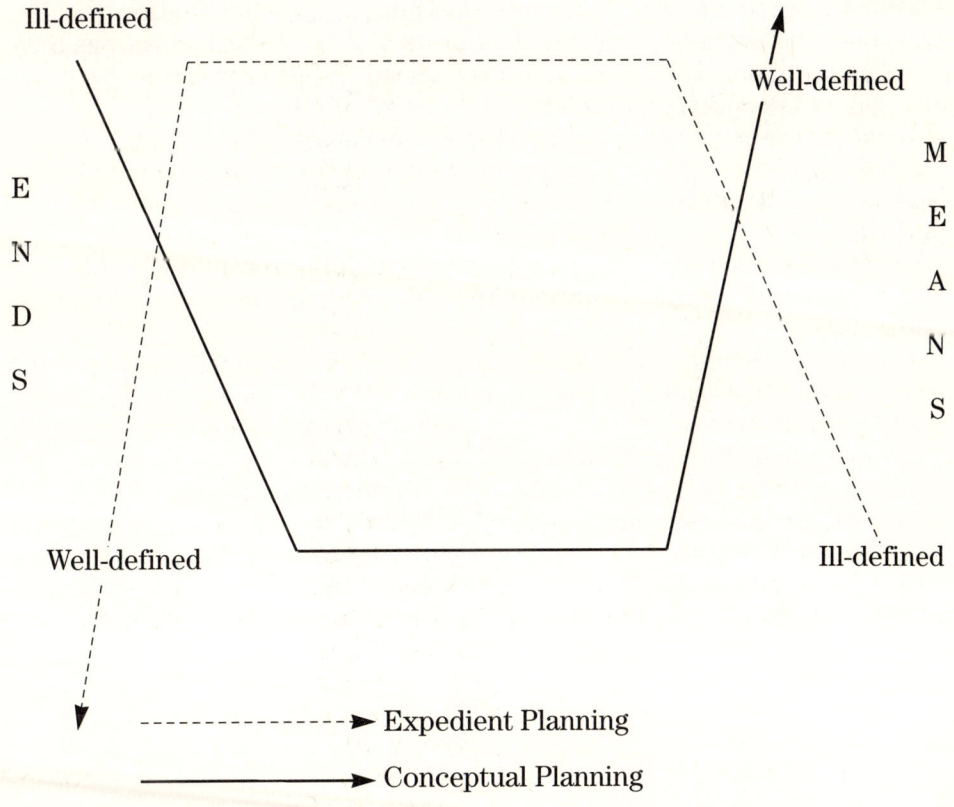

Ill-defined

Well-defined

E
N
D
S

M
E
A
N
S

Well-defined

Ill-defined

Expedient Planning

Conceptual Planning

Figure 4

Some of the distinctions between norm-referencing and criterion-referencing may be drawn as follows:

Norm- vs. criterion-referenced measurement

A *norm-referenced measure* is used to identify an individual's performance in relation to the performance of others on the same measure. A *criterion-referenced measure* is used to identify an individual's performance with respect to an established standard of performance.

In *n-r* the meaningfulness of an individual's score emerges from comparison with the scores of other individuals. In *c-r* this is not so (for example, a swimming/life-saving test): *c-r* is crucially used to make decisions about learning–training programmes and a *c-r* test can reflect training objectives (though *c-r* can be used to select also).

Variability: with *n-r* the more variability the better, but this is not a condition for a good *c-r*, where meaning comes from the connection between the items and the criterion. Item analysis in *n-r* is aimed at getting discriminatory items for a good spread (variability). Item writing in *c-r* has the different aim of seeing that the item is an accurate reflection of criterion behaviour.

Reliability: in *c-r* zero internal consistency does not matter, that is, everyone who takes the test *can* get a perfect score. If the *c-r* test has high average inter-item correlation, if it has high test-retest correlation, both are nice, but not necessary and relevant to *c-r* tests.

Validity: again adequacy of criterion representation is paramount.

Item analysis: negative discriminators need to be closely examined but neutral discriminators need not in *c-r* *if* they reflect an important attribute of the criterion.

Information reporting: degree of approximation to criterion behaviour about which information is needed depends crucially on what use is made of the data.

Ideal c-r: depends on knowing immense amount about subject matter of test – also homogeneous (that is, up to now only formal areas, mathematics and so on): but now with Munby's communicative needs analysis a specifying tool is available.

It was possible on the basis of the SCS to build up a system of *bands* or *performance levels*. Taking bands 8/9 as 'control' or ideal end, placement tests could be devised at lower levels, with band 4 frequently highly relevant to placement. Target performance cells could be specified, involving particular media/activities/tasks at particular levels. (See Fig. 5).

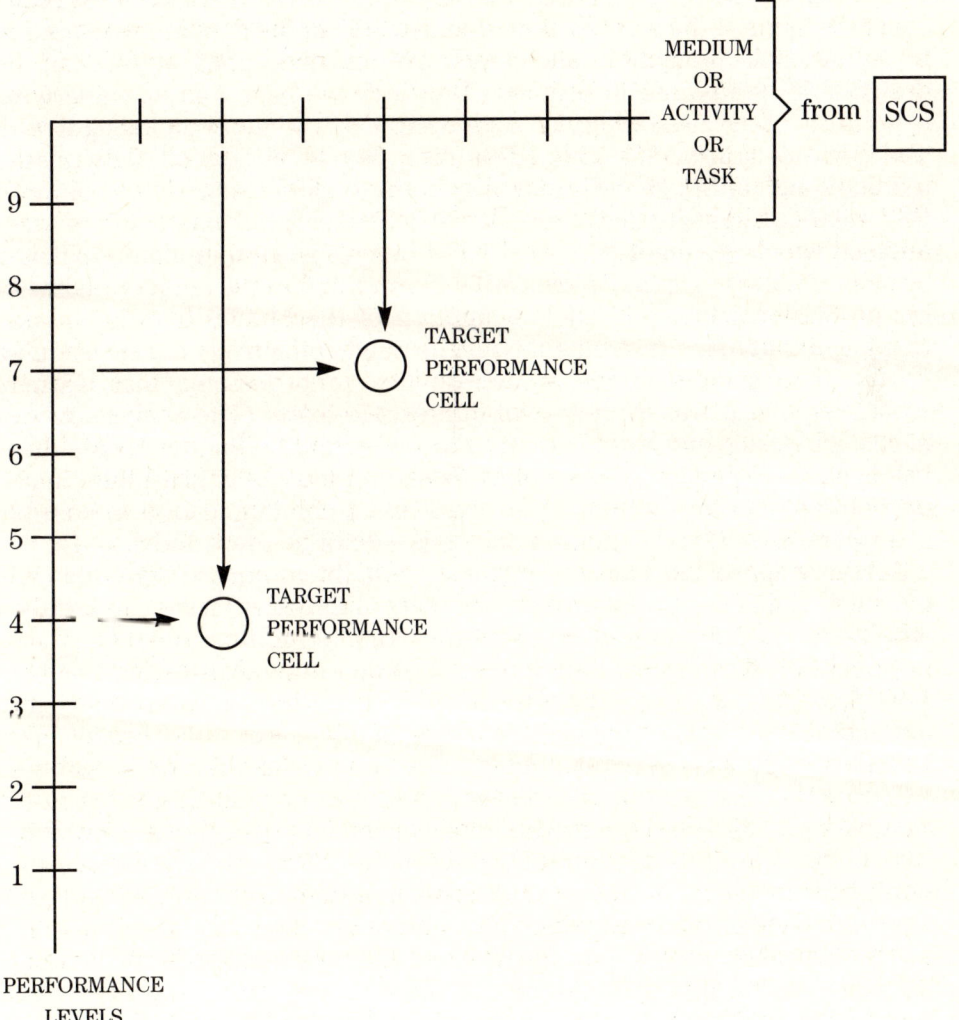

CELL DESCRIPTION

MEDIUM
OR
ACTIVITY
OR
TASK

from SCS

9

8

7 — TARGET PERFORMANCE CELL

6

5

4 — TARGET PERFORMANCE CELL

3

2

1

PERFORMANCE
LEVELS

derived from

CNP6
Targel level
Dimensions and tolerance

Figure 5

3.2 The project approach: the human dimension (1981)

PATRICK EARLY

The prevailing view of language teaching in the 1970s was that what really counts is input to the learner, both linguistically defined and then extended by situational, pragmatic and functional criteria. Such input can be designed in depth, and in previous Dunfords we have had an underlying hypothesis of the desirability of such design. Are we now replacing it with 'the cock-up approach'? The 1970s view led to enormous faith in the textbook and, although we can hardly point to global success or failure of ESP textbook development, we can at least say that expectations were aroused which were not fully met. Widdowson's work found an organising principle in the cognitive world of the learner and in the subject matter of his professional interest. The assumption of the Munby Instrument was that the output of the Instrument could be taught effectively because course content had been rendered so relevant by preprocessing that learners would see that it was in their own interests to learn. (The analysis was of needs, and needs and wants are not the same thing). Simultaneously there has been an explosion of textbooks, based on loosely defined 'functional' or 'notional' designs, which try to teach what communication is possible even when specific communication needs cannot be predicted closely.

All three approaches have reorganised content without looking radically at what happens in classrooms. Where ministries have undertaken wholesale curriculum reform by translating structural objectives into notional/functional ones, they have succeeded only in throwing teachers into despair at their impotence to turn their classrooms into communicative environments. Munby's model was, of course, only intended to process syllabus content, not to undertake the whole process of curriculum innovation and renewal, and it is our fault rather than his that we have neglected the methodological element over the last ten years. The Munby model looks ahead to the point at which the learner is a confident member of the target speech community. We should pull attention back to the route which gets him or her there, and to some of the psychological factors which characterise learners: sex, stage of learning, educational background, experience of learning other languages and motivation, and the role of the teacher. Constraints affecting teachers are discussed in several papers in *ELT Documents 110*, including Jane Willis's work on teachers' language skills (Willis 1981). The recent (1981) SELMOUS Conference dealt largely with the problem of how a teacher teaches a subject matter which is not part of his own specialisation (see *ELT Documents 112*). The learning environment and the curriculum context are also important. Such factors cannot prescribe, but should certainly inform, our methodological approach.

Method, in the last resort, is the set of rules that applies to classroom discourse, that determines the understanding that exists or should exist between teacher and learners as to what goes on in the classroom. Method is the level at which classrooms are organised and classroom discourse proceeds. If the content has changed in ways which demand changes in organisation, for example to a developed classroom in which group and pair work predominate, then the rules of classroom discourse have to change too. Can this be designed? Perhaps all we can do is set in train a language teacher/learning process, informed and enriched by our knowledge of the needs and wants of learners and, through minute by minute evaluation and adjustment, reach the kind of appropriacy and compatibility of course design that we want. This is not evaluation in the rigid sense of measuring parameters and securing replicability. It is sensitivity to feedback, knowing what works or what has gone wrong. There is a danger that a heavily designed project will induce loyalty to that design, leading participants to gloss over the cock-ups. Information on what has gone wrong and why can be enormously valuable; unfortunately it is often locked away in filing cabinets under confidential seals.

The speaker then showed 'Teacher Training Observed', a video film of a curriculum innovation project in Germany which began with teacher training, and only then proceeded towards syllabus changes, the writing of materials and the further training of teachers to interpret them. In the discussion of the film there was doubt whether, in a developing country, one would ever get funds or support for such a project, but enthusiasm for the involvement of the body of teachers in the planning, where this could be achieved.

3.3 Extracts from consultancy reports (1981)

ALAN MOUNTFORD

a. Sudan: some key ELT concepts

1 A perspective on evaluation Evaluating – descriptively and judgmentally – what is produced by a KELT programme as teaching materials is of great importance and value, not only for the institution concerned but also for other similar institutions within the country and/or in other countries. However, the criteria for such an evaluation are far from clear.

Materials are not theoretically pure artefacts. They originate as a response to needs of various kinds which are defined in various ways. They are produced within a curriculum context, which involves a view of curriculum innovation, conditioned by an organisational setting – relationships within a structure – as part of an institutional framework, with its own policy and resources. It would seem, therefore, only proper to evaluate materials as part of, and in relation to, a larger evaluation programme or project design; and that the criteria used to evaluate them should systematically relate to, and indeed derive from, the design factors that originated the programme or project.

It is commonplace that operations that are designated KELT are referred to as *projects*. It thus behoves us to consider in what sense, and to what extent, such operations can and should be defined in project terms. Central to such a consideration is the assumption that such operations need to be characterised by a distinctive approach. A project approach carries with it certain implications for the way a particular operation is set up, organised and run, whatever the post title. Above all, it seems to me, such an approach requires explicit statements enshrined in a project design document of:

- time related *objectives* in relation to *aims*
- available and needed *resources*
- organisational *structure* and relationships
- participant *functions* of all staff including support staff, and
- a set of operating *strategies* including course/materials design rationale, systems for feedback and evaluation, research requirements and capability, training requirements and procedures, procurement and use of equipment etc.

The virtue of looking at KELT programmes in this project-orientated way lies in making available for reference and scrutiny a clear specification of what a programme is all about: who does what, with whom, to what ends and why; with what resources; on what time scale; and how. Indeed, without such a design statement or project specification as an operating framework, it is not at all easy to see how programmes can be effectively evaluated. And in the absence of criteria by which programmes can be evaluated – either internally or externally – their justification and continuance is threatened, as informed strategic decisions can only be made on a relatively *ad hoc* basis.

There is little evidence that the KELT programmes at present in the Sudan are conceived in any thoroughgoing way in project terms, though they are referred to as 'projects'. No 'design documents' exist for our KELT involvement in ELSU, SELTI, the Polytechnic, or for the University of Juba, comparable with the documentation that exists for the CSE project at King Abdul Aziz University or UMSEP, for example. Allowing for differences in scale and scope, it seems to me that the design rigour that has gone into these projects should be applied to our approach to KELT projects. All the programmes in the Sudan are developmental, and all are susceptible to organisation in project terms with explicit statements of objectives, resources, structure, functions and strategy. Such an approach would only enhance the excellent work that has been done, and is being done, by structuring it more coherently and by making it more amenable to evaluation.

2   Other key KELT concepts   Three concepts would seem to derive from the key concept of viewing KELT as project-oriented activity. They are: time-boundedness; counterparting; and levels of staffing.

2.1 Time-boundedness There has been a tendency to conceive of KELT involvement as lasting four to five years. This is reflected in the length of contract of KELT officers. Clearly, open-endedness of KELT involvement is contrary to what is implied by a project approach. Equally clearly, however, it is not possible to set an arbitrary time limit on the life of a KELT project without reference to the objectives such a project seeks to achieve. It would perhaps be more appropriate to consider KELT projects in terms of *phases* which may or may not correspond to a life expectancy of four to five years.

2.1.1 A *feasibility and design* phase: such a phase is the core of the involvement when the design strategies are implemented to fulfil a set of objectives. During such a phase counterparts are trained and the dynamics of innovation are set in motion. Such a phase has to last until trained counterparts return and local capabilities are created to allow independent take-off into self-sustaining growth in the host institution and environment. Generally, at least three years are needed for this phase, depending on the project, during which additional KELTs may be recruited.

2.1.2 An *implementation* phase: such a phase is the core of the involvement when the design strategies are implemented to fulfil a set of objectives. During such a phase counterparts are trained and the dynamics of innovation are set in motion. Such a phase has to last until trained counterparts return and local capabilities are created to allow independent take-off into self-sustaining growth in the host institution and environment. Generally, at least three years are needed for this phase, depending on the project, during which additional KELTs may be recruited.

2.1.3 A *maintenance and monitoring* phase: this phase begins when it is judged that short to medium term objectives have been met, and medium to longer term objectives take over as the motivating force for the project. Clearly different aspects of a project evolve at different rates depending on the scope and scale of the enterprise. However, this phase should be seen very much as 'safeguarding the investment' and local BC office and HQ ELS/MD resources may need to be marshalled to ensure an appropriate level and degree of support. Such a phase may last at least as long as the implementation phase, that is, three years.

2.1.4 A summative *evaluation* phase: during each of the previous phases progress needs to be evaluated. Such evaluations will inevitably be formative although there is scope for summative evaluation at the end of phase 2. It must be emphasised that it is only in relation to project aims and objectives that such evaluations can be made, quantitatively and qualitatively, descriptively and judgmentally. Such a phase may well be short – weeks rather than months – and may well be conducted by external agents.

2.2 Counterparting

Counterparting is a key project concept in relation to the withdrawal of expatriate expertise and the assumption of responsibility by trained local professionals. It is recognised that certain ELT involvements that fall within the scope of KELT are more or less amenable to counterparting. Four phases in the training of counterparts can be identified, making use of the notion of apprenticeship.

2.2.1 *Pre-training* apprenticeship, when someone identified as potentially suitable for counterpart training (who may or may not be initially trained and experienced) is led to perceive and understand what the project is about and how he/she fits into it.

2.2.2 *Training* at an appropriate UK institution following an appropriate course leading to an appropriate level of qualification (diploma, MA or even PhD) which can/should involve research in relation to local needs.

2.2.3 *Post-training* apprenticeship, when the trained counterpart is reintroduced to the project at a later stage in its development and applies his/her training to the developing project. This period should be seen as the time when the counterpart is prepared for the crucial task of assuming responsibility for the implementation and maintenance of project tasks and goals. It is also the time of greatest vulnerability for the counterpart (and for the project), when expertise is not necessarily in status in the host institution, thus leading to frustration.

2.2.4 The *assumption of responsibility* during which periods of orientation, updating and consolidation of expertise are needed through attendance at conferences, seminars and courses to reinforce professional commitment and capability. Assumption of responsibility for self-sustaining growth should be seen as a gradual process during which ELT managerial skills need to be fostered.

The first three periods of counterpart training generally fall within phases 2 and 3 of a project life-span. The fourth period occurs during phases 3 and 4 and continues throughout the after life of the project.

2.3 Level of staffing

A third key concept relates to the level of staffing within a KELT project, arising out of feasibility studies and reflected in a design framework.

2.3.1 What expatriate ELT staff are needed within a KELT framework, to support a KELT project? This is the issue of 'junior' KELT staff in support of project aims and objectives, but having a more classroom-orientated brief in relation to the implementational strategy of the project or the developmental role of 'senior' KELT officers.

2.3.2   What type and level of non-ELT expatriate support staff are required to give infrastructural depth to a KELT project? For example, what size and scope does a KELT project have to be to warrant the appointment (on what terms) of a full-time project assistant to handle the administration demands of a well organised project?

b.   Somalia: textbook project

1   Project objectives The stated objectives are realistic and realisable, and consonant with those set out for the Yemen project. They provide a broad, principled framework within which the course can be specified in more detail as it progresses. The key objectives are 1 and 6:

1. That the course should be rooted in the Somali environment and reflect Somali norms and values and the interests of Somali pupils;

6. That the methodology should take account of established teaching and learning strategies . . . incorporating a considerable degree of explicitness as to classroom procedures and tactics, thus extending the teachers' repertoire of practices.

These objectives, as attributes, seem to me to characterise what a new textbook should aim to be like: an instrument for learning (and changes in practice) that is sensitive to the ecology of the social and educational environment in which it has to flourish.

2   Project equipment We are now much clearer about what equipment is required for textbook writing projects. It may be more extensive and expensive than for other KELT projects but if we are to do this kind of work (and the reasons for doing it cannot be doubted on the grounds of the extra equipment required) we should have available as soon as the project is agreed a list of what will be needed, formulated as part of the project feasibility study. What is needed, it seems to me, falls into four broad categories:

2.1   independent means of *production for trialling materials*, including a stencil cutter, typewriter, duplicator, voltage stabilisers, ancillary equipment etc;

2.2   independent means of *production for preparing camera ready copy* for offset litho, including IBM electronic golfball typewriter, plain paper copier, illustrator's equipment, polaroid camera, ancillary equipment and software;

2.3   *general office equipment* including staples, felt-tips, correcting fluid, ribbons, clips, files, glue etc;

2.4   equipment in support of pre- and in-service *teacher-training* orientation and support, including OHPs, tape-recorders, projectors, transparency makers, video-tape equipment and a portable camera.

3   Textbook design   The two key objectives in the design document influencing textbook design have already been commented on (1 above). The *cultural mutuality* is mainly achieved through the expertise of the illustrator; the *participatory methodology* is mainly achieved through an explicitness in the construction of rubrics, so that both teachers and learners are aware, in a single course book, what is expected of them in the classroom.

Basically the four-year course will be structured in two stages. Books 1 and 2 will comprise a *Foundation course*: Books 3 and 4 will comprise a *Development course*. The former will focus on developing oral interaction in Somali settings; the latter will shift attention towards developing reading skills in 'cultural contact' settings: Somalia and the world. The effect of an adaptation to a six-year course will be to shift the Foundation course down into the primary sector, and extend the Development course throughout the secondary sector. The first year of the Development course would thus become a 'bridging' course, while the last year would become an 'extension' course with optional units of work.

With much of the methodology made explicit in the course books, the teachers' books will consist mainly of summaries of unit content and a glossing of that content and class activities, plus additional exercises. This rather than a detailed step-by-step outline of procedure – which seldom gets read by teachers, and rarely remembered, let alone enacted.

A key part of the structure of a unit will be the 'workbook' element which will be designed not as a true take-away workbook, but as a prompt towards using the students' exercise books. The workbook element will mainly consist of 'five-finger' language exercises.

The topic/structure sequence should be designed with reference to the Yemen textbook although clearly, because of the distinctiveness in socio-cultural setting, there will be differences in the selection and ordering of functional and structural items. It should be possible, however, after the first two books of each course, to construct a unified syllabus at an appropriate level of *generality* consisting of thematic, functional and structural sequences. Inevitably, at this stage in both projects the syllabus design will be 'light' and predictive; design 'in depth' will be done retrospectively as a rationalisation of the design features. As I have said on previous occasions, it is dangerous to fix objectives too early, lest they inhibit and constrain development rather than initiate and sustain it.

What is important is to keep clearly in focus the interests, knowledge and experience of the learners on the one hand, and the expectations and capabilities – communicative and professional – of the teachers on the other. To balance, in other words, the needs and wants – in educational terms – of the Somalis (from Ministry to parents of children), with the resources and constraints in the environment, and then to reflect them quite explicitly in the content and organisation of the text, and the roles and strategies assigned to learners and teachers in the teaching process. Hence, the crucial criterion for the success of any curriculum innovation is *compatibility*. Is the strategy compatible with the skills possessed by the agents of change (the school teachers), the attitudes, motivation and intellectual awareness of the subjects of change (the pupils) and the substantive features of the environment in which the innovation takes place (the Somali school system)?

To achieve this balance requires the exercise of judgement and skill, knowledge and insight, and organisation and flair of the highest order.

Textbook projects are, therefore, major educational ventures representing an investment the return on which is visible only over a ten or twenty year period, but which require in their early years considerable support and monitoring costs, both locally (Ministry, Council, Embassy and teachers) and from headquarters (Council and ODA). They also require a willingness to suspend judgement until an appropriate time, to allow the writers opportunity to assimilate the values of the community, appreciate the sensitivities of the people involved, and judge the strength of the web of relationships.

4   On evaluation   The purpose of this section is to dwell upon the issues involved in evaluating projects. Much evaluative comment has already been made in this report. This comment has been about:

1. what the project should be like;
2. what it can be like;
3. what it is like.

1) has to do with predictions – the conception of textbook project and our expectations of what it will achieve. 2) has to do with perceived realities acting as constraints on our predictions – the balancing of design and environmental variables – from which emerges 3) an achieved structure and visible accomplishment, susceptible, if necessary, to retrospective rationalisation. Evaluation is concerned with observing and commenting on the matching – or mismatching – of these three perspectives: of defining, describing and passing value judgements on what the project can be like in the light of what we would like it to be like, viewed from the perspective of what we can see it is like.

However, central to any evaluation is the problem of deciding what it is that is being evaluated, using what criteria, for what purpose. With this project we are clearly in the area of formative evaluation. Equally with any products that have issued, or will issue, from the project. The criteria we use are the objectives made explicit in the design document, and the design parameters used in the creation of the textbooks that make up the course. The purposes of any evaluation are to facilitate decision making about the implementation of objectives, and to make predictive judgements about the likely success of the course when used by teachers in schools. There is thus a relationship between criteria and purposes which is cyclical: objectives enable decisions to be made about design parameters which result in material that is tested in representative school environments. The evidence of trial testing may

lead to objectives being reformulated, or, more usually, to design parameters being modified, the objectives remaining essentially valid and
intact. The figure below summarises this:

WHAT IS BEING EVALUATED	CRITERIA USED IN EVALUATION	PURPOSE OF EVALUATION
Design	Objectives	Decision making
Products	Design parameters	Successful use in schools

The process is one of *reality realisation,* as outlined above, and there is
plenty of evidence of the process being alive and well in both Yemen and
Somalia. There are three important generalisations to be made:

1. Given our experience of the Yemen textbook project, and others with a
   similar remit, for example the Tunisian project, and what we have
   learnt from the Crescent course, our conception of what textbook
   projects (or any materials development projects) should be like
   corresponds much more closely with what we know they can be like,
   that is, the various ways the tasks get shaped by a recognition of the
   constraints. These include the socio-educational environment, on the
   one hand, and the administrative and professional controls exerted by
   London (ODA/BC) on the other: how constraints, in short, get elevated
   into design as positive rather than negative factors.

2. In a very important sense, one of the visible – though less easily
   promotable – accomplishments of any education project is its own
   design – a close definition of its objectives and operating strategy, and
   how these get formulated, acted upon, and modified in the process of
   their realisation.

3. There is an inherent difficulty in this sort of work of quantitative
   evaluation. So many variables are at work in improving the actual
   performance of students in English which lie completely outside the
   control of any Ministry let alone a textbook writing team. What is
   important, it seems to me, is to modify attitudes qualitatively to
   teaching and learning English by means of a new textbook in order to
   make the process more imaginative and humane by making it connect
   more perceivably with the whole socio-cultural-educational experience.
   Hence, the desirability of improving the precision of our qualitative
   judgements in evaluating the success of textbook projects.

3.4 Evaluation of curricula and syllabuses (1984)

CHARLES ALDERSON

Any consideration of curriculum and syllabus design must begin with two questions. What do we intend to achieve with our curriculum and syllabus, and how are we going to know what we have achieved and how we have achieved it? As Wiseman and Pidgeon (1970:20) put it: 'The fundamental task of constructing a curriculum is manifestly that of devising an instrument for successfully achieving a set of educational aims.'

In other words, designers are necessarily and essentially concerned not only with establishing curricular aims, but also with evaluation, and ensuring adequate means of evaluating success (or otherwise). This means not only taking evaluation seriously in curriculum development, but also and importantly integrating evaluation into design projects from the very beginning, rather than leaving it until the design has been finalised and the curriculum implemented. As Wiseman and Pidgeon point out, evaluation must be considered and built in to projects at the same time as the aims and objectives and the means of implementing these are being developed. Typically, however, and not only in language teaching projects, evaluation is left until the end of a project, at which point evaluators are invited in to pronounce judgements on the worth of a project (which can, not surprisingly, cause considerable resentment). Despite the attention paid to evaluation in the Cameroon Textbook project, for example (Wilson and Harrison 1983), it appears to have been the case that the lack of priority given to evaluation in the planning stages of the project led to inadequate provision and above all to the results of evaluation being ignored. Wilson and Harrison clearly show how the almost daily changes in constraints on development projects make it essential that evaluators work as closely as possible with developers from the inception of a project. Unfortunately, however, theorists may often recognise the importance of evaluation, yet fail to show how such evaluation could or should be implemented (see, for example, Breen and Candlin 1980). This is, indeed, particularly a problem in language teaching, especially in EFL. As Murphy (1985:8) says:

> The crux of the matter as far as the development of language teaching is concerned is that the theoreticians are content to maintain a non-empirical approach, and their competing designs, for all their academic weight, fail to produce the improvements sought.

He suggests that this is precisely because they fail to take evaluation sufficiently seriously as to specify procedures for evaluating designs and innovations. To quote Murphy further:

> We need to know how well the theory works in practice. To acknowledge the need for 'thoughtful experimentation' (Wilkins' phrase), for the 'test of practical application' (Widdowson's phrase) is insufficient by itself. Since no results are given, no indication of

what a practical test would be like and no source for guidance on how to conduct such tests, we are left thinking that the phrases may be no more than enjoinders to 'give it a whirl'.

There is, indeed, considerable evidence that evaluation is either simply ignored, or has lip-service paid to it, or is added as an afterthought, once materials and methods have been designed and established. Yet if evaluation is to guide the curriculum process and decisions, then it must be incorporated *ab initio* – so that it can take account of the developing aims of the project, and even contribute to such aims, and also so that its findings can be fed back into the design process in a continuous dynamic interaction.

What is evaluation? There is a regrettable tendency, within ELT, to equate evaluation with testing. The two are not synonymous, however, since tests are only one means of gathering information. Evaluation is, in fact, a very generalised area. To paraphrase Cronbach (1975: 399-400): 'Evaluation is a diversified activity where many types of information are useful for making many types of decisions.'

This usefully emphasises the plurality of possibilities for procedures, and draws attention to evaluation as an information-gathering activity intended to inform the decision-making process in a curricular context. Cronbach also says: 'Evaluation should be used to understand how the course produces its effects and what parameters influence its effectiveness.' In this view, evaluation is much more than 'just' measuring: it is part of the process of understanding.

There is, however, a regrettable tendency also to view testing as simply the administration and interpretation of pen and paper tests. I prefer to take a wider view of testing, and see it as a two-part activity: elicitation and judgement. A test is essentially a device for eliciting relevant behaviour – which then becomes describable – and some procedure for judging that behaviour – which implies the establishment of criteria for adequacy and acceptability. This wider view of testing allows us to consider as a suitable instrument any procedure which elicits and allows for description, and then provides for comparison and judgements. It is interesting to compare this definition of a test with Nisbet's view of evaluation (Nisbet 1972).

> Evaluation is not only a judgement: it also sets out the evidence and reasoning which led to that judgement, and if evaluation is to be accepted as valid we need to be sure that the evidence reported is a fair sample, and the reasoning from it is logical, and that alternative interpretations have been considered and disproved.

In other words evaluation, like testing, is concerned with explicitness of evidence, with its validity and with the validity of the comparisons, criteria and judgements. It is important to emphasise that there is no one way of evaluating, rather that different sorts of evidence, elicited by different instruments, will be appropriate for different purposes. There is a close and crucial relationship between what and how one evaluates, and one's purpose in evaluating. The procedures one adopts and the content one selects for the evaluation will depend upon why one is gathering the information and who it is intended for. As Rea (1983) points out: 'Different areas of evaluation are important to different people at different times and for different reasons.'

Examples of three different procedures

The Bangalore/Madras Communicational Teaching Project provides an interesting example of the use of fairly traditional language tests to provide some means of external evaluation of an innovative teaching programme in order to convince outsiders and sceptics of the value of the Project. Details are available in Beretta (1984) but briefly the instruments chosen were two tests intended to favour one or other of the experimental and control groups of school children who had or had not taken part in the Project, and a group of three tests intended to be neutral as to bias towards one or the other group. In addition, the performances of both groups on public examinations were compared to see whether the experimental groups showed any disadvantage on 'traditional criteria' however irrelevant they might be to the aims of the Project.

What is interesting is not so much the results (although these tend to show limited advantage for the experimental group over the control group) as the fact that the evaluators might be said to have stacked the dice against the experiment by selecting tests rather than engaging in extended analyses of attitudes, of classroom discourse or of subsequent use of English 'in the real world' or whatever other procedure might have found more potentially favourable results. Instead, traditional criteria were used to convince sceptics.

Unlike the Bangalore Project, which conducted an 'external' evaluation only after four years of experimentation, the work of the Communication Skills Unit (CSU) in Dar es Salaam is interesting as an example of evaluation in action precisely because it has incorporated evaluation through language tests from the very beginning of the design of the courses for which the Unit is responsible. In this case, too, it is noteworthy that outside 'experts' were not invited in to conduct an external evaluation. Instead the team members themselves built in the externally verifiable evaluation procedures and instruments, not simply in order to convince outside sceptics of the value of their work but in order to prove to themselves that what they were trying to achieve was or was not being achieved. Again, there is no space to go into detail; but in summary, students were given entry and exit tests to determine the amount of learning during CSU courses, the performance of students taking CSU courses was compared with that of those not taking such courses and a range of subjective assessments by language and subject tutors was gathered on both CSU and non-CSU students, in order to investigate whether students benefited from the CSU courses. Again, what is important is less the results of the evaluation, but rather that:

- the evaluation was internal, but externally accountable;
- the evaluation, even though rather traditional in design, was included in course design from the very outset;
- formative as well as summative aspects of evaluation were included; and
- the design was essentially intended to answer the question: Do our courses meet externally and internally defined objectives?

Both the Bangalore and the Tanzanian projects are notable because their use of language tests as instruments allows for public scrutiny and criticism and the operationalisation of objectives they represent.

In the Institute for English Language Education at Lancaster I am responsible for the pre-sessional language and study skills courses we run for overseas university students, and we have evolved a rather extensive set of evaluation procedures for our courses. These involve an initial pencil and paper test for the students, a questionnaire on their expectations and wants regarding the course and an interview with course tutors. During the course each tutor fills out an activity report on which he not only describes what he has done in class, but also provides an initial evaluation of its effectiveness. This is done for each lesson. Weekly planning meetings allow for more reflective feedback and discussion. The students fill out a mid-course questionnaire and have the opportunity to give feedback to their personal tutors in tutorials. At the end of the course they fill out an individual questionnaire, discuss their evaluations in groups without tutors present and then finally report to tutors in plenary what was felt about the course. Tutors make a written record of the discussion, fill out their own final evaluation questionnaire and then write a report on their own area of responsibility and the materials they have used. In addition, students are given a further test of language and study skills, which enable us both to assess progress during the course and to make recommendations to sponsors and subject tutors about the need for and nature of follow-up help. Finally, ex-students are canvassed some six months after leaving the course for their opinion of its effectiveness in the light of their experience in their target study situations.

A great variety of information is gathered here by a variety of means. Some proves to be more useful than others: the activity reports tutors write prove to be very valuable for teachers wishing to repeat or modify the course in subsequent years. For immediate course steering the discussions in tutorials are most valuable, whilst the mid-course questionnaires allow us to spot widely-felt areas of concern. The group discussions after students have had a chance to record their individual opinion provide a very rich source of information for future course design.

It is interesting to note that while our procedures do allow us to get a great variety of information about our course, they also present us with a real problem. The 'opinions' and results are so diverse that it is almost impossible to quantify or indeed adequately report them, let alone to take decisions on the basis of the information gathered. Indeed we have not yet solved one of the more intractable problems of evaluation, namely: having gathered apparently reliable and publicly accountable data, what is one to do about it? As Murphy (1985: 16) says: 'Without doubt the hardest part (of evaluation) is to develop our ability to interpret and act on the findings an evaluation produces.' However, the difficulty of making the judgements that evaluation requires does not absolve us from the responsibility of gathering believable, relevant and accountable information. In conclusion, I wish to offer a few thoughts arising from my experience of evaluation as an evaluator and teacher, and as a reader of other people's evaluations.

Firstly, we need to be sensitive to and aware of the existence of different perspectives among the various participants involved in the project or course one is evaluating (be they administrators, designers, inspectors, teachers, students or the lay public), and we need to devise a variety of ways in order to collect and take account of these. Secondly, there is a need in many evaluations for an increased involvement of the student, not only as a contributor of opinions and performance but also as an involved participant: for example in the design of the evaluation procedures, in the interpretation of the resultant data, in drawing up recommendations and in evaluating the evaluation. Thirdly, it is extremely important to monitor what is going on during a course, description being the first phase of evaluation. Thus self-monitoring by students, teachers and course designers (for example by recording their rationales for decisions as they develop a course) will be of central value in assessing the value or even development of a course. Fourthly, evaluation must involve the participants: they should be interested in and closely connected with the search for signs of success or otherwise, in systematic and accountable ways.

Thus, fifthly, evaluation needs to be built into course design from the very outset, and needs to be sensitive to the ongoing necessary modification of plans as the project progresses. Moreover, evaluation needs to be conducted by insiders on a project, or outsiders working closely with the project team, in publicly accountable ways. Sixthly, we need to recognise, as Rea (1983) says, 'the evolutionary nature of an educational project' and the ensuing need to observe and describe that evolution. This includes a recognition that evaluation procedures need to be flexible and responsive to changed circumstances. Lastly, since 'what constitutes success for one party may well be insignificant to the concerns of others, it is important to recognise contributions from a variety of contexts' (Rea 1983). Since such contexts may have conflicting goals, it is important to take account of the fact that the content and method of evaluation will vary according to its audience and its purpose, and, if I may follow the time-honoured custom of quoting myself as if I were an authority, 'what we need is not Evaluation by Standardized Procedures but Evaluation for Specific Purposes' (Alderson 1979).

4.0 Teacher Training

MIKE BEAUMONT

This section offers a juxtaposition of perspectives. It incorporates the keynote addresses of the 1982 and 1983 seminars, both devoted to the subject of teacher training. The first, by Strevens, is an extract from a paper that ranged over rather wider issues before concentrating on teacher training; Morrow's paper is included in its entirety. Alternating with these overviews are the concerns of practitioners working in the field: a set of questions elicited from participants for discussion in the final plenary session of the 1982 seminar, and a teacher training course design proposal offered as a case study in the same year.

A number of shared concerns can be distilled from the questions. First, there are issues related to the methodological model to be presented to trainees. The first question, for example, wonders whether a 'standard methodology' is ever justified. Other questions seem to assume that a communicative approach is desirable, but are concerned about how to introduce it in circumstances that are constrained by classroom conditions, examinations or trainee resistance. Linked to, but distinct from, this issue is that of the appropriate role of the 'foreign expert' in the process of local teacher training and development. A third concern is the educational and/or linguistic level of trainees in some contexts. Finally, there is the fundamental problem of effectively instituting long term educational change through pre- and in-service teacher training programmes.

All these four issues are addressed to some degree by the Angolan course design proposal. It does not seem to commit itself, at least overtly, to a particular model of teaching. It rather talks of an approach that is 'easily transferable to local counterparts', that is 'sensitive to the trainees' needs' and 'emphasises their individual strengths'. The 'foreign expert' syndrome is mitigated by the involvement and specialist training of local personnel. Successful applicants for the course must show evidence of minimum language and educational levels. The proposal also emphasises the need for an infrastructure to ensure the continuation of training after the life of the project.

Strevens' and Morrow's papers both provide useful frameworks within which to consider these issues. Strevens' somewhat algebraic formulation highlights the important complementary roles of theory and experience in all training, perhaps foreshadowing the subsequent emergence of Wallace's Reflective Model (Wallace 1991). Morrow pursues the parallels between language teaching and teacher training, supporting our contention in the introductory paper to this volume that developments in the content and process of teacher training have tended to follow, rather than lead, developments in ELT. In a sense, this is a fitting paper with which to close Part 1, since it incorporates discussion of all our themes: syllabus design, methodology, evaluation and teacher training.

4.1　Some problems (1982)

SEMINAR PARTICIPANTS

- Shouldn't we develop individual teachers along lines they are most happy with, rather than superimpose a standard methodology?

- What procedures can be adopted for helping students on a 'basic' teacher training course whose own level of English is only at that of the book they are teaching?

- How to encourage communicative language teaching among untrained but experienced teachers who have large classes, few resources, and little material incentive to change and who know they are being 'preached' to by 'experts' who have done little or no teaching in their circumstances?

- How can we get teachers to change attitudes and perspectives? How do we develop an attitude to teaching and learning which is at variance with all their previous personal experience and often in the context of prevailing attitudes among other subject teachers in the same system as themselves?

- How can we help teachers to develop sensitivity to learners' difficulties and through this to find efficient ways of continuously checking learning?

- How to create a teacher training syllabus to cover all aspects of the teacher's own needs?

- Does the communicative approach help the drop-out from the state secondary system in any more efficient way than the conventional structural approach?

- What are the characteristics of a 'good' language teacher?

- What are the possibilities for an approach which seeks to compromise between a communicative methodology and teaching towards an external structure-based examination?

- How can the trainee be encouraged to relinquish classroom authority?

- How to make communicative teaching acceptable to older conservative teachers?

- What can be done concerning teacher motivation, attitudes, flexibility and commitment when local conditions of service are unrealistic and unattractive?

- Does a well-paid foreigner have the right to harass very badly paid colleagues with giving up what they have been doing for years and putting in vast amounts of extra time in order to make life more complicated for students whose school-leaving grades were good enough only for them to become chronically badly paid school teachers?

- How much point is there in launching a programme that attempts to teach and train trainees along the lines of communicative methodology when you know very well that their ultimate fate is to teach school children from prescribed books written according to a very restrictive methodology?

- How does one make the most effective use of individual observation and guidance visits to the classes of teachers already in service?

- How can students, who have been through eleven or more years of schooling in a formal classroom with chairs in straight rows facing the teacher, and have been accustomed to regarding a teacher as someone who stands at the front of the class and lectures, best be encouraged to adopt a less teacher-centred approach when most of their other teacher training college subjects are taught in an equally teacher-centred way?

- How can we ensure that ideas and techniques which are discussed and practised in teacher training sessions are actually adopted and adapted by teachers on a long-term basis?

- How can you train teachers whose general level of education, including the ability to think independently, critically and creatively, is extremely low as is also their competence in English, in a very short period of time and with very limited resources: that is, finance, hardware and trainers?

- How can we implement a problem-solving approach with learners whose previous experience of language learning and whose expectations about what should happen in the English class do not significantly include problem-solving?

- What assistance can be offered to the teachers wishing to improve their own linguistic sensitivity – for example, to be more confident in their judgement of students' communicative efficacy?

- How do you convince teachers that some form of innovation is possible in the classroom, when circumstances prevent your being able to demonstrate its practicality with a class of students equal in number to the size of the class that the teacher is likely to have to contend with in the schools – perhaps up to 60–70 students?

- How does one persuade teachers to see the relevance of others' experience to their own?

4.2   Teacher training: nature and choices (1982)

PETER STREVENS

1   Nature

Too often, teacher training is viewed, even by those who organise and carry it out, as something rather simple and self-evident. But the comparison of teacher training programmes in different institutions, in different countries, under different leadership, reveals that a great many courses merely continue without change whatever has been offered in that institution for the past ten, twenty or thirty years. Nor is there sufficient awareness or discussion of the important points of choice. And when discussion does take place, it is frequently on the basis of 'our course is better than X's course', rather than on a basis of a rationale or model for teacher training. Most practitioners of teacher training, then, appear to regard teacher training as a simple sequence: *training* followed by *experience* as a teacher. This can be formulated as:

$$1)\quad T\text{ - }EXP$$

There is, however, a great difference between *initial* training, given to a trainee before ever he sets foot in a classroom as an autonomous teacher, and *further* training, given to a teacher who has trained earlier and then earned considerable experience. Further training is followed by further teacher experience as in 2) below, where I = initial and F = further training. But not all teachers have the opportunity of further training, hence the brackets.

$$2)\quad I\text{ - }EXP\text{ - }(F\text{ - }EXP)$$

The concept of training as a single homogeneous activity obscures important elements which imply choices. One set of elements is organisational, the other is educational. The organisational elements of teacher training comprise: the process of selection for training (since not everyone who decides they would like to become a teacher will necessarily be selected even to enter the training process); the evaluation of the individual's performance during training and potential for the future as a teacher, and in consequence of this evaluation, acceptance – or not, as the case may be – as a trained teacher, with the consequent licence to take employment as a teacher.

3)   *SEL - T - EVAL - ACC?*

The educational elements of teacher training, which constitute the content of a course, contain the mixture I have elsewhere (Strevens 1981) categorised as *skills, information* and *theory*. In the context of this paper it may be preferable to distinguish not three elements but four, which occur as two linked pairs: *general* and *special* training; and *practical* and *theoretical* training. That is to say, there are aspects of learning to become a teacher that are broadly similar whether one intended to teach Biology or English as a foreign language: these are the general elements, and they may include an important amount of continuing personal education for the trainees, especially the widespread 'teacher training college' model. The *special* elements include not only how to teach EFL, but also continued improvement of the teacher's command of English and his or her familiarity with the language and its internal mechanisms. It is important to be aware that the mixture of general and special elements varies widely from one training course to another: indeed it is precisely in drawing up this part of an initial teacher training syllabus that some of the most important decisions present themselves.

Similarly with the mixture of *practical* and *theoretical* elements. Here the amount of time available – the duration of the course – will have a great influence on the course, but so also will the philosophical outlook of the training course designers upon the relative weight to be attached to the 'how' of teaching as distinct from the 'why' of principle and theory. The content part of initial teacher training, then, can be represented as comprising variable mixtures of the two sets of elements.

4)   *G   PR*

+   +

S   TH

It may be worth adding to the formulation we have built up a mention of one particularly valuable form of initial practical training: an *apprenticeship*. This occurs when, after the end of a period of intensive initial training in a special institution, but before final evaluation and acceptance as a teacher, the trainee is placed as a probationary teacher in a school, but in a special relationship with an experienced teacher. The teacher does not interfere with the trainer's work, but is available for advice and encouragement, to help the trainee at times of difficulty and strain; and to add a professional, chalkface opinion to those practical and theoretical evaluations which will be taken into account in deciding whether a trainee is to be accepted into teaching. Apprenticeship, however, is far from universal, let alone obligatory.

5)   *T - (APPR) - EVAL - ACC*

The formulation as a whole is presented in the following table:

Teacher Training: a Formulation

$$(\text{EXP}) \left(\text{SEL} \left[\text{I} \left\{ \begin{array}{cc} \text{G} & \text{PR} \\ + & + \\ \text{S} & \text{TH} \end{array} \right\} (\text{APPR}) \ \text{EVAL} \right] \text{ACC?} \right) \text{EXP (F) EXP}$$

Signification

(EXP)	Some aspirants to the profession obtain teaching experience before being selected for initial training
(SEL.....ACC?)	Entry to the teaching profession is begun by a process of selection for training, and completed by a decision of acceptance or non-acceptance
$\left[\text{I} \ldots \ldots \right]$	Initial training: total sequence
$\left\{ \ldots \ldots \right\}$	Core content of initial training
G **+** **S**	G = general teacher training, irrespective of subject S = specialised training to teach EFL + = a mixture of the two, in proportion, according to circumstances
PR **+** **TH**	PR = practical training, including supervised teaching TH = theoretical training – or at least based on principle and generalisation
(APPR)	Apprenticeship: not universally offered or required
EVAL	Evaluation: practical and written
EXP	Experience as a teacher following successful training and acceptance
(F)	Further training: not universally taken or required. (Often taken as 'in-service' training)

2 Some crucial choices

a) *Selection* Recalling Beeby's (1968) insistence upon the general level of personal education among teachers as a major influence upon the possibility of change, either criteria for the selection of trainees need to be kept at a high level, or alternatively a major element of personal education must be built into initial training courses. (In British EFL this is nowadays taken care of either by the expedient of requiring trainees to be graduates before selection, or alternatively to have taken a BEd degree, in which personal education and professional training go hand-in-hand.)

b) *The mixture of general and special training* It is customary for EFL specialists to disparage conventional Postgraduate Certificate in Education courses – with the exception of those few which incorporate specialist EFL elements. The argument is often put as an affirmation that the RSA Cert TEFL is more valuable than a PGCE! And certainly the specialist EFL component of the RSA course is immensely valuable and is absent from most PGCE or Dip Ed courses. But equally a training consisting solely of a course to take an RSA qualification may lack some of the essential *general* component of learning what is involved in being a teacher.

c) *The mixture of theory and practice* The following factors determine the appropriate mixture:
- time available: the shorter the training course, the less theory can be imparted;
- personal education of the trainees: the possibility of theory being meaningful depends on the trainees' previous educational history;
- experience of teaching: without some awareness of what is involved in teaching, theoretical knowledge is of limited value.

It is easy, following these rules of thumb, to fall into an anti-intellectual attitude and say 'Never mind the theory: teach them to be good practical classroom teachers' but as they mature and develop they should also be offered a growing intellectual framework for the understanding of what they are doing, which in turn will always improve their classroom performance.

4.3 A case study: course design proposals for teacher training at the National Language Institute (INL), Angola (1982)

MARGARET TARNER and ANDREW MCNAB

1 Aim

To introduce an initial English language teacher training capacity in Luanda province by designing and implementing a course that will accept selected candidates and prepare them for teaching or teacher training careers in the INL, the secondary education system and other language teacher organisations in Angola.

2 Objectives

2.1 To design and implement a programme that meets the teacher training needs identified in the above aim and that satisfies national requirements for certification.

2.2 To employ an approach and methodology that provide trainees with techniques that can be exploited in a wide range of prospective teaching situations.

2.3 To create an infrastructure for the continuation of teacher training support after the completion of the project.

2.4 To develop the basis for the creation of an in-service teacher training capacity.

3 Assumptions

3.1 That the programme will be under the administrative and academic control of the INL.

3.2 That the INL will begin the process of recruitment for this course as soon as the general framework is approved.

3.3 That the training course will involve a minimum commitment of five hours per day at the INL (exclusive of private study time);

3.4 That candidates can be identified who will show evidence of:

3.4.1 the necessary personal qualities and commitment;

3.4.2 a minimum level of English language competence equivalent to Band 3 on the INL's scale of assessment;

3.4.3 a minimal educational level equivalent to the ninth class. (Exceptions may occasionally have to be made to this requirement in the case of outstanding candidates.)

3.5 That candidates selected for training will undertake teaching and/or teacher training responsibilities for their sponsoring organisations upon completion of their training programme.

3.6 That adequate facilities can be made available for the successful operation of the programme.

3.7 That during the period of training, trainees will have access to classes in their prospective teaching situations.

3.8 That an adequate level of staffing is available and that at least two Angolan teachers can be identified to work with the project team.

4 Strategies

4.1 Design and implementation

4.1.1 Preparation (April-June 1982) The first priority is to create the necessary infrastructure for teacher training activities, and to achieve this it is most important for the team to be able to gain some insight into regional and national training needs. This will involve visits to other institutions concerned with the teaching of English. It will also be necessary to ascertain how training activities can be integrated into the mainstream of the educational system to ensure that national certification requirements are met.

It is proposed that a detailed programme design will be developed during this period so that a pilot course can be put into operation by the start of the 1982–3 academic year.

4.1.2 Basic design framework Duration: 1200 hrs distributed over five three-month modules. Intensity: Four days per week, five hours per day (two hours to be devoted to language improvement, and three hours to training related activities). The fourth module will consist of teaching practice and follow-up activities. Maximum intake: 25 trainees.

4.1.3 Content Language improvement: to improve general fluency, and increase the trainee's confidence when using English in the classroom. **Language sensitisation:** to introduce trainees to aspects of the communicative functions of language and to develop a perspective of language as a network of inter-related systems. **Theory and practice of language teaching:** to develop the trainee's competence in:

- classroom management
- materials selection (where relevant) and exploitation
- use of teaching aids
- applying evaluation procedures
- preparation of supplementary material and activities;

to create an awareness of the past and current methodologies and their theoretical base.

4.1.4 Implementation The course will be piloted over a period of 15–18 months as from the beginning of the 1982–83 academic year with a view to its full implementation by March 1984.

4.2 Approach and methodology

4.2.1 The principal concerns involved in the design and implementation of the programme are that it should:

- be developed in such a way as to be easily transferable to local counterparts;

- always be sensitive to the trainees' needs and provide them with an approach to teaching which emphasises their individual strengths;

- produce trainees who will be able to operate in a variety of prospective teaching situations.

4.2.2   In order to fulfil these requirements it will be necessary to organise training in such a way that:

- is is practically based, that is, on a principle of 'learning through doing', in the process of which a methodology applicable to a variety of learning contexts will be established;

- the progress of each trainee is carefully monitored;

- full documentation is available for future use. (This would include the INL's handbook for core courses.)

4.2.3   Guidance in methodology and teaching techniques will be organised through the use of approaches which will be: 1) Observation based: for example, exercises and discussions of model lessons leading to simulations in practice. 2) Experience based: that is, through an examination of the trainees' own experience. This can be combined with a task-based approach in which the trainee is required to perform specific tasks within a given period of time. A combination of these two approaches is termed *micro-teaching*. As students grow in confidence and expertise they move from their peer group to work with full-size courses.

It can be seen from the above that theory is constantly related to and never divorced from practice.

4.3   *Infrastructure for the continuation of teacher training*

4.3.1   Maintenance of the teacher training capacity after the conclusion of the current agreement can be achieved by:

- full documentation;

- a continuation of limited 'co-operante' input into the programme;

- the identification of key personnel to undertake periods of specialist training abroad

4.3.2   Assuming that suitable candidates can be identified the following would be a reasonable time-scale to adopt. *September 1983:* A period of specialist training abroad for up to five candidates. Suitable candidates will be selected from among those who have worked with the project team. On their return they would assume some of the functions of the present project team. *September 1984:* A similar programme of training for selected candidates from amongst the first group of trainees to complete the full training course.

4.3.3   Dissemination of the teacher training capacity can be achieved by the attachment of successful trainees to run in-service and/or pre-service training courses in English Language Teaching for the INL, the Ministry of Education and other language teaching organisations according to national rather than regional needs.

4.4   *In-service teacher training capacity*

4.4.1   A national in-service training programme will be dependent upon the successful execution of the pre-service course. On a regional basis, discussions have indicated that only a limited number of practising Angolan teachers will be available for retraining. It is proposed therefore to offer occasional seminars which would serve to update the methodology of these teachers. These seminars would also serve to develop links between the project team, the trainees, and practising teachers.

4.4.2   Obviously the main local resource for in-service training lies in the ability of successful trainees from the pre-service programme to take up 'leadership' or 'key responsibility' posts. It would be impracticable to offer a major retraining programme until there are sufficient manpower resources available to make such a programme effective. The competence of these leaders could be extended by occasional short courses conducted by visiting ELT specialists. A network of in-service training programmes requires the creation of an adequate national infrastructure. It is beyond the present capacity of the project team to advise on how this should be achieved and it is recommended that an examination of this question should be one of the functions of a forthcoming consultancy visit – preferably to take place before June 1983.

4.4   Teacher training courses: design and implementation (1983)

KEITH MORROW

I'm a charlatan; you're a charlatan

To be asked to give the keynote talk to a gathering of this distinction is a golden opportunity to raise issues without having to solve them. My role is to provide food for thought, but I am offering it in a deliberately raw state; over the next fortnight there will be ample opportunity for you to chew it over.

A charlatan is defined by the Advanced Learner's Dictionary of English as 'a person who claims to have more skill, knowledge or ability than he really has . . .'. How many of us involved in teacher training can, by the very act of being involved in teacher training, escape the charge? For what do we actually know about the design and implementation of teacher training courses? What is the basis of the 'skill, knowledge or ability' that we lay claim to? Crucially, how have we been trained as teacher trainers? Presumably we believe that training is important, or else why are we trying to train teachers? But who has trained us?

Such questions can easily be dismissed as pious rhetoric, but if we are serious about what we are doing then I think they deserve investigation and discussion in order to make clear in an explicit way the assumptions on which we base our work. Only if the assumptions are made explicit can they be challenged or improved. Fortunately for me, it is not my role to state assumptions, though I hope they will emerge from follow-up discussion; rather I hope to indicate areas in which assumptions need to be stated, and to suggest some sources from which we might draw them.

A useful maxim in this field is 'start with what you know'. This is the approach I want to follow in suggesting that many of the issues that confront us in teacher training are recognisably the same issues that confront us in language teaching. In a sense this is hardly surprising since both language teaching and language teacher training are educational activities and can be expected to share a large number of common and indeed wider educational concerns. But how much of the copious literature on language teaching is consciously considered by those involved in teacher training for guidance on the design and implementation of courses? Let us look at some accepted truths and contentious issues from language teaching and see what relevance they have.

Language teaching and teacher training: some fundamental parallels

Perhaps the most basic parallel is that the design and implementation of courses in both areas require decisions to be made about *what* and *how*, about content and methodology.

WHAT

Syllabus   In language teaching there has been much debate in recent years about what the content of a teaching programme should be. Should syllabuses be prescribed or negotiated? Should they be analytic or synthetic (cf. Wilkins 1976)? If synthetic, what are the elements of which they should be composed? How are these selected or graded? All of these questions seem to be equally relevant to teacher training courses, and I feel we are missing an important aid in design and implementation if we fail to take conscious account of them.

The answers we arrive at will be different in particular circumstances – as in language teaching – but the issues are constant.

Definition of objectives   The specification of intermediate and terminal objectives for language teaching courses is now an accepted part of good pedagogic practice. Their value is seen as twofold: firstly they act as a chart to the student of his progress through the course and an incentive in terms of setting an attainable goal; secondly they help to reduce for teacher and student the infinite possibilities of the language into something more tangible and realisable. Again this seems to be an area where there are clear implications for teacher training courses. What the objectives of a particular course should be cannot be pre-judged *in vacuo* and indeed may be amended as the course progresses. But there should be objectives. What would they look like?

One of the most interesting areas of debate in language teaching recently has been the relationship between accuracy and fluency, and form and function as intermediate and terminal objectives. It may not be immediately clear that such concepts have any relevance for teacher training, but it is useful, in my view, to pick up any issue from one field and examine it carefully for implications for the other. Even if definitions have to be stretched, occasional illuminating insights can make it worthwhile. What could an 'accurate' teacher be, as opposed to a 'fluent' one? Or, expressed rather more aptly in language use terms, what are the complementary characteristics of a skilled teacher which might be identified as 'accuracy' and 'fluency'? And what might the 'forms' of teaching be as opposed to the 'functions'?

HOW

Learner-centred vs. teacher-centred   The impact of 'communicative' language teaching over the last ten years has perhaps been most remarkable (though least debated) in the area of methodology. Procedures such as role-play, techniques such as pair-work or group-work, concepts such as the 'information gap' are now part of the common currency of language teaching. Fundamentally they represent a shift from a teacher-centred towards a learner-centred methodology. But what impact ought this to have, and indeed has it had on teacher training?

My own feeling, somewhat perversely in view of the previous section, is that this is an area where ideas have been transferred too glibly. The lecture on 'communicative methodology' is universally derided as a nonsense; but in terms of economy in disseminating ideas and information a good lecture has a lot to recommend it as opposed to yet another worksheet to be discussed in groups. Group discussion based on a worksheet is a procedure whose value in language teaching derives from the practice it offers in handling the processes of language use, ie promoting fluency. What is discussed is normally secondary to the act of discussion. But in teacher training, discussion is no longer the end but the means of acquiring insights into ideas. My point is that it may not often be the best way of acquiring such insights. This is not intended as a reactionary call for Victorian values, but rather as a reminder that although many issues are common to these two areas, it should not be an uncritical assumption that a procedure appropriate to one will necessarily be appropriate to the other.

Acquisition vs. learning   In many ways this is perhaps the most central area of debate in language teaching today. Unlike the communicative vs structural debate, which is concerned with different approaches to how to teach a foreign language, this is concerned with whether it can be taught at all in any meaningful sense. According to proponents of the acquisition hypothesis, language use is based largely on data which is unconsciously acquired through exposure to meaningful language; language which is consciously learnt has only a marginal role as a monitor of performance. The implications of this for future teacher training would be considerable if the same hypothesis were applied to teaching performance as to language performance. Testing the hypothesis is of course extremely difficult in language terms, and would be equally so for teaching. But as professionals, we have to decide where we stand. After all, if the acquisition theory was accepted, the worksheet would be under attack from the other end of the spectrum!

DOGMA AND ECLECTICISM

This is the last area where I want to consider parallels between language teaching and teacher training. In general most British teachers of EFL are proud to be eclectic; Krashen has referred to eclecticism as 'a moral obscenity'. There is clearly a divergence of view and tradition.

In teacher training, the issue affects both the content and the methodology aspects, but it is particularly interesting in terms of prescriptivism. Most teacher trainers are only too aware that teaching is a very complex business, beset with many variables and few certainties. Yet in order to give initial trainees a foothold on the ladder, it is often felt necessary to give very firm guidelines about what should and should not be done in the classroom (Gower and Walters 1983). Do such guidelines represent a safety line or a straightjacket? Discuss.

In the preceding sections we have seen three ways in which there may be a relationship between ideas and issues in language teaching and teacher training. Firstly, on a very general level, there are questions of syllabus design and methodology, which reflect the common educational concerns of the two activities. To point to these similarities is almost to utter a truism, but it is worthwhile if it casts fresh light. More tenuous is the link between the two activities in terms of particular issues raised in connection with just one. Fluency and accuracy are examples of this, with little obvious direct relevance to teacher training, but perhaps a heuristic value in leading us to ask questions and search for implications. Finally there are areas where an activity quite justified in language teaching is transferred over-enthusiastically and uncritically to teacher training. My homily against the worksheet syndrome is an example. In the next two sections I want to look at the question of design and implementation more directly, again drawing on language teaching as a source of ideas.

Teacher training as ESP

Teacher training is in essence a goal-oriented educational activity. As implied above, the formulation of the goals may sometimes leave something to be desired, but all would agree that in general they relate to the equipping of individuals with a set of skills which will enable them to function more effectively in a professional environment.

This is also a reasonable working definition of the goals of ESP, and so it might well be profitable to see how far a model of course design from ESP can be applied to teacher training. This is a simplified version of the ESP model applied in the Bell Educational Trust.

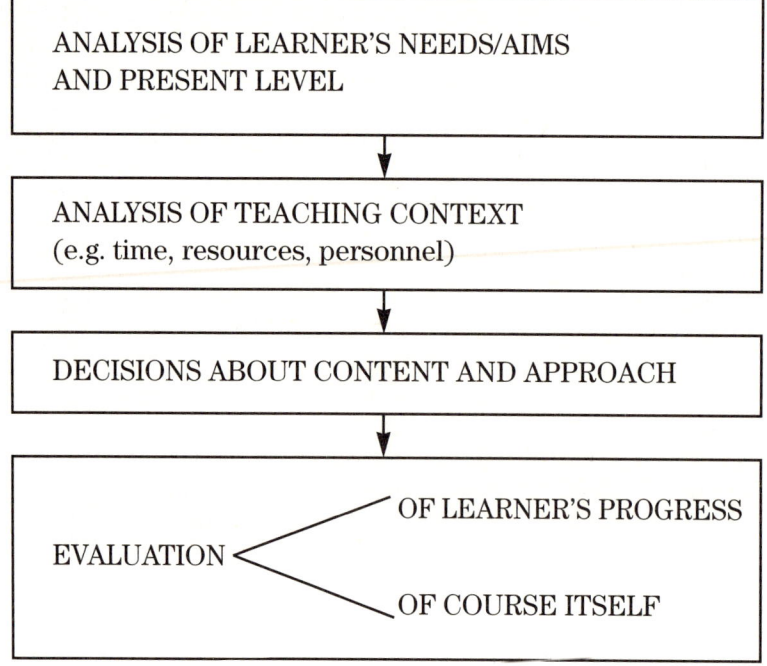

I make no claims for originality for this model, but in fact its value in the present context lies precisely in the fact that it is well established. For it seems to me to represent in essence a process of design which is as relevant to teacher training courses as it is to ESP. The focus on the needs and aims of the particular group of learners, leading to the construction of 'courses for horses', is a useful reminder that in teacher training there is no single body of content that is appropriate to all trainees. Similarly the emphasis on the teaching context is important both in terms of the context in which the trainees will subsequently have to operate and in terms of the context of the training course itself. But perhaps the most significant aspect of the model – significant in the sense that in practice it is often overlooked – is evaluation. It seems to be absolutely essential that evaluation is built in as a key component of the design model right from the start. All too often it is tacked on as an afterthought, or glossed over completely.

Evaluation of teaching performance and language performance

In view of the importance of evaluation in the design of teacher training courses, let us see what language teaching can offer in the way of parallels.

Recent work in the development of criteria for the evaluation of language performance has yielded a set of categories which might well inform the evaluation of teaching performance. At the very least, consideration of these criteria might force the issue of evaluation of teaching performance into central prominence and lead us to state explicitly where they fall short of what is needed.

The criteria I have in mind are those formalised for the RSA Examinations in the Communicative Use of EFL. Language production (in writing and oral interaction) is assessed in terms of, *inter alia*, accuracy, appropriacy, range, flexibility. The question of what might be meant by 'accurate' teaching has been broached earlier. It is arguably the least easy of these four terms to transfer directly to teaching performance. But appropriacy (in selecting the appropriate way to deal with the needs of a particular group or individual), range (in terms of the repertoire of skills, techniques and materials that can be handled) and flexibility (in dealing with the unexpected in the lesson) are surely at the heart of good teaching, and it might fairly be argued that a teacher training course might be evaluated in terms of its success in developing the participants' skills in these areas.

What does 'training' mean?

In his paper on 'Teacher Training and the Curriculum' given at Dunford House last year (see this volume), Peter Strevens pointed out that 'education' and 'training as a teacher' do not necessarily, or indeed often, co-exist in a given individual who is a teacher. The following possibilities may be found and all can be instanced in different countries of the world.

	Educated	**Trained**
A	+	+
B	+	−
C	−	+
D	−	−

This is very helpful in reminding us of the range of backgrounds that participants on our teacher training courses might encompass. But it clearly begs a number of questions, particularly by representing 'educated' and 'trained' as either/or categories. It represents in essence a static view of training (and education) as opposed to the dynamic view implicit in the last section.

Acceptance of the evaluation criteria set out there is one way of formalising the notion that one never stops learning how to be a good teacher. Leaving aside for the sake of illustration the question of 'accuracy', it is clear that 'appropriacy', 'range' and 'flexibility' are dynamic concepts in terms of which teacher development could be described, and in terms of which differential levels of performance could be located. This is indeed the essence of the RSA language examinations, which ask the candidates to perform tasks on the basis of which their language performance is deemed to meet (or not to meet) the different specifications in terms of these criteria for Basic, Intermediate or Advanced level.

How feasible would it be to adopt such a scheme for the evaluation and development of teaching performance? A bandscale might be imagined with a number of levels which would define both the range of teaching skills and the degree of skill expected in their execution at each level. In the interests of exemplification, but with no greater confidence, let me offer a sample of what the very top and the very bottom of the scale might look like.

---

0   Below the bottom of the scale.

1   The first point on the scale.
    Teacher can use a given coursebook at one level with minimum
    adequate skill (i.e. flexibility, appropriateness/range of techniques).

●

●

●

●

n   The top of the scale.
    Teacher can select, adapt and use appropriate material for any
    group of learners with a very high degree of skill.

The most immediate attraction of such a scale is that it would give us the chance to evaluate intending trainees in terms of the 'level' of a particular course, and decide where effort could most usefully be put in the context of the system in which we are operating. My own feeling is that worldwide the greatest benefits would accrue from concentrating on bringing as many teachers as possible on to the first point on the scale. After that, development is a luxury. But where would we place RSA Preparatory courses, or the RSA Cert TEFL? Do MAs in Applied Linguistics or TESOL find a place? And what is the position of the many short courses for overseas teachers run each year in the UK by a number of institutions including the Bell Educational Trust?

Evaluation is a key element in the design and implementation of teacher training courses. It involves evaluation of the participants, in terms of making judgements about their performance as teachers, and of the course itself, in measuring how far it has achieved its goals. The last is also a sort of performance evaluation, which is why I feel that the model I have tentatively advanced may be worth exploring further. In the end, of course, it may be rejected; but it will have to be replaced with something better.

Conclusion

Our experience and training as language teachers equips us with a wealth of background and insight with which to examine critically the design and implementation of teacher training courses. We should constantly seek parallels between the two activities, and consider carefully the potential relevance for one of the ideas and issues from the other. Above all, in both areas we should be extremely wary of charlatans.

ELT in Development
1985–92

Part 2: ELT in Development 1985–92

Gerry Abbott

> The reasonable man adapts himself to the world; the unreasonable one persists in trying to adapt the world to himself. Therefore all progress depends on the unreasonable man.
>
> (George Bernard Shaw)

Pressures on global ELT

In the early 1980s, British ELT experienced two very different but potentially convergent influences – the one external and administrative, the other coming from within the profession itself.

The first was the impact of the general 'value for money' movement generated by the government of the day. Up to this time, funds for ELT aid administered by the British Council had come from an ODA budget earmarked solely for that purpose. Although there was no doubt that the Council had achieved and maintained a very high standing in ELT world-wide, there was a growing feeling in the ODA that ELT aid objectives were too often imprecise and that in consequence accountability was problematic. Another aspect of this unease was the conviction that ELT should be regarded not as a separate field that was *sui generis* but as one among many other kinds of aid activity with which it should a) co-operate in regard to broader aid objectives and b) compete so far as funding was concerned.

The other influence was also a sense of unease, first expressed by Rogers (1982) but soon echoed by some other ELT practitioners in the developing world who, in evaluating their own work, thought that ELT in such areas might have some undesirable socio-political consequences and might even work counter to efforts at development. For instance, the pursuit of English as a language of power might work against the maintenance of mother tongues and thereby make literacy (a useful tool in development) harder for minority groups to achieve; among more literate groups the learning of English might be seen as an entrance ticket to elitehood, in which case it would merely help to perpetuate social inequalities; and in the eyes of some, ELT might even be seen as a channel for cultural imperialism. This healthy self-questioning included misgivings about the assumed superiority of the teacher who was a native speaker of English over the teacher who was not, as well as doubts as to the suitability of 'native' (for example British) Englishes over 'nativised' (such as Nigerian) varieties, though the latter doubts had been expressed much earlier (see, for instance, Kachru 1976). While the government (through ODA) was concerned that development funds should be used as efficiently as possible, its ELT fieldworkers were beginning to question whether ELT aid was necessarily conducive to 'development' – though the causalities, if any, were by no means clear. The 1991 Dunford seminar was devoted to a discussion of the question but produced no clear answer; this was hardly surprising, given the nature of 'development' and 'education'.

Concepts of 'development'

As we saw in the introduction to this book, the concept of global development had been with us since 1949, when President Truman spoke of the 'underdeveloped areas' of the world and pioneered the Four Point Program, which offered technical aid. The 1960s had been designated 'First Development Decade' by the UN; a second and third had passed, with 'development' becoming an industry in itself, based in what was first called 'the west' and then 'the north'[1]; and still there had been no general agreement on the meaning of the term. Some had dismissed the concept as mere westernisation, intentional or incidental, while others – seeing it simply as a process of becoming more wealthy – had looked for a rise in GNP or per capita income, though such figures are only averages that can disguise huge disparities between the rich and poor of one nation. Whereas some had equated development with industrialisation and recommended a transfer of technology, others were now insisting that true and sustainable development involved 'empowerment' and a fairer distribution of social benefits. The favoured approach therefore came to be a 'people-centred' one in which the beneficiaries of aid projects would act as participants rather than mere recipients of what others deemed suitable; and since a people-centred approach would not by definition be valid if it systematically undervalued 50 per cent of a target population, development agencies recognised that women have a vital role to play.

These, then, were some of the main currents in 'development' thinking up to the time of the 1991 Dunford seminar. Concepts of development are not culturally neutral, however, and the two most prominent exponents of cultural identity are religion and language. The Bangladeshi writer Taslima Nasreen has (at the time of writing) been obliged to flee her country because of her championship of women in what she sees as the development of her country. As one of her countrywomen – herself an aid worker – had earlier observed: 'Development organisations undermine the power of the mullah' (*The Guardian* 1 August 1994).

With regard to overpopulation – seen by many as a cause of continuing underdevelopment – religion is of course a potent influence. The Vatican for example refused to endorse UN declarations on population in 1974 and 1984 and, when doing so again in 1994, found itself joined by Islamic fundamentalists, who saw in the UN draft proposals an attempt to impose

---

[1] Such broad geographical labels are of course misleading. The homeless who sleep on London's pavements and the women working in Manchester's sweatshops are surely part of 'The Third World' – another unsatisfactory label?

western sexual values upon the rest of the world. While such events have made the headlines from time to time, surprisingly little has been written about the relationship between *language* and development – a topic to be dealt with below.

Education and culture

Whatever their views on development, most authorities have agreed that education is a crucial component, despite the fact that in the rapid development of Europe it was the industrial revolution which gave rise to national education systems, rather than the reverse – though it is likely that the adult literacy rate (possibly 50 per cent in Europe at the time) was a favourable and perhaps necessary precondition for industrialisation (see for example Roberts 1993: 537–9). In any event, more than two decades of massive investment in education by the poor countries of the south failed to bring about the expected economic returns.

But then, what is *education*? Most people associate it with formal instruction in schools and colleges, and it was into these that most of the south's initial investment was poured; but it can be viewed as a cradle-to-grave experience, the sum of the processes that contribute to an individual's development; and this is how it is interpreted by many of those engaged in development programmes involving non-formal education, including adult literacy activities. Which, then, is most deserving of development funds – primary, secondary, or adult education? Whichever is selected, should aid be confined to producing the middle-order technicians generally believed to be needed in order to establish and maintain the country's infrastructure (sewage, road, rail and other systems) as a necessary basis for development? Would such a policy lead to the provision of something other than 'education'? And if so, would it matter?

These and many other basic questions arose especially in the case of schooling – a time-honoured and universal institution, we tend to suppose, forgetting that there are, for example (but for how long?), plenty of Amerindian cultures in which schools are unknown; the same was until comparatively recently true of all indigenous sub-Saharan cultures, in which it would have been quite unthinkable to allow a child to leave home and village in order to learn things. The school as we know it is a recent invention[2] – that was even more recently introduced into school-less cultures, often along with a curriculum designed by a colonist and a working language that was European. Culturally, then, schooling in most parts of the south has been alien in structure, in that it divides children by year of birth for example; in content; insofar as it excludes local skills and knowledge in favour of European school subjects; and in the very medium in which teacher and pupil are required to think. During the 1980s there was a growing loss of confidence in schooling as an agent of development

---

[2]British 'public' schools of the late 17th century consisted of one large schoolroom in which the instruction was very loosely organised by a master. It contained 'forms', but these were not determined by age, and there was no simultaneous instruction for all. Not until the late 1800s did this system die out, the schoolroom being ousted by a new invention: the classroom. (See Reid, 1990).

and a growing feeling, strong if unsubstantiated, that *mal*development might be the result of a kind of cultural invasion in which language was implicated. Language teachers are involved in what Simon (1987) calls 'cultural politics': if learners are to be 'empowered', they need not only to learn a language but to learn how to put it to good use in their own way of life. But what if the language one learns to operate in is *alien* to one's way of life? Ngũgĩ wa Thiong'o (1986: 14–15) describes the culture/language nexus in this way:

> Culture embodies . . . moral, ethical and aesthetic values, the set of spiritual eyeglasses through which (people) come to view themselves and their place in the universe. Values are the basis of a people's identity, their sense of particularity as members of the human race. All this is carried by language. Language as culture is the collective memory bank of a people's experience in history. Culture is almost indistinguishable from the language that makes possible its genesis, growth, banking, articulation and indeed its transmission from one generation to the next.

The effect of imposing the language of the colonist on African children is, says Ngũgĩ, 'the domination of the mental universe of the colonised', so that

> the colonial child was made to see the world and where he stands in it as seen and defined by or reflected in the culture of the language of imposition (p. 17)

and therefore 'The language of his conceptualisation was foreign'. It seemed probable that the imposition of English had contributed to the socio-economic and political instability of anglophone nations in Africa, and some would even agree with Djité (1991), who concludes:

> *Nous prétendons donc que la langue, et plus précisément la réforme linguistique en Afrique est l'une des préconditions au développement . . .*

Djité (perhaps wisely) attempts to go no further, but one winner of the Nobel prize for literature has seriously suggested (Soyinka 1994) that the arbitrary imperial boundaries agreed in Berlin a century or so ago should be redrawn along *cultural* lines, thus greatly reducing dependence on European languages as media of education, broadcasting, jurisprudence and so on, and – if this linguistic argument is valid – opening the way to development of a more suitable kind at a more rapid rate. However, it is surely unrealistic to expect such a mutually agreed rearrangement of international borders to take place.

The role of the vernacular
If the views of Djité and others are valid and if British donor agencies are interested in generating development disinterestedly rather than in waving the flag or seeking markets, might not better value for money be obtained by encouraging ELT to take a seat in the back row, behind

vernacular and national languages, rather than by 'pushing' English? Attempting to empower foreign populations in this way would be dangerous because it would challenge the system of power-politics operating in the recipient country; for while imperialism on the international stage has waned, it is alive and well *intra*nationally in many a multicultural country where sizeable minority groups are systematically marginalised, not least by a deliberate demotion of their languages. Nevertheless, such a challenge might well be necessary if development funds are not to be wasted. In a book aimed at teachers of multicultural classes in Britain, the first 'working principle of effective teaching' put forward by Hulmes (1989: 153) is the 'principle of continuity and development':

> It emphasises the continuing significance of tradition for a sense of cultural identity. At the same time it allows for reflection, for adaptation and for changes to meet present needs. It allows, in other words, for decision-making, and facilitates personal choice.

This principle for dealing with the individual surely holds true for dealing with a language community, which should be given time for reflection, discussion and decision-making *in its own language* about its own development priorities, and should be enabled to implement desired changes in its own way and at its own speed. Relevant empirical evidence in support of this view is admittedly hard to come by but Robinson (1991), for example, has investigated language use in rural development communication in the Ombessa area of Cameroon, where development activities were interventional, the language of power was French, and the local language Nugunu. The general hypothesis was as follows:

> If the aim of development is to enhance people's capacity to take charge of their own destiny, then attitudes to the way they see themselves within their own culture help in identifying how far development intervention is actually touching people's lives. If language attitudes are not taken into consideration by development intervention, we may expect a certain lack of harmony between what is actually happening and what development hopes for (ibid: 81).

In the Ombessa area as elsewhere, development activities were seen as so exogenous and 'transitive' that even indigenous development agents assumed that they had to use French rather than the local language. The effect was counterproductive.

> Strong opinions were expressed by villagers that agencies and agents, in encounters and meetings, should use/learn the local language. At the same time, development services were felt to be distant and removed from the real needs of the villager, even unavailable to them (ibid: 84).

Further research of this sort in anglophone areas would be of great value. In the meantime, the truism that people operate and co-operate best in their own language is surely justification for a 'bottom-up' development policy in which communities could establish their own aims and priorities. Innovations carried out in this way would accordingly be small-scale, people-centred, culturally non-destructive and comparatively cheap. Such an approach may sound utopian; but even if it were to be a total failure, the result would be less *dystopian* than seeing one's way of life disrupted and perhaps destroyed by outsiders (even of one's own nationality) operating in a resented and perhaps even incomprehensible language. We should also bear in mind that for three decades traditional approaches have had no great success.

Ideally, then, a development project should be locally conceived, discussed and designed even though certain foreign skills and equipment would have to be imported. The following little fairy story contrasts sharply with an account of a real development project which I read recently, and may add some colour to the views put forward above.

> After a careful ODA survey of the hinterland of Morphiamania a hydro-electric scheme was proposed which necessitated the flooding of a large valley. Thanks to a vernacular literacy programme for adults, the local Dawn people had come to understand and favour the scheme but had specified the smaller Valley of the Night rather than the Valley of the Dawn which, though preferred for reasons of engineering, contained a village famous for its storytellers, a revered old temple and very good grazing. Their elders were present at meetings in which the scheme was discussed in Morphian and English but rendered into Eogloss by local interpreters, who also interpreted the Dawn elders' questions and comments. Explanatory leaflets in Eogloss were prepared in consultation with the elders, who saw to their distribution and held subsequent meetings to discuss the content. This participation continued until the project was approved in turn by the Council of Dawn elders, the Morphiamanian Ministry of National Development and the ODA. Dawn labour was employed as far as practicable in the extraction of timber from the valley, the management of its wildlife and the construction and operation of the dam; and most important of all, Dawn villagers were linked into the electricity supply grid – a detail curiously omitted from the original plans.

ELT in aid projects

If the views reported above have any validity, ELT aid donors and their field staff need to ask themselves first what the implications are for national language policies, for it is within these that ELT has to operate. For the sake of argument, let us assume that a multicultural country's policy-makers do not accept what many authorities have been saying for three decades, 'that the human being ought to be the goal of development' (Verhhelst 1990: 160) and that they are unwilling that 'programmes and projects should be based explicitly on the cultural identity of each people' (ibid: 159); let us assume that in their view development is achieved not by an 'open-ended quest and interaction of free and questioning persons' (Rahnema 1992: 128) but by the enforced acceptance of ready-made solutions, and that their ideas on human rights include neither the right to study one's one language nor the freedom to learn and to publish in that medium.

The next question presumably would be: What should the aims of British educational aid be in such a context? Only now does the question of ELT aid policy arise; and by now one might have concluded either that no aid should be given at all, or that funds should be withheld from ELT and offered as support for any vernacular teaching schemes that might be acceptable to the host government. However, this is not an either/or matter: what is being (and has long been) advocated is vernacular literacy as a *basis* for further language learning, not as a substitute for it. On the one hand the case for saving a language from extinction is surely as strong as the case for saving the whale or the Madagascan periwinkle; but on the other, as I have argued elsewhere (Abbott 1984: 99), it would be inequitable to withhold ELT from youngsters in a country where even the slightest knowledge of English can lift one from squalor to employability. The ideal school syllabus would enable children to use languages incrementally as they move from the domestic to the national and international spheres, but economic arguments are put forward against the use of a minority group's mother tongue as the initial medium of education. Fasold (1984: 305-6) suggests five criteria, four of them socio-linguistic: a language would be deemed unsuitable unless it was already

- used as a medium of wider communication in the area;
- used by at least 100,000 people;
- suitable for use without extensive language engineering;
- wanted by most speakers as the medium of schooling.

Such hard-headed decisions may be considered necessary, but they will surely contribute to language death on a large scale.

By Fasold's fifth criterion, however, a high primary school drop-out rate may well indicate a need for initial mother tongue literacy teaching. Drop-out rates are indeed so high in many of the poorest communities that it is possible (as I suggested at the beginning of this Introduction) that greater attention to the causes of this problem might not only yield better value for aid money but at the same time remove some of the unease that has been expressed by the ELT profession.

Conclusion

However it might be construed, 'good development policy' presumably has to be weighed against 'enlightened self-interest' and 'economical use of funds', a balancing act that necessarily affects ELT. In the following Dunford papers we begin with considerations of economy, since the political climate during the period under review affected ELT profoundly. The contributions in Section 5 deal with the need for efficient investment of development funds in ELT overseas, while those in Section 6 go on to consider how such investments should be used – that is, how best to administer ELT in aid projects so that innovations are not only established but also sustained after the injection of aid. Since innovations, like plants, need to be suited to their environment if they are to flourish, questions of cultural and methodological *appropriacy* are debated in Section 7. Finally, the cultural/linguistic unease outlined above is given an airing in Section 8. The breadth and depth of the psychological, social and political issues involved are such that it is far too soon to expect any resolution of the policy problems that arise; but the issues themselves are sure to reappear in future seminars.

5.0   Values and Costs

GERRY ABBOTT

In 1989 an international conference in Beijing recognised the immense importance of preserving 'the rich cultural heritages embodied in the world's variety of languages' and reaffirmed what had been stated decades earlier (see for example, Unesco 1953): that the first years of schooling should be conducted in the language of the home wherever possible, not least because literacy in the mother tongue 'can later be built on in the context of lifelong education'. However, immediately following these fine words came a let-out clause conceding that countries 'will need to decide their own language policies in conformity with their national objectives' (Unesco 1989: 13). This amounts to a perpetuation of the status quo and will do nothing to lower the appalling levels of illiteracy and consequent educational drop-out in the South that were noted in the report of the following year's conference in Jomtien (Inter-Agency Commission, 1990) and are summarised by Iredale in paper 5.1 below.

Iredale reports that the ODA's first criterion for donor support is, as one would expect, 'How will the proposed intervention benefit the country's development?' We have seen that many authorities have found such simple, fundamental questions virtually unanswerable either because of differences in the interpretation of 'development' or because they have no faith in 'intervention' – see for instance Carmen (1996). However, most would agree with Iredale that high priority should be given to projects of benefit to girls and women.

In the following paper, MacBean explains to his audience of non-economists how cost-benefit and cost-effectiveness analyses might be applied, along with other forms of appraisal, to ELT projects. Much of this information is new to those engaged in English teaching, and is especially relevant to those with managerial roles in ELT, whether in aid projects or in commercial enterprises. In view of what comes later in section 8, MacBean's question 'Do ELT projects have externalities?' is perhaps of particular interest. Nuttall then summarises the findings of an enquiry into the relationship between education (ELT in particular) and development. Not surprisingly, the researchers were unable to establish firm causal relationships involving ELT, but they did reach one encouraging, if tentative, conclusion.

Nuttall mentions more than once the concept of 'educational development' – a process which is presumably to be measured in economic terms. Taking language planning issues of the kind that had been discussed by Fasold (1984) and Abbott (1984) among others, Turner offers a timely caution against any assumption that we are yet in a position to make safe economic forecasts in matters as complex as those involving educational decision making.

In an attempt to end this session on a down-to-earth note, we end with a brief summary by Thomas. Acting as a rapporteur of a Dunford group discussing matters raised above, he lists some of the group's conclusions and suggested implications for ELT professionals in the field.

5.1   Investing in education (1992)

ROGER IREDALE

The situation

The World Conference on Education for All in 1990 firmly set the agenda for education throughout the decade. The Conference focused attention on the remarkable inequalities of provision in many countries, and the extent to which education systems had failed to meet the challenges inherent in the 1961 Addis Ababa Resolution that 100 per cent primary education enrolment ratios would prevail by 1980.

This is not to say that donors and recipients wish to invest in basic education to the exclusion of other levels of education. There is continued evidence that many are deeply concerned about the quality of secondary and higher education. The Commonwealth Higher Education Support Scheme, though based on essentially political rather than economic considerations, provides an indication of the degree of concern that exists about management of universities in Africa and elsewhere.

But the general thrust is towards improving access to basic education, finding ways to make it more cost-effective, and improving its quality. UNESCO's World Education Report (1991) provides reminders, if we need them, that education remains in a perilously weakened state in many parts of the world. In 1990 gross enrolment ratios at secondary level for Sub–Saharan Africa were 17 per cent and 38 per cent for South Asia, compared with 99 per cent in North America. In the 1980s expenditure per pupil in 26 African countries declined by an average of 33 per cent. The survival rates in 1988 of children entering first level education between grades 1 and 4 were only 67 per cent for Sub–Saharan Africa, 55 per cent for Latin America/the Caribbean, 65 per cent for South Asia, and 78 per cent for East Asia (ibid: 31–37).

These sobering figures underline the need to do something major to improve the situation at primary level, and among younger illiterate adults. The school system has to address the brutal fact that in Sub–Saharan Africa under 50 per cent on average of adults are literate, and only just over one-third of women have achieved literacy. Cold statistics like these do not adequately portray the huge waste of human talent resulting from repetition, failure, drop-out, illiteracy, and the consequent and subsequent inability of young people to be able to access services, facilities, forms of employment, rights, privileges, and other enabling structures which we take for granted but which are crucial to health, welfare and the quality of life.

A donor's perspectives

Virtually every analysis of the rate of return from basic education (certainly primary) suggests that investment at this level produces a high (often the highest) return. Moreover, in countries where there have been structural adjustment programmes which have not sufficiently addressed their adverse effects on the social sectors, it is primary school provision that has suffered. UNESCO's figures indicate a general decline in teachers' salaries throughout the 1980s, with consequent loss of morale, often combined with the need to 'moonlight' in order to maintain family income (though this is not only at primary level, and there are stories of university staff and civil servants in Uganda taking different jobs in order to make ends meet).

Cost-benefit analysis has traditionally been employed by economists to determine whether it is worth putting more resources into educational facilities. Individuals make an informal cost-benefit analysis whenever they decide to invest in more education at the expense of earning more money; they assess that the additional training will produce promotion or some other opportunity. Similarly, governments and donors can look at the costs and benefits to society as a way of investing taxpayers' money in education rather than in other forms of infrastructure or service.

Not that cost-benefit analysis (CBA) has proved to be an exact science in relation to educational investment. CBA is widely employed for the enumeration and evaluation of all the relevant costs and benefits of education, but there is a degree of unease over its use, largely because of the number of unquantifiable variables that crop up. One of the traditional weaknesses of CBA has been the assumption that everyone educated or trained will take up employment and that their likely earnings can be ascertainable, measurable and quantifiable. In addition, CBA has not yet derived any measure for the value of the education of women who do not appear to enter employment, but whose skills and influences extend to their family.

Nevertheless, a substantial body of empirical study suggests that the rates of return to primary education are generally higher than for other levels of full-time education, both in terms of the social rate (that is, the usefulness of the education to the community at large) and the private rate (that is, the value of the education to the individual in enabling him or her to benefit personally). Not only that, but there is some evidence that investment in education produces at least as good a rate of return as does investment in other sectors such as health. It is worth noting in passing that part-time education, because it usually does not interrupt work, delivers a high rate of return.

To sum up, effective investment in education is an important element in social, economic and political development as well as a consequence of it: improved economic conditions will in turn lead to a demand for social services, including education. The extension of education to all parts of the population is an important role of the development of health, population and environmental awareness, good government (through popular participation in political processes), and economic activity via the development of a skilled workforce. The questions are: 'How much should be invested, and what is the best way of doing it?'

The nature of the response

The process by which money is allocated to one sector rather than another will vary considerably across aid agencies. In the case of the ODA, the main arbiter of allocation is the Country Review Paper (CRP), a majority policy document produced biennially and updated in the alternating years. The paper is produced as a result of wide consultation within the ODA and with the UK representation in-country, is discussed formally by the ODA's top management, and finally submitted to the Minister for approval. It is an internal document and is never available publicly.

The paper outlines the rationale for UK investment, reviews the efforts of other donors, considers where the UK has a particular relative advantage, and examines the match between what is desirable and what can be achieved within existing or potential manpower resources. Naturally it takes as a starting point the expressed priorities of the recipient. It should be remembered that the provision of technical co-operation (manpower, consultancy, training) tends to be much more demanding of administrative resources per pound spent than capital aid (the building of dams, power stations, roads, railways, etc.) or programme aid.

To an extent sectoral allocations are part of an historical process, but the CRP provides an opportunity for policy-makers to review the directions which advisers and programme managers have taken during recent reviews. The paper also allows a review of allocations between sectors, and an examination of the extent to which interdisciplinarity is possible. At the present time discussions on the social sectors concentrate increasingly on population, health (including AIDS), and basic education, all within the context of poverty alleviation which is one of the ODA's main overall policy thrusts.

Identification and appraisal criteria for donor support

Identification and appraisal of projects are normally what the ODA calls 'core tasks', and are therefore performed by in-house professional advisers in combination with administrative colleagues ('desk officers'), advisers from social sector disciplines and engineers (where appropriate), economists and the representatives of line ministries in the recipient country. The combination will vary from project to project according to the terms of reference of the mission. The kinds of criteria which the team will have in mind are:

1) **Benefit:** How will the proposed intervention benefit the country's development? (This would normally be reflected in the 'wider objectives' section of the project framework.) What contribution will it make to the development of manpower, industry, health and environmental awareness, or the personal development of people?

2) **Costs:** Will the economic benefits outweigh the costs? Will the proposed intervention lead to improved performance and facilities or other outcomes that represent a genuine degree of increased productivity? Or will it impose system and other costs that are unacceptable or unmanageable? Will it leave a burden of cost that outweighs the advantages long term?

3) **Sustainability:** (which is closely related to the above): Will the proposals be viable in terms of the recipient government's capacity to maintain the work once the donor has withdrawn? Does it offer methodologies that are consistent with the general goals and philosophies of the system? Will its general approach to be acceptable to those most closely involved, and therefore implementable? Will institutions involved have the capacity to absorb and implement the proposed strategies? How can ownership and commitment by the recipient government be assured?

4) **Alternatives:** Have all the alternative approaches been considered? Are there more cost-effective ways of achieving the objectives than those currently suggested? For example, is in-country training (ICT) or third-country training (3CT) an equally effective way of approaching staff development as bringing people to Britain for training (UKT)? What combinations of UKT and ICT are possible and how will they affect the design of the project?

These considerations are reflected in the appraisals which appear before the ODA's Projects and Evaluation Committee when a major educational project is put forward for approval. Typical headings in the relevant part of the project document are:

● Labour, inputs and services required (on the part of the recipient government);
● Social and environmental appraisal (which looks at gender issues among others);
● Economic justification. As well as technical appraisal this third element typically includes five sets of criteria:

i) Does the project fit in with the recommendations of ODA's Education Sector Review for the country concerned and the broader reforms being undertaken and proposed for the education sector?

ii) Does it promote or improve the sustainability achieved in an earlier project on which this particular project builds?

iii) Are the project and post-project cost implications manageable for the recipient government?

iv) Is the institutional capacity of the executing agents adequate to ensure sustainability?

v) Is it the most cost-effective means of achieving project objectives? Can the benefits be defined and compared with those of alternative approaches?

It will be seen that these questions (drawn from an annexe to a document dealing with a Tanzanian English Language Teaching Project) reflect exactly the questions asked in the paragraphs above. They examine the proposal within a broad policy context, look at the key issues of sustainability and cost/manpower burden, and they ask questions about alternatives.

Some implications

It will be evident that while the above criteria offer a model for approaching the appraisal of education projects, the analysis will vary considerably from place to place.

The intervention will depend on a large variety of extraneous factors, beginning with the position of other donors. (Despite our desire to increase our basic education portfolio we have come across countries where so many donors are already involved in the primary sector that there is no room for us, and we are instead considering a secondary level intervention.)

It will obviously depend on the recipient's stated goals, though we are always free to reject these if we do not accept their validity. (Recently we declined to enter a literacy project, much as we wanted to, because we did not believe that the 'top-down' methodology proposed was the right way to approach the problem and that our aid would consequently have been dissipated had we accepted.)

It will reflect the UK's capacity to assist in the area chosen, and will be in an area where we have particular strengths to offer. It will include a careful analysis of the capacity of the recipient to accept and use the offered intervention. It will look for ways of helping both systems and networks of institutions to improve their overall capacity, which includes management, administration and research. It will have considered (and rejected) alternative solutions to the problem. It will take into account the contributions of other donors, and will, where possible, complement their interventions (for example by offering a technical co-operation element based on a World Bank capital project).

Most important, it will have considered the field management implications of what is proposed and looked at how the project will be handled on the ground, how responsibilities will be distributed and defined, and how much that will cost. This is important, since the cost of field management adds to the overall cost of the project and consequently reduces the amount of aid available to the recipient government.

Conclusion

It will be apparent that tertiary level projects must be appraised very carefully indeed. With the high unit costs attaching to university education, projects aimed at this level should be demonstrably high priority and cost efficient. Likewise, the placing of long-term UK staff in the field in any project needs to be carefully examined. Again, UK training is an expensive option, and its use must be carefully considered and its relative value examined against alternative forms of training. Priority must be given to poverty-focused interventions and those that benefit girls and women; and projects that improve efficiency and/or quality in sustainable ways are the only ones that will attract funding.

This does not mean that we will not support higher education projects; nor does it mean that we want to cut down the number of British staff in the field, or to reduce the numbers of trainees brought to the UK, or to penny-pinch on the costs of field management. On the contrary, all have their place in the order of things, and will continue to be seen as important. But they must be subjected to the kind of scrutiny that ensures that they represent the most justifiable strategies for approaching the kinds of major problem referred to in the opening paragraphs of this paper. Otherwise, how do we justify them?

5.2   Economics and ELT (1992)

ALASDAIR MACBEAN

Introduction

> 'An economist is a person who knows the price of everything and the value of nothing.'

That is a not uncommon view of economists. But it is quite false. Explaining why market prices sometimes fail to measure social value has been a major activity of economists. The value to society of many activities exceeds the price consumers are willing to pay. In many other cases (for example chemical industries) the costs to society from pollution can exceed considerably the direct input costs measured by the firms in producing the products.

Monopoly, external costs such as pollution, or incidental benefits such as reduced congestion on old roads when a new turnpike is built are examples of market failure and can justify government controls, or taxes and subsidies designed to correct market price distortions. The growth of environmental concerns and the need to improve efficiency in health services and in education as rising expenditures press on government budgets have accelerated the economist's interest in finding ways of valuing benefits and costs in areas where explicit markets seldom exist. This is relevant to the concerns of this seminar. If English language teaching has to compete for resources against projects where benefits are readily valued then it will be at a disadvantage. A general appeal to the self-evident merits of foreigners learning English will not cut much ice. What is required is a systematic way of setting out, and where possible valuing, the contribution which ELT will make in achieving a set of objectives. These objectives could be very specific, as for example when an agency lays down the objectives and invites tenders. Or they could be much more general if the aid agency has been approached by the host government for assistance to many projects over several fields and where the demands exceed the finances allocated for aid to that country. Fortunately cost-effectiveness analysis and cost-benefit analysis are two techniques which conveniently provide a framework for the economic appraisal of a project or programme.

The real difficulties of these approaches lie not in the formulae but in the welfare economic theory which underpins the methods of valuing the outputs and inputs of the activity being appraised. There will always be a large element of judgement involved in any economic appraisal. The merit of the cost-benefit approach is that it makes these explicit and can force consistency across projects.

I can do no more than sketch the main outlines of subjects that have whole textbooks devoted to them. Most people find cost-benefit analysis easier to follow if one starts with the way in which a commercial firm would be expected to evaluate a possible investment. I shall start there, and then show how the method is adapted to become an appraisal which seeks to estimate social rather than private benefits and costs. I choose to do this with a health project which shares some of the problems of estimating and valuing benefits likely to be faced in ELT. Next, I discuss the economic analysis of the value of education and training in general, and finally I turn to ELT.

Commercial appraisal of a proposed investment

We assume a firm whose objective is to maximise profits and whose managers are rational in the pursuit of that aim. We also assume that two potential projects (A and B) have already cleared technical and legal hurdles. Both are do-able. The first step is to estimate all the costs and revenues which would accrue to the firm as a result of each project in each year over the assumed life of the project. The net revenues (revenues-cost) for projects A and B are set out in Table 1. The decision-maker has to decide whether either or both the projects are worth doing. If they were mutually exclusive, for example, alternative ways of producing the same service, the firm has to choose between them. How should it do so?

Crude methods like the number of years it would take to repay the original capital invested, or the annual average percentage return, are rough guides; but they are not really satisfactory because they fail to take account of the timing of the costs and revenues and may therefore mislead. Both firms and individuals have a preference for net earnings sooner rather than later. Most of us expect our incomes to rise over time, so diminishing marginal utility of income alone provides a reason why, on the average, people will value an extra £100 to spend today more than an extra £100 in a year's time. This helps to explain why we demand interest to persuade us to cut our consumption today and lend the money saved to financial institutions. If the market interest rate were 10 per cent then we should be indifferent between £100 now and £110 in a year (ignoring tax complications). Equally we can express this as 'the present value of £110 in a year's time is £100'. This is the clue to the use of Discounted Cash Flow (DCF) analysis which is the standard way that accountants and economists take account of time in comparing projects. By discounting the net revenues as they appear in the yearly cash flows and summing them over the life of the project we arrive at the net present value of each project. The firm should choose as its test discount rate the rate at which it can borrow. If both projects have a positive net present value (NPV) then both pass the financial test. If they are mutually exclusive projects for example, two ways of producing the same service or if the firm for some reason cannot raise enough capital for both, then it should choose the one with the higher NPV. The effect of discounting is to reduce the weight given to money earned or spent in later years compared with earlier ones. In our example both projects are viable at 10 per cent of discount and, if they are mutually exclusive projects, B is to be preferred. The higher the rate chosen, the more will projects with a quick payoff be favoured. From the viewpoint of the firm, the opportunity cost of later rather than earlier revenue surpluses is that the earlier they come the more they could have earned when reinvested.

Commercial Appraisal: Discounted Cash Flow Analysis (£m)					
Year		Net Cash Flow	Discount		Present Values
	A	B	Factor at 10%	A	B
0.00	-20.00	-10.00	1.0	-20.00	-10.00
1.00	3.00	5.00	0.909	2.727	4.545
2.00	+5	+7	0.826	4.130	5.782
3.00	+6	+8	0.751	4.506	6.008
4.00	+6	+8	0.683	4.098	5.464
5.00	+6	+8	0.621	3.726	4.968
6.00	+6	-5	0.564	3.384	-2.820
7.00	+6	+4	0.513	3.078	2.052
8.00	+6	+3	0.467	2.802	1.401
9.00	+6	+2	0.424	2.544	0.848
10.00	-5	-10.00	0.386	-1.930	-3.860
Net Present Values of Projects					

Table 1

These projects and data are entirely imaginary but one could think of A as an underground mine with a heavy initial expenditure on sinking shafts and then a slow build-up of mineral extraction as the shafts extend, while B is an open-cast mine to extract the same mineral from the same source with lower start-up costs, but a need to replace heavy earth-moving machines and trucks in the sixth year, and heavy costs for restoring the area at its finish. At the 10 per cent discount rate both projects would pay, but as they are mutually exclusive B is to be preferred because of its higher NPV. If you can lay your hands on a set of present value tables you may like to experiment with different rates of discount, e.g. 5 per cent and 20 per cent, to see if this makes a significant difference. NB: Without discounting, A has the higher net cash flow.

All investment decisions are forward-looking. All of the figures are forecasts and they may be surrounded by much uncertainty. Risk is something we do have to take into account in both private and social investment appraisals. So far we have ignored the issue of risk. But all these estimates of revenues and costs are only forecasts and subject to uncertainty. Some projects are inherently more risky than others. Given two projects with equal net present values, we would choose the less risky one. There are various ways of taking risk into account but there is not time here to go into them.

Cost-benefit analysis

If a public sector industry is given the instruction to maximise profits or minimise the required subsidy then it would appraise a new activity in the same way as the private firm. Presumably that is pretty much what Railtrack is having to do at present. But let us suppose now that we are considering a project in a field such as health. Like education (or teaching English) the services produced are generally not sold in a free market. Let us also suppose that the project is in a large African country whose domestic prices are very distorted because of price controls in some areas, subsidies and taxes in others and high import barriers. This is one among many projects put up to an aid agency whose resources are much less than the total demands placed on it. The agency needs a rational decision-making process which enables it to make the best possible selection of projects which would use up the budgeted resources for that country. Its objectives are, broadly, to promote social and economic development. That could of course embrace quite a lot of subsidiary objectives: increasing consumption, increasing resources available for reinvestment, increasing job opportunities, reducing inequalities in income distribution, improving the status of women, reducing the prevalence of child labour and so on. This is where judgement and common sense come in. You cannot expect every project to contribute to the solution of every problem and no one has the time or the resources to track down and quantify every effect of a project. One just has to do one's best given these limitations. Collecting and analysing information has its cost too.

Most economists would try to measure the effect on increasing the present value of consumption and they would try to identify which groups in society would benefit most. If it was a very large project and its income distribution effects were likely to be important, then one could weight the benefits going to the relatively poorer members of the society more than those benefits accruing to the better off. Other effects which are too difficult to quantify can be listed and left to the qualitative valuation of the final decision makers. But we should quantify in money values as much as we can. It is essential to express the benefits and costs in money values in order to add together different benefits and costs.

'Shadow' prices or social accounting prices

As market prices are distorted we need some guiding principle to help us in valuing the inputs used (materials, labour, capital) and outputs produced (improved health, lives saved). For inputs the basic principle is opportunity costs. If workers for this project are drawn from the ranks of the unemployed or from underemployed rural labourers, the cost to the economy is the output that would be sacrificed by shifting them from their present situation to working in the project. But that is likely to be much less than the wages which will be paid to them in the government health service. We need to estimate a shadow wage which would include the value of output lost by taking workers from the rural economy or from the informal sector in the towns to work in the project. We should also have to add the costs to society of putting them to work in the project such as provision of housing, water and electricity and the costs of their extra consumption due to their increased incomes.

The shadow exchange rate

Medical equipment and vaccines will have to be imported. The financial cost in local currency will be the cost in foreign exchange times the official exchange rate. But in most developing countries foreign exchange is very scarce. Their export earnings and net capital inflows fall far below the amounts they could usefully spend on imports for consumption and investment. So they ration the use of foreign exchange by controls and high barriers to imports. This rationing of foreign exchange holds down the number of units of local currency needed to buy a dollar. The local currency may be overvalued by as much as 50 per cent. The existence of parallel markets and illegal black markets for foreign currency is evidence of this tendency. What this implies is that a unit of foreign exchange is worth a great deal more than the official number of units of local currency that the central bank will give for it. So we need a shadow rate of foreign exchange to enable us to value any input or output of the project which uses or saves foreign exchange, requires imports, increases exports or replaces imports. Normally the shadow rate would be calculated by a central planning body for consistent use by all project analysts.

The shadow interest rate

The same would be true of the rate of interest or discount used in calculating the NPV of the project. Most developing countries do not allow interest rates to be market determined. They hold down interest rates to public sector borrowers. But this means that there is a large excess demand for capital in the private sector, which means that many potentially highly productive ventures are thwarted. Again a planning agency will usually provide a test discount rate to be used for all projects. The aid agency providing the funds will often have its own test rate. These rates are in real terms, that is, they ignore inflation. In fact in most project evaluation we carry out all the calculations in the prices of the initial year.

Other price adjustments

Other price adjustments that may have to be made are to deduct any taxes paid on goods and add back any subsidies. We wish to allow for the real costs of any electricity used in the project. These may be significantly higher than the price charged by the national power company. In most developing countries electricity prices do not cover the full costs of production and distribution. Taxes on vehicles bought for the project should be deducted. They are a mere transfer within the economy, not a real cost. Let us now turn to the outputs.

The direct outputs of a health project would be in terms of numbers of vaccinations given, numbers of patients seen, diagnosed, treated and so on. But the ultimate goals are lives saved, sickness reduced, suffering of victims and relatives avoided or alleviated. A technical appraisal would attempt to put numbers on these. Questions to be asked at this point would include whether these objectives could be achieved in other, possibly cheaper ways: preventive rather than curative approaches, treatment in large city hospitals, in small township centres or in the home, carefully targeted, or broader approaches, and so on. This requires interchange between technical and economic appraisers. It requires experience and imagination from the analysts. They need to be familiar with the institutions, politics and customs of the area where the project would be.

Valuation of the benefits would be in terms of the gains to the economy from prevented loss of work due to death and sickness. This would involve multiplying work years by the market, or the shadow wage rate, depending on whether the workers involved were fully employed at wages which reflected the value of their marginal product, or were likely to be unemployed, or underemployed. Estimation gets more difficult as we move on to wives and mothers saved. We ought to put some monetary value on the costs to the society of losing them. We also ought to put some value on the reduction of suffering. This may offend sensitivities or seem impossible, but law courts already tackle both of these issues in compensation claims and damage suits. Actuaries and economists are called in as special witnesses to help the courts on such matters, particularly in the USA. Implicitly, police and local authorities do it when they decide on whether to install a pedestrian crossing or traffic controls. Whether we do actually attempt to add these benefits into the monetary calculus or simply list them is a matter of time, resources and taste.

Externalities (side benefits or costs)

In addition to direct outputs the project may have some external effects or side effects. Suppose it were to control malaria through spraying breeding areas with DDT? As is well known, DDT kills many beneficial insects as well as harmful ones. It also builds up in predators such as birds and fish, reducing their populations. The economic losses associated with these effects should go in as costs of the project. But a health project may have external benefits as well. It may train health auxiliaries who, when this project is finished, become available for other projects which do not have to incur the costs of training them. This may be worth including as an extra benefit if it can be reasonably anticipated. (Do ELT projects have externalities?)

Once all the direct and indirect costs and benefits of the project have been identified they should be valued wherever possible and set out in an annual cash flow exactly as for the commercial appraisal. Calculation of the NPV of the project then provides a major input into the decision-making process which determines whether the aid agency finances this or some other project. The non-quantifiable factors, politics, the special preferences of the agency and so on may still play key roles. But the project appraisers should have done their bit towards reducing the 'hunch' factor and increasing the rationality of the decision process.

Cost-effectiveness analysis

In this approach one omits the benefit side. The output objective is agreed and the economic question becomes one of setting out the relative costs to the society of different means of achieving the objective. This is much more limited in that it does not question the merits of the objective as compared with other objectives which could be achieved with alternative uses of the resources. As benefits are usually much the more speculative and difficult to estimate, a cost-effectiveness appraisal is simpler to do. It still, however, involves the same 'shadow pricing' methodology outlined above.

Returns to education

The economics of education has been heavily influenced by the human capital approach. This treats education and training as similar to investment in physical capital such as machines, factories and roads. Individuals are viewed as investing in additional years of education as long as they expect the NPV of their future earnings to be increased by an amount at least equal to the cost. Most of the cost to the individual is sacrificed earnings when education is free or heavily subsidised by the state. For the nation similar considerations apply. It should invest in education and training up to the point where the returns just equal the marginal return on investment in physical capital. For an optimum, marginal returns on all types of training and all types of investment should be equalised. Otherwise it would always pay to reduce investment in those activities where the marginal return is relatively low, and shift the resources released to activities where the marginal rate of return is relatively high.

Country	Year	Primary	Social Secondary	Higher	Private (a) Primary	Secondary	Higher
Latin America							
Brazil	1970	na	24	13	na	25	14
Chile	1959	24	17	12	na	na	na
Colombia	1973	na	na	na	15	15	21
Africa							
Ethiopia	1972	20	19	10	35	23	27
Ghana	1967	18	13	17	25	17	37
Kenya	1971	22	19	9	28	33	31
Asia							
India	1978	29	14	11	33	20	13
Indonesia	1978(b)	22	16	15	26	16	na
Pakistan	1975	13	9	8	20	11	27
South Korea	1971	na	15	9	na	16	16
Developed Countries							
Japan	1976	10	9	7	13	10	9
UK	1978	na	9	7	na	11	23
USA	1969(c)	na	11	11	na	19	15

Source: Psacharopoulos (1985)

a) Income measures before payment of income taxes;
b) Social rates refer to 1978, private rates for 1977;
c) Private rates for secondary and higher education have declined since 1969; 1976 estimates are 11 per cent and 5 per cent respectively. For social rates, no later estimates are available

Table 2: Some estimates of rates of return to education

Empirical evidence on returns to education

Much empirical evidence shows a significant association between education and higher incomes both for individuals and nations. Table 2 shows statistical evidence for both private and social rates of return to primary, secondary and higher education in selected regions and countries. The social returns are lower than the private ones because in most countries the main costs of education are met by the state. As these returns are higher than in most physical investments at the margin there seems to be a strong case for spending more in education, and favouring primary education in developing countries. But on further examination the evidence is less strong than at first appears. Could it be that the number of years in education typically correlates with higher innate ability and/or social class? If so, much of the association with extra years of education could be spurious since ability and social class are also likely to play a powerful role in generating ambition, gaining good jobs and influencing promotion. Also employers may use educational standards less as evidence of useful knowledge and training than as a screening device to select candidates for jobs which require some generalised ability and stamina.

Much evidence suggests that very few jobs make use of knowledge gained in education or even in vocational training. If these criticisms carry weight we have to consider whether some of the resources currently devoted to education by governments might not be better devoted to devising cheaper screening methods. Fortunately for educationalists, like me, some recent studies give strong support to the view that cognitive skills such as literacy and numeracy account for much of the difference in earnings associated with higher levels of schooling (Boissiere *et al.*, 1985). A recent paper also makes out a strong case that evidence published in the last few years shows that quality in education, as measured by expenditure per pupil and by pupil-teacher ratios, has a positive and stable relationship with earnings in later life. This finding probably comes as no surprise to you, but educational economists have expressed scepticism about the benefits of both the quantity and quality of education (Card and Kreuger 1991).

At the macro level the consensus among development economists is that technology and human know-how are more important factors in explaining differences in rates of growth among nations than investment in physical capital. Countries like Japan, Korea and China are clearly convinced of it. They have invested heavily in education and continue to do so. Their growth may justify their faith. But much wider studies also bear out this view (World Bank 1991: 43 and 55–59). There are good grounds for thinking that most of these calculations actually under-estimate the social and private gains from education. Most omit the gains from the influence of educated parents (particularly mothers) upon their children, and add nothing for the consumption gains from education such as access to literature, better appreciation of art and culture generally. They also ignore much of the socialising effect of education in integrating societies and making democratic systems of government more workable.

This section has, I hope, illustrated the kinds of benefits which one would like and seek to quantify in an educational project. The costs, as we have noted, are not simply the tuition, accommodation and materials. Often a major cost, both for pupils and parents as well as society is the sacrificed output of the years spent in education beyond the permissible age of employment. This will differ between societies and bears heavily on family decisions in farming communities or where child labour is widely used and very productive, such as hand-woven carpets. These ideas will, I hope, be useful when thinking about ELT projects, to which we now turn.

The economic appraisal of ELT projects and programmes

A characteristic of the acquisition of a language (or for that matter mathematics) is that it is both an end in itself and a key which provides access to much else. It is hard to be good at physics or engineering without a fairly good grasp of maths. But maths is also an end in itself. Similarly people may learn English because they enjoy the language and its literature. But probably the majority of the foreigners who study English to a reasonably high standard do so because they want it for a special purpose. If we can demonstrate that English is essential for a particular purpose then a major element of the justification for ELT will depend on whether the purpose itself would pass an economic appraisal. If the social return on some doctors acquiring a special surgical technique is high and a good working knowledge of English is essential for them to communicate with the English-speaking surgeons who can teach it, then one should treat the ELT provision as part of the project. Its costs are simply added to the costs of bringing the trainees and trainers together and effecting the transfer of knowledge. We should then check that the combined project meets the required criteria: for example, that it has a positive present value when discounted at the test rate.

Suppose an overseas Ministry of International Trade sought aid for the provision of ELT up to translator level for the sales staff of a large number of trading companies. An immediate question would be why, if they believe that this will raise the profits from exports, should they not pay for this themselves as a commercially profitable investment? But perhaps they do not have the necessary foreign exchange. Next, why do they need such a high level? They reply – because they need staff who can write attractive sales literature in English. But then one must ask whether this could not be done better and more cheaply by simply hiring some part-time native English writers to polish up the texts and eliminate the howlers committed by their present staff. Economic appraisal is not just about feeding numbers into a formula, it is asking questions about objectives and the means proposed for attaining them. These are the areas where the ELT expert has an enormous advantage. Experience of previous projects gives knowledge about common pitfalls, common problems that arise, staffing, and essential materials and back-up. One should seldom take any claim for granted. In reviewing a project proposal in agriculture we found that a proposal to increase output by moving from single cropping to triple cropping was unworkable, even with new irrigation, because there simply was not enough time to harvest one crop and plant the next. In preparing a proposal one has to put oneself in the position of the aid agencies' appraisers and try to anticipate their doubts and questions about the technical and economic feasibility of the proposal. There is little point in training ELT teachers in the use of the latest teaching aids if there is little prospect of their education ministry providing the equipment, or if the general standards of maintenance are such that the equipment will be useless in a few months, or if there is too little money in the educational budget for photocopying paper, or replacement bulbs for projectors.

Practitioners or sponsors of ELT will be much better placed than I to suggest how ELT benefits can be assessed. Clearly many countries and many private citizens believe it has a high utility. Why else would they or their parents be prepared to pay the high fees demanded for courses in English mounted by both the private sector and the British Council? But for countries where poverty prevents the commercial purchase of ELT it is necessary to demonstrate that the gains from an ELT project are likely to be greater than alternative uses of the funds. The net present value of an extra £100,000 worth of ELT provision will differ from country to country, depending on the need for English as a lingua franca or merely as a second language for special groups within the population. Each of the case studies presented at this seminar may come up with very different lists of benefits and costs because of the differing circumstances of the economies and projects with which they are concerned. But I would suggest that they should find it helpful to adopt the framework of cost-benefit analysis and the ideas which the work of economists in educational, health and environmental sectors have thrown up in the last 30 years. The ODA's *Planning Development Projects* (1983) has some helpful guidelines and a check list of questions in a chapter on appraising educational projects (pp. 85–91) and the report from the Australian 'Workshop on Guidelines and Criteria for Overseas English Language Training Programmes' (1992) does the same for ELT. They relieve me of attempting that task from my basis of considerable ignorance.

One issue I should like to emphasise. Economic appraisal is not in competition with appraisal of the technical, sociological, or political appraisal or a project policy. They are complementary. A project has to meet all the criteria which would determine whether it can be done before trying to decide whether it is a better project than some alternative use of the funds. A proposed project or change of government policy which is likely to involve large costs and potential benefits should be appraised by a team which uses all the relevant disciplines.

5.3   Evaluating the effects of ELT (1991)

DESMOND NUTTALL

Background

The British Council and the Overseas Development Administration invest very substantial sums of money in supporting English language teaching. They do not do this simply as an act of charity or simply for cultural reasons; they do it in the belief that ELT investment will contribute to economic and human development, for example, by giving university students access to technical literature, and possibly to make it more likely that countries will wish to trade with the UK, or send its students to the UK rather than, say, to France. Of course, the UK is by no means the only English language-speaking country in the world, so others like the USA, Canada and Australia might benefit from the aid efforts of the UK (and vice versa).

The British Council asked the London School of Economics to prepare a report into the relationship between ELT aid and educational, social and economic development. This report was also to propose a model or framework for analysing the relationship between ELT and development, identifying key indicators and potential means of evaluation. The report was also to summarise its findings in relation to a justification for ELT aid. The chain of links between studying English in the classroom and any later economic and human development that can be uniquely and unequivocally attributed to those English lessons is fragile. To demonstrate that ELT investment 'pays off' one has to eliminate other possible reasons for a country's economic and human development. The aim of the present study was to explore that issue in more detail, to establish whether or not the issue would be amenable to more elaborate research.

Executive summary of LSE study

1) There are arguments which suggest that within an aided country ELT aid is fungible and that it should be cut wherever it causes domestic funds that *would* have gone to ELT to be invested in less aidworthy projects. Such arguments appear very dubious on both theoretical and empirical grounds. In particular, there is very little evidence to suggest, on either theoretical or empirical grounds, that private returns to tertiary education, and by extension to ELT, are significantly higher than social returns, or that returns to education are significantly higher than returns to the economy at large. It is therefore possible to conclude that educational aid is needed.

2) Evidence from Africa suggests that the use of English as a medium of instruction makes for a cheaper delivery of education. Using UN data, a case study compared educational attainment in 50 African countries, distinguished on the basis of whether English is used as a medium of instruction or not. It was found that when wealth (GDP per capita) and commitment to education (per capita expenditure on education as a proportion of GNP) is taken into account, the use of English as a medium of instruction emerges as a significant factor in determining educational attainment. Countries that use English as a medium of instruction were likely to have a higher degree of educational attainment than those that did not. This would indicate that, given the resources at their disposal, delivery of education in countries that use English as a medium of instruction was more efficient than in those that did not.

3) While the results in 2) above demonstrate the usefulness of ELT, they do not in themselves demonstrate the cost-effectiveness of ELT aid. Further research will be required to develop models and acquire data which can be used to assess cost-effectiveness in this area.

Conclusions and proposals for further research

This study has reinforced the difficulty of demonstrating any causal line between ELT investment and educational, human, social and economic development because of the mass of other variables potentially involved in contributing to development and the time taken for the improved ELT capability to feed through to development. Nor is it easy to demonstrate a causal link between ELT provision and improved educational standards where one might expect a close connection and a shorter causal link.

Council projects are required to specify their aims and objectives, together with the proposed success criteria (or indicators) and means of measuring them. The analysis of these shows that, although broad aims are often stated (linking ELT aid to development) indicators are almost always tied to shorter-term objectives, and that the indicators and evaluation methods are specified in very general terms. It is difficult to see how ELT aid could fail to achieve its shorter-term objectives and yet contribute to development, but it is necessary to examine this statement carefully to see if other mechanisms contributing to development might be present. If not, one can view the attainment of these objectives as a necessary, but not sufficient, condition for contributing to development.

The second part of the study examines the much broader issue of the empirical relationship between education and development, and the justification for aid. It demonstrates that there is very little evidence to suggest that private returns to tertiary education, and by extension to ELT, are significantly higher than social returns, or that returns to education are significantly higher than returns to the economy at large. These findings imply that the less developed countries, by and large, could not readily afford to pay more for their education systems or support their own ELT programmes.

It also demonstrates that, in Africa, the educational attainment (as defined by the UNDP) in English-using countries is significantly higher than in non English-using countries for a given financial commitment to education. This suggests that using English is an economic and an educational asset, but does not demonstrate a causal relationship. It might be, for example, that legacies of British rule other than using English, such as the continued use of a British educational system, could be the cause (or part of the cause).

Together, the studies have not taken the topic of the relationship between ELT provision and development much further, though encouragement may be taken from the relationship between educational attainment and use of English in African countries. To make progress, further modelling at the micro-level and the macro-level is needed.

More specifically, the framework used by the OECD International Education Indicators Project should be expanded (and possibly adjusted) to encompass a wider range of outcomes, including impact on development, and to introduce ELT expenditure and ELT aid as inputs. This could lead to a regular monitoring of key indicators (most of which are already available through the UNDP and Unesco), and the time series would provide more power by allowing the study of the relationship between changes in output and changes in input. At the micro-level, more attention should be given to the careful specification of project objectives and indicators, as well as the means to measure them, and to examining the extent to which the objectives are achieved. These exercises might also assist in the refinement of the concept of educational development. Finally, further research should be undertaken into the more detailed issues put forward in the second part of the study. For example, the rates of return to ELT provision and aid at different levels of the education system should be examined, as should the rates of return for males and females separately.

It is important to determine the investment of other English-speaking countries in ELT aid, and the division of these contributions in each less developed country. This division could then be related to the numbers of students from the less developed country studying in each of the donor countries, or to the proportions of LDC's foreign trade going to each of the donor countries. Other analyses of ELT and trade could establish whether there were more trade opportunities for English-speaking than for non-English-speaking countries in Africa.

These diverse examples suggest that a first stage of further work should be to develop a conceptual framework of the possible effects of the different kinds of development and the links between them, and macro-indicators of the type described above that would detect these effects, together with other possible explanations (such as the 'free-rider' effect of gaining from another country's investment in ELT aid), some of which might be eliminated or held constant in the analyses. This framework could be linked to the educational framework referred to above, the notion of educational development being the linking concept, which should therefore be clarified and expanded. This is a substantial programme of work. It might serve to improve the focus and quality of ELT aid, and maximise its beneficial effects, but it is over-optimistic to hope that it will be capable of providing an unambiguous estimate of the impact of ELT on educational, social and economic development.

5.4a   The value of ELT in development projects (1992)

JOHN TURNER

Where English is chosen as a lingua franca, this choice gives access to a world language of communication and scholarship. This is clearly a tremendous benefit for a variety of reasons. It is valuable in all aspects of diplomacy including aid diplomacy. It is useful for students to have access to the vast literature available in the English language. Indeed at higher levels of scholarship, it is now an essential requirement for scholars of all subjects of all nationalities. Moreover, even at lower levels of education, it may be necessary, for purposes of publishing economy, to use a lingua franca to produce suitable books at reasonable prices even at junior school level. Even when using English as the medium, commercial publishers often find it necessary to produce textbooks for groups of countries with a few specific country-oriented pages and with different covers. By producing cheaper, more utilitarian textbooks, curriculum development centres and national literacy agencies can often publish books more cheaply for a smaller number of consumers, though below a certain number, which will differ in each country considered, such publication can only be done with a government subsidy.

We are treading here in territory of which the main parameters have hardly been drawn and in which we have little research evidence. Some of the questions are detailed; for example, what is the smallest language group for which it is realistically possible to produce vernacular school texts up to a) the end of primary school or b) the end of secondary school? If such books were produced, would there be sufficient teachers whose mother tongue was in that particular language to teach in all the schools concerned? Others are more important philosophical points; for example, is it necessary to teach all pupils English in order to provide for the needs of diplomacy, scholarship, etc. or should one concentrate on providing the high quality language education which is necessary for the relatively small cadres concerned? How would the selection of these particular individuals be made and at what stage? Questions of equity enter the debate at a very early point. Moreover, a good deal of the evidence needed to answer such questions would be country-specific, larger scale comparative studies only being of use for very general guidance.

Even the impact of using English as a lingua franca on the intellectual development and cultural identity of the nation has hardly been systematically examined, though loud assertions are frequently made. The impact of multilingualism on individuals has been frequently explored. The general conclusion seems to be that children brought up in a country or countries in which several languages are spoken can become proficient in several of them, providing all the languages are regularly exercised. Where this is the case, the evidence would seem to indicate that a higher proficiency is reached at any one time in the language which is most used but that the languages can change position if there is a movement from one language environment to another. This sort of evidence is very useful. It does not, however, help us in countries where the models of one or more of the languages, for example, English, are inadequate models and in particular where the school teachers who are teaching the target language have an inadequate grasp of it themselves. Questions relating to the feasibility of introducing English as the national language and the language of education in Namibia therefore in terms of the provision of materials, the retraining of teachers and the effect of the change on school standards cannot in my view by answered with any degree of certainty in our present state of knowledge, nor can we know with any precision what it will cost or whether that cost is worth paying. Some guidance may be sought from comparative studies but the differences of population numbers, mix of vernaculars, history, political orientation and existing educational frameworks are so variable that the results of such studies must be treated with extreme caution. The consequences of making one choice rather than another are likely to be of great importance, yet the outcome of such choices depends on a great variety of factors which we find it difficult to understand and even more difficult to control.

Nevertheless, choices have to be made and methodologies have to be developed to make such choices possible and effective. Indeed both parts of the term 'cost-effectiveness' have to be unpacked if adequate comparisons are to be made. In terms of cost, for example, a basic programme of a relatively simple type (for example, to build and equip a training college for a given number of students to teach certain subjects up to a specified level and to train local staff to teach in that college) would produce greatly varying estimates from those tendering for the project. An American and British team would be likely to quote very different prices because of the different rules of AID and ODA and their different styles of operation. Moreover, the cost of a British project to a developing country changes completely when the rules governing aid operations also change, as they have done frequently in the past. Is it, for example, necessary to use British carriers for the transport of staff or could one go for the cheapest carrier? Are there restrictions on the provenance of equipment? Can it be bought from the cheapest source, or must it be bought either from the donor country or from the country in which the project is placed? Must a proportion of the training be done in the donor country or can some or all of it be done in the project country? Must all the aid personnel be citizens of the donor country or can they be drawn from any country in the world? These are just a few of the questions which can totally change the cost of any project and they are all questions relating to national policy, rather than to the substance or quality of the programme.

Questions of effectiveness are equally difficult to define. The project system through which we have just been passing and from which it appears that we may be about to emerge has built into its structure definitions of effectiveness by which the success of a particular project can be evaluated. Very often these are expressed in terms of the achievement of certain targets by specified dates. For example, draft textbooks up to certain class levels in certain subjects may have to be completed by a certain date and be in the schools by another date; a certain number of head teachers may have to have completed three-week training programmes in school management by a certain date; a certain number of future lecturers in primary education are to have completed appropriate degrees in British or American universities to enable them to do their task by a certain date. Measures of this kind can very easily be evaluated. Whether, however, the curricula and textbooks produced are in fact the best that could be produced for the pupils to learn what it is intended that they should learn is an entirely different question. Whether the new lecturers in primary education are able to teach so well in their own primary schools that they can provide a convincing and wholesome model to their students is a different level of evaluation which we find it difficult to embark on. Yet these are the questions which really matter and which are themselves dependent upon the future economic prosperity of the country which will enable the accompanying needs of the children to be met, the necessary books and equipment to be bought and teachers paid sufficiently to persuade some of the brightest young men and women to enter the teaching profession. Answers to these questions in turn may depend upon whether the rainfall over a particular period is average or whether scientific and industrial developments require a particular mineral which is available in the country concerned.

I would not wish the general tenor of these remarks to be mis-understood. I am certainly fully committed to the notion of exploiting existing methodologies and developing new ones to ensure that we derive the best value from a stated expenditure in giving aid to developing countries or indeed in answering questions on social issues in our own country. What I am trying to say, however, is that the technology for making educational decisions at the present time with any degree of accuracy in our forecasts is still in rather a crude handicraft stage. Even on a global scale the estimates, for example, at Jomtien, of the cost of providing Education for All by the year 2000 can only be regarded as showing that a certain level of activity is not totally beyond the bounds of possibility and that the social and egalitarian aims underlying such provision are aims that can, and should, be striven for. To do this in a way which produces the motivation which is already evident in order to make changes in this direction is an amazing achievement. To imagine, however, that the costs forecast will fall in any way as anticipated by the various economic projections presented at the conference would be to court bitter disappointment. Nevertheless, we must attempt to produce 'best guesses' on the basis of the maximum amount of information gathered from the best study we can make of similar situations if our decisions are to have any rationality whatever.

5.4b   Towards a synthesis of outcomes (1992)

ANDY THOMAS

A 40-minute plenary participant-led discussion, chaired by Andy Thomas, attempted to capture some of the major general issues emerging from the 1992 seminar. The following nine issues emerged.

1)   The ELT profession should define its 'scope of accountability' to extend beyond immediate to wider objectives to which it contributes. For example, a justification/evaluation of a language-oriented teacher-training project could measure not only teacher improvement but also consequent learner preparation for higher education or employment, as a result of improved teaching across the curriculum. Similarly, a justification/ evaluation of a language training project linked to a fisheries training project could measure not only the improvement in language skills of the trainees but also their consequent improvement in the area of fisheries, the latter in collaboration with fisheries experts. The extent to which these

'intermediate' wider objectives contribute to 'remote' or longer term national aid objectives of socio-economic development cannot be measured by ELT professionals alone, or even ELT professionals in collaboration with other (such as fisheries) professionals, without the help of macro socio-economists, who are ultimately responsible for such justification.

ELT professionals can, however, identify probable national socio-economic benefits in logical rather than strictly quantitative terms for the quantitative consideration of macro socio-economists. A 'cumulative' accountability model, using fisheries as an example, may be diagrammatically represented as follows:

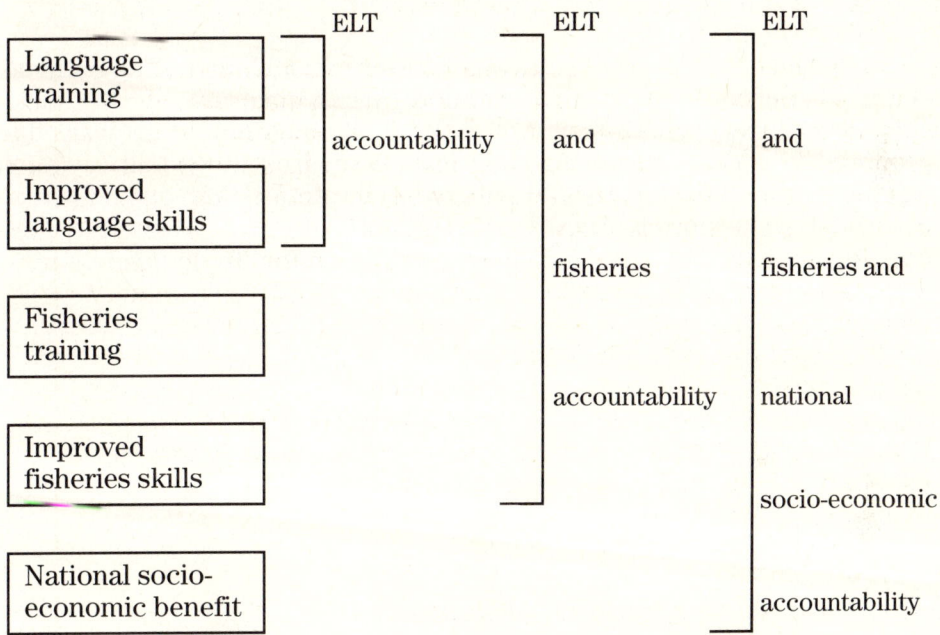

If, as is often the case, prior socio-economic justification exists for investment in, for example, education or fisheries, then the task of the ELT profession becomes justification of investment in ELT in terms of the contribution it makes to improvement in these sectors. (A complementary alternative to this indirect national benefit model, specified in terms of direct individual or group benefit, is proposed in 9 below).

2)   An essential measure of the value of investment is that of the cost-effectiveness of such investment.

3)   In the light of 1) above, it is clear that the ELT profession needs to establish working links with others, both inside and outside education.

4)   In establishing such links and adopting an interdisciplinary approach, the ELT profession must establish itself as a credible participant in discussions on development by demonstrating an awareness of all levels of development.

5)   Such credibility may be established if the ELT profession can clearly define its place and role within the world of information and knowledge.

6)   When engaging in cost-benefit analysis, the costs and benefits to UK institutions are a significant part of the equation.

7)   Given that there are both 'soft' (qualitative) and 'hard' (quantitative) benefits to be derived from investments in ELT, we should look at the relationship between soft and hard indicators.

8)   We should not forget that English is the language of international communication, which is itself a significant justification for investment in ELT.

9)   In terms of aid priorities (given this international, and often national, status of English) an alternative, more direct measure of the socio-economic impact of ELT at the individual or group level than that proposed in 1 above at the national level, would be the extent to which equal opportunities that would otherwise be denied are opened up to individuals or groups by access to English.

6.0   Administering ELT Aid

GERRY ABBOTT

Iredale opens this section with an outline of the shift of ODA policy mentioned at the beginning of Part 2 (see page 92). His main point is that ELT must, if it is to be an accountable aid activity, be seen to serve a practical purpose. It may be objected that a rigid application of this policy would leave unsupported the teaching of EFL in state schools where the aim is purely educational and no clear practical purpose identifiable. Here the value of the outcome, though likely to be unquantifiable, may nevertheless be substantial.

In the drive for cost-effectiveness, 'projectisation' and 'sustainability' were the new buzz words. By and large, ELT would find itself projectised in one of two ways, either:

i)   as a service input to a project with a wider occupational or post-school academic purpose (EOP or EAP) or

ii) as an activity within a national education system that used English as a medium of instruction.

One example of type i) was the Ecuador fisheries project mentioned by Iredale, and a brief description of that project immediately follows his contribution.

If projects are to succeed they need to be well designed, appropriately managed and carefully monitored; in this regard, Harrison and Munro sketch out the ODA's policies and procedures with especial reference to the 'project cycle' and the 'project framework' being used at the time.

Finally come two reports that give us the benefit of practical experience in the 'on-site' management of ELT in aid projects. St John offers guidance in the management of innovation in communication skills projects; and, since awful warnings can be as useful as positive guidance, we end with Ahrens' observations on the breakdown of a project in India. Both warn that the degree of intended innovation should not be too great, and that the existing circumstances must be taken fully into account; this question of appropriacy of aims and methods is to be taken up in Section 7.

6.1   The English language as aid (1986)

ROGER IREDALE

In 1983 the ODA made an important decision to shift its funding from a functional scheme, which was called the Key English Language Teaching (KELT) Scheme, to the geographical funding on which virtually all of the ODA's other programmes rest. This decision was taken after the issue and discussion of an evaluation report had recommended against an alteration of the funding pattern, on the grounds that ELT was a resource which needed special protection. The ODA gave considerable thought to this recommendation but concluded otherwise: not that ELT was not a special resource, but that it did not require special protection. We saw no reason why the teaching of English should uniquely seek to pre-empt the resources available to developing countries, rather than compete for funds against such important other areas of activity as agriculture, health, water, or, if it comes to that, the teaching of science and mathematics. But, more importantly, we had every confidence that our pre-eminence in ELT would ensure that our work in the English language field would prosper; in the event, even in the context of increasing pressure on the bilateral programmes, the number of ELT posts has actually risen from 114 to 127 and there is little sign that this trend will be reversed. The diversification of the funding throughout the whole range of geographical desks in the ODA has effectively ensured that ELT cannot be singled out as a target for expenditure reduction.

But there have been more important consequences than these. Before we put the KELT scheme into the general pocket of money available to each Geographical Desk Officer in the ODA, not only did some desk officers tend to regard themselves as having no responsibility for ELT, their attitude being that ELT was something which the British Council did with money that had nothing to do with the desk officer, but also – even more importantly – it was actually very difficult to integrate ELT into the broad pattern of ODA activities within any given country. There were very significant dangers in this. The bilateral aid programme for any particular country ought in logic to be a unity. Britain has undertaken to help that particular country, discussing with its government the ways in which we are best equipped to offer such help, and the two governments should have made a rational decision about the most economical and relevant ways in which that help can be targeted. In logic, it does not make sense for a donor like Britain to be scattering small packets of assistance like seeds here and there across a large landscape in the hope that the odd patch of green may appear; what makes sense is to concentrate on one or two significant plantations and try to get them established.

Increasingly our ELT work is being defined in clear project format, with the KELT post perceived as only one instrument in the achievement of a strategy. With KELT funding springing from the same source of funds as for the other parts of the programme, it is much easier to develop a strategy looking forward over a number of years with planned steps towards a quite clear set of objectives, and using a number of complementary approaches. Thus, we are gradually moving from the old concept of the 'KELT post' to the idea of the achievement of certain objectives by a number of methods which might include, *inter alia*, a fully-funded British person who is an ELT specialist. This makes it easier to define exactly what we are aiming at, quantify results, and ensure that other people in the ODA (some of whom may not have much sympathy at all for ELT) are convinced that our efforts are aimed at a sensible developmental objective.

A considerable amount of discussion has taken place within the ODA this year about the Project Framework. This is a paradigm which those planning projects should be prepared to develop from the beginning of their thinking about a particular project. The Project Framework is a grid which obliges the originator of a project to look at all the various inter-locking parts of a project and state precisely what it should achieve, how this is to be brought about, what measures for monitoring are to be taken, and how 'success' is to be evaluated. The Framework measures not only the inputs, in other words the various items that are contributed by the donor and the effectiveness and efficiency by which they are put in, but also the outputs, or in other words what is actually expected to result from the particular aid. It is a valuable intellectual discipline, and one which should put a stop to the age-old problem of putting someone in post and then discovering that additional inputs needs to be provided for which no financial provision has been made and over which there are then frustrating and lengthy delays, affecting the morale of the officer; I hope that it will lead to a more business-like way of setting about achieving our ends.

I hope that we would all agree that ELT is not an end in itself. ELT in a developing country under the Aid Programme is ELT for a purpose. It may support the work of students of Science and Technology at a university, where the acquisition of English is an essential tool for student and tutor in acquiring a proper mastery of a subject where many of the textbooks are printed in English. We are involved in this kind of work all over the world, from Brazil through Turkey to China. Or it may be an essential tool in secondary school classroom teaching in a country where English has been adopted as the common medium, as in Kenya and in many parts of Africa. Even more specifically, it may be developed, as in Ecuador, in order to enable local people involved in an ODA fisheries project to use technical texts printed in English and to come to Britain to study as counterparts for those personnel. Whatever the form a particular element of assistance takes, it will have a clear enabling objective. Increasingly, that objective is related to matters that are less narrowly educational and more broadly developmental, as in the Ecuador example which I have just cited. Thus in planning this conference with our council colleagues, ODA's Education Advisers asked that we should enable those present to talk about the role of English within the broader process of communicating ideas, skills and techniques. Focus must be increasingly upon *why* English is being provided and what will be the consequences of its provision.

Here we return to the Project Framework, where outputs have to be quantified and shown to have some relevance to a developmental process. Of course, you may feel that I am being dogmatically narrow in my definition of what is 'developmental'. I am fully aware of the importance of mastery of language for its own sake; but where the resources available to developing countries are so limited, and where we have pitifully small sums of money to offer for the solutions of such huge problems, we are obliged to focus on the essential. And the essential is the immediate economic development of a country's resources, including the human ones. Naturally, when people learn English, for whatever purpose and by whatever method, they acquire something of the flavour of our culture, our institutions, our ways of thinking and communicating. This is all to the good, and it is a worthwhile objective that can happily co-exist with the specific purpose for which the language skill is being imparted.

6.2   ELT in a fisheries training project: work in progress (1985)

KATHRYN BOARD, ROBIN CORCOS, JOHN HOLMES, OLIVER HUNT, STUART MATTHEWS, MIKE SMITH and ANDREW THOMAS

Introduction
The project, which is already in existence, aims to develop the fishing industry in Guayaquil (Ecuador), and it is this programme which forms the content that the English course is to support. The fisheries training necessitates four categories of language use:

1) using the technical literature in English so as to consolidate the training and remain able to use such sources after the departure of the TCOs*.
2) interacting with TCOs during training, which in the project is done in Spanish.
3) tackling the ELTS exam and, for the few candidates selected, proceeding to further training in the UK – a process handled by the British Council in Quito; and
4) for these few, interacting with overseas visitors.

Although the language of training is Spanish, English being needed only for certain of its components, within these an understanding of written English is an essential skill; in the long term too, the trainees will need access to specialist literature in English. The ELT support will therefore confine itself to 1) above, using texts in the target domain so as to ensure face validity and thereby maximise motivation.

*TCOs: Technical (here 'Fisheries') Co-operation Officers

Since the components of the English syllabus must serve those of the existing Spanish-medium training programme, the initial ELT planning involves:

i) itemising and specifying the TCO training programme through the fishing-skills project design and implementation;

ii) identifying areas within each training unit where technical and innovative details could feasibly be used to improve or consolidate the existing fishing practices and procedures;

iii) matching each selected area with a use-related task;

iv) selecting appropriate reference material to act as an enabling resource for each allotted task; and

v) constructing a set of activities that enable the learner to move from resource to task completion.

Constructing the English Language (EL) units

More specifically, the designers of the EL course will need to:
- make an inventory of all the units and stages in the existing fisheries training schedule;
- identify those components that could be enhanced by EL input;
- establish performance objectives for each of the *occupational* units;
- design EL units to help trainees attain the occupational objectives with the aid of resource tests in English which in turn will entail:

    a) selecting appropriate texts
    b) creating tasks that link texts to objectives and
    c) devising various levels of task;

- design self-access remedial materials for under-achievers; and
- produce an introductory module that will familiarise the trainees with the structure of the EL course.

The training project deals with the major aspects of the fishing industry (harvesting, processing and so on) and, since its design is already established, the EL course takes it as 'given'. Each of its units does include tasks whose successful completion depends upon reference to information written in English. It is these reference tasks that form the basis of the EL component, whose own units (though restricted to the task in hand) will cater for differing levels of linguistic competence so that each learner can progress at his own pace.

The effectiveness of each EL unit will be assessed not by the English teaching staff but by the TCO dealing with the occupational unit concerned, so the major criterion will be the degree of success in the *fisheries* task. Only through liaison between TCOs and EL staff will changes in course content and/or procedure be effected. Similarly, TCOs will report to EL staff on the need for individual self-access remedial work for any under-achievers.

English will be used only when necessary. Since the TCO/trainee relationship at this stage of the project is essentially that of craftsman/apprentice, much of the workaday interaction will be in Spanish; only when the TCO feels the need for tests in English to supplement the day's work will that situation change, and even then Spanish will be used when mediating (for example, in the form of instructions and questions) between the resource material and the occupational task.

Sample EL component

In conclusion, here is just one specific example of the way in which the English language support system feeds into the fisheries training programme.

TCO SYSTEM   **ELT SUB-SYSTEM**

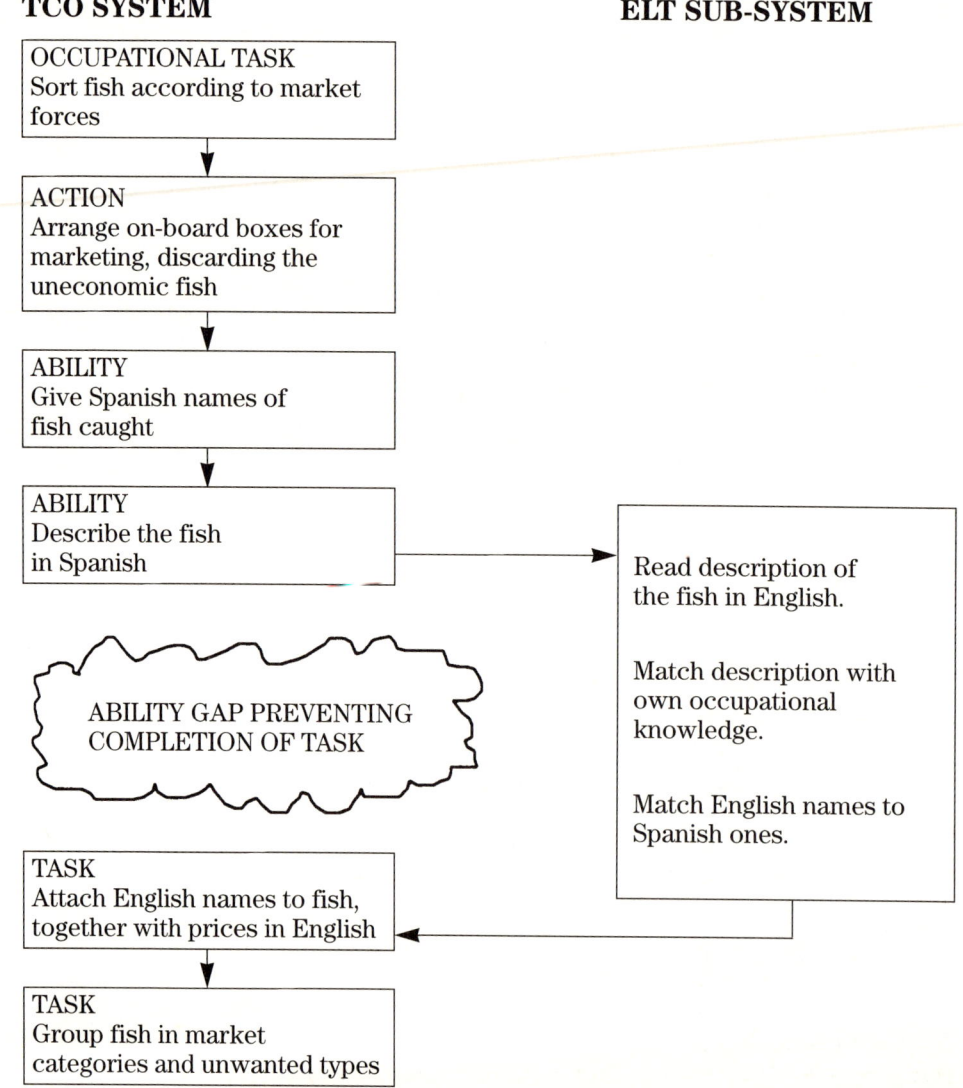

6.3   Project administration (1989)

MYRA HARRISON and HECTOR MUNRO

An important new development in the management of aid worldwide is that the development agencies, including both the World Bank and the ODA, are using the 'project cycle' as a scheme for describing projects from beginning to end. As used by the ODA the project cycle identifies five major stages:

- identification
- preparation
- appraisal
- implementation
- evaluation

At the appraisal stage, the ODA must take into account the following factors:

- ODA policy (country/sector)
- recipient government policy
- economic viability
- social impact
- environmental impact
- political context
- commercial considerations
- institutional development considerations
- professional viability
- management viability.

Economic considerations which merit attention include a comparison of benefits against costs (that is, both actual costs and the shadow/opportunity costs). In this context the following questions are pertinent:

- Who benefits?
- How do you compare benefits 'with the project' as opposed to 'without the project' (meaning, what would the difference be if the project were not implemented)?
- What does the project actually fund?
- What are the manpower benefits derived from a project?

In order to arrive at some answers to these questions economists include the following among their approach:

- cost-effectiveness analysis
- unit cost per trainee in institutional development
- target-benefit analysis.

To improve management and design of aid projects, ODA has adopted the project framework. This is a document approximately two pages long, which provides an easy overview of a project under the following headings:

- wider objectives
- immediate objectives
- outputs
- inputs

By presenting project content in a matrix under these headings several advantages are achieved. It clarifies the objectives of the project; it brings the key project components together; it is systematic; it establishes key stages of the project under 'indicators of achievement'; and it makes provision for monitoring. The second part of the project documentation required by ODA is the project memorandum, which is divided into twelve sections. The most important of these sections are those which refer to means of monitoring the project, to evaluation, and to implementation arrangements. One source of confusion in drawing up project frameworks and memoranda is the distinction between immediate objectives and project outputs.

An output is what the project directly produces by its use of the inputs, and it is the direct responsibility of the project manager to achieve it. The immediate objective is the impact that the project is aimed at producing. For example, if the project trains and supports agricultural extension staff, the *output* will be the effective delivery of agricultural extension systems; the *immediate objective* will be improved.

Most agencies use the 'project framework' (or 'logical framework') approach to project management.[*] The four columns are labelled project structure; indicators of achievement; ways of assessment; assumptions/risks. The vertical path through the framework show the logical progression from the bottom row 'inputs' to the next row up 'outputs', which keep to the 'immediate objectives' of the project in the third row up. The logical path is completed by the contribution of the project to the wider (national) objectives.

One of the major points of discussion following this presentation was how far project framework ideas and drafts need to be shared with aid recipients. The question of how much of the ODA's plans, views and commitments could be shared was asked; sensitive items might be involved in the final column of the project framework, where assumptions and risks are listed. The general feeling of the group was that as much information as possible should be put into the framework and should be shared with the host government where this could be done without offending sensibilities.

[*] One Dunford seminar group was given some papers describing a proposed Nigerian Junior Secondary School (JSS) project and asked to formulate its terms within the framework. The result of this exercise is shown opposite, not as a 'model answer' but merely for illustrative purposes.

The 'Project Framework': a trial exercise based upon Nigerian Junior Secondary School Project documents

	Indicators of achievement	How assessed	Assumptions
Wider objectives			
To improve the English ability of students from Nigerian secondary schools	Post JSS performance	Grade & exam WASC Feedback – tertiary institution Feedback – employer	GoN policy on English unchanged Exam system harmonises with methodology of INSET
Immediate objectives			
An adequate level of professional competence in the cadre of English teachers in junior secondary schools	In-life of project opportunity for all teachers	Increasing number annually being trained Post-course evaluation	Career incentives established by GoN Commitment of GoN to fund INSET Centre (recurrently)
A sustainable INSET for teachers of English in JSS	Staff, premises, budget in place and plans for future decided	Inspectors' reports (including classroom observations) Centre reports and monitoring reports	School teachers released and funded for attendance on courses
Outputs		Centre programmes, including job descriptions, travel schedules, organogram courses run (increasingly annually)	Centre remains an autonomous body
Establishment of a national INSET centre			Funds and personnel released on time (for training teachers)
Establishment of a cadre of competent INSET teacher trainers			
Inputs			
Training – UK and in-country	UK	Host	Suitable ELTOs can be recruited Suitable Nigerians can be recruited for training, administration and counterparts
Personnel, equipment and materials	2 ELTOs 6 TCTPs 2 Land Rovers Equipment and materials	2 counterparts Administrative staff Accommodation – office – staff Consumables	Counterparts bonded after training Adequate GoN budget provided Equipment, accommodation, etc. delivered on time

6.4a   Managing change in communication skills projects (1991)

MAGGIE JO ST JOHN and DAVID CLARKE

Introduction

Failure to develop adequate communication skills in English – which is arguably the foremost language of development and international co-operation – can have a deleterious effect on the efficiency and effectiveness of projects in almost all sectors. Within any organisation three variables are integrally linked – people, work and systems; and three factors that affect the decisions relating to these are politics, language and culture.

- *Politics* is to do with who has power, status and authority, and how these are obtained, wielded and influenced.
- Within *language* two aspects seem particularly interesting for our concerns; the role of English in the wider community, as a natural language, official language, language of an educated elite etc.; and the position of L1 and L2 teachers of English.
- *Culture* is the set of values, norms and beliefs which affect how groups and individuals perceive and act. A project (Lee and Field 1985) must fit the existing culture (unless it is a project whose specific objective is to change the culture). If it does not then it will fail at the outset or wither away; we cannot graft together unrelated species.

It is important to recognise the dynamic interaction between these categories. At the implementation stage of a project, we have variables concerning people, work and systems operating dynamically with each other and the wider environment, which includes language, politics and culture:

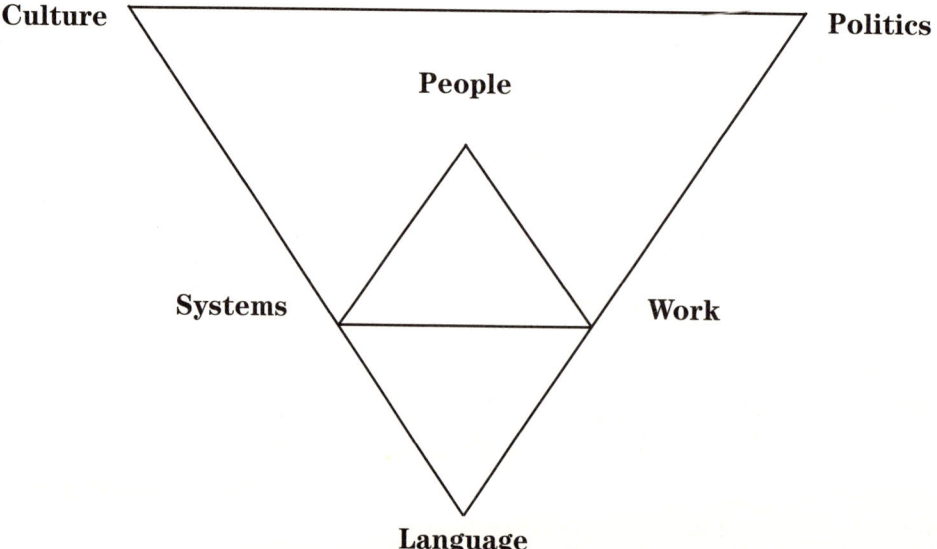

Communication skills projects involve change and innovation. Factors relating to change are thus important. In general, change is met by inertia and resistance; successful change processes are those which can minimise resistance effectively. Change has been quite extensively studied within industrial and management contexts and of the factors that research has shown to be influential in reducing resistance to change there are six which I have found valuable as an ESP/Communication Skills Consultant. These are:

1) degree of ownership
2) perceived benefit(s)
3) participation/involvement
4) understanding
5) an innovation champion
6) support from the top

These can impact on people, work and systems.

People: Format of external personnel   One of the major resource provisions within a project is human, that is, personnel and their expertise and knowledge. There are a number of formats which can be adopted. For example:

- full-time personnel only
- part-time (+ consultants)
- full-time + consultants
- consultants/links only

Full-time means present for the duration of the formal project time; *part-time* means present for an extended length(s) of times; and *consultants* means those providing short, intensive periods of input. *Links* means a formal arrangement between at least two institutions with exchanges on both sides.

Typically we seem to be seeing a shift from 'full-time personnel only' to other formats. Outsiders can play valuable roles: they can operate outside some of the constraints, they can add the weight of shared opinions and approaches, they can provide impetus; and they can extend the available expertise. Full-timers are often expected to be superpersons, fulfilling the roles of managers, teachers, course designers, materials writers, testers, evaluators, facilitators and counsellors; so it can be a relief to have support, an alternative view, and perhaps to devolve some responsibility.

In deciding on a suitable format for personnel the resistance-to-change factors are relevant. Degree of ownership means the extent to which those on the ground feel that the project belongs to them and that they are making decisions and influencing the direction of activities. This can be easier to establish if there is no full-time external presence. Similarly, participation and involvement may have to increase if there is no outsider to whom matters can be left. However, in the absence of full-time personnel it is also possible that understanding will be lower or take rather longer to reach a particular level. The format of the human resource input is less likely to affect the perceived benefits but the chances of a local innovation champion emerging can be higher in the absence of a full-timer.

Work: Sources of teaching material and time spans   Inevitably communication skills projects are concerned with teaching materials, and three options (or some combination of them) present themselves: the use of published material, the adaptation of such material, and the development of in-house material. (Years ago a scheme was proposed for collecting the mass of material developed on projects around the world but not made available to others. Such a system would have enabled us to adapt other people's project material rather than continually redevelop our own; but nothing came of that valuable fourth option).

Within the crucial work variable in our diagram we have a dichotomy between the concepts of local ownership, involvement and participation on the one hand and the demand for immediate results on the other. Often materials are written largely by outsiders in order to have something to show at the end of the project. This is in part a product of the lifespan of projects as perceived in the past. My visualisation of the typical project as carried out on the ground is of a defined start and an abrupt finish, with a period of intense activity in between. But projects occur in contexts and within sets of existing systems, and I would prefer to see a project's beginning and ending as blending processes. We should be concerned with the process of a project rather than just with a product. I think we need to view the formal project stage as only one phase, a phase which should in many cases be more extensive that intensive; indeed, I believe that the processes of change are such that, instead of thinking in terms of three-year intensive projects, we should be considering a lifespan of five, seven, even ten or more years, though often on a less intensive basis. This would reduce the pressure to come up with a product.

We know that the experience of ownership and participation results in increased understanding and commitment; and our experience of resistance to change tells us that what is needed are courses and materials that have been designed by locals, not by outsiders. The perceived benefit is particularly great if publication results, as this raises profile and status. But during a three-year project we can expect good materials to be developed locally only when the participants are highly experienced, and this is rarely the case. The project format must therefore allow time for the acquisition and application of new knowledge and processes, a matter which is either ignored or placed too low on the list of crucial determining factors.

Systems: Evaluation   Though evaluation has become an integral part of project frameworks, there are some aspects that need further thought.

1)   Although project documents detail performance indicators, they are not distributed to all those who will actually do the work that provides the results and the data. If people know what is expected of them, they are

more likely to reach that point. for this reason, and to facilitate the systematic collection of appropriate data, all those involved will need to know the performance indicators if we are serious about evaluation, whether as an ongoing developmental influence or as a summative assessment.

2)   What of the indicators themselves? The majority (by using 'better', 'more', etc.) require comparisons to be made, yet the initial collection of baseline data and its dissemination are not built into the project start-up. The very words 'better' and 'more' are so general as to be problematic. How much better? How much more is it reasonable to expect? And whose interpretation of 'better' and 'more' is to be given most credence and weight?

3)   Action plans - in which we specify how much we hope to achieve, by when, in what way and with what support   will provide later on a real measure of whether we have exceeded expectations, fulfilled them or failed to realise them. What will be most important is how and why we have achieved our results, as it is this that will affect our future efforts. Yet the why of evaluation seems to be ignored, only the what being built into the frameworks and indicators that I have seen.

4)   If we are to be genuinely serious about evaluation, rather than just 'follow the book' because it is a good thing, we shall have to consider more appropriate timespans. In the case of communication skills work in higher education courses, most programmes are taught in the first year. The first students to experience the early stages of change will probably graduate three or four years later – that is, four or five years after the project began – yet the duration of the project may only be three years. How, then, could evaluation of its effects be validly determined? If we reckon on at least three years being needed for any changes to become really influential on the programmes; and if we then allow for that group of students to complete their studies; then it will be seven or eight years before we can truly assess the impact on graduating students, and even longer before their impact (for example, as contributors to the economy) can be assessed.

Stronger dynamic links between the key variables and the project's environment would strengthen the long-term impact of the project itself. Our current approach to project design, including timespans and evaluation procedures, takes insufficient account of the process and pressures of change.

6.4b   How a project can break down (1990)
PATRICIA AHRENS

The decision to extend the teaching of English to Classes 5, 6 and 7 in Gujarat State in the 1970s entailed the in-service training of 30,000 teachers. These teachers were non-graduates who had studied English for only two years at school and had no EFL training. There was an immediate need for widespread teacher training and radio was chosen as the medium. The first programmes appeared in 1979. Three institutions were involved in the programme:

a) All India Radio commissioned scripts, paid script writers, recorded programmes and broadcasts on the local network in open time.

b) The State Institute of Education (SIE) published and distributed support material, organised teachers' and script writers' conferences and elicited evaluative feedback on programmes.

c) The H M Patel Institute of English, which functioned as the English wing of SIE, designed the radio series, recruited script writers, accepted scripts, edited the support material, ran workshops for scriptwriters and teachers, and carried out evaluation.

There were problems associated with the work of each institution. One common problem was that none of the institutions and few of the individuals concerned with the project had experience, expertise or informed interest in work at the primary/middle-school level. Most of them worked at a higher level in the education system and with more advanced language learners.

a) All India Radio could commission any one scriptwriter only twice in six months: they therefore had to use a great many scriptwriters. The fee for a script was not high, but writers enjoyed the publicity. The completed programmes for teachers were broadcast either during school hours, when teachers often used them as class input, or on Saturdays when no-one listened.

b) The State Institute of Education was obliged to use the government press to print the support material for teachers. The press took a long time to process orders. As a result the support materials sometimes had to be written well before the programmes they related to: on other occasions they were published after the programmes had been broadcast. The distribution of the materials to schools was also erratic.

c) The H M Patel Institute of English had to find large numbers of script-writers who had good ability in English, an understanding of current ELT approaches and knowledge of work in primary/middle schools. In practice this combination was almost impossible to find. Although H M Patel Institute was the focus and generator of most of the work, it had no executive authority in the project: the radio work was in no-one's job description.

Unfortunately, despite many good ideas and much hard work, the project broke down. A number of possible causes of the breakdown can be identified.

- There was a lack of focus in objectives and in executive authority. A large project like this might be handled as a cluster of smaller projects. Each project must have clear objectives and executive authority must be lodged with a stated person or people.

- There was a lack of adequate management structure; such a structure must be evident to and accepted by all concerned. Without it there is no clear place where change can be initiated.

- There was a lack of motivation and incentives for participants in the project. A project plan should take these into consideration. For example, the training should lead to some reward, such as enhanced job satisfaction or financial reward.

- There was a lack of adequate evaluation and/or feedback. Procedures for regular evaluation should be included in the plan and these should lead to the plan being amended where necessary.

- There was a lack of interest in and awareness of the project. This problem could be overcome if everyone concerned with the project were better informed and involved in it.

- There was over-anxiety about project materials. Where the work of a project depends on materials such as books or radios, the people accountable for the materials must have the confidence to use them, even lose them.

- There was a lack of follow-up. Project plans should allow for maintenance work, for example, replacing materials. They should also aim to develop long-term spin-offs from the main project such as self-study packages, better PRESET and teacher support groups.

- There was a lack of commitment by key people. Such people must be prepared to support the work of the project.

- The degree of ELT innovation was too big. The project should plan to deliver only the degree of innovation which the receiving system can tolerate.

- The general educational innovation was too big. Account must be taken of how the ELT innovation fits in with the general education ethos of the receiving system.

- The language skills of the English teachers were low. Support for the development of teachers' language knowledge and skills, as well as for their professional knowledge and skills, must be included in the project plan.

- The mode of project transmission was not suitable; in India radio is seen as a source of entertainment rather than education. All aspects of the chosen mode of project transmission must be examined in the local context.

7.0 Appropriate Methodology

GERRY ABBOTT

The term 'appropriate methodology' has sometimes been understood (perhaps by analogy with 'appropriate/intermediate technology') to refer to methods that are 'low-tech' – for example, limited to the use of blackboard and chalk, pen and paper; but clearly the use of overhead projectors, computers and video would also be 'appropriate' in more privileged circumstances. The term also embraces (as Ahrens reminds us in the previous section) what is culturally, as well as technologically, suited to the teaching context. It would, for instance, be inappropriate (even improper) to expect most teenage Chinese girls to participate willingly in uninhibited role-playing activities because this would require them to break the cultural rules of decorum. Both of these aspects, the technological and the cultural, also need to be borne in mind when training multinational groups of teachers in Britain where, although one's training methods might include 'warming-up' activities and a frequent use of handouts, one must remember to get the trainees to come up with appropriate substitutes for these if the teachers back home have no access to photocopiers, and the warm-up exercises would be impracticable either culturally or because of overcrowding in the classrooms.

Perhaps with such classrooms in mind, Bowers open this section by taking issue with 'communicative' methodology, challenging Widdowson to a duel over ten statements drawn from the latter's published work (Widdowson 1978 and 1983). This contribution should be read as a lightly edited record of an informal exchange of views and it is for the reader to determine how far Widdowson, cast in the role of 'theoretician', counters the objections of the 'practitioner' as played by Bowers. Tonkyn then reports on some problems of overseas students in Britain, among which are some interesting culturally determined preferences concerning their own experience of studying English.

Most of those studying English in the world's state school systems are taught in classes that the teachers feel are too large – so large in some cases that methods appropriate to the circumstances are bound to differ considerably from those generally recommended by ELT pundits. Using case study material, Coleman reports some of the problems as perceived by the teachers; he concludes that in attempting to implement such borrowed methodologies these teachers are engaging in a futile pursuit.

These methodologies are borrowed from what Abbott calls 'the anglocentre'. He suggest that while they can perhaps usefully be transferred to classrooms in what he calls the privileged 'paid' sector of the ELT world, they are not transferable to the underprivileged 'aid' sector. Abbott contends that for most of the world's schools, a reading method would be more practicable and sustainable than one based on oral communication.

7.1 A debate on appropriate methodology (1986)

ROGER BOWERS and HENRY WIDDOWSON

Relevance to context provided the focus for an unrehearsed encounter in which Henry Widdowson responded to a critique by Roger Bowers.

Roger Bowers

The term 'methodology' can have two meanings for the purposes of this seminar – classroom methodology (M1) and project methodology (M2). Each can be represented by a 'fishbone' diagram with four labelled points:

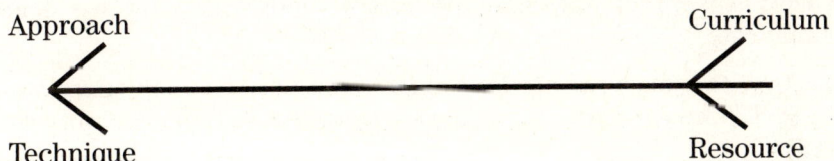

Approach   Curriculum

Technique   Resource

In the case of M1, we may ask 'Is the methodology consistent with an approach to education and curriculum as a whole?' and 'Is it carried out using techniques and resources that are feasible and employable?' M2 is analogous with M1, but the questions are: Are the development aims (approach) compatible with the overall development programme (curriculum), and do they make the best use of the technical expertise and resources locally available? In other words, is the programme/project appropriate to the context? In both cases appropriacy is thus directed by contextual variables.

Questions regarding who makes the judgement concerning appropriacy are difficult to answer, since there are generally 'clashes of interest', and deviation from the planned line in order to reconcile such differences should be expected and accepted. What is clear is that we operate, in the classroom and in the project environment, in a context-dependent situation, while theory, even applied theory, is context-free. It is judged in terms of coherence and rigour: it doesn't have to 'work' to be right. Some of Henry Widdowson's views may thus be questioned as to their relevance to the contexts in which we work. I propose to take and comment on ten powerful quotations from Henry Widdowson as an opportunity to explore the notion of relevance to context. The sources of all these quotations are Widdowson (1978) and (1983).

1)   'I think it is important to recognise that language teaching is a theoretical as well as a practical activity, that effective teacher materials and classroom procedures depend on principles deriving from an understanding of what language is and how it is used.'

Understanding of language is irrelevant. What we need to understand is teachers, students, administrators, and how they react to change.

2)   'Discourse can only be taught in relation to actual areas of use.'

The vast majority of learners do not, and will not, need to use the language. They are perfectly satisfied with usage. Discourse can be taught in these terms like any other level of language.

3)   'Language teachers are often represented by themselves and others as humble practitioners, essentially practical people concerned with basic classroom tactics and impatient of theory. Such a representation is unnecessarily demeaning.'

There is nothing demeaning about being practitioners impatient of theory. Why is it assumed that theory makes practice respectable?

4)   'Only by practising communicative activities can we learn to communicate.'

All sorts of things can contribute to learning about communication. And how much communication really goes on in the classroom in any case?

5)   'A communicative methodology will differ significantly from traditional methodology.'

There is no such thing as 'traditional methodology' and probably no such thing as 'communicative methodology'. Any contrast is too ill-defined in its practical dimensions to be any value.

6)   'If any language teaching is to be concerned with language use, then it cannot be entirely based on the linguist's idealisation of data which is concerned with the decontextualised sign as symbol.'

'To incorporate . . .', yes, 'to be concerned with . . .', no. Generations of language users have been brought up on a diet of decontextualised signs.

7)   'Sound ESP pedagogy requires that course design should service methodology and not, as seems to be the prevalent view, the other way round. It does not actually matter very much, I think, what language the learners are presented with. What does matter is how they can put it to effective use.'

Why assume that one way of proceeding negates another? And where is the evidence for preferring one to another? Without such evidence, the argument proceeds by whim, and is won by the most articulate.

8) 'It might be objected that I have not dealt with the particular practical problems that the ESP teacher is faced with – problems which call for immediate administrative decisions about what and how to teach, and which allow little leisure for indulgence in theoretical speculation. But such decisions cannot be dealt with in advance: all one can do is to indicate the kinds of consideration that they need to take into account. To the extent that they are informed by principle and not merely controlled by expediency, these decisions must depend on the teacher taking bearings on the theoretical issues that I have been raising here.'

There is nothing 'mere' about expediency: and decisions about what and how to teach are the very nub.

9) 'Where compromises are called for to accommodate local constraints, they can be based only on an understanding of how the principles of language teaching pedagogy are being compromised.'

All pedagogy is 'constrained'. To think of some pedagogic ideal from which the wayward teacher is compelled to depart because of his benighted condition is to devalue performance and its context in favour of metaphysical speculation.

10) 'All this may seem excessively elaborate – a glass bead game of over-nice distinctions remote from the reality of practical teaching. But I do not see that anything less complex can provide us with the essential conceptual bearings we need to locate and describe ESP as an area of language education.'

Well, OK if we are trying to 'locate' and 'describe'. But if that is all that we are doing, we are remote from the realities. We have got enough maps: let us have some blueprints.

Henry Widdowson

The concern of Applied Linguistics is to provide a theoretical perspective for practical and applicable courses of action. Thus, in the diagram for M1 above, approaches are the theoretical backing for a set of techniques, and resources are the pedagogical tools of an educational perspective which establishes a curriculum. Applied Linguistics is concerned with all these areas. Roger Bowers sets up an opposition between what I say as representing the purveyors of theoretical ideas, and what the Council does as representing the agents of practical action. But is it the Council he is talking about? Who is the 'we' that he refers to? The resources and their agents are often distinct entities, as is the case of the ODA and the Council. The relationship between the providers and the executors is central to the discussion and thus cannot be encapsulated in a single pronoun.

It is, further, somewhat unfair to hit out at Applied Linguistics Departments as 'theoreticians' or as 'out of touch'; such departments must demonstrate the relevance of the general principles they teach when they are involved in teaching practice observation and in discussions with the practising teachers who attend their courses. With reference to Roger's critique of the remarks that he has quoted (out of context, may I add), I should briefly like to make the following points in reply to each of his:

1) We need to understand language too, since this is what we are involved in teaching.

2) Discourse cannot be taught as 'usage'. This is a contradiction in terms.

3) Indeed it is damaging for teachers to deny the importance of theory, for in doing so they deny themselves opportunities for development.

4) I was concerned here not with learning about communication, but with learning to communicate. A good deal of communication does really go on in the classroom. The question is the extent to which it is real, and by what criteria you define its reality. What is real for the native speaker user is not necessarily (and not usually) real for the non-native speaker learner.

5) There are general but essential differences of principle, which can be and have been identified, which distinguish different approaches. Such identification is of very considerable value since it is important to relate particular practices to more general principles.

6) The operative word here is 'entirely'. The pedagogic idealisation of language for instruction is not the same as the linguistic idealisation of language for analysis. This does not mean that decontextualised signs (symbols) may not figure in teaching as contributing to a development of language use, as I think is argued in the paper from which this extract is taken.

7) Methodology accompanies course design in a flexible relationship, but change in the students' handling of language is brought about by how that language is presented and activated in class, ie by methodology.

8) There definitely is something 'mere' about expediency; it is not supported or informed by principle.

9) Agreed, all pedagogy is constrained. The important thing is to recognise how. Local constraints are conditions which influence the way principles are applied. 'Compromise' was not a well-chosen world, perhaps; 'modification' would be better. But the point is that we need to understand the relationship between abstract ideas and the actual realisations of them. To do this is not to compel people to conform to an ideal but to provide a basis for modification, so that there is no such compulsion.

10) Blueprints are something fixed, unchangeable, inflexible. We certainly do not require those in the contexts in which we are working. We require maps, and Roger's M1 and M2 are indeed maps of the kind that Applied Linguists use.

Three further and more general points need to be made:

a)   Appropriate Methodology is not new in terms of learning-goals; what is new in our considerations of methodology is the socio-cultural context in which language teaching takes place. We need to understand more fully the process of learning and, more importantly perhaps, the process of enquiry, which is where universities can make a meaningful contribution – particularly through teacher education, which is central to any discussion.

b)   'Constraints' implies a view of Appropriate Methodology falling short of some ideal in particular contexts. The ideal was thus inappropriate and wrong in itself. We should think in terms of 'conditions', and particularly local enabling conditions which define our own needs and possibilities. Projects require a flexibility of approach and should be seen as networks of collaborative effort.

c)   Council personnel are mediators; they are complementary to academic enquiry since they represent a range of unique experiences which inform research and theory. They should thus see themselves as complementary to, rather than in conflict with, the universities.

7.2   Overseas students' views on language learning in the UK (1986)

ALAN TONKYN

While the stressful environment of studying may cause emotional problems for all, there are particular problems for overseas students; there are thus implications for making our teaching appropriate to those with possibilities of studying in UK. The factors contributing to academic success or failure for overseas students might be categorised as follows:

a)   Intrinsic:

>   Age
>   Race
>   Health (physical and psychological – especially psychological maturity)
>   Personality (degree of extroversion)
>   Experience of other systems
>   Motivation (especially commitment to the host culture)
>   Knowledge of subject
>   Language proficiency.

b)   Extrinsic:

>   Climate
>   Diet
>   Accommodation
>   Cultural differences (politico-economic, social, religious, cultural, language, distance)

Degree of closure in Culture 2 (including racial discrimination)
Course content
Course study methods
Finance
Ease of withdrawal from course.

Success or failure will depend on how the student uses his intrinsic qualities to deal with the extrinsic problems. How the qualities and problems interact is clearly a complex area. For example, an extrovert personality may lead to more language practice and learning, but may also be distracted more easily from academic matters. Lack of commitment to the subject studied or of empathy with the local culture are likely to militate against success, but lack of linguistic knowledge might be compensated by a good subject knowledge.

Many overseas students feel that British students are unfriendly, and this can lead to suspicions of racial bias. Others comment that British students are equally unfriendly to each other. A survey conducted by Hawkey (1982) found that overseas students had three times as many overseas friends as British friends. This is all related to the degree of closure in a society and it may be that Britain is a relatively 'closed' society in which people are reluctant to become involved. Zwingmann and Gunn (1983) assert that the typical overseas student's expectations of satisfaction with life and study in UK follow a U-curve. Expectations are likely to be unrealistically high at first and then drop to a 'trough of despondency' before climbing and eventually levelling out either above or below the original level of expectation/satisfaction. The curve for some students, however, may level out at a point around the bottom of the curve.

Factors leading to success

I recently gathered some students' perceptions of the importance of factors contributing to academic success; half way through a ten-week course, I asked them to rank a series of factors. Although the standard deviation for each ranking was high, the factors at the top of the list which were perceived to be important were mainly academic factors. Social factors were seen as less important. The list is as follows:

1   Knowledge of subject
2   Hard work
3   English language skills
4   Guidance from academic staff
5   Understanding British study methods
6   Personal comfort (food/health/accommodation)
7   Personality/character
8   Good relations with fellow students and British people
9   Freedom from homesickness.

Since these students were working together on a pre-sessional course it may be that they would give less weight to social factors than overseas students working with British fellow students on their academic courses. Three areas deserve attention:

1 Pre-departure briefings
2 Pre-sessional courses
3 In-course provision of support.

One means of addressing the first issue is for returning overseas students to brief those about to come to UK, but different briefers can disagree markedly with each other, and are bound to have different levels of satisfaction which might be passed on. Pre-departure briefings are, however, often given at too abstract a level and more anecdotal evidence should be given to demonstrate how acceptable behaviour differs in the host culture. A British briefer speaking the local language would be a great asset. One area that requires particular emphasis is religion, as students coming for the first time to a secular society might well be disgusted and alienated by an unprepared-for 'godlessness'. This was connected with the tendency of people to expect other societies to mirror their own. If they were given information that suggested that this was not so (for example, that many people do not believe in God), then it would simply not be taken on board. A further factor about briefings that caused many problems was that students were often unsure about how long they would be away from home.

Pre-sessional courses should break the 'cocoon' and involve students with real life, perhaps by involving British students in obtaining historical or geographical information from overseas students. Overseas students' clubs provide much-needed support for the outsider, but they can be an easy way out of integration for the overseas student. It was felt that there was a marked lack of awareness amongst tutors of the need for adequate and appropriate support for overseas students after the pre-sessional courses.

Student reports on language training
At this point the group watched three videos of students from Yemen, Turkey and Hong Kong talking about their learning experiences. The following points emerged from the interviews.

Video 1 (Yemen) Positive attitudes to English and speakers of English were evident. The pace of learning at school was considered too steep but English teaching at university level was valued since it provided more and better opportunities for practising the language. The language skills were broken down by the student interviewed into grammatical, speaking, listening and reading categories. Reading was characterised by reading aloud and pronouncing the words. It was felt more useful to follow grammar structures sequentially rather than 'jumping around'.

The Koran encourages perfection and accuracy, which raised questions about the possibilities of transference to other areas of learning. The interviewee felt that learning the Koran involved understanding as well as rote learning.

Video 2 (Turkey)   Language learning was seen as unrelated to general educational issues. The interviewee considered there to be three major skills – reading, writing, listening, with writing as the most important area.

Video 3 (Hong Kong)   Divergent attitudes were expressed about the relevance of grammar and rules in language learning. Views varied: a 'natural approach', with no focus on structure or explanation, was favoured by a European interviewee; the importance of English for communication with emphasis on fluency rather than accuracy was stressed by a Hong Kong primary teacher; and there was a general tendency to expect language teaching to use 'grammar' as a necessary base for learning to be built on. It was felt that rules were essential for learners from a Chinese/Japanese L1 background since the language systems bear no relationship to each other. Memorisation was again a fairly major issue, but interviewees favoured contextualised learning rather than simple rote learning. As regards the four skills, while the importance of speaking and using the language were recognised, interviewees still saw writing as a measure of ability to use language accurately. There was a request for more structured written exercises to help internalise rules. From the above, it was concluded the learners do not always break the language down into the same skills as we do, or alternatively, relate them differently.

Skills and Activities Favoured   Findings from surveys on pre-sessional courses at Reading University were then presented as follows:

1a)   Students were asked to rank the four skills areas in order of importance for success on a future academic course; results were:

    1   Listening and speaking
    2   Writing
    3   Reading

1b)   The necessary language 'factors'

    1   Vocabulary
    2   Fluency (speech/writing)
    3   Grammar
    4   Pronunciation

1c)   Problem areas (in descending order of importance)

    1   Speaking/listening (social)
    2   Writing
    3   Speaking (academic)
    4   Listening (academic)
    5   Reading (academic)

1d)   Pre-sessional course feedback

    i)   Top six materials/activities (in descending order)

        1   Academic writing course

2   Listening comprehension and note-taking course
3   Mini presentations
4   Listen to This
5   Maxi presentations
6   Project (own subject)

None of the materials were scored as being less than 'useful'.

ii) Bottom five (ascending order of importance)

1   Pronunciation practice
2   Project: information sheet on reading
3   Project: TV/radio programme
4   Pronunciation practice (clusters)
5   Extended writing in class

Appropriate methodology

The following points (anecdotal) were drawn from the reading course.

1   There may be a need to explain one's approach: for example, Omani students expected a reading class to relate to reading aloud.

2   There is a tendency towards a teacher-centred view, since we start from *our* expectations of what is learner-centred.

3   Textbooks should be 'transparent', that is, demonstrate the approach.

4   There is a need for appropriacy in the balance of oral accuracy/fluency. Individualised self-access oral materials were suggested in feedback on oral presentations. It was felt necessary to avoid too overt seminar skills (e.g. language of interruption).

5   Note-taking skills, on the other hand, should be handled more overtly.

6   Writing should focus on process rather than product.

7   Inadequate vocabulary inhibits the development of skimming/scanning skills.

7.3   Teaching large classes and training for sustainability (1990)

HYWEL COLEMAN

1   Introduction

In observing teachers working in large classes in different parts of the world over the last fifteen years, I have been struck by the frequency with which teachers undertake cumbersome and exhausting classroom routines. It is my intention in this paper to enquire where these apparently in-appropriate routines come from, and to consider how teachers can be helped to escape from them.

The paper begins with an extract from my classroom observation diary which describes a lesson typifying this tendency to employ awkward and tiring teaching procedures. It then looks at four specific aspects of the behaviour of teachers or large classes and in each case attempts to draw a link between that behaviour and the advice which is given by recognised authorities on TESOL methodology. It will become apparent that published advice is frequently inappropriate for the large class contexts in which teachers work; it may even be dangerously counterproductive. The paper ends with a discussion of the way in which we need to move forward.

2   *The cumbersome classroom*

The following description of a lesson is taken from my classroom observation diary. The lesson was observed in Country A, in a girls' secondary school in a working class area of a major city. There were 40 girls in the class; this was a number which the teacher considered to be large.

> On Monday morning, from 0900 to 1000, I visited a girls' secondary school in a suburb in the north of the city . . . I observed a complete lesson taught to Class 9 . . . The class consisted of 40 girls, sitting in heavy desks in a reasonably spacious though rather full room. There seemed to be one book per desk (i.e. one per pair of pupils). The lesson was based on a passage about the life of the founder of the nation. This is a topic used at various levels, in slightly different forms; . . . one of the lessons observed the previous week was also based on the same biography.

The teacher's standard procedure was as follows:

- T reads a sentence

- T occasionally asks pupils to read a sentence from the text

- T asks pupils for an explanation – sometimes in English, sometimes in L1 – of individual words or phrases (an example was 'matriculation exam', but nobody succeeded in providing a suitable explanation)

- T provides the correct answer

- T occasionally asks a question about the content of the sentence

- T occasionally asks pupils to chant sentences

- T provides a single word prompt and asks pupils to produce a new sentence, based on the model of the sentence which has just been chanted but incorporating the new vocabulary item.

Students were expected to stand up every time an adult entered the room. Individuals stood up whenever they were addressed or when they were nominated to provide a response. They remained standing, sometimes for agonisingly long periods, even when they had provided the required response, until the teacher told them to sit down again. The convention appeared to be that a correct response allowed one to sit down again immediately, but it frequently happened that the teacher gave no clear indication as to whether their response was correct or not; consequently the pupils remained standing. Towards the middle of the lesson, the emphasis changed;

- T *Open your copies* [i.e. the exercise books] *please now and write your answers.*

She then copied on to the blackboard two questions which were already in the students' book and which the students could see easily (in exactly the same way as the teacher observed the previous week had done):

1) *When was the founder of the nation born?*

2) *What do you know of his early life?*

The pupils had to close their textbooks and write answers to these questions from memory in their exercise books. The teacher patrolled the room while the girls worked. She made frequent 'tsk-tsk-tsk' sounds to stamp out murmurings. If the pupils finished this exercise before the end of the lesson they had to hand in their books to the teacher for correction later. I am not sure what was to be done by those who had not finished (about half the group). Finally, the teacher wrote up a homework task on the blackboard:

And all the words and meaning

At the same time, the teacher gave this oral instruction:

- T *Write your homework. Now copy it.*

The bell indicating the end of the period was ringing at the same time; the teacher was also preparing to leave the room. The girls stood up, looking somewhat confused. At this point I left, together with the teacher.

I have described this lesson in detail because it reveals so clearly three of the most common characteristics of large class teaching. Firstly, the teacher is obviously deeply concerned with the maintenance of control in her lesson. This is particularly clear in the requirement which she imposes for learners to stand up when they are addressed, and in her policing of the classroom while the students are working individually. Next, much of the activity in the lesson is routinised to the extent of being ritualistic; this can be seen from the teacher's tendency to answer her own questions, and from her copying onto the blackboard questions which are already available to the learners in their textbooks. Thirdly, several features in this teacher's lesson are similar to lessons taught by other teachers in the same context. If the lessons which occur in the same context but which are taught by different teachers do share similar features in this way, then this suggests that we must avoid simplistic criticism of 'poor teaching' and seek instead a comprehensive explanation for the observed behaviour.

In summary, this observation indicates that the teacher (in common with her peers) is taking it upon herself to perform certain routinised actions in the classroom. Many of these actions do not have obvious pedagogical value and they are exhausting for the teacher to undertake. Why, then, do they occur?

3   Specific behaviours in the large class

It seems likely that the distinctive patterns of teacher behaviour and classroom management – which, to the observer, may actually appear quite inappropriate for use in a large class – reflect the teacher's fundamental conceptions of his or her duties. That is to say, I am hypothesising that many teachers possess deeply held views about their responsibilities in the language classroom which, objectively, are incompatible with the realities of the large class. I am also hypothesising that these fundamental beliefs are transmitted through pre-service training and, to a lesser extent, through in-service training. Ultimately, however, I suspect that many of the tasks which teachers are attempting to carry out in their overcrowded classrooms derive from ideas which were developed in very different contexts – in much smaller classes in very privileged teaching contexts.

I examine this hypothesis through four case studies. In each case, I will attempt to trace the individual teacher's behaviour to a commonly held view of the duties of the language teacher. This will be done by examining the literature on language teaching methodology published in the UK over the last half-century. This is not, it must be emphasised, because I intend to attribute the behaviour of a particular teacher at a particular point in time to the influence of a particular publication, but rather because I am taking the published idea simply as an exemplar of perceptions which are taken for granted in the smaller and better resourced classrooms of Britain.

The first case study reveals a teacher who is excessively concerned to monitor individual performance. The second study discusses the difficulty which teachers have in marking written work in large classes. The next case examines teachers' concern to maintain control, and the last looks at attitudes towards memorising the names of large numbers of students.

3.1 Monitoring individual performance   The first case study is taken from my observation diary of a first-year Engineering Diploma class taking compulsory English in a university in Country B. My diary records the following events:

> Although this is only one third of the original class . . . which is supposed to have had only 46 participants in all, I counted between 85 and 90 people present. . . . [The teacher] was using *Kernel Lessons* Unit 3, Situations 4 and 5. His method consists of the following stages.

1 Reading aloud (hurriedly and rather quietly) one of the stories accompanying the situations . . .

2 Reading the story again.

3 Asking the students, 'Do you understand?' which leads to some 'no' responses.

4 Reading the story for a third time.

5 Walking very slowly round the class, asking every single student individually a question concerning the passage.

The individual question asking and answering takes at least 30 minutes for each story (i.e. *c*. 30 seconds per student). While all this is going on, the rest of the class is extremely restless and noisy – not surprisingly, since there is in effect no teacher present. This must be an extremely exhausting method for the teacher, and it is obviously frustrating and inefficient for the students.

Why was this teacher teaching in such an inefficient and exhausting way? Look at the advice offered by French (1948: 41):

Out of 100 English sentences, 97 will be in the form of statements; and (these) . . . must therefore be taught and drilled very early and very thoroughly. In this drill, because the pupil learns by saying and doing things himself, the teacher's object will be, not to make statements of his own all the time, but to get the pupils to make statements. This is done by asking questions:

Teacher: What is that?
Pupil: That is a red book.

It may be thought that I am being anachronistic in referring to a book published more than 45 years ago. However, I was issued with a copy of it by Voluntary Service Overseas when I began my own English language teaching career. This was in 1972, when the book was already 24 years old. It is reasonable to suppose that the influence of the ideas which French was proposing could still be felt in 1981 when the lesson described above was observed.

The observed lesson indicates that the teacher was trying very hard to implement precisely what French is proposing; doggedly, diligently, he gave every individual learner in his large class an opportunity to answer a question and he then monitored the performance of every individual. Although there is no suggestion that this particular teacher had read that book, it does appear likely that the teacher had in some way absorbed the principle that monitoring individual performance is of supreme importance. However, his attempt to implement this principle, in a very large class, was pedagogically unproductive. He ended up creating a severe classroom management problem for himself and at the same time reduced his students' learning opportunity to just a couple of minutes in every session.

3.2 *Marking* Marking and giving feedback on students' written work is also, understandably, a major task for teachers of large classes, as the following evidence (from Coleman 1989:56–7) testifies. These comments come from university lecturers in English in Country C who work in classes which have an average of 53.8 students and which in some cases accommodate up to 200 students:

> *'It is difficult to mark all their scripts within a short period of time.'*
> *'Marking students' scripts after examination or assignments consumes a lot of my time.'*
> *'I also find it difficult to mark their assignments and examination, especially composition'.*
> *'Marking also is dreadful, so it limits the number of essay work I give.'*
> *'Much time is required to assess the learners.'*
> *'I find it difficult to correct students' essays and assignments.'*
> *'More time is spent on thinking about marking the assignment and less time is spent on planning and varying activities.'*
> *'Immediate feedback from looking at written exercises is difficult.'*

What advice might these overloaded teachers find if they were to consult the literature on ELT methodology? Haycraft (1986:123) warns:

> There is little point in your students working away if they are not going to learn as much as possible from any mistakes they make. The 'reward' for doing written work is the feeling that something is being learnt. If students sense that their teacher is too indifferent to correct efficiently, they follow his example and become reluctant to do any written work. . . . In my experience, students prefer clear assessment and there is no need to use this invidiously. . . . You underline mistakes so that the student can still see what he originally wrote. At the end, you add up the errors under each category, and list them. (. . .) From intermediate level on, you can plan much of your teaching round these mistakes. Before returning the written work, go through the compositions or exercises, one by one, and comment on mistakes which you think are common to most of the class, without of course saying whose homework you are looking at. Remember to return written work as soon as possible. If you delay, interest will wane. At the same time, the fact that you return written work promptly shows that you care.

There is a clear conflict here, between the advice which is being given and the constraints of the situation in which the teachers in Country C are working. Nevertheless, despite these constraints, the teachers continue to struggle to carry out what they perceive as their duty: to provide detailed feedback on every individual student's written work. As in the first case study, it is not being suggested that these teachers have necessarily read Haycraft's work, but rather that they have through their training, through their reading, or simply through the unformulated ethos of the teaching context, internalised an assumption that it is part of their duty to read and provide detailed comments on all the written work which students produce, even though this assumption is clearly an impractical one in their teaching situation.

For some teachers, the burden of trying to fulfil their responsibilities becomes too great. As the following teacher (also from Country C) admits, in such cases they may then reduce the amount of writing which they ask their learners to undertake, as a way of reducing their own marking load: 'It creates a great burden for the teacher to mark too many scripts of afterclass assignments – thereby making the teacher give less written assignments.'

Thus, in trying to carry out their perceived responsibilities, teachers find that they face a huge task. To compensate, they reduce the amount of learning activity which the learners are asked to perform. The advice, therefore, has a direct counterproductive impact on the learners' learning experience.

3.3 Maintaining control The third case study concerns the maintenance of control in large primary classes. A group of primary teachers of English in Country D, talking about their classes (average size 43.5 up to 60), made these complaints (Coleman 1991: 158 and unpublished questionnaire responses).

> *'It's so hard to control the class.'*
> *'I can't control the class very well.'*
> *'Students are too many, it's difficult to control them by making noise, arguing, quarrelling each other.'* [sic]
> *'Too difficult to control unless some sought of force is applied. Using such force deters teacher-students interaction in class.'* [sic]
> *'I always lost control. . . . 1. Always lost control. 2. Unintentionary hurt chn (beating and scolding). 3. When teacher is unfriendly, chn will not like to attend lesson.'* [sic]

But on consulting the authorities, these teachers are likely to find advice such as the following:

> During the presentation stage teachers tend to act as controllers, both selecting the language the students are to use and asking for the accurate reproduction of new language items. They will want to correct the mistakes they hear and see at this stage fairly rigorously.

> . . . teachers as controllers are in complete charge of the class. They control not only what the students do, but also when they speak and what language they use. . . .Certain stages of a lesson lend themselves to this role very well. The introduction of new language, where it makes use of accurate reproduction and drilling techniques, needs to be carefully organised. Thus, the instruct-cue-nominate

cycle is the perfect example of the teacher acting as controller. All attention is focused on the front of the class, and the students are all working to the same beat. (Harmer 1991: 41 and 236)

The published advice here emphasises the importance of maintaining control. The ideal teacher is in perfect control, selecting language input, determining everything that the learners are to do, deciding who is to speak, and generally co-ordinating everything that happens in the classroom. This advice might be feasible in a small class, of say, a dozen young adults (though I refrain from commenting on its pedagogical value). The harassed and overworked teacher in a class of up to 60 young learners, on the other hand, finds it impossible to 'control' them in the total way which is being recommended. Indeed, the advice is likely only to increase the teacher's sense of inadequacy.

3.4 Learning names   There is ample evidence that teachers in large classes in many parts of the world find it difficult to memorise and use the names of all the people they teach. This is not in any way surprising. Moreover, many teachers feel very guilty about this difficulty. For example, a teacher in Country E (quoted by McLeod 1989:4) said that it was difficult: 'I can't get to know their names or to know them individually.'

A teacher in Country F (Coleman 1990:) said: 'I may spend and certainly will spend the whole year without knowing my students' names. Knowing pupil's names is of great importance in our culture.'

And a university lecturer in Country C again (Coleman 1989:59) said: 'Sometimes I am not even sure if everybody is present.'

What advice are those people given? Nolasco and Arthur (1988:10) observe that in large classes:

> It is always very important to find out about your students and the first step in this process is learning names. . . . Observation has shown that a teacher's inaccurate use of, or failure to use student's names has a direct correlation with inattention and discipline problems. Knowing the students' names allows you to nominate students with confidence as well as to identify trouble-makers. It also indicates that you care about what the students are doing and this helps to contribute to a positive learning environment. It does not matter how you go about learning names as long as you do it efficiently and put them to use quickly.

Of course, teachers of large classes – like their colleagues in more privileged situations – long to be able to pay individual attention to all their learners and to address them all by name. But in reality, with perhaps several different classes to teach in one week, each of which may have 60 or more learners in it, there is a limit to the number of names that the average teacher can memorise. Here, asking the teacher to pay individual attention to all learners and (cf. Section 3.3 above) to orchestrate a classroom conversation and to sensitively correct every tiny error which crops up is unreasonable. It is very likely, then, that this sort of advice simply serves to make teachers feel even more inadequate and incompetent than they do already.

4   *Implications for sustainability*

Of course, it is very easy to pick out extracts from the work of writers who probably did not have large classes in mind and show how inappropriate their advice is for teaching with large numbers of learners. On the other hand, as we have seen here, ideas which almost certainly derive from small-class contexts in privileged teaching situations do filter through to very different situations, and often carry with them very considerable authority. When this occurs, the dangers are twofold. Firstly – as we say above in the case of monitoring individual performance and marking written work – teachers may actually adopt cumbersome roles which are pedagogically counterproductive; and secondly – as we say with the call on teachers to memorise the names of all their learners and to maintain perfect control – the advice may make teachers feel guilty. It contributes to their sense that their teaching situation is not a 'legitimate' one because it does not permit the implementation of the imported and authoritative teaching procedures. The advice, in other words, helps to create in teachers a sense of alienation from their teaching situations.

We need now to consider what routes are open for teachers who have to work with large numbers of learners and – more broadly – what needs to be done to ensure the sustainability of pedagogical innovation. I would argue that a universalist or 'autonomous' approach to language teaching methodology is highly vulnerable and that the essentially anecdotal 'teaching tips' approach which still characterises much discussion of large classes is also inappropriate. Methodological innovation must, therefore be context-sensitive or 'ideological'. Specifically, teachers will have to derive methodologies from within their large-class contexts rather than attempt to modify imported ideas. The great challenge will be in the area of teacher development. Teacher educators – including pre-service teacher educators – must recognise that it is the large class which is the normal teaching context for the majority of the world's English language teachers. The parameters of the large class, therefore, must be taken for granted throughout all teacher development activity. (The small class is a relatively unusual set of circumstances. A corollary, then, is that the specific requirements of teachers of small classes should be dealt with in specialised modules.)

Teacher development programmes, therefore, must have at their core the development of skills which will empower teachers to analyse their classroom contexts and to derive appropriate modes of classroom behaviour from their analysis. The teacher's analysis of his or her own large-class context will need to include at least the following elements:

The parameters of class size   How many learners are on the roll in one class? Does actual attendance tend to be larger or smaller than this? How stable is attendance? (that is, is it the same 70 people each week?) In total, how many learners does the teacher have contact with across the time-table? What is the teacher-learner ratio in the institution? Are any 'para-pedagogues' – for example, teaching assistants, parents – available to help in the classroom? How typical of the teacher's local and national situation are the answers to these questions?

The potentialities of class size In what ways can the identified para-meters of class size be exploited for the pedagogical advantage of the learners?

Pedagogical objectives and appropriate methodology What is feasible in the circumstances? How appropriate are procedures derived from other contexts?

Roles Who should do what and who should take responsibility for what, in the circumstances? In particular, what is least burdensome for the teacher and most productive for the learner?

The constraints of class size What difficulties are apparently caused by the number of learners in a class and by the density of those numbers in the space available?

The etiology of class size Why are classes the size that they are? Which of these factors are amenable to influence by the teacher alone or by the teacher in co-operation with colleagues or parents?

5 Conclusions

In this paper, I have looked at a number of classroom settings in six different countries. These settings have in common the fact that large numbers of learners are trying to learn English (or, at least, that the teacher concerned believes the number to be large). In each case, too, the teacher is battling to reconcile two elements which are essentially irreconcilable: a strong sense of duty, incorporating fixed ideas of what sort of behaviour is appropriate in the language learning classroom, versus a classroom context which is not conducive to the implementation of these ideas.

It has been suggested that teachers find themselves in this situation primarily because of the influence of their initial training. Ultimately, however, many of the principles which teachers attempt to implement, even in the most extreme and difficult of circumstances, derive from very different classroom environments and are inappropriate in other situations. The consequences, as we have seen, are frequently counterproductive.

In order to help teachers avoid – or to escape from – this conflict between duty and context, it has been proposed that both initial and in-service teacher development need to be firmly rooted in the realities of the teaching context. A teacher development programme must have as its central agenda the analysis and critiquing by teachers or prospective teachers of their present or target teaching situations. Without a pivotal role for analysis and the development from that analysis of appropriate methodologies – by teachers themselves – the effects of teacher development activity cannot be sustained. At least in the context of large classes, if teachers are not helped to become the authors of their own methodologies, then teacher education is futile.

For ideas developed since this paper was given, see Coleman (1995) and Coleman, ed. (1996). Holliday (1994) is also pertinent.

7.4   Sustaining ELT in normal circumstances (1990)

GERRY ABBOTT

British-sponsored ELT overseas can be viewed as comprising two 'wings', or sectors. On the one hand we have an aid sector in which, directly or indirectly, the vast majority of recipients are schoolchildren in developing countries, most of them living in rural areas and attending state schools. Here, even in the cities, the standards of provision are low. The teachers are poorly trained and poorly paid, and generally speak poor English; the schools are poorly equipped and supervised; and the classes are large and poorly motivated, there being little if any felt need for English and few if any opportunities for speaking the language outside the classroom. On the other hand we have a private paid sector in which the customers are older, more urbanised and much more motivated, where the teacher is much better trained and supported, where the class is small and where there is heavy reliance on such equipment as photocopiers and cassette recorders. The circumstances that I consider 'normal', and the learners I am concerned with here, are those in the impoverished aid sector; and I see two dangers.

The first is the danger of assuming that what is good for the privileged paid sector is also good for the 'normal' aid sector. Methods and materials designed in the 'anglocentre' (mainly North America and Britain) may well transfer to the overseas paid sector without much modification, especially where the learners belong to an elite; but they are largely unsuitable for the mass of English language learners and teachers. Naturally, Ministries of Education staffed by elites in the capital cities will tend to follow the anglocentre's ELT orthodoxies, believing them to be the best available, and may consequently prescribe unrealistic syllabuses, methodologies and attainment targets; this in turn gives rise to the phenomenon described so vividly by Hawes (1979) – the gulf between the 'official' and the actual in schoolteaching. It is not only in developing countries that uncomfortable realities are excluded from the political agenda, of course; but in impoverished settings the disparities show up much more, and nowhere more clearly than in ELT.

For the 'normal' teacher whose own English is very limited and far from fluent, interactive oral work is an embarrassment if not an impossibility, whatever the Ministry might specify; and in the usual large and crowded class, speech-work is difficult and tiring to conduct. Creative written work is hard to monitor and entails a great deal of marking. Listening is a little more manageable. Assuming that the class can indeed hear the teacher, short monologue scripts can be used to good effect even when the teacher's own pronunciation leaves much to be desired. (Listening to dialogues is less feasible: the teacher might own a cassette-recorder, but who will provide the cassettes . . . and, where there is no mains electricity, supply the batteries?) The skill that lends itself most easily to both teacher and learner in these circumstances is reading. It is also, in areas with low or no exposure to English, the skill through which both learner and teacher can be enabled to sustain and improve their knowledge of English. Instead of exporting undiluted 'communicativeness' therefore, perhaps we should develop a reading method – albeit a more communicative one than that devised so long ago by Michael West – and develop it in the field, rather than in the anglocentre.

Now that ELT is one of the UK's leading industries in terms of profits, a second danger is that our ELT pundits – academics, examiners, textbook writers, publishers and (above all) consultants, advisers, English Language Officers and the like – will become more and more seduced by the privileged conditions obtaining in the paid sector and less and less mindful of those in the aid sector. Third World teachers themselves, during their short stay in the UK on a Masters degree course, have produced for me assignments and dissertations that specify splendid communicative activities for use in schools back home, and I have had to remind them that such daydreams cannot be realised in those circumstances. Similarly, British Council-recruited ELT advisers have on occasions advocated activities or produced materials which have been rejected by teachers on the spot as unsuited to their own culture, or their own capabilities, or their students' interests, or their institution's meagre facilities.

Such inappropriacies result, I believe, from the seductiveness of privileged circumstances. Perhaps our diploma and degree courses in ELT should shake themselves out of what I call 'the handout culture' and pay more attention to the realities of teaching as experienced by nine-tenths of our profession. Perhaps, too, the ODA policy of funding ELT only at 'multiplier effect' levels (teacher-training, syllabus designing, etc.) should be revised so that such posts include substantial school teaching duties. In this way, the assistance offered by our experts would make for greater sustainability in that it would be geared to normal circumstances.

For a brief and interesting introduction to the important but neglected work begun by West in Bengal, see Howatt (1984: 245–50). More particularly, in an article published since the above paper was presented, Tickoo (1992) puts forward an argument similar to the one above; he too believes that in 'normal' circumstances a reading method would be more realistic and produce more sustainable results. For further thoughts on the inappropriateness of ELT methods, materials, etc., see Abbott (1992).

8.0   ELT, Culture and Development

GERRY ABBOTT

In the introduction to this second part of the book it was noted that many authorities view the sort of global development so far achieved as 'mere westernisation' – Latouche (1989), for example, calls it '*l'occidentalisation du monde*' and Shiva (1989) sees it as 'the new colonialism', a 'project of western patriarchy'. Where such widespread misgivings occur it is right that personnel involved in development projects should pause to consider the nature of (mal)development and the part they play in it. If 'development' that involves ELT necessarily entails westernisation, are ELT personnel willy-nilly agents of cultural imperialism? If they are, how might they minimise this presumably unintended involvement?

This section begins with a brief summary of just one of several thought-provoking activities organised by Burke and Bolitho for the 1991 seminar. They confirmed the existence of a confused uneasiness among the participants, who saw a need to modify ELT policy in the context of development aid. The 'cross-cutting' issues that they summarise diagramatically clearly deserve further investigation.

There follow two reports on how culture-clash can affect classroom experience. Holes shows how Arab conceptions of language, language-learning and education differ from those current in UK, and Bellarmine reports on the sort of cultural mismatches that can make project administration difficult for British expatriates.

We end with another disagreement. This time Bowers takes issue with Phillipson's firm convictions concerning linguistic imperialism – or linguicism, as he prefers to call it. Phillipson sets out a case for regarding ELT activities of the kind undertaken by The British Council as a form of neo-imperialism. It is hardly surprising that Bowers should beg to differ, but in doing so, he usefully picks up many of the strands running through this part of the book – demand and supply, education and training, top-down and bottom-up approaches, the case for intervention, and so on. Interestingly, he recognises that development efforts must lead us outside ELT, 'beyond language and education, into the areas of decision making'. Might it be that the decision-making process in language-in-education planning is a possible target for development aid?

8.1   Socio-economic roles and ELT (1991)

JOHN BURKE and ROD BOLITHO

The theme for the day was 'ELT: socio-economic roles and their implications – views from the grassroots'. The primary purpose was to look to the socio-economic, and indeed cultural and environmental aspects of ELT aid for development through the eyes of some of those most directly involved in receiving and providing ELT, including English teachers from other countries, advisers and UK trainers and institutions.

Two key articles by Rogers (1982) and Abbott (1984) present differing views of, and perspectives on, the role of ELT in developing countries. Seminar participants were asked to read them and to state (in a secret ballot) whose side they were on. Surprisingly, perhaps, twelve sided with Abbott and nine with Rogers. The subsequent debate highlighted both the confusion felt by participants over many of the issues and the emotive nature of some of them. Numerous points for development and further consideration emerged. These were summarised in the conclusion, and included the following.

1)   There was a need to recognise that ELT had to provide clear and identifiable socio-economic, cultural and environmental benefits. Simply to assert its relevance was no longer acceptable. 'Cross-cutting' issues such as the environment, women, poverty, employment, population, democratic processes and so on applied as much to ELT as to any other aspects of aid for development.

2)   There was a need within that framework to see ELT as part of education and as a service subject.

3)   There was a need to fine-tune ELT provision to particular contexts to enable cross-cutting socio-economic issues to be accommodated. There are wide-reaching implications of this for ELT course design, for training patterns, project design, and so on (see Fig. 1).

4)   There was a need to demonstrate links between ELT and the various socio-economic and cultural issues and to establish measuring instruments and evaluation measures of those links. This will require ELT specialists to work closely with specialists from other fields.

5)   There was an urgent need for ELT to look beyond its now traditional areas of interest to focuses and activities which may more readily help it meet socio-economic demands. These focuses and activities well may include some of the following.

- literacy (in English and in the L1)
- language across the curriculum
- translation and interpretation
- broader educational contexts for ELT

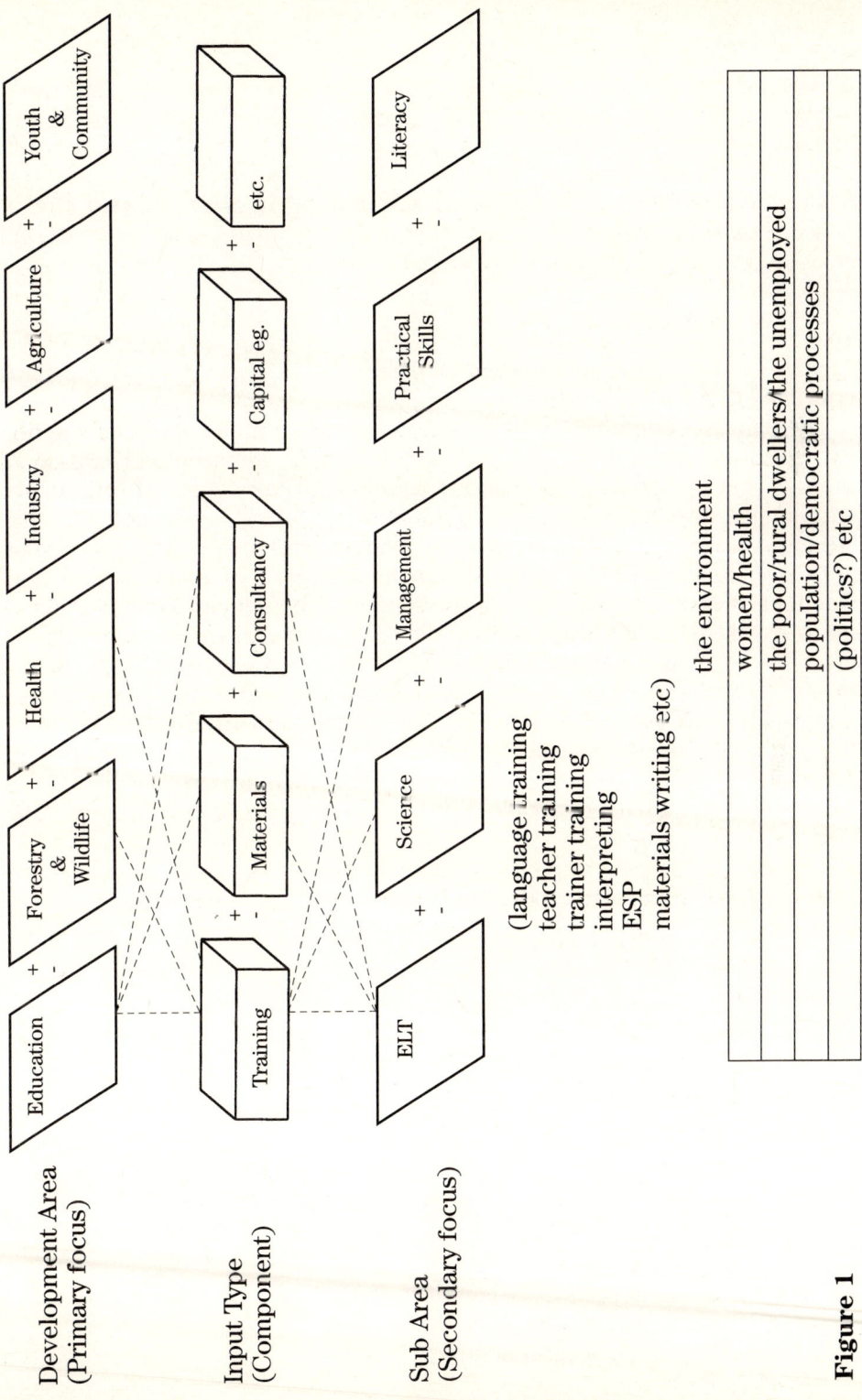

Figure 1

- narrow-focus ESP
- approaches to managing change
- approaches to (and extensive application of) classroom and other relevant research.

8.2a   Attitudes to language and learning in Britain and the Arab world (1985)

CLIVE HOLES

This was a discussion presented in the context of an MA course in Applied Linguistics at Salford University organised with special reference to the Arab world.

The Salford course developed as a result of two areas of dissatisfaction with traditional courses of the kind, the first an apparent separation of theory from application, the second a failure to take cultural differences sufficiently into account when dealing with foreign students who are studying in Britain. Such students are usually not familiar with the British approach to higher education, in which a degree of responsibility and freedom of choice is expected of the student. The educational tradition of many overseas students is one in which they are more or less told what to do, what to read – indeed, what to think. These dissatisfactions resulted in an attempt to offer a contextualised MA course in which theory and practice are inextricably linked. The course aims to teach students to be aware of their own assumptions and to enable them to discuss the cultural preconceptions they bring to bear on teaching and learning. Let us first consider what some authentic quotations suggest about Arab attitudes to language.

Some Middle Eastern attitudes to language and learning

1) T: I've just now been there . . .
   S: You can't say that, sir.
   T: Pardon?
   S: 'Now' takes '-ing'
   (Bahrain secondary school student, 1971)

2) 'Give us the good grammar'. (Dean of the Faculty of Engineering, KAAU, 1975)

3) 'I will teach you the good Arabic'. (Bahrain headmaster, 1984)

4) 'We don't have the time to watch *Coronation Street*, and anyway we are here to learn correct English'. (Salford MA student, 1984)

5) 'Arabic is a richer   language than English'.
               more complex/difficult
               more beautiful/poetic
   (Most Arabs)

6) People in Salford always use slang language so we shouldn't learn from them'. (Arab student of English, Special Studies Unit, 1984)

In similar fashion, let us now consider some culturally determined expectations concerning the teaching/learning process:

7) S: I want to talk to you about my dissertation.
T: Fine, go ahead.
S: Please tell me what my topic is going to be.
(Most students, most of the time)

8) *Examiner* (in viva): Why is there no bibliography to this essay?
Candidate (after pause): Dr Holes didn't say I needed one.
(Syrian student, Salford 1985)

9) T: But you can't talk about the 'social structure of society', it's tautological. You mean either 'the structure of society' or 'social structure'.
S: (in triumph): But look here, sir, on p. 20 of Trudgill's book, '. . . the social structure of society', so it must be right.
(Jordanian student, Salford 1985)

10) T: By and large, I think it's true to say that Arabic makes less use of ellipsis than English does, especially in the verb phrase –
S: (interrupting) How would you translate /biʕtukaha/?
T: (puzzles) 'I sold it to you'.
S: (in triumph) OK. That's five words in English, in Arabic we have only one!

11) /fil ʔiʕāda ʔifāza/
'In repetition, there is benefit'.
(Arab proverb)

12) 'It is disquieting that, in any human activity, we often seem to be waiting a breakthrough before which nothing of significance can be postulated let alone tried out. At such a time something of a deadlock develops, and things come to a relative, if not virtual, standstill. The deadlock may continue for a few years or a few centuries. Then someone steps forward, takes things into his own hands and systemizes the fuzziness by stamping out order and establishing the rule and defining the trend of the given activity. Things develop steadily, later on. Human individuality, it seems, keeps popping up to direct the course of events and lead in all spheres of activities to our life. To the chagrin of communist and materialist thinkers alike, this fact serves as a reminder that it is the individual man, as such, who is the focus of events and the pioneer who emerges from the crowds to assume the role of leadership . . . [10 more lines in similar vein] . . . Try to visualise with me, that according to the previous common belief, the earth was flat and stretched infinitely and that the sun went round it. Can you think of anything more naive?'

(Opening paragraph of an essay on 'Intertextuality' by a Syrian MA student, Salford, 1984)

13) (a) /ʔuṭlub il-ʕilm wa law fi ṣi:n/
'Seek knowledge even in China'
(Qur'ān)

(b) /ʔuṭlub il ʕilm min ilmahd ila llaḥd/
'Seek knowledge from the cradle to the grave'
(Ḥadīth)

Finally, let us contrast some of the expectations of a typical British academic with the corresponding expectations of the typical Arab postgraduate student:

What the typical British academic expects/does	**What the typical Arab postgraduate expects/does**
Contact	
'Come to see me when you need to.'	'Summon me (and tell me what to do).'
Teaching style	
Relaxed chat with a few blackboard notes plus occasional handouts.	Note down what is written, store all handouts. Ignore much of what is said.
Content	
Review and critique of conflicting views: personal, critical synthesis.	Read all, learn all, construct 'patchwork quilt' of quotes and conflicting theories.
Verbal style	
Oblique, understated, indirect, ironic, rhetorical (written/oral).	Direct, overstated, often sweeping generalisation, 'wordy' (written/oral).

It is necessary to understand the cultural situation of the Arab-speaking student. The Islamic view is that there is only one solution to questions in the physical world, and this is to be derived from the Qur'ān, which offers the right, the only path. The traditional Muslim understanding of 'knowledge' is of a set of unquestionable facts, and it follows that in education the teacher is the unquestioned 'knower'. Arab students consequently have difficulty in reconciling opposing theories when both appear in respectable literature and therefore bear a stamp of approval. This difficulty, together with the transfer of a written style that conflicts with the depersonalising and economic style of Western academic writing, makes it hard for the Middle Eastern student in Britain to present information in an acceptable form in assignments and examinations.

In discussion it was generally agreed that many of the value judgements and expectations illustrated were to be found in many parts of the world and not simply among speakers of Arabic, but that it is particularly difficult to stop Arabic-speaking students transferring to English the values that they associate with their own language. It may be that their great loyalty is made more intense by the threatening cultural force of English, with its cargo of implicit Western values.

8.2b Cross-cultural constraints on sustainability: a view from South India (1989)

ROBERT BELLARMINE

In order to achieve project sustainability, it is necessary for the donor and the recipient to have an adequate understanding of each other's culture, particularly the work culture. It may be desirable even to assimilate certain features of the local partner's culture. In any South Indian project, it will be particularly important to take account of three features of South Indian culture to maximise project sustainability: 1) weak occupational motivation; 2) an ancient perspective on time; and 3) the distinction between politeness-driven and fact-driven replies.

1) In India the link between occupation and personal identity is loose and therefore occupational motivation is weak. For instance when social groups are formed among teachers, professional interests rarely form the basis. Important factors are religion, caste and physical proximity. This is evident in South India projects where, between the UK consultants' visits, there is little follow-up discussion in teachers' groups. More importantly, six of the eight teacher-development groups started up three years ago are now defunct.

2) Perspectives on time differ radically between the UK consultants and the local participants. Project teachers as Indians see time chiefly as an 'inexorable cosmic frame of reference', whereas the British consultants as westerners see it as a resource.

3) A common communication problem occurs when an Indian project teacher says 'Yes' purely out of politeness and the British consultant takes it as its face value. The latter misses the point because the politeness-driven 'Yes' is equal to a fact-driven 'No'. The choice between the yes and the no is determined by factors such as hierarchy, gravity of the request, insistence on explicitness, the number of times the request/question is repeated, and the publicness/privateness of the speech situation.

How might a UK consultant overcome the cross-cultural constraints? As regards the loose coupling of occupation, identity and motivation, all teachers should be involved in project planning from the very outset to get them to have a stake in the project. They should also be given career counselling emphasising the project's relevance to their individual lives and to their family.

Both sides need to understand the time perspective problem and to work at changing each other's attitude so as to facilitate an assimilation of the two perspectives. This can be done by specially designing a project diary that accommodates these differing time perspectives. Thirdly, the project staff should openly discuss the subtle uses of yes/no, to increase mutual understanding. They can even arrive at a code of conduct with special reference to this communication problem, clear and quick communication being crucial to project success.

8.3   Linguistic imperialism (1991)

ROBERT PHILLIPSON

My forthcoming book (Phillipson 1992) attempts to place issues of language and power, language and dominance, the ethics of aid, ELT professionalism, and the overt technical agenda and the covert political agenda of global ELT within an explicit theoretical framework. This links up the macro level of English as a world language to the micro level of the pedagogic and linguistic principles which underlie ELT professionalism. Such a theory can hopefully help to reduce the subjectivity of much evaluative analysis, and might help to clarify the 'cross-cutting' of ELT with other dimensions of 'development'. It presupposes a coherent trans-disciplinary approach drawing on many traditions in the social sciences and the humanities.

A key concept is linguicism, which is defined as ideologies, structures and practices which are used to legitimate, effectuate and reproduce an unequal division of power and resources (material and immaterial) between groups which are defined on the basis of language. Linguicism is affirmed in similar ways to racism. In linguistic discourse the dominant language is glorified, dominated languages are stigmatised, and the relationship between dominant and dominated is rationalised, always to the advantage of the dominant. This was the pattern in colonial education, which had the following characteristics.

- It lowered the status of local languages.
- It ignored local educational traditions.
- It lay stress on the civilising properties of the master language.
- It was western-oriented and bookish.
- From secondary level upwards, it copied European education, which was monolingual.
- It claimed to play a key role in introducing 'science' and 'civilisation'.

The rationalisation of the linguistic hierarchy was implicit in the colonial power structure, and explicit in many policy papers on colonial education. This pattern of linguicism was also imposed domestically, *vis-à-vis* dominated indigenous languages (Welsh, Breton, Navajo) and is currently being asserted *vis-à-vis* immigrant languages. The linguicist characteristics also apply very generally in postcolonial societies, that is, most 'Third World' countries have perpetuated colonialist language policies. World Bank studies of education neglect the language issue. IMF structural adjustment policies involve a continued emphasis on the learning of the former colonial language.

What rights should all languages ideally enjoy? A great deal of effort is being put into determining and codifying linguistic human rights at Unesco, the Council of Europe, the European Parliament and in applied linguistic circles (FIPLV, AILA). Existing international covenants and most national constitutions do not guarantee the rights of minority language speakers to learn the mother tongue fully, as well as the dominant language, to identify with the mother tongue, and use this in dealing with officialdom. There is an increasing awareness that such matters are inalienable human rights, and that according such rights to minority language speakers does not represent a threat to dominant languages. A proposed linguistic charter for Africa (Dalby 1985) proclaims the equal linguistic rights of every individual, granting these the status of national languages, and giving one African language the status of official language in each country, to replace or be used alongside the existing 'foreign' official language.

The reason that the speakers of few languages in former colonies enjoy such rights is that the educational and linguistic policies of such countries are locked in a structure which has replaced the colonial one, and which can be called imperialist. Imperialism can be conceptualised as a structural relationship whereby one society or collectivity can dominate another. The key mechanisms are exploitation, penetration, fragmentation and marginalisation. There are six interlocking types of imperialism: economic, political, military, social, communicative and cultural. The principal sub-types of cultural imperialism are media, educational, scientific and linguistic imperialism. English linguistic imperialism can be defined as the establishment and continuous reconstitution of structural and cultural inequalities between English and other languages. Characteristics of ELT in this structure are the following

- Anglocentricity
- Professionalism
- Political disconnection
- Narrowly technical training.

An example of ELT operating in a linguicist way at the macro level is the way arguments are marshalled in a language planning policy paper for Namibia. The variables selected gave far greater prominence to European languages than any Namibian languages, and placed excessive emphasis on the use of language for international purposes rather than for intranational purposes.

An example of ELT operating in a linguicist way at the micro level is the tenets which served as pillars of the rising ELT profession and which were given a seal of approval at a key conference at Makerere in 1961. There were five tenets, which held that

- English was best taught monolingually
- The ideal teacher of English was a native speaker:
- The earlier English was introduced, the better the results;
- The more English was taught, the better the result; and
- If other languages were used much, standards of English would drop.

All five are scientifically false, and can be better labelled as:

- the monolingual fallacy
- the native speaker fallacy
- the early start fallacy
- the maximum exposure fallacy
- the subtractive fallacy.

Adhering to these tenets has had major consequences, structural and ideological, for the entire ELT operation in aid contexts. There is a clear need for more empirical studies to test the theoretical apparatus in a variety of contexts and refine it. Linguistic hierarchies have been successfully challenged in minority education in several parts of the world (see examples, and theoretical analysis, in Skutnabb-Kangas and Cummins 1988). There is a challenge for ELT to reconnect politically and work out anti-linguicist strategies which can empower speakers of dominated languages.

8.4   ELT and development: projects and power (1991)

ROGER BOWERS

Introduction

As I am not at present directly involved in curriculum innovation, I shall be referring to several projects which have been reported elsewhere (Bowers 1987: Celani *et al.* 1988). My primary concern is with curriculum innovation in which there is interaction between a 'host group or institution and an 'external' agency or advisers, and in particular with the hundred or so ELT projects currently managed by the British Council on behalf of Britain's Overseas Development Administration: but some of my comments on insider/outsider roles and power relations can apply to any innovation context including curriculum development which is initiated, funded and conducted wholly within a national education system.

A recurrent reference point will be Phillipson's (1990) study *English Language Teaching and Imperialism*. Though I disagree profoundly with much of Phillipson's thesis there is no doubt that the issues which he discussed are relevant and deserve debate. 'Language pedagogy', he says (ibid: 29), 'must attempt to place its activities in a macro-societal theoretical perspective and analyse the historical, political and intellectual roots of the profession'. I agree. In this seminar much discussion will centre on the agenda for change itself, in what directions curriculum innovation proceeds, with what intentions and results, and by what processes. My concern here is with two prior questions; a) Who is empowered to set the agenda for change? b) On what grounds do they exercise this authority?

Linguicism

Phillipson's central concern is defined as follows (ibid: 41):

> English linguistic imperialism is one example of Linguicism, which is defined as 'ideologies, structures and practices which are used to legitimate, effectuate and reproduce an unequal division of power and resources (both material and immaterial) between groups which are defined on the basis of language'.

It will come as no surprise that I do not consider this an appropriate description of the work of agencies such as the British Council and its bilateral and multilateral analogues in the areas of educational development and promotion of the English language. But there is an issue here which is central to the diffusion of innovation. A central problem for me in addressing Phillipson's argument may be illustrated by a further and final quotation (ibid: 7).

> In language pedagogy the connections between English language and political, economic and military power are seldom pursued. Language pedagogy, and theory and practice of language teaching and language learning, tends to focus on what goes on in the classroom, and related organisational and methodological matters. In professional English teaching circles, English tends to be regarded as an incontrovertible boon, as does language policy and pedagogy emanating from the core-English countries. It is felt that while English was imposed by force in colonial times, contemporary language policies are determined by the state of the market ('demand') and the force of argument (rational planning in the light of the available 'facts'). The discourse accompanying and legitimating the export of English to the rest of the world has been so persuasive that English has been equated with progress and prosperity. In the view of the Ford Foundation's language projects officer, 'English as a Second Language (ESL) was believed to be a vital key to development by both the United States and by countries like Indonesia, the Philippines, Thailand, India, Turkey, Afghanistan, Pakistan, Egypt, Nigeria, Colombia and Peru' (Fox 1975:36). The arguments in favour of English are intuitively commonsensical, but only in the Gramscian sense of beliefs which reflect dominant ideology (Gramsci 1971).

There are a number of elements in earlier parts of this passage which I would disagree with. But my real problem is with the last sentence. Not only does it remove any obligation on the part of those on the other side of the argument to listen to my views, since I am in the chosen terminology a representative of the 'Centre'. but it also provides a pretext upon which any proponent from the 'Periphery' of similar views can also be ignored, on the grounds that their perceptions have been distorted by subjection to precisely the process of intellectual hegemony which is at issue. I cannot accept that restriction of debate.

But let me turn away for the time being from Phillipson, with the observation that his concern with the political and cultural aspects of the promotion of English language and international involvement in educational development is a well-placed concern. I cannot claim that bilateral and multilateral aid is directed solely towards the developmental interests of the 'recipient' with no attention to the interests of the 'donor' (terms whose semantics we do not have the time to discuss here). In my work and that of parts of the British Council there is no doubt that terms such as *promotion, market, investment* and *long-term return* are now a part of the rhetoric of cultural relations, as they are indeed of national education and the international development agenda. If there is a single lexical item which sums up the tensions between interests it is perhaps the word 'demand': for demand can be stimulated as well at satisfied, and it is the extent to which we believe we are doing the first or the second of these when we engage in international programmes for curriculum innovation in English that places us on one side or the other of the linguicism debate.

So who sets the agenda?
Inevitably our personal engagement in educational innovation is likely to colour our views on this issue. My own long-term experience (I have been involved more tangentially in a number of countries) has been in Ghana, India and Egypt, and it is on this last context that I primarily draw. Hyde (1978) reports President Anwar El-Sadat's summary of the major concerns of educational policy in post-revolutionary Egypt under five headings:

1) national integration

2) secularisation

3) education of the masses

4) revival of Arabic

5) modernisation (this last term being widely defined).

Hyde reports also recognition within Egypt of the role which the import of educational ideas, of science and technology, and of language (primarily English) would play in the pursuit of these aims. It is interesting to note, if we are prepared to accept Hyde's observations, that *at least at the policy level* no conflict was felt between the revival of Arabic and the promotion of English and other international languages. The import of ideas and a communicative medium from outside was seen as a part of the revolutionary process, not as a representation of it. In the Egyptian context, my own observation suggests, ideas and processes drawn in from outside were not in themselves seen as threatening or intrusive; foreign ownership of those ideas, and foreign influence over decisions as to which ideas and processes should be accepted and indigenised, certainly would have been. In the Egypt of my experience there was never any danger that the fundamental decisions regarding education policy and language policy would be outside the control of national politicians and administrators: far from it. The boundaries between local policy and external professional advice were firmly drawn, and the advisory role itself tightly circum-scribed. To suggest otherwise would insult the independence and integrity of those to whom, as well as with whom, we worked.

Even so, in a major aid environment (such as Egypt has been over twenty or more years) there are operational tensions. Some of these are described in *ELT Documents 125* (1987) which discusses a range of teacher education programmes at the Centre for Developing English Language Teaching, Ain Shams University, Cairo – a joint Egyptian/American/British project. I can best resummarise them as follows.

Appropriate methodology

As I pointed out at a previous Dunford seminar (see 7.1 in this volume) all innovation involves a measure of mediation, of matching ideas to contexts of curriculum innovation. This requires the development and implementation of a two-fold methodology which we may label M1/M2.

M1 methodology is a set of principles for the management of the classroom, informed by a desired approach to language teaching and learning. M2 methodology is a set of principles for the management of change, informed by an approach to social development in general and curriculum development in particular. Both M1 and M2 need to be appropriate in terms of four features – two 'internal' and two 'external'.

INTERNAL

Approach   Is the methodology (M1) consistent with a set of beliefs about education which are both in principle valid for the local context and in practice held by those involved in and accountable for a methodological innovation?

Is the project methodology (M2) consistent with a set of development aims which are both in principle valid for the local context and in practice ascribed to those involved in and accountable for the development?

Techniques   Is the classroom methodology (M1) realisable through a set of techniques which are in principle feasible for those responsible for implementation and in practice performed by them? Is the project methodology (M2) attainable through a set of techniques which are both in principle feasible for those responsible for implementation and in practice performed by them?

EXTERNAL

Resources   Can M1 be implemented within the resources locally available, and does it make the best use of them? Can M2 be implemented within the resources locally available, and does it make best use of them?

Curriculum   Is M1 compatible with other components of the curriculum, and does it maximise the effect of the curriculum as a whole? Is M2 compatible with other components of the development curriculum (that is, the aims and processes of the total developmental agenda) and does it maximise the effect of the development programme as a whole?

A programme of innovation, in our case of curriculum innovation, has to be appropriate in terms of both M1 and M2. And to be appropriate it has to be valued within the set of aims and beliefs actually held by those locally responsible for endorsing the innovation. Failure to achieve that endorsement, through disagreement or default, sets the programme as a whole on a course to failure, and may well earn accusations of attempted linguistic or pedagogic imperialism.

Let me turn to a second example. The Brazilian ESP Project reported in Celani *et al.* (1988) incorporates a detailed and well documented description of how this project was initiated in order to ensure from the outset maximum participation in framing its objectives and in agreeing and enacting its processes. In general, Celani reports (ibid: 7).

> The main characteristic of the Project is perhaps its participatory quality. It derived from the needs of practising teachers and these same teachers have been closely linked with most of the operations involved in implementing the project. This collaborative feature ensured active participation from the start and influenced the design of the evaluation of work carried out in Phase II. The Project is a loose federation of interested parties, not a rigid structure imposed by a Ministry or an outside agency.
>
> Another characteristic is the allowance made for preserving local features. Teachers who work with students of tourism will thus teach oral skills, while the majority concentrate on reading only. Some teachers feel the need to put more emphasis on structural aspects of language than others do. There is a consensus tempered with variety. The decision not to produce a Project textbook contributed to this atmosphere.

Approaches to innovation

This notion of 'consensus tempered by variety' captures well one of the approaches cited by Straker Cook in assessing the Egyptian project mentioned above (Bowers 1987:18):

> Reviewing the literature on educational innovation, Nicholls (1983) reduces a number of approaches to three basic models.

Model 1: research – development – diffusion

> In this model, an active researcher-theoretician, as innovator, perceives a problem and presents his solution to a passive receiver. However, he takes no part in the implementation process.

Model 2: social interaction

This has essentially the same ingredients as Model 1, but focuses rather on the means of diffusion. The innovator determines both who the receiver shall be and what his needs are. The receiver is seen as active, in that he may provide feedback to the innovator, but the innovator has no role in the implementation of the innovation nor in any subsequent modifications.

Model 3: problem-solving

In this model, users' needs are paramount, and innovation emerges spontaneously from discussion and transactions between users. In effect, the users are at the same time the (collective) innovator and the recipients. Innovation thus becomes a non-directive process, and the outcome is unpredictable

There are several comments to be made. The first two models are variants of the same basic approach: innovation is conceived as a product, an artefact to be sold to the recipient. There is a high degree of control over design, little or none over implementation. The feedback allowed for Model 2 does not amount to evaluation, since there is no mechanism for systematic adjustment of the innovation to the system or of the system to the innovation.

Model 3 is superficially more attractive: it treats innovation rather more as a process, or at least as the sum total of changes wrought on the system of spontaneous perturbation. However, it denies the role of an instigator, either among the users or operating on the group from outside: and one wonders therefore just how the innovation is generated. Changes may indeed occur spontaneously, but it is less likely that genuine innovations would. For who are the users, if they are not teachers and educators within the system? And hierarchical systems such as educational institutions have an inherent stability and exert a powerful inhibiting influence on innovators operating from within.

Straker Cook goes on to analyse the components of an innovating environment and to set out his own categorisation of strategies for diffusion (co-operative: inertial, self-adaptive; multi-level; precedence). But this is not the place to delve deeper into the theory. Let us rather return to evidence from the Celani example, where characterisation of the project as a 'Model 2' approach is supported by detailed evaluation results. One of the questions asked, to over 100 teachers and over 200 students, concerned their attitudes to the introduction of an ESP approach. The findings of Celani *et al.* (1988:33) are shown in the Table overleaf.

These findings do not seem to me to support charges of either linguicism or (dare I mint the term?) pedagogicism. The approach which a programme of innovation adopts includes definition of ownership of the project, the decision-making powers of the participants in it. The Celani example may not be representative of all such projects, or even of such projects as are supported by British agencies: but it is reasonable to suggest that projects are by and large (like the Celani project) sensitive to the issues which Phillipson raises and guided by procedures for identification, design and implementation which ensure that the 'donor' is employed in roles which are defined by the 'recipient'.

We may ask therefore to what extent the 'recipient' is equipped to assume the role of authority which a participative model requires. Here we may again find ourselves employing some of the models and terminology discussed by Straker Cook: we immediately confront issues of 'top-down' and 'bottom-up' of pre-planned and organic development objectives, of the 'external' and 'internal' initiation and management of change.

Learning ESP seems to you to be:	ESP (1)	Teachers (2)	Students	Ex-students
• preparation to suit the interests of the consumer society	8%	6%	12%	13%
• a means of spreading the imperialist domination of other peoples	5%	0%	8%	7%
• a way of knowing other peoples	20%	15%	16%	10%
• access to specific bibliography	75%	71%	49%	66%
• access to any bibliography	85%	91%	60%	46%
• useful for getting a job	20%	18%	10%	12%
• other	5%	6%	3%	2%
(N)	(84)	(34)	(2008)	(224)

The role of training

Change involves choice; and choice involves both displacement (distancing from what is) and discernment (awareness of what might be). It seems to me that a part of the solution to the dilemma which Straker Cook defines comes through the provision of what we may term developmental training, either in preparation for a proposed innovation or as the indirected cause of it. Such training will incorporate the following features (Richards and Nunan 1990:xii) – for 'teachers' read also 'trainers', 'inspectors', 'materials writers', 'curriculum developers' etc.:

- a movement away from a 'training' perspective to an 'education' perspective and recognition that effective teaching involves higher level cognitive processes, which cannot be taught directly;
- the need for teachers and student teachers to adopt a research orientation to their own classrooms and their own teaching;
- less emphasis on prescriptions and top-down directives and more emphasis on an enquiry-based and discovery-oriented approach to learning (bottom-up);
- a focus on devising experiences that require the student teacher to generate theories and hypotheses and to reflect critically on teaching;
- less dependence on linguistics and language theory as a source

discipline for second language teacher education, and more of an attempt to integrate sound, educationally based approaches.

and

● use of procedures that involve teachers in gathering and analysing data about teaching.

I have no answer to the dilemma that might arise where, in order to train a recipient group out of over-dependence on an authoritative external group, we attempt to train them in an independence from authority which is itself not a part of their cultural set. It is my belief that developmental training can play a part within the identification and design of all projects in ensuring that local authority is engaged, project aims and processes subject to local constraint, and the project as a wholly locally owned and sustainable.

What kind of training?

Given the need to avoid providing training which creates rather more than diminishes dependence by the 'Periphery' on the 'Centre' (another of Phillipson's concerns), what features might appropriate training display?

One approach (which I will not expand upon today) would be to draw upon Kachru (1986) as Phillipson does in recognising four basic areas in which the power of English might manifest itself – linguistic, literary, attitudinal and pedagogic – and to develop ways in which training can address these.

A second approach is to focus training on the management of change itself, not in relation to education and ELT but in general, in relation to any organisational setting. Hunt (1986: 255–60 identifies these seven components:

Data collection   What is the evidence of the problems? What are the symptoms?

Definition of the problem   What precisely is the problem?

Diagnosis and identification of the cause(s)   What is causing the problem?

The plan   What shall we do?

The action   Implementation of the plan of action to correct the deviation.

Consolidation   Stabilisation of the revised action.

Evaluation   Measurement of the continuing effect.

Hunt goes on to argue that much change is not so rationally and sequentially initiated and conducted. Nevertheless a part of the process of ensuring that authority for change rests with those likely to be most affected by it must be to ensure that a reasonable number of them are individually empowered by training and experience to ask Hunt's questions, within whatever ideological or institutional framework they choose or are required to operate in. If this approach to training is seen in itself as a perpetuation of cultural or linguistic or pedagogic imperialism, the withholding of such training is surely more damagingly so.

Interestingly, while continuing to dispute Phillipson's premises, I find myself agreeing with some of his conclusions. The process of empowering those who should be so empowered to take decisions regarding curriculum innovation in ELT must take us outside the technical concerns of ELT, beyond language and education, into the areas of decision making and the management of change in general. The place of management training for educational administrators and policy formulators deserves attention, and it is significant that management training is coming to the fore in a number of professional courses in Great Britain – including courses designed primarily for the overseas student, teacher and researcher.

I end on a cautionary note. Though training may be a large part of the answer to undue external influence, that training too must be sensitively deployed and conducted, and *seen from the viewpoint of the recipient*. In a forthcoming article Parrott (1991) gives graphic descriptions of cases where this has not been the case and the process of training has damaged individuals and thereby the educational programmes and contexts in which they operated.

Ultimately, as with all aspects of project planning and performance, the responsibility for ensuring that projects and project components do not preserve and enhance inequality, but rather improve access to opportunity, is a shared one. it would be an odd argument that, in seeking to increase respect for our 'recipient' colleagues and to enhance their rights and authority, failed to pay them the respect of assuming that they will display the authority vested in them by their local standing, knowledge, sensitivity and continuity of being there. In the best projects that is exactly what they do: and they, more than us, carry the can if a project fails to meet its appropriate objectives or succeeds in achieving the wrong ones.

Looking into the Distance (1993)

Part 3:   Looking into the Distance (1993)

Gerry Abbott
Mike Beaumont

The single remaining Dunford seminar in the period under review introduced a new topic, the 1993 theme being *Language Issues in Distance Education*. A single seminar might be thought insufficient to warrant adding a third part to this book, but we consider that in the context of global development Distance Education (DE) has such potential that it merits a whole section to itself.

By the time of writing (1996) the concept of DE has already become better known and its practice more widespread. Not that it was by any means a new phenomenon at the time of the seminar: correspondence courses had become popular in Europe and the USA as far back as the late 1800s; with the advent of radio the BBC and other networks were soon broadcasting, at home and abroad, educational programmes that included language lessons; and by 1969 Britain had an operational Open University whose techniques included the use of television. But although the use of various media to disseminate knowledge was not new, the concept of DE had become more clearly defined. Keegan's (1990) list of its characteristics might serve as a working definition of good DE practice. He describes it as a system in which (we paraphrase):

1) the education is not private study but learning that is guided by an educational organisation;
2) teacher and learner are usually not in each other's physical presence;
3) teacher and learner are linked by written and/or electronic media;
4) the learner can communicate both with the teacher and with other learners; and
5) teacher and learner may occasionally meet.

By that definition DE would appear to be a poor substitute for face-to-face methods. Why then have DE courses for ELT proliferated over the last ten years? It is difficult not to be cynical in answering this question. The few institutions in the state sector of the British education system that were running ELT training courses in the mid-1960s had three main sources of students. The first was teachers from overseas; the second group was British teachers working abroad – directly employed by local institutions, whether in the state or private sector, or by UK-based organisations such as the British Council or one of the main private sector institutions which operate internationally; the third source was British teachers working in schools in the UK, either serving as language support teachers for bilingual pupils in the state sector or as teachers of EFL in private language schools. Provision for these three groups increased within the state system, but even more so in the private sector. However, two factors, both economic, have affected the resourcing of these groups leading, we would argue, to the recent and rapid development of DE programmes in Britain.

The first was the decision by the British government in the early 1980s to increase substantially the fees paid by overseas students for higher education courses. The purpose was to encourage HE institutions to compensate for cuts in recurrent funding by recruiting more students from overseas. One result of this was that institutions which had not previously run courses for English language teachers recognised the potential of the market. Courses mushroomed and competition for students intensified. One long-term effect of this competition has been the search by institutions for more flexible and 'user-friendly' modes of course delivery; hence, amongst other developments, DE. The second factor was the general economic climate. Up to the mid-1980s many of the teachers in all three groups had been able to obtain some support for their studies. Teachers in the British state sector had been able to apply for secondment, their schools obtaining some government support for their replacement. The successful schools in the private sector had been able to earmark some funds for in-service training. There were scholarships for British teachers working abroad and for overseas students, either from their own governments or institutions, or from aid budgets administered by the British Council or the ODA. By the end of the 1980s things had begun to change. The recession and cuts in public funding both in Britain and overseas reduced the funds available for in-service teacher education. Professionally, however, the need for training and for further qualifications had not diminished. Indeed, political developments in certain parts of the world, notably China and Central and Eastern Europe, had created substantial new opportunities. DE programmes provided an economical solution both for individual teachers faced with paying for their own professional development and for funding bodies still keen on stimulating educational innovation.

Though important for understanding the context in which Dunford participants debated the issue of DE, this pragmatic and essentially economic perspective is unduly narrow, first because it concentrates on the British dimension and second because it undervalues the educational potential of DE programmes. The 1993 Dunford participants included representatives not only of Britain's Open University but also of the Indira Gandhi National Open University, and at this point it is perhaps useful to distinguish 'distance education' from 'open learning'. The two concepts overlap a great deal, of course, but the latter term emphasises the loosening of those restrictions usually place upon a learner, restrictions as to who has access to the education on offer, what is studied and how and for how long, and even how the learner is assessed. Bearing in mind the theme of 'development' that runs through the preceding pages, it is worth dwelling upon the immense potential of open learning in any process of 'empowerment'. Snell (Hodgson, Mann and Snell 1987: 166–70) clearly recognises the possibilities.

> When conceived of as development, open learning is a matter of removing the constraints on a learner . . . (. . .) By conceiving of open learning in terms of development dissemination we may in fact achieve an educational provision that not only has its roots in the individual's creation of his or her own meaning and understanding but is also widely accessible and available.

Although, therefore, DE programmes have invariably arisen out of economic necessity, the notion of 'empowerment' is frequently advanced as a philosophical reason for their existence. Where DE comes close to open learning and many of the constraints to which Snell refers are removed, this argument may be justified. However, for this to be the case DE programmes need to address a number of issues. First, there is an understandable tendency for distance learning tasks to be 'objective' and 'closed'. Distance educators need to make sure that feedback on tasks, while being both clear and helpful, is not professionally prescriptive. Second, since professional development feeds on interaction, programmes need to work hard to counter the 'isolation' factor felt by many distance students. Third, DE invariably means following a course in order to gain a qualification. The concern of course providers for reliable assessment can also be a constraining factor on professional outcomes. Fourth, where distance materials are provided by institutions outside the educational context of the participants, sensitivity needs to be shown to local conditions, priorities and values. Finally, with the rapid development of technology, we need to ensure that the benefits of DE do not simply accrue to those with the resources to pay for them.

Meanwhile, as the world has been busy developing and exploiting new means of communication (from the postal system to the telephone to the radio to the TV to the computer to the Internet) the question of the *language* of communication has been largely neglected. Given the necessary installations, the means make it possible to send sophisticated messages to any part of the globe and to receive responses; nevertheless, for most of the world's poor such systems will not offer 'open learning' until the messages are sent, and the replies monitored, in their own languages. Once again, political as well as economic questions arise. Will Ministries of Education be willing to open up learning experiences by making use of the learner's own language? If so, do the necessary personnel and appropriate materials yet exist? If not, how are they to be produced? Where they do exist, will the learners and their tutors have any freedom to establish their own aims, curricula and procedures? And with regard to assessment, will the learner's certificated achievements be given due recognition?

One does not have to agree totally with Phillipson (see Section 8.3 of this book) to acknowledge the growth of linguistic imperialism and anglo-centricity in Britain's aid activities. The former is practised *within* most of the recipient (and some of the donor) countries by governments intent on achieving internal cohesion by means of cultural suppression, and both are practised unaggressively by aid agencies such as the British Council, which in spreading British culture abroad is simply fulfilling the terms of its royal charter. We could not help noticing, for example, the opening paragraph of a publicity document issued by the Council's own Language and Development Consultancy Group.

Language and Development

Why is language important?

● All development projects, whatever their focus, ultimately depend on effective communication.

● Neglecting language training endangers effective in-country and overseas training.

● Effective language training yields many benefits:

to projects themselves
to staff involved in projects
to society at large

The truth of these statements appears to be self-evident until you realise that 'language' means 'English'. We also could not help contrasting this document with a decision made in 1814 by the directors of that eminently imperialistic institution, The Honourable East India Company. Having just been given an annual grant for 'the introduction and promotion of a knowledge of the sciences among the inhabitants of the British territories in India', the directors decided to spend much of it encouraging their younger staff – no, not to teach English – to study Sanskrit:

> We are informed that there are in the Sanskrit language many excellent systems of ethics with codes of laws and compendiums of the duties to every class of the people, the study of which might be useful to those natives who may be destined for the judicial department of government. There are also many tracts of merit, we are told, on the virtues of drugs and plants, and on the application of them in medicine, the knowledge of which might prove desirable to European practitioners; and there are treatises on astronomy, mathematics, including geometry and algebra, which, though they may not add new lights to European science, might be made to form links of communication between the natives and the gentlemen in

our service, . . . and by such intercourse the natives might gradually be led to adopt the modern improvements in these and other sciences. (Quoted by Thomas, 1891:24)

True, the grant was a large one, Sanskrit was a classical language rather than a vernacular, and there was a body of indigenous written literature to use as a starting-point – hardly a typical set of factors in overseas development contexts. But the Company's intention in this instance was surely a commendable one, and the fact that little came of it was the fault not of the proposers but of an anglocentric policy implemented soon afterwards. The point that concerns us here is that given sufficient funds a highly experienced company that virtually ruled over British India considered it worthwhile to reverse the usual flow of information in order to 'form links of communication' so that people 'might gradually be led to adopt . . . modern improvements' – a development policy that we consider deserves further consideration, not least in the context of Distance Education.

9.0   Language Issues in Distance Education

GERRY ABBOTT and MIKE BEAUMONT

We begin with a survey of some of the major educational and logistical problems that DE faces in 'the developing world'. Turner's field of reference is English-medium education, especially within the formal educational systems of Africa south of the Sahara; much of what he says, however, is valid in any context. The failures of primary education in anglophone Africa, where English is a passport into the modern sector, lead him to conclude that non-formal education (including DE – presumably in the medium of English) may be the only way of creating equal opportunities for all.

Dodds then deals with non-formal adult education projects as carried out for different purposes in three nations: in Ghana, mother-tongue literacy courses in fifteen local languages; in Pakistan, rural education – presumably carried out in the national language, Urdu; and in Namibia, English by Radio for teachers, English being the recently designated national language. He ends with four very down-to-earth questions, answers to which would go some way towards the realisation of 'equal opportunities for all'.

Smith's contribution serves to give us a salutary reminder that, whatever the input that DE might deliver to a learner, it will be the recipient's own learning preferences that largely determine the quality of intake. Smith's dimensions of cognitive style (holist-analytic, verbaliser-imager) should of course be seen as clines rather than as mutually exclusive polarities: one can learn both holistically and analytically (for example, by a combination of 'look-say' and 'phonic' methods) and a visual image can undoubtedly reinforce the spoken or written word.

There follow descriptions of two DE programmes for teachers of English, both mounted in British universities. Walsh's very practical contribution concentrates on the nuts and bolts of overcoming the distancing effect and producing appropriate materials; and it is encouraging to find Edge and Ellis focusing on the *empowerment* of the distant teacher, the course philosophy being the sharing of a 'spirit of development'.

Webber closes this book with a succinct summary of the forward-looking observations of the 1993 Dunford participants. They clearly believed DE capable of catering for the individual's educational needs and wants, and that 'the language requirements of students could be met exactly and efficiently'.

We would add our hope that 'language requirements' does not simply mean 'English requirements'. Indeed, we wonder whether our thinking about *societal* development projects might benefit from a consideration of that branch of psychology which deals with *individual* needs. Where classical behaviourism assumed that a person was little more than a physical mechanism seeking to satisfy selfish ends, humanistic psychology objected that this view failed to account for many of the most important qualities in human life: for altruism, the sense of wonder, aesthetic enjoyment, mystical experiences and so on. It was felt necessary to incorporate *human* values into the psychologist's scheme of things, and Maslow proposed a hierarchy of needs: above the basic 'deficiency needs' (for example, for shelter and sustenance) which can be satisfied from outside, there were layers of 'being-needs' that constitute a desire for the fulfilment of one's perceived potential, a desire for 'self-actualisation' (see Maslow 1954). It is possible to view the development policies pursued by First World donors hitherto as attempts to deal with deficiency needs. We suggest that while continuing to acknowledge the importance of satisfying these, future policies might try to take the overlying needs much more into account. The implications for DE might be startling and far-reaching; but so might the effects.

9.1   The logistics of distance language teaching

JOHN TURNER

I learned to be sceptical about the value of distance language teaching over 40 years ago. In 1953, I was visiting primary schools in northern Nigeria to see the use to which English teaching by radio was being put in some of the few classrooms which had radio receivers. In one of them I saw small children imitating perfectly the received pronunciation of the radio teacher, only to be corrected in turn by their Nigerian teacher, who insisted on 'correcting' their pronunciation and getting them to imitate his own impenetrable accent. Not only did this demonstrate the superior skills of children in language acquisition, but it also showed beyond any doubt the key role of the teacher where oral language skills are being taught by distance methods as a supplementary resource in the classroom. The experience had remained my reference point in all discussions of English language teaching by distance learning methods.

It can, however, be argued persuasively that in order to evaluate the potential of mass instructional methods, we cannot afford to concentrate on one particular situation. We are dealing in effect with a number of continua. The first of these is the continuum of school provision. We are all aware that in all developing countries there is a tremendous range of educational provision, even if we exclude the private provision which is generally available in the capital cities to the richer citizens and the international community. The physical provision is sometimes the equal of, and occasionally superior to, similar schools in developed countries, and the teachers are usually the best qualified in the system. Such schools can easily be identified by the density of new cars clustered outside the school as the children leave at the end of the day.

At the other end of the continuum are rural schools, usually of poor construction with a little crude furniture, and sometimes with no furniture; sometimes they have no windows and no teaching equipment other than cracked or pitted blackboards. It is by no means uncommon to find that the school buildings are no longer adequate for the growing numbers of children and that classes have to be taught under shade trees. In wet weather, teaching is hardly possible at all. Often children walk several miles in each direction to obtain this poor educational experience, mediated to them by unqualified or poorly qualified teachers. Schools may be situated at all points of this continuum, the average varying from country to country. In general, however, there is a great preponderance of schools at the more deprived end of the scale.

The second continuum is a continuum of teaching ability. This ability is not necessarily identical with, but is closely related to, the amount of education and training of the teacher. In many countries the proportion of unqualified teachers, which had fallen during the 1960s and 1970s, has been rising again during the 1980s and 1990s as the population increases and the financial position of the countries declines. Chance factors, however also come into play. When I was teaching at the Nigerian College of Arts, Science and Technology at Zaria, during the 1950s, I was impressed by two students in successive years, whose English was remarkably fluent and with an accent which was so typically English that it seemed almost a parody. On enquiry, I discovered that they had both been taught in a remote bush school in the far north of the country where there just happened to be a primary school teacher who, because of his own education at the hands of a well-disposed expatriate family, was able to have a tremendous influence on the language acquisition of all these pupils who came within his care. One of the students subsequently used his language skills by becoming a successful politician, while the other entered the Nigerian Broadcasting Corporation and became nationally known, particularly in news and current affairs programmes.

Having recognised the immense variety of schools and teachers in each country and the way in which countries differ from each other, it is still clear that there is an urgent need for distance learning programmes in English language throughout the world. As I have indicated above, my main interest is in developing countries and here the need is clearly immense. The following reasons may be regarded as particularly acute.

- In spite of the Jomtien Conference's emphasis on Education for All by the Year 2000, there are still many countries where, at the present time, less than half of primary children attend school. In Ethiopia, for example, 20–25 per cent of children attend school, though in some parts of the country, the percentage is below double figures. Even in countries with a high primary school attendance rate, the quality of their educational experience may be poor. Kenya, for example, has enrolled 94 per cent of its primary-age children in schools but 40 per cent of primary teachers are unqualified. For this and other reasons, only 38 per cent of girls and 46 per cent of boys complete the entire primary school programme. Throughout Africa therefore, there are very large numbers of children who do not secure even a complete primary school education and whose educational deficits must be made good by some other way later in their lives. Moreover, for those in school a distance learning component could hardly fail to enrich their learning.

- The birth-rate has still not steadied, let alone declined, in most developing countries. This is one reason why the per capita expenditure on schooling is falling in virtually every country in Africa and why the proportion of the age group in schools is also declining. It is difficult to envisage any likely change in this pattern, though the impact of AIDS, both on child enrolment and on teacher supply, is difficult to evaluate.

- Many countries in Africa are in a precarious financial position. Structural readjustment programmes may, in the medium to long-term improve the economic position. In the short term, however, there is little prospect of the decline in the percentage of GNP devoted to education being reversed.

- The consequence of all these factors is that many children are not accessing good quality primary education at all and that for many of those who do leave school without completing a full primary education programme, their only chance of acquiring the necessary language skills is by taking part in non-formal, including distance learning, education. The percentage of the adult population which will require non-formal educational provision is also continuing to increase.

Taking into account the magnitude of the problem, one is driven to the conclusion that the needs cannot be met by traditional teaching methods, whether formal or non-formal. An entirely new approach has to be adopted. The only feasible methodology is distance learning, though our knowledge of language teaching at a distance is barely adequate for our needs.

Moreover, the number of specialists in distance learning methodology currently available is tiny in proportion to demand. The number who have had experience in producing and directing successful programmes is even smaller. Consequently, the main difficulty in the great majority of countries that are most dependent upon distance learning solutions is the acute shortage of skilled personnel. It is one thing to be able to talk about strategies in distance learning; it is quite another to be able to sit down and give the extremely detailed assistance required to enable subject specialists to convey their expertise in the appropriate form.

In developing successful programmes, we need to be aware of the different situations in which such materials may be used. In the first place, distance learning materials may be used to supplement teaching. In other situations, a variable amount of teaching may be provided to supplement the distance learning programme, while in others there may be no teaching input whatever, the whole programme being conveyed by distance learning. While some materials could be used in all three situations, it is clear that different approaches and packages would be needed for each of these situations.

Another major problem relates to the most desirable media for specific courses. Commercial correspondence courses have relied for the most part on the printed word, coupled with an efficient postal service and skilled in-house tutors. The British Open University model, which is an example of a highly successful programme with relatively small dropout rates and a high success rate, has accustomed us to think of multimedia programmes including not only printed work and distance tutors but also support through radio and television and their accompanying recorded equivalents.

These programmes are also supported by residential courses, some of which, such as certain science programmes, are compulsory for all students. These techniques have been adopted by a number of programmes in other countries that have also used satellite technology in order to increase the market. New media are also becoming available with an apparently unlimited potential for distance education, for example CD ROM, computer-assisted learning and interactive video programmes.

The fact remains, however, that for most of the potential users of distance education, advanced technologies are virtually inapplicable. Even in those countries that have used them, questions arise as to whether the money would be better spent on increasing the users of the system, rather than on providing high-cost resources for a small fraction of those who need to learn. This implies that the solutions we are seeking should depend on low-cost techniques as much as possible and especially on printed materials. Indeed, even with printed materials, choices may have to be made between varieties of programmes with different costs. An inevitable trade-off has to be made between spreading distance learning packages of lower quality around a much greater market, and making programmes with a high success rate and a high cost available to a smaller proportion of the population. Such decisions may vary according to the nature of the audience and whether it is indeed a mass audience or a select audience to which particular programmes are directed.

We must also differentiate between various legitimate purposes for distance learning. The one which tends to be uppermost in our minds is the purpose of making education available to students for whom there are insufficient teachers or for whom teachers cannot be afforded under a traditional system. A second purpose is to provide additional tools to teachers who are inadequately trained and who cannot teach to the required standard. A third is to extend the provision of learning to a very much larger number of people who are not registered students but who 'overhear' the studies provided for others. With some programmes (such as those in primary health care), the existence of the larger audience may make audio or video programme transmissions cost-effective, which would not be cost-effective if they were being provided only for registered students. Similarly, the provision of written or cassette-recorded materials to schools for class use by inadequately trained teachers may make the production of such materials financially viable where that would not be the case if one were only costing the provision of totally distance education programmes. It is necessary, therefore, in considering distance education in any particular situation, to provide a total strategy wherever this is possible, rather than a partial and narrowly focused one. What students appreciate in distance learning programmes includes the following:

1) Regular assignments which are rapidly marked and returned to the student. These help to maintain commitment, allow students to diagnose and monitor their own progress, and take some pressure off the final examination. The continuous assessment element is regarded by most students as of the utmost importance.

2) Support from locally based tutors where this can be organised. This, of course, can be a costly benefit unless a substantial number of students are grouped together.

3) Residential schools. Residence need not be of great length and should be directed where necessary to those aspects of the programme which it is difficult to undertake at home. Residential courses at the beginning of each unit are of particular value.

4) Student self-help groups. It is difficult to organise these, however, without central support, since individual students are unlikely to know which other individuals near them are undertaking the same studies in the same subjects at the same time. Such groups, however, are very highly motivating and are a low cost means of providing remedial help. Central assistance may also be required to locate suitable premises for self-help groups if none of the homes of the participants are suitable for informal meetings.

Language teaching suffers from some of the same problems as science teaching by distance learning methods. Perhaps it is largely for that reason that we have acquired less experience in these areas than in other subjects. Just as it is essential for a scientist to have laboratory practice under skilled supervision, so some areas of language instruction can best be undertaken in a tutorial or workshop situation. This is especially the case in a second language situation where the models of language available both in the community and from classroom teachers may be detrimental to the learner. Even in the case of the teaching of French in primary schools in Britain, where corruption by inadequate second language speakers is not a problem, direct language teaching through unsuitably prepared teachers has proved to be an inadequate way of teaching the language. Moreover, language skills, whether those of the learners or of their teachers, require constant refreshment if they are not to deteriorate.

As in most distance education, it is desirable to target programmes as precisely as possible. In many countries, such as Namibia, it is teachers who are in greatest need of help so that they might, in turn, mediate their knowledge to their pupils. As in all successful skills teaching, it is desirable to use a competency-based technique. The first step in an improvement programme for teachers would be to analyse the language skills required for primary teachers at each level of instruction, bearing in mind the class books (if any) currently being used in schools. The knowledge and skills required would then be placed in hierarchical order and dealt with in discrete but ordered programmes which might be taught with varying degrees of support. Each package should have a pre-test and a post-test: at the start of each package, the learners would be tested to see whether or not they already have competence in the contents of that package. If they have, they move on to the next package without receiving the earlier one until they reach a point at which substantial deficits began to occur. At this point, the teaching starts. Teachers who already have the skills taught in later packages would not need to receive further instruction in them. After each successful testing, whether with or without the learning package, the appropriate competence would be marked in the competency grid ('passport') possessed by each teacher. It is hoped that when the entire course had been completed for any given level of teaching, the teacher would receive a certificate together with some small salary increment.

The advantage of such a programme is that is can be taught efficiently with only those parts of the course being taught which each individual teacher specifically needs. Moreover, the support and face-to-face teaching for each component, where this is available, could be undertaken by specialist teams at weekend courses or during vacation periods. The face-to-face support for different packages could be allocated to different groups, including NGOs, for different sections of the work and for students living in different regional areas. Such a programme could be economical and effective if the necessary preliminary analysis is well conducted and if the administration of the programme is efficient. In comparison with the normal 'blunderbuss' approach to nationwide language improvement, this might well prove successful and cost-effective. Certainly, every programme as it is put in place must at least aim at the greatest amount of instructive support that can be achieved. In summary, I believe that the following guidelines should inform all our work in distance education.

1) Even where there is abundant access to the media and sufficient technical assistance to maintain the equipment required, a minimal approach should nevertheless be maintained. Only those media which are absolutely essential for the success of a programme should be used. There is no country that is so rich that it can afford to waste scarce

resources. Where a very large increment of cost is necessary to provide a very small increment of knowledge or skill, the necessity of that increment should be closely studied.

2) There should be a realistic attempt to evaluate the existing resources of the country in terms of the technical infrastructure. If the postal system is totally unreliable, alternative means must be found of distributing course materials. If radio transmission is poor, it is impossible to rely on audio assistance as an integral part of the programmes though it may be used for purpose of enrichment. The same is true *a fortiori* for the visual media.

3) If it proves necessary to use audio cassettes as part of the programme, the repair facilities must be realistically surveyed. It may well prove necessary in some countries to provide a central servicing facility as part of the distance learning infrastructure.

4) It is wasteful of effort if teachers and lecturers, however highly skilled, are asked to write distance learning materials when they have not been specifically trained to understand the distinction between textbooks, lecture notes and distance learning materials. A high priority should therefore be given to the employment of distance learning specialists who can both train and work with subject specialists as they undertake their work.

5) There is no point in producing materials from scratch if materials already exist which can be used without adaptation: there is no point even in adapting materials which are already completely adequate for the job. Similarly, there is no point in writing new materials if existing materials in another country can be effectively adapted. Different subject areas and indeed different topics within subjects have highly differential cultural loading and it is necessary to diagnose carefully the needs of each module.

6) Proper attention should be paid to the learning needs specific to the job for which the students are being prepared. In particular where the courses are part of a teacher training or upgrading programme, only those aspects of the subject should be taught which are essential for the teachers to do their work. The principle of selectivity in subject matter is important in every subject in every country and too little attention is paid to the principles of such selectivity. What is relevant and what is irrelevant must be clearly distinguished from each other.

The guidelines mentioned above are by no means subject specific. There are in addition general organisational criteria which must be met whatever the subject, level and purpose of the teaching may be. Among these criteria are, for example, the following.

1) Political will. If the politicians (who for many jobs, including teaching, represent the employers) believe that distance education is an inferior form of learning, it is unlikely either that adequate financial provision will be made or that the motivation for securing sound learning exists.

2) The availability of recurrent resources. Nothing is more dismal than for students to embark on a course which cannot be continued because of lack of finance. This implies that self-sustainability should be built into the programme so that it does not remain a constant drain on the education budget.

3) Immaculate administration, an essential prerequisite of success in distance learning. Great care must be taken in the design of headquarters and regional offices and in the choice of hard- and software needs.

4) Training of all those involved in the distance education programme. Even those who are well prepared in distance education technology (and there are hardly any in most countries) will still need specific training in the aims and administrative patterns of each specific course which is established.

5) Remuneration of all part-time tutors, most of whom will also be full-time teachers or lecturers. Without this the programme will fail.

6) Quality assurance mechanisms built into the system. The work of every tutor/marker must be regularly and randomly evaluated, as should all other aspects of the programme such as the continued writing of new materials which takes place and the efficiency of the record maintenance.

At the beginning of this paper, I expressed concern about the poor and deteriorating position of primary education in most countries in Africa and have come to the conclusion that for many people there will be no alternative to non-formal and especially distance education if the aims of Jomtien are to be realised. This gives a special urgency to the solution of the many problems in the training of teachers of English in all those countries in which English is an important means of entry into the modern sector. Improvement and greater accessibility of English teaching is not just an issue of improving knowledge and skills but also has important applications for the creation of equal opportunities for all.

9.2   Distance learning for non-formal education

TONY DODDS

Introduction: a clarification of terms

Literacy education by correspondence quite rightly seems to be a contra-diction in concepts. Yet for many, non-formal education is thought to consist mainly of adult literacy classes and distance education is dominated by correspondence courses. So how can distance education make a significant contribution to non-formal education? The purpose of my presentation is to suggest that it can and to explore some of the ways and circumstances in which this can be achieved. But let us first clear away the misconceptions with which I started.

What is non-formal education – other than a rather unsatisfactory phrase?   Most people correctly see it primarily as adult basic education. This does include adult literacy and in this way is concerned with language issues, but it also includes such things as health education, agricultural education, basic skills training and community education. It is concerned with organised learning whose primary objective is not examinations, which does not necessarily follow school curricula and which often takes place outside and independent of the traditional institutions of education. It is concerned with life improvement rather than qualifications.

Most of my examples in this paper will be drawn from this kind of education. But it also covers a wide range of learning aimed at people whose education is beyond the basic. It has included, in the past, for example, education aimed to facilitate Sweden's decision many decades ago to change from driving on the left to driving on the right – and that particular example used distance education. My own examples will also include an English language course for Namibian teachers, which is not aimed at an examination. So non-formal education can cover a wide range of subjects and levels.

What is distance education?   This too is an unsatisfactory phrase, but one we appear to be stuck with at least for the time being. When the IEC started in 1971, we talked about 'three-way teaching' – a combination of correspondence courses, educational broadcasting and occasional face-to-face tuition. In the 1970s our sister organisation, the National Extension College, invented 'flexi-study'. The Open University popularised the phrase 'open learning', which might eventually oust 'distance education' though it is at present largely limited to the UK in its popularity.

All these phrases are in my opinion preferable to 'distance education' because they stress flexibility, the extension and opening up of education rather than the distance between teachers and learners; they put emphasis on purpose rather than on technology. So I wish to avoid purism and pedantry in my interpretation of distance education in the examples I use to point to the conclusions I hope we will draw. In fact, some may wish to query whether these are examples of distance education at all.

What will the presentation consist of?   I must point out that I am not primarily concentrating on language issues in this paper. However, insofar as non-formal education includes language issues, they are also raised in what follows. First I will present three case studies: a functional literacy project in Ghana, a functional education project for rural areas in Pakistan and the English language programme for teachers in Namibia to which I referred earlier. Two of these are specifically concerned with language teaching. In the first two, we will look at videos about the project and I will summarise some conclusions from recent evaluations. In the last, we will listen to a radio programme and consider evidence of the results. Finally, I will round off the presentation by inviting you to discuss four questions, which I see as central issues in an examination of the potential of distance education for non-formal education.

'Breaking the culture of silence': Ghana's national functional literacy campaigns

Background: Ghana had run quite large-scale adult literacy campaigns both before Independence in 1957 and in the Nkrumah era of the 1960s. But disillusionment with Nkrumah led also to widespread disillusionment with literacy, community development and adult non-formal education in the 1970s and 1980s. Evidence suggests that many lapsed back into illiteracy in the absence of reading material, and that adult illiteracy grew. When Gerry Rawlings came to power, the cry for mass education regained popularity. This was reinforced by the World Bank's belief in literacy as a prerequisite for development and by its enforcement of economic readjustment policies in return for loans. When recognition dawned that readjustment to Reaganite/Thatcherite economics could lead to social disaster and starvation in rural areas, the concept of PASCAD dawned (Programme of Actions to mitigate the Social Costs of Adjustment!) and the Ghana government skilfully enlisted international donor agency support for its national literacy plans, as an essential element in its drive for economic recovery. Distance education techniques – or at least the use of radio – became incorporated in these plans almost by accident. Ghana's literacy campaigns are being conducted in fifteen Ghanaian languages. Primers, radio programmes and post-literacy materials also therefore have to be written and produced and supervised in all these languages.

Assessment: A recent IEC/Ministry of Education review of the ODA pilot support programme concluded that, while enormous logistical problems remain in the path of achieving large-scale improvements in adult literacy coverage, great strides had been made in creating motivation, providing primers, organising classes and making large numbers of people literate. It recognised the important role that radio had played in the mobilisation of support for the literacy classes and in promoting the functional themes of the campaigns, but it also recognised the limited contribution it had made to the actual learning taking place in class and the difficulty in measuring its overall impact on the levels of literacy achieved in those areas where radio coverage was available. In its proposals for improvement the review laid stress on the need for organised post-literacy activities and urged the wider use of rural newspapers as well as specially developed post-literacy readers as the basis for organised reading clubs, and post-literacy learning forums. It suggested radio could and should also play a more direct 'teaching' role in such forums. In these ways, it suggested that distance education methods could play vital roles in mobilisation, promotion of functional themes and, especially, in providing the basis for post-literacy activities.

'Functional education for rural areas': Low cost, appropriate media for basic function education in Pakistan

Background: The Allama Iqbal Open University of Pakistan is an open university – or indeed any kind of university – with a difference. It has, since its foundation as the People's Open University during the elder Bhutto's regime, had a commitment to provide education for the 'uplift of the rural masses', most of whom remain illiterate. So it has sought to develop programmes to cater for illiterate and newly literate adults. The ODA, early in AIOU's history, undertook to support an action research experiment, and establish effective distance education methodologies to provide functional education for the predominantly illiterate adults in village communities. In order to do so, the project recognised the need to find out what the rural masses needed for their educational uplift. Hence it developed (and retains) a commitment to social research as an essential part of the project at all stages – needs assessment, materials development and testing, evaluation and replication.

Assessment   Evaluation studies, both internal and external, at the end of the pilot project in 1985 and 1986 assessed that the methodologies developed were effective and should be replicated on the same model in other parts of the country as a permanent programme of the university. The programme has continued in this form under the management of the University's Bureau of University Extension and Social Programmes from 1985 to date. A more recent evaluation, while stressing that the methodology continues to provide effective learning at pre-literacy level, points out that these methods continue to be used on a very limited scale, failing to achieve the economies of scale of which distance education is supposed to be capable. It again proposes (as did the 1985 evaluation) that, for its programmes to have a major impact, AIOU must find ways of working together with the major national extension and non-formal education agencies.

'Let's Speak English': a radio-led English language communication course for primary school teachers in Namibia

Background   When Namibia achieved independence in 1990, the new government moved to implement the language policy that had been worked out in exile, and endorsed by all the major political forces in the country. This was to make English the country's national language and to introduce it as the language of instruction for primary grade 4 onwards. But most primary school teachers in Namibia had very poor communication skills in English. The Ministry of Education invited the ODA to support and 'English by Radio' project to help alleviate this problem. A series of workshops were run jointly by the Ministry, with the support of the Namibian Broadcasting Corporation and by the IEC, with the support of BBC's English by Radio and Television Department. A course was planned, written and produced consisting of a year's worth of weekly radio programmes, and two accompanying self-study textbooks. It was planned and organised that these materials would predominantly be used in study groups of teachers meeting regularly in their own communities, assisted by selected and trained group leaders. The course was first offered in 1992, on its completion, and again in 1993.

Assessment   Unfortunately, the IEC was not allowed to carry out a detailed evaluation study of the project, on the grounds that, having been involved in setting the project up, it would be incapable of setting up an objective evaluation. As a result, no detailed evaluation has been published, though an initial evaluation was carried out by the British Council in Namibia. (Initial hearsay results of this evaluation suggests that quite large numbers used the course in one form or another – though many had difficulty systematically following the radio programmes, and the study groups were spasmodic or non-existent. It is hoped that a more detailed and up-to-date assessment can be given in discussion.)

Key issues

The following questions seem to me to be the key issues. What can we conclude from these case studies by way of guidance in answering them?

a)   Does distance education have a role to play *i)* in literacy and numeracy education and *ii)* in adult basic and non formal education more generally? If so, what?

b)   What methods and media of distance education are appropriate for adult basic and non-formal education? What are the essential elements for success and effectiveness?

c)   How can programmes be organised which extend these approaches to 'the masses' and thereby realise economies of scale and mass impact?

d)   In what ways, if at all, do distance education methods lend themselves particularly well to non-formal language teaching?

Subsequent to consideration of the case studies, there was broad discussion of a number of general, overarching issues relating to the nature, role and practices of distance education. Various questions were considered. These included the following.

● *Where should the decision-making process start in considering how to proceed with a distance education project? The argument put forward was that the process should begin with consideration of the objective. Thereafter, the processes, methods and media needed to attain the objectives could be considered. These might – or might not – include distance education methods. Subsequently, the point was made that invoking the notion of 'distance' in any circumstances might well be a total distraction. The key question is appropriateness and effectiveness of methods and approaches. If using radio or television or local newspapers and so on is appropriate (with or without a teacher), then that approach should be adopted.*

● *What should the nature of the end-product of a distance learning programme be? Does there need to be an examination and a certificate of attainment or is the actual achievement itself (for example, of becoming literate, or being successful in farming), sufficient 'end-product' motivation? (It was noted that the question of certification or success, as desired end-products to participation in a programme, was a matter of considerable debate in South Africa.)*

● *When should evaluation of a distance learning project take place? There was evidence that some evaluations were undertaken too soon after the completion of a project. A longer-term view was often necessary, though it was important to recognise that the longer one is away from the actual implementation, the more difficult it is to measure the results of a programme or, indeed, to isolate the results from other possible contributory factors. This applied particularly to socio-economic and environmental charges.*

● *What sorts of external constraints directly affect the implementation and quality of distance education provision? A number of factors were mentioned in this respect, with one being developed in some detail relating to the uncertainty, and even suspicion, with which some authorities, including politicians and governments, viewed distance education. It was also suggested that in some cases distance education, on the contrary, might be used by some authorities as a safety valve and as a way of diverting difficult educational pressures.*

An interesting concluding observation was made concerning the funding of distance education. It was suggested that the potential demonstrated by distance education (as evidenced by the projects under consideration here), justified a reconsideration of how resources allocated to education generally might be redistributed to provide distance education with greater support than hitherto and thus enable it to convert its potential into a major and real force for change and development.

9.3   Cognitive styles and the design of instructional materials
EUGENE SADLER-SMITH

The effectiveness of instructional materials is determined by many factors. For example:
● the characteristics of the learner (What is their habitual mode of thinking and processing information?);
● the mode of presentation of the instruction (Is information presented as words or pictures or an equal balance of both?); and
● the organisation of the contents of instruction (Is information presented repeatedly at greater and greater levels of detail? Are the links between discrete topics and the learner's existing knowledge made clear?)

The characteristics of the learner
Many different terms have been used to describe differences between individual learners. A simple scheme based on Gorham (1986) and Curry (1983) gives a threefold classification:

- instructional preferences (What method of learning does an individual prefer, e.g. group based, individualised, etc?)
- learning styles (What approaches does an individual adopt in a new learning situation, e.g. active, reflective, conceptual or pragmatic?)
- cognitive styles (How does an individual habitually represent and process information in the memory during the learning process, e.g. in words or pictures or both, in wholes or in parts?)

Verbal–imagery dimension of cognitive style

The verbal–imagery dimension of style is a description of an individual's habitual mode of representation of information during thinking. Verbalisers 'represent' information in words; imagers on the other hand, when they read, listen to or consider information, experience fluent spontaneous and frequent mental pictures (Riding 1991).

Holist–analytical dimension of cognitive style

The holist–analytical dimension of cognitive style is a description of the habitual way in which an individual processes information: some individuals (described as analytics) will process information into its component parts; others (described as holists) will retain a global view of information. For holists there is the danger that the distinction between the parts of a topic may become blurred. For analytics the separation of the whole into its parts may mean that one aspect of the whole may be focused on at the expense of the others and its overall importance exaggerated.

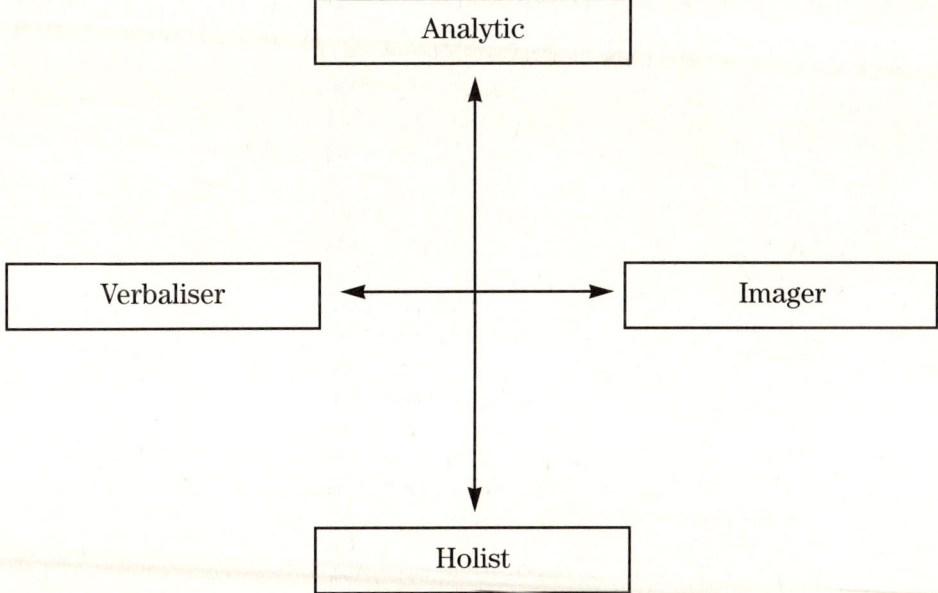

Figure 1   The two dimensions of cognitive style

These dimensions may affect learning in two separate ways, as shown in Fig. 1:

- the verbal–imagery dimension of cognitive style determines the most appropriate mode of presentation of information for a particular individual (e.g. textual, diagrammatic/pictorial); and
- the holist–analytic dimension of cognitive style determines the most appropriate way in which the contents of instruction may be structured or organised (e.g. with or without a particular type of advance organiser).

Cognitive styles and learning performance

Since the holist–analytical and verbaliser–imager dimensions of cognitive style affect the processing and representation of information respectively, one may anticipate beneficial effects on learning performance if the mode and structure of that information is congruent with, or anticipates the weaknesses of, the learner's preferred mode of thinking.

Mode of presentation

It is possible to match the mode of presentation of information to the verbaliser–imager dimension of cognitive style. A model for the interaction of cognitive style, learning performance and mode of presentation has been suggested by Riding: imagers may be expected to benefit from the presentation of information in a diagrammatic or pictorial form; verbalisers may be expected to benefit from a textual presentation (Riding and Ashmore 1980; Riding, Buckle, Thompson and Haggar 1989). This model was not wholly supported by Riding and Douglas (1992) who investigated the effects of text with textual and diagrammatic supplements. Fig. 2 below shows the hypothetical interaction and that revealed by Riding and Douglas.

Hypothetical interaction

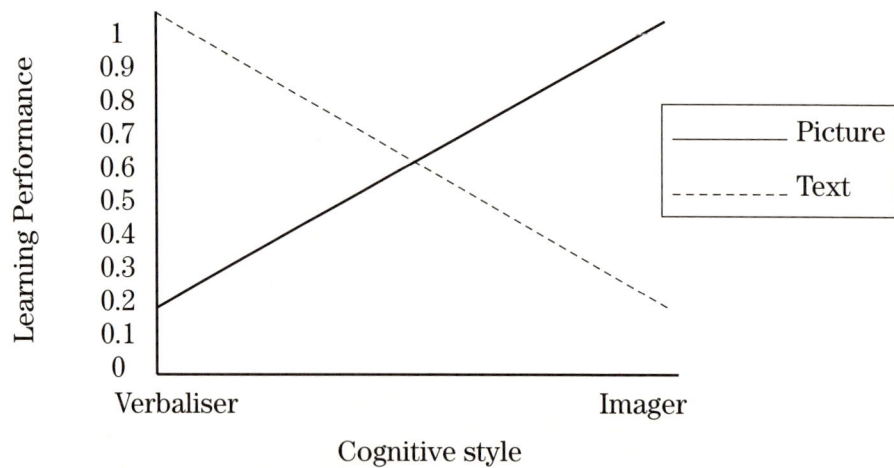

From Riding & Douglas (1992)

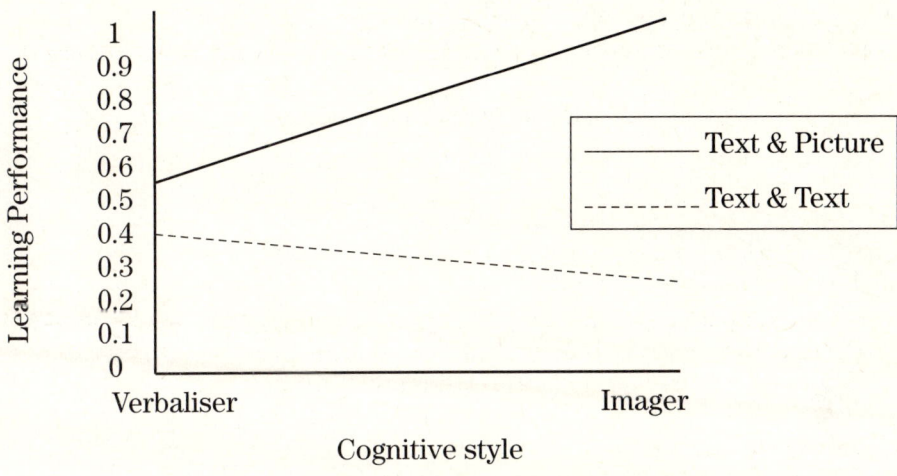

Figure 2   Interaction of verbaliser–imager dimension, mode of presentation and learning performance

Hence mode of presentation of information may be matched to the verbal–imagery dimension of cognitive style.

Structure of presentation

In the case of the holist–analytical dimension, the concept of matching instruction to the learner (as for example, in the presentation of information in a visual mode for imagers as shown in Fig. 2) does not apply. Both holist and analytical styles are not ideal in the sense that neither leads necessarily to the optimum organisation of the contents of memory, that is, an integrated version of the whole of a new piece of information, with links to the learner's existing knowledge. Therefore, in the case of the holist–analytical dimension, instruction should be designed in order to compensate for the deficiencies of each style so that an optimum organisation of the contents of memory may be achieved. It is suggested that an advance organiser may facilitate this linking of new information with that already in memory (Ausubel 1963). Furthermore, the present author would suggest that different types of advance organiser may be appropriate for the different cognitive style types. One may expect that:

- holists may benefit from an advance organiser which shows the structure of the content in terms of its divisions into parts (that is, an analyser-type organiser); and
- analytics may benefit from an advance organiser which gives a global view of the whole (that is, an overview-type organiser) – see Fig. 3.

Hence, to accommodate individual differences in cognitive style it may be necessary to:

- match instruction to the verbaliser–imager dimension;
- provide a compensatory strategy for the holist–analytical dimension.

Hypothetical interaction

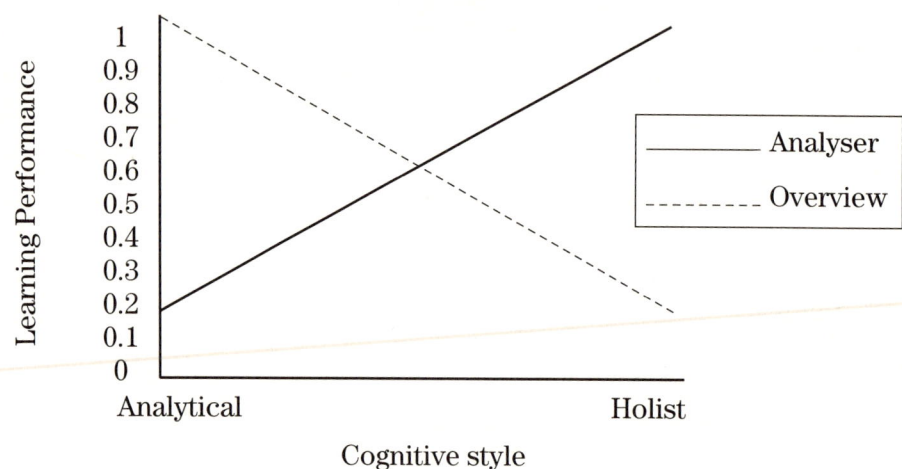

From Riding and Sadler-Smith (1992)

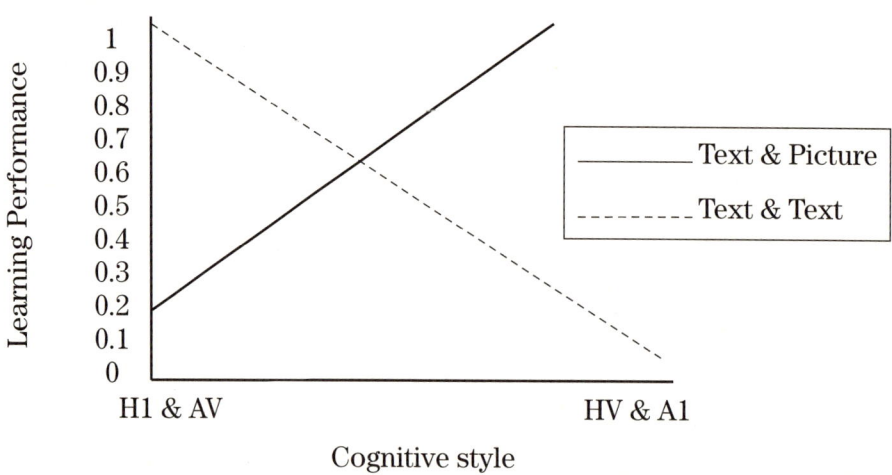

Figure 3   Interaction of holist–analytical dimension of cognitive style, mode of presentation and learning performance

Instructional prescriptions for the four cognitive style types

The model outlined above suggests that instructional prescriptions can be formulated to match the learner's cognitive style. The table below summarises the instructional prescriptions for the four cognitive style types.

	Holist verbaliser	Holist imager	Analytic verbaliser	Analytic imager
Textual mode	■		■	
Pictorial mode		■		■
Preview type organiser	■			
Linker type organiser		■	■	
Analyser type organiser	■	■		
Overview type organiser			■	■

Adapting instruction to the learner's cognitive style The cognitive style differences outlined above may be accommodated by the use of a variety of instructional media which may use a non-adaptive or an adaptive approach in the presentation, organisation and structure of the content of the instruction.

Adaptive approaches Adaptive approaches are designed to customise the instructional materials to particular cognitive style attributes. An adaptive approach would rely on the computer-based identification of a learner's cognitive style. The computer, acting as an 'intelligent tutoring system', could present instruction in the manner prescribed for the particular style of the individual learner.

Non-adaptive approaches Non-adaptive approaches cater for the whole range of cognitive style differences by:
● dual modes of presentation or content structures within a package, *or*
● the development of two or more sets of instructional materials of contrasting designs.

Contrasting designs Rather than try to accommodate style differences within the same package, it would be feasible to have two or more physically separate packages, each designed for particular cognitive styles. A number of instructional treatments would be necessary in order to accommodate both dimensions of cognitive style.

Balanced designs   This is a cognitive 'belt and braces' approach; a variety of modes of presentation and structures may be built into the design on the assumption that learners will focus on those attributes which best suit their preferred mode of thinking. However, it may be prudent for learners to be informed as to their cognitive style and advised as to which modes of aspects of the instructional materials are best suited to their style. Without proper advice there is the potential of a balanced design to be used in a way which is inappropriate to the style of the learner. Balanced designs may be delivered via the medium of the printed page or the computer screen.

England (1987: 13) in a discussion of Pask's (1976) learning style, suggest designers can make their materials more versatile by 'build[ing] different levels into their materials. The overall structure should have enough cohesion and coherence to allow a linear progression through the material, which would suit serialist [analytic] learners. But other levels . . . can be infused to offer holists and versatile students [analytic imagers and holist verbalisers] the opportunity to explore concepts in their own ways.'

The concept of the balanced design assumes that there will be no conflict or interference effects between simultaneous presentations in different modes. Further research is required to investigate the effectiveness of balanced designs.

Computer-based balanced designs   Presentations could consist of a mixture of text or diagrams. Alternatively, two or more modes of presentation could be available to the student, who is free to 'toggle' between the text version and the picture version of the teaching material. The structure of a topic, and hence holist analytical dimension of style, could be addressed in a number of ways:

- the learner could 'toggle' between a number of different types of organiser, for example, preview type or linker type, analyser or overview type, and focus on the one which he/she had been advised best suited his/her style; or
- the learner could be given the option to view a concept map which provides both a whole view and a breakdown of the topic into its parts; or
- the package could be designed with overview, outline and detail levels, each available at any one time for the learner to 'toggle' between.

Print-based balanced designs   The development of balanced print designs may be technically more difficult and the end product less elegant (as a result of the inherent inflexibility of print) than a computer-based design. However, within a balanced text design one could envisage:

- dual modes of presentation; and
- alternative content maps/advance organisers

Dual modes of presentation could be achieved by mapping text and picture/diagram on the same page or facing pages in a logical and consistent manner in order to facilitate learner access to the information. A sample page from a prototype balanced design and a template for the design of such a page are shown in the Appendix to this paper.

Alternative strategies   While it is recognised that both adaptive and non-adaptive approaches offer great potential for the improvement of learning effectiveness and efficiency, it is also acknowledged that it may not, for a wide variety of reasons (both technical and commercial) be possible to adapt instruction to the learner. If it is not possible for technical, pedagogical or commercial reasons to produce instruction to cater for all cognitive styles, then cognitive styles information may help to identify those individuals who, by virtue of their style, may not be able to succeed with certain tasks or with certain instructional treatments. For such individuals alternative or remedial instruction may be necessary. Through an awareness of how they learn, each individual can assume some responsibility for their own learning and take appropriate actions in those circumstances where learning is not taking place as effectively as it might.

Learners, under the guidance of a tutor/counsellor, could employ a variety of strategies in order to intervene in the learning process and accommodate their own cognitive style.

Conclusion

The holist–analytical and the verbaliser–imager dimensions of cognitive style may have important implications for the ways in which instruction is designed and delivered. Indeed a casual inspection of currently available self-instructional materials suggests little cognisance is taken of individual differences between learners. Hence it could be argued that conventional instructional design methodologies assume that individuals represent and process information in similar ways. A corollary of this is that the mode of presentation and structure of instructional materials should attempt to accommodate individual differences in cognitive style. A number models of varying degrees of technical complexity have been suggested here which describe how instructional materials may be adapted to individual differences in cognitive style. These differences could be accommodated by means of an instructional system capable of presenting information in a variety of ways using text, diagrams, still and moving photographic images, speech and sound in a manner appropriate to the user's cognitive style.

However, at the present time, the most practical approach would appear to be some form of balanced design in any medium or combination of media. The development of both non-adaptive and adaptive systems would be subject to commercial constraints. Further research and development work is required in designing and validating the hypothetical system described herein.

Appendix

Section	Sub-Sections	Section Contents	Picture/Diagram Window
Content header		Text Window	
		Activity Window	
Keywords		Location Bar	

Template

Combustion

What is Natural Gas?

Overview
Natural gas, Hydrocarbons; The alkanes; Non-combustibles

Natural Gas

Natural gas is a mixture of a large number of gases. Some of these are combustible (i.e. they will burn), others are non-combustible (i.e. they will not burn)

The composition of a typical North Sea gas is shown in the table below:

Component of dry gas		% by volume
Combustibles	Methane	94.4
	Ethane	3.22
	Propane	0.59
	Butane	0.21
	Pentane	0.07
Non-combustibles	Carbon dioxide	0.05
	Nitrogen	1.46

Remember! These figures are for a North Sea gas, natural gas from other parts of the world may have a different composition

Keywords
combustibles
non-combustibles

MODULE 1: Combustion/Section 1: What is Natural Gas?/Page 1

Think of 100m³ of natural gas in a pipe.....

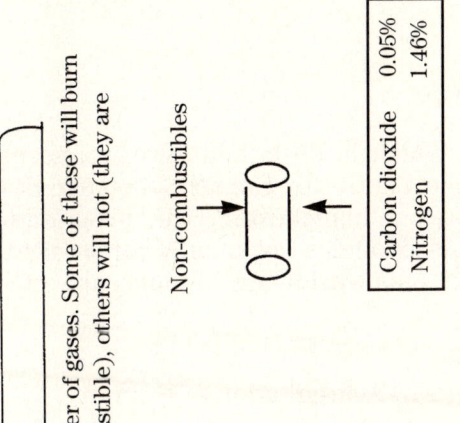

It is made up of a number of gases. Some of these will burn (we say they are combustible), others will not (they are non-combustible).......

Combustibles

Methane	94.4%
Ethane	3.22%
Propane	0.59%
Butane	0.21%
Pentane	0.07%

Non-combustibles

Carbon dioxide	0.05%
Nitrogen	1.46%

Remember! These figures are for a North Sea gas; natural gas from other parts of the world may have a different composition.

Look at the table and/or the diagram above. Write, in the space below, three things about the composition of the North Sea gas shown:

1
2
3

Sample page

9.4a   The practicalities of running a distance learning programme

GILLIAN WALSH

Context

The distance TESOL programme which is described here is one of the postgraduate courses offered by the Centre for English Language Studies in Education (CELSE), University of Manchester. The programme is modular, with ten units per module. Modules are mainly print-based and materials are posted monthly to students worldwide. Modules are offered:

- as part of a Masters level course;
- as part of a Diploma level course;
- as free-standing modules with APEL (Accreditation of Prior or Experiential Learning) potential;
- as in-country courses, partially tutor-led, for groups of overseas students.

The distance programme is currently being followed by over 100 students, approximately three-quarters of whom are based overseas. In addition, single modules are being taken by several groups in Eastern Europe and a group in Sri Lanka. The programme aims to maximise the choices available to individual students in terms of: modules, start dates and the sandwiching of distance and contact modules. This description of the practicalities will focus on four points:

- distance education is not the norm;
- distance students are distant;
- distance students are not students;
- distance materials are special.

Distance education is not the norm

For the University   Various faculties within the university have distance learning programmes, but these are all working separately. The university administration is not set up to deal with distance learners, so each programme has separate administration. This administration is not funded by the university's central finance; the funding has to be a bolt-on cost element to distance modules. However, since a distance module is recognised as equal to a contact module of the university's Masters or Diploma courses, the university requires distance programmes to comply with rigorous academic and administrative procedures.

For the Student   Most of CELSE's distance learners have no previous experience of distance learning. Many begin their Masters course by distance, having applied by post, and so have no knowledge of Manchester, the university, CELSE or its tutors. The students can be seen as having two central requirements – information and support. These requirements and ways of meeting them are the focus of this paper.

Distance students are distant

This may seem to be stating the obvious – of course they are distant. But they are distant in different ways. CELSE has very few students who are UK-based: there are single students in Laos, in Brazil, in the Gulf States, in Japan. All have their own particular problems with distance. Some have no ready access to phone or fax facilities, others find their materials detained in customs. Some have restricted access to libraries, some are fortunate enough to have fellow teachers who are interested in discussing points from the distance materials with them. For many, isolation is a key problem, and of the two requirements that need to be met, the first is the need for information. A general information pack was therefore developed to provide answers to the four questions most commonly asked (or rather, written) by CELSE's applicants.

 How much does it cost?

 When can I start? When will I get the materials?

 How does the programme work?

 Where can I stay during the contact block?

Of course, not all applicants ask these and only these questions; to enable us to respond to other queries a database of questions and answers has been built up. For advice on module choice and scheduling, the distance learners' point of contact is the distance learning co-ordinator. In order to be able to deal with all the queries it was decided that the co-ordinator would need to have:

- experience of learning at a distance;
- work experience in TESOL;
- knowledge of the contents of TESOL MEd modules.

Once they have the basic information about cost, and about when and how they can start, distance learners need to know about which modules they can choose, and about when and how to pay. Once the choice is made, the administration need information about the modules to be taken in order to:

- notify the module tutors;
- inform the university's central administration;
- print materials.

The distance materials themselves are printed on a 'just-in-time' basis to avoid:

 having a backlog of outdated stock;

 storage problems;

 costs of printing large stocks before they are required.

Having decided which module(s) to follow and when to start, distance learners will have further information requirements, but more pressing is likely to be their need for support as they encounter the advantages and disadvantages of studying at a distance.

Distance students are not students

That is to say, they are not only students – they have, in all probability, chosen to study by distance because they have job and/or family commitments which prevent them from following a full time, face-to-face course of study. In the case of TESOL distance learners, working while studying may be as much an advantage as a disadvantage. Students following the programme at post often have the advantage of being able to experiment with new approaches and techniques, to apply their new knowledge and gauge its effectiveness with their own classes. On the other hand, working at home can bring its own disadvantages.

Distance learners beginning the programme frequently express anxiety about assessment. The materials contain self-assessment questions (SAQs) with answer keys, and the SAQs are objective or semi-objective in form, so that the students can perceive their progress. However, each module requires that they complete an assignment – often to produce, analyse and evaluate materials – and it is this assignment that causes anxiety. There are many possible reasons for this anxiety: the students have, after all, no classmates against whom they can measure their progress and many will not have undertaken any form of academic writing for several years. To meet students' requirements for support in this area the distance learning 'Introductory Information' pack includes guidelines for assignment writing and a set of criteria, with descriptors, for assignment grading. The criteria and descriptors are illustrated in the table opposite.

Distance students, with no seminars or tutorials and no peers to engage in fruitful discussion, are essentially learning from reading. There are exceptions to this – CELSE's Educational Technology modules, for instance, have computer and/or video based delivery systems – but the majority of distance students will be learning from print-based materials, and this implies a heavy reading input. Here too, distance students require support.

Distance materials are special

Just as two types of student requirements have been identified, so distance learning materials may be seen to be special in two ways:

- they need to provide information (about programme structure as well as academic content);
- they need to provide support for students (facing isolation and a heavy reading input load).

Many distance programmes keep the two information requirements separate. Many offer study skills (academic reading and writing) support

Criteria for essay-type assignments and dissertations		
Content	**Structure**	**Grade**
is sufficient, and relevant to issue being discussed shows critical understanding of relevant facts and issues shows originality in thinking and breadth in reading	integrates detail into a coherent whole guides reader through to a reasoned conclusion is supported throughout by appropriate and accurate language	A (70% or more)
is sufficient and relevant to issues being discussed shows good grasp of relevant facts and issues shows breadth of study and some originality	reveals an attempt to create a coherent whole attempts to guide reader through to a reasoned conclusion is rarely affected by inappropriate or inaccurate language	B (60–69%)
is sufficient to cover the subject but has a few irrelevancies shows satisfactory grasp of relevant facts and issues shows adequate reading but little originality	links parts together but falls short of creating a coherent whole does not always guide reader and does not always have a conclusion is weakened in places by inappropriate or inaccurate language	C (50–59%)
does not fully cover subject specified and/or is sometimes irrelevant shows a weak grasp of relevant facts and issues suffers from inadequate reading and thinking	sometimes fails to link parts to each other shows little regard for reader and does not come to a justifiable conclusion is weakened by inappropriate or inaccurate language	D (40–49%)

modules separately. In CELSE's case the information and support are all built in to the modules; this requires the co-ordinator to work as a member of the design team. It was mentioned above that CELSE modules consist of ten units. Actually they consist of ten units plus a unit 0, an introductory unit which contains information about:

● the programme;
● the structure and organisation of the module;
● reading requirements for the module (including an annotated bibliography); and
● the assignment.

In addition the unit provides support for students in the form of:

● a glossary of key terms used in the module;
● explanation of icons used as signposts throughout modules;
● introductory SAQ tasks to provide a 'taster' for the module proper; and
● a combination of input reading and SAQs to provide study skills support.

The following icons are examples of signposting used for student support.

Objectives   Pre-reading   Input Reading

SAQ   Answer Key   Assignment

Once students have started a module, record-keeping becomes important. The administration and the tutors need to know what has been sent, where, and when. Clearly a computer database with student addresses and other details can be of use here. However, the tutors are not necessarily going to be able to access computerised data, so print records may also be of use.

During the module students may be confronted by some of the disadvantages of studying at a distance. Examples of these have been given earlier, but I should like to return to the point that was made at the beginning. Distance students are *distant*. They may be distant from academic facilities, so that a postal library and photocopy service may be required; they are also distant from their tutors, and may be able to communicate only through the post; the 'less distant' student may have access to phone, fax, or even e-mail, but in the case of CELSE students these last two facilities are still uncommon. Post, then, is the means by which feedback on the module is communicated from students to tutors and feedback on their work passed from tutors to students.

The isolated distance learner, with no facilities, is wholly dependent on the arrival of a distance module. Materials in distance education must therefore encompass the support that the isolated distance student requires, and CELSE is currently researching means of including the required support in the input reading materials.

9.4b Teacher education and empowerment: a view from a distance

JULIAN EDGE and MELANIE ELLIS

After some introductory comments, the first part of the presentation put forward arguments concerning the potential relationship between distance learning and teacher education. The second part indicated how one particular course, Aston University's MSc in Teaching English, attempts to realise this potential.

Introduction

There is no attempt here to make universally valid generalisations about distance learning, or to work towards any kind of definition of what distance learning is. The presentation is made from the perspectives of one specific attempt to help course participants reach their educational goals. In this attempt, almost all the learning and teaching takes place in distance mode.

From the perspective of this experience, it was disappointing to hear an earlier speaker refer to education itself in terms of the old container/transmission metaphor, and I felt an emotion more akin to despair when I heard distance education described as 'merely a delivery system'. Similarly, while one can sympathise with the specific circumstances which led another guest speaker to refer to distance education as better than nothing in desperate circumstances, it is inevitably to the continuing detriment of distance education to have it so described, when the description might be misunderstood as having some general relevance.

In contrast to the above, the attitudinal tone of this presentation is celebratory. Distance learning and teacher education involve mutually supportive processes towards mutually coherent ends (Richards 1991): participants increase their awareness of the contexts in which they live, they increase their potential for creating autonomous meaning in those contexts, and they increase their control over their contexts – a complex of outcomes which Paul (1990) refers to as 'self-actualisation'.

This process works at many levels. Following an Open University course, for instance, can lead a person to recognise time spent doing the ironing as a good time for listening to study-cassettes. Working on the personality development component may lead a person to appreciate an infant daughter as an important informant for academic research. Studying the Enlightenment may bring a different understanding of the attack on fundamental cultural values implied by current threats, reported perhaps dismissively in the daily press, to the life of a novelist. It is correct to say that such awareness-raising can take place through traditional education, but distance education not only makes the experience available to a whole new community of learners, it brings the process into the learner's home environment.

Teacher education

It can be useful to think of teacher education as made up of the twin elements of training and development – see for example Freeman (1992), where 'training' refers to technical, professional, or project-oriented learning, while 'development' is seen as person-oriented, helping an individual grow towards their own potential. Useful as this analysis is for purposes of reflection, we must also seek to work for a fusion of the two elements in action. This fusion is what is being referred to here as *empowerment*, where individuals are helped to become increasingly aware of themselves in their own context, both as persons and as professionals.

As the term empowerment is also used by others whose more-or-less overt project is the de-skilling of teachers and the centralisation of educational power (see, for example, Smyth 1989 or any statement by Her Majesty's Secretary of State for Education at the time of writing), it is worth saying a little more about how it is being used here.

Empowerment

Empowerment is a complex term which, again for the purposes of reflection and discussion, can be considered from three perspectives, in terms of an increase in authority, ability and responsibility.

Authority: As people become empowered, they extend their range of authority, perhaps officially by gaining promotion, or interpersonally in that they behave with a greater sense of sureness, or internally, in that they simply feel more confident. They become more the author of their own narrative.

Ability: Empowerment involves increasing one's skills and abilities – becoming more able in what one does, and thereby more prepared to take on more authority and responsibility.

Responsibility: One needs to be ready to take responsibility for one's actions and for their outcomes. This responsibility becomes greater as authority and ability increase. At the same time, the taking on of more responsibility needs to be done in such a way that it will neither disempower others, nor threaten those who are in power.

This last point emphasises the overlap between a discussion of empowerment and a discussion of other types of innovation: it is often unwise to confront those in power. Their positive engagement is greatly preferable if one's purposes are evolutionary rather than revolutionary.

Aims of the Aston MSc in Teaching English

These aims are as follows:

Professional development in the sense both of the individual's professionalism, and also of the development of the profession via the contribution of empowered individuals.

Local development brought about by helping participants deepen their understanding of the situation in which they are working. Inquiry is set in the context of the participant's own practice. Here there are echoes of 'theorising from the classroom' (Ramani 1987), 'teachers theorising their practice' (Smyth 1989) and 'reclaiming our own theory' (Naidu, Neeraja, Ramani, Shivakumar and Viswanatha 1992), where teachers empower themselves through a process which begins with a description of their own work.

Co-operative development, that is, the building of co-operation between teachers as they develop the discourse with which they describe and then shape their practice.

How the programme works

DE materials   Individuals receive course components in the form of ring bound files. The files contain custom-written textual input, individual and group tasks, and reference material. Video material is also available at the Local Resource Centre.

Local resource centre (LRC)   An LRC is established before the course begins. There are currently LRCs in UK, Spain, Greece, Turkey, Abu Dhabi, Malaysia and Japan. LRCs are located in places where there is already a library which can be supplemented, library staff where possible, and a readily accessible facility open at weekends. This has so far meant either a British Council Centre or a co-operating university.

Local Group   The course is open to groups of ten to fifteen from one of the countries where there is a local centre. Although it would be possible for someone from the group to elect to work alone, the course is not open to individuals where no centre is available. If a group from a country where there is not a local centre expresses interest, there is the chance that a new local centre could be started. Group meetings are voluntary, but those who attend find the support helps counter the emotional isolation of the distance course, as well as providing an intellectually stimulating forum for individual and co-operative development.

Course tutor   Each group has a tutor, based in Aston, who has teaching duties as well as acting as a mediator between the participants, other colleagues, and the university. Participants and tutor communicate via post, fax, e-mail or telephone. It is important to note, especially when discussion focuses on the 'delivery' of distance education, that communication is frequently initiated by participants. The tutor also makes regular visits to the local centre to run workshops.

Support   The provision of multiple support systems is taken very seriously. An introductory workshop is run so that the tutor has a 'face' and becomes a real person for the participants to correspond with. Responses to affective concerns are built into the design of the course and there is a conscious attempt to compensate for the emotional stress a distance course can generate.

Visits   As well as the initial, introductory visit and subsequent visits by the tutor, subject specialists visit LRCs, especially in support of components assessed by examination, as these can generate high stress.

Newsletters   These are written individually by tutors for their groups and go out approximately every two weeks, with information, news and general interest items to keep the lines of contact open.

LSU bulletin   This is published twice yearly, providing a forum for participants to publish their work. Help is given in producing the register necessary for academic writing and participants are encouraged to go on to publish in journals.

Study companion   This provides an overview of all components of the course, and a breakdown of what they contain, along with a description of the assignments to be completed. Reading lists are also included. This gives participants the chance to read ahead and plan their study – also the chance to shift focus if they have had enough of what they are studying in detail at any one time.

Course guide   This provides an administrative overview of the course, for example the dates of examinations and when assignments are due, as well as relevant university regulations and a guide to academic writing conventions.

Course structure   The course is offered in two variants: MSc in Teaching English or MSc in Teaching English for Specific Purposes. Group members opt for the variant they want and they receive appropriate materials. Two units are sent out concurrently until the dissertation phase. The course is arranged in five phases and two strands: pedagogic and linguistic. The linguistic strand is evaluated by examination, while the pedagogic strand is evaluated by assignment based on action research in context.

Phase	Linguistic	Pedagogic
1.00	Text & Discourse Analysis	Methodology
2.00	Linguistic Varieties (Exams)	Course & Syllabus Design
3.00		Materials Analysis & Production
		Options
		Currently: Management of ELT, Business
		English, Classroom Research, Self-Access
		& Distance Learning, Teacher Development,
		CALL, Computational Linguistics
	(End of Diploma Phase)	
4.00	Descriptions of Modern English	
	Lexical Studies	
	(Exams)	
5.00	Dissertation	

The following points emerged from discussion.

Tutor feedback on written work

Feedback should be viewed as written teaching. One effective method tried and popular with course members is the provision of a brief and general written response accompanied by an audio cassette on which more detailed comment is made. This satisfies two potentially conflicting needs – the academic institution's requirements for documentation and the human need for personal and developmental support.

Timing *The course begins in January and ends in November of the second year. Initially two components are sent out and then the next two before the first assignment is due.*

Study time *Graduates report greatly varying amounts of time spent studying, from a minimum average of eight hours a week to a maximum of twenty.*

Resources *If additional resources are needed, participants have full use of Aston's library and inter-library services, although this involves expense and careful planning ahead.*

Particularly at the dissertation stage, there is the danger that a course member might have problems tracking down resources when pursuing a line of thought in great detail. Tutors advise on this, but do not actively limit choice of topic on these grounds. Comments from the Open University representative showed that the OU insists course members complete assignments and dissertation only from materials provided. This is done to ensure the course can be completed by anyone receiving the material. Aston's position is that the assignments and dissertation formats provide a framework, but that it is the participants' concerns in context which must make up the content. This should not be more constrained than is absolutely necessary. Lack of reference material is usually more an understandably perceived problem than a truly crucial one.

Standards *A question was asked as to whether the distance dissertations were not of a lower standard ('impoverished') as a result of the potential shortage of material. On the contrary, it is in-house dissertations which often suffer in comparison, due to their being removed from the context of the practice they refer to.*

Methodology *If the course is advocating a reflexive approach then the tutor needs to be seen to be practising this. If participants are expected to theorise from their own practice, then the tutors too need to carry out investigations into the nature of distance learning as a teaching method. An example was given of investigating ways of giving feedback on written assignments, where the tutor put himself into the vulnerable position of asking for comment on a variety of feedback modes. By opening up,* *showing that the interaction is a dynamic one, the tutor enters into the spirit of development, which is the essence of the course philosophy.*

Throughout the session, inspiration was drawn from the Shona proverb provided by Moses Mulabeta and Bill Louw in another session: 'Your feet will get you somewhere, but your backside won't'. With this in mind, we covered some distance.

9.5   Where do we go from here?

RICHARD WEBBER

This paper is the product of a rapporteurs' report-back session which formed the final session of the 1993 Dunford seminar. Rapporteurs for each of the topic areas covered during the seminar were asked to review the sessions for which they had been rapporteurs, and to guide the participants towards discussion of likely new directions which might develop in Distance Education (DE) relating to language issues. This paper is an account of participants' ideas relating to these possible new directions.

The seminar was structured around two very basic areas of interest in DE, educational sub-sectors and means of delivery. Sub-sectors covered were secondary, tertiary, teacher-training and non-formal, and means covered were materials design, conventional broadcasting, costing DE options and the opportunities presented by new technology.

Tertiary and secondary
Discussions revealed that nearly all the new directions envisaged from the tertiary and secondary sectors were very closely related and included:

1) An increased exploitation of the potential offered by learning through a mix of media ('pluri-modality') whether print, broadcasting by radio and/or TV, use of pre-recorded audio and/of video material, telephone or new technology.
2) An increase in the use of new technology, whether teleconferencing, satellite narrowcasting, interactive video or whatever new technology may develop.
3) Resulting from 1) and 2) above, a new body of expertise amongst materials writers to exploit the opportunities offered by the new technology, in association with existing materials production methods.

Looking ahead, participants noted the following points.

4) Materials developed for non-language teaching topics will increasingly build language learning into their subject materials as an integral (not add-on) element of the instruction package.
5) As a complement to 4) above, learning programme designers will increasingly include direct teaching of language as an essential support for non-language learning subjects.

6) To render instructional packages at the tertiary and secondary levels cost-effective, there will be an increased number of consortia.

7) As a result of 6) above, materials will have to contend with two opposing forces. Firstly there will be pressure from consortia to reduce unit costs by 'internationalising' materials so that they are acceptable to as many markets as possible. Secondly, there will be pressure from end-users (foreign governments and students) to make materials culturally and pedagogically suitable for them specifically. Materials will vary between the range of responses suggested by these forces.

8) Increased numbers of consortia and the internationalisation of learning will lead to an increase in modularisation and the use of credit transfer systems.

9) An issue which was seen as having specific relevance to the secondary sector was the expected increase in the use of distance methods in ELT for cross-curricular purposes.

Teacher training (TT)

Distance techniques in the training of language teachers were seen as having considerable potential advantages over non-distance methods and because of these advantages, together with perceived economies, it was felt that teacher education by distance was going to grow even more rapidly than it has already done in the last few years both in the UK and overseas. Reasons given by participants for this projected growth were as follows.

1) TT at a distance will allow teachers to remain in the workplace during training and thus allow them to apply new ideas immediately to their classroom, to conduct research using immediately available data and to avoid depletion of national staff strength while absent on overseas training.

2) Distance TT will require trainees to learn not only the substance of their instructional programme but also the necessary study skills involved, and will thus be an instrument of teacher improvement in national human resource development within and beyond the education sector.

3) Distance TT courses will use the fact that trainees are in daily contact with their classes to incorporate assessment of actual teaching ability into the overall assessment scheme by relating study tasks to day-to-day teaching duties.

4) Distance TT will integrate the new technology into instructional programmes with caution, proceeding from the readily accessible to the more esoteric, to ensure that fear of technology does not interfere.

5) Distance TT will, by making new technology available to an important sector of society, not only empower teachers but contribute to national development through a more widespread understanding of the use of, and demand for, modern communications technology.

Non-formal education

1) The participants felt that distance learning for non-formal education would enjoy an expanding future as part of the post-Jomtien interest of ILOs in large scale basic education programmes.
2) The need for economies of scale, together with the commitment of ILOs to national rather than regional development, would ensure that DE non-formal programmes would be large in size.
3) New technology (cheaper local radio transmitters, cheaper satellite reception equipment associated with higher-powered satellites and the development of narrow-casting, higher production quality via Desk Top Publishing, etc., for rural newspapers in local languages) will improve the quality of access to non-formal education by distance and reinforce literacy skills learnt.
4) Non-formal education will use study groups increasingly as a means to support the associated language learning needs of students.
5) Together with plans to target large numbers, DE in non-formal education will seek to address the wide variation in effectiveness of current literacy programmes by increased use of assessment and evaluation techniques and by corrective measures based on the findings of these techniques.

Materials writing

Participants made the following predictions.

1) With the integration of language learning into the Education Sector of ILO lending, distance materials would inevitably be part or parts of multi-disciplinary programmes rather than 'stand-alones'.
2) In a climate of increasing attention to costs and a plethora of existing high quality products, ways could be found to adapt existing materials to new environments rather than starting from scratch.
3) Developments in the field of educational psychology would impact on the style and content of materials production for distance language learning programmes and this would cause an improvement in the effectiveness with which the varying cognitive styles of learners would be addressed.
4) The outcome of 3) above would be an increase in 'multi-channel' approaches to language issues in DE whereby skills would be imparted via a wide variety of techniques and presentation styles.
5) Interest in DE by ILOs would lead to more funds being available for materials production; in consequence, the quality of the content and physical production of materials would improve significantly.

Broadcasting

Two sessions of the Dunford 1993 seminar were devoted to broadcasting, and participants' judgements as to likely new directions in this area are listed in this section. However, participants generally felt that broadcasting was not really a discrete topic area but was another form of materials production disseminated through the airwaves. They foresaw as follows.

1) The future will bring more international collaboration in language learning through broadcasting in terms of delivery systems and materials production. Participants wondered if, as a consequence of this, Third World skills might not be stifled by international consortia.
2) The international collaboration envisaged in 1) above would lead to two conflicting tendencies: firstly that there would be more cross-cultural awareness and secondly that cultural imperialism by international consortia would tend to ride roughshod over local sensibilities. Participants saw future language learning-related broadcasting veering between these two poles.
3) In order to market more successfully, broadcasting companies will undertake and make better use of market research.
4) A probable consequence of 3) above will be an increase in 'narrowcasting' via satellite, whereby very specific audiences can be targeted with specially designed materials.
5) The penetration of broadcasting will become more widespread and more intense and will form a significant part of the 'cultural backdrop' of more and more countries.
6) There was a danger that in the longer term the current and impending glut of educational broadcasting might be rationalised by the well-established process of concentrating capital into a rather restricted range of options, which would neglect less prominent minorities.

Costing

This question was considered of vital importance by participants in considering what developments might occur in the means of delivery of DE language programmes. Participants felt that:

1) The combined pressure of increasingly restricted budgets and ever higher governmental expectations would inevitably lead to a more stringent costing of distance programmes in terms of monetary, institutional and individual inputs.
2) Pressure on costs and human pressures would lead to more collaboration between institutions and individuals.
3) Opportunity costs for the learner would be taken more into account: for example, a student might prefer a low-cost in-country distance programme (whereby he/she could keep working and maintaining a family) to a high-cost overseas programme, perhaps partially funded by an ILO.
4) The whole range of potential options will be considered very carefully for each DE programme in order to maximise effect and keep down cost. The inventory of options considered will include the wide range of possibilities currently emerging from the new technology.
5) The drive to keep costs down will lead to an increase in the hire of casual materials writers, course planners, tutors and others. However,

this 'casualisation' will allow the number of individuals involved in mounting distance programmes to increase together with an increasing demand for distance programmes.

The new technology

The application of existing but relatively recent, and of impending, technology of DE and its applications to language was a topic which provided discussion throughout the seminar. Relatively recent possibilities included teleconferencing by PC using telephone links and satellite television broadcasts. Impending technology included 'narrowcasting' (a satellite transmitting a narrow but powerful footprint to a specific audience), interactive satellite broadcasting and the transmission of video images via cable and with the assistance of compression technology. Participants felt that new directions relating to the new technology would include the following:

1) An increased use of individualisation ('bespoke materials').
2) A valuable synergy between existing classroom practice and the opportunities presented by the new materials.
3) The spread of technical literacy both within and outside the education sector.
4) An increasing electicism in choosing delivery methods, whether from the technology menu or from the conventional menu.
5) An understanding that the potential use of technology would remain uncertain. Technological advances (who had heard of the Walkman twenty years ago?) have often headed off in unpredicted directions, and this trend would continue.
6) A need for educationalists to ensure that their interest in and involvement with technology is founded on sound educational considerations, and not based on naive belief in the applicability of new technology or the persuasiveness of salespersons.
7) A need for educationalists to ensure that language is explicitly on the agenda of educational programmes produced for the new media and that the manifold possibilities offered by the new technology are used to maximise effective language learning.

It was felt that since the new technology was perceived as having a tremendous potential to assist developing countries to overcome their skills shortages in education, governments would inevitably exploit this potential. There was, however, a strong caveat to this: it was felt that a forceful case would have to be made to ILOs and governments that to disseminate content programmes together with their language support materials was not in itself an answer but that such materials, to be effective, would have to be planned with the same degree of commitment in terms of finance and logistical forethought as would in the best circumstances be applied to conventional classroom-based instruction programmes.

Conclusion

In brief, participants felt that DE and the language issues that it involves would be an important growth area in the field of education both in the short and longer term. The twin factors of a general drive for cost-cutting and the potential being opened up by new technology would ensure this for better or worse. The drive for cost reduction would, it was felt, lead to a general concentration of resources in all DE sectors, with the emergence of a greater number of consortia; within these there would be a greater use of teams in which the language expert would work alongside media and content specialists to produce learning packages. If things turned out badly, the field of DE could be dominated by all-purpose materials of little value to anyone in particular. However, it was felt that with care and perseverance and the correct exploitation of the new technology, the future of DE would allow a more exact matching of learner materials to learner needs whereby materials were tailored to individual needs and the language requirements of students could be met exactly and efficiently.

Bibliography

Abbott, G. 1981. 'Approaches to English teaching'. In Abbott, G. and P.G. Wingard (eds) *The Teaching of English as an International Language: A Practical Guide.* London: Collins.

Abbott, G. 1984. 'Should we start digging new holes?' *English Language Teaching Journal* 38/2:98–102.

Abbott, G. 1992. 'Development, education and English language teaching' *English Language Teaching Journal* 46/2:172–9.

Abbott, G. 1992a. 'The proper study of ELT.' In van Essen, A. and Burkart, E. (eds), *Homage to W.R. Lee: Essays in English as a Second or Foreign Language.* Berlin & New York: Foris Publications.

Abbott, G. 1994. 'Language rights and duties in our education systems.' *FIPLV World* News, No. 31.

Alderson, J.C. 1979. *Materials Evaluation.* Proceedings of the Second Latin-American Regional ESP Seminar, Cocoyoc, Mexico.

Alexander, L.G. 1976. 'Threshold level and methodology'. In van Ek 1976: 148–65.

Ausubel, D. 1963. *The Psychology of Meaningful Verbal Learning.* New York: Grune & Stratton.

Beaumont, M. and Gallaway, C. 1994. 'Articles of faith: the acquisition, learning and teaching of *a* and *the*'. In Bygate, M., Tonkyn, A. and Williams, E. (eds) *Grammar and the Language Teacher.* London: Prentice Hall.

Beeby, C. 1968. *The Quality of Education in Developing Countries.* Cambridge, Mass: Harvard University Press.

Beretta, A. 1984. 'Evaluation of the Bangalore/Madras Communicational Teaching Project'. (Unpublished ms) The University of Edinburgh.

Berko Gleason, J. (ed.) 1993. *The Development of Language.* New York, Macmillan.

Boissiere, M. *et al.* 1985. 'Earnings, schooling, ability and cognitive skills.' *American Economic Review* 75/5.

Bowers, R. (ed.) 1987. 'Language teacher education: an integrated programme of ELT teacher training.' In *ELT Documents* 125. Basingstoke: Modern English Publications / Macmillan.

Breen, M.P. and Candlin, C.N. 1980. 'The essentials of a communicative curriculum in language teaching'. *Applied Linguistics* 1/2: 89–112.

British Council, 1981. *ELT Documents 110: Focus on the Teacher*. London: The British Council.

British Council, 1981. *ELT Documents 112: The ESP Teacher: Role, Development and Prospects*. London: The British Council.

British Council, 1983. *ELT Documents 116: Language Teaching Projects for the Third World*. Oxford: Pergamon Press in association with the British Council.

Brumfit, C.J. 1984. 'Key issues in curriculum and syllabus design for ELT' *Dunford Seminar Report: Curriculum and Syllabus Design in ELT*. London: The British Council. Part 1: 7–12.

Brumfit, C.J. and Johnson, K. (eds) 1979. *The Communicative Approach to Language Teaching*. Oxford: Oxford University Press.

Button, J. (ed.) 1990. *The Green Fuse*. London & New York: Quartet Books.

Card, D. and Kreuger, A. 1991. *Education in the Labor Market: a Partial Survey*. (Mimeographed conference paper) Princeton, NJ: Princeton University.

Carmen, R. 1996. *Autonomous Development: Humanizing the Landscape*. London: Zed Books.

Carroll, B.J. 1980. *Testing Communicative Performance*. Oxford: Pergamon.

Celani, M. *et al.* (eds) 1988. *The Brazilian ESP Project: an Evaluation*. São Paulo: Centro de Pesquisas, Recursos e Informação em Leitura.

Coleman, H. 1989. *Large Classes in Nigeria*. Language Learning in Large Classes Research Project Report 6. Leeds: University of Leeds.

Coleman, H. 1990. 'The relationship between large class research and large class teaching.' *SPELT (Soc. of Pakistan English Language Teachers) Newsletter* 5/1: 2–10.

Coleman, H. 1991. 'Primary ELT teachers and large classes.' In C. Kennedy and J. Jarvis (eds) *Ideas and Issues in Primary ELT*. Walton-on-Thames: Nelson.

Coleman, H. 1995. 'Appropriate methodology in large classes.' In R. Budd (ed.) *Appropriate Methodology: from Classroom Methods to Classroom Process*. Paris: TESOL France.

Coleman, H. (ed.) 1996. *Society and the Language Classroom*. Cambridge: Cambridge University Press.

Cronbach, L.J. 1975. 'Course improvement through evaluation'. In Golby, M. *et al.* (eds) *Curriculum Design*. London: Croom Helm and The Open University.

Curry, L. 1983. 'An organisation of learning styles theory and constructs.' *ERIC Document* 23:51–85.

Dalby, D. 1985. 'The life and vitality of African languages: a charter for the future.' In K. Mateene, J. Kalema and B. Chomba (eds) *Linguistic Unity and Liberation of Africa*. Kampala: Organisation for African Unity Inter-African Bureau of Languages.

Dakin, J. 1973. *The Language Laboratory and Language Learning*. London: Longman.

Deyes, T. 1980. 'Stop press review' *Dunford Seminar Report: Communicative Methodology*. London: The British Council. Part 8: 109–10.

Djité, P.G. 1991. 'Langues et développement en Afrique.' *Language Problems and Language Planning* 15/2: 121–138.

Dore, R. 1976. *The Diploma Disease: Education, Qualification and Development*. London: Allen and Unwin.

Dore, R. 1980. 'The future of formal education in developing countries.' In J. Simmons (ed.) *The Education Dilemma: Policy Issues for Developing Countries in the 1980s*. Oxford: Pergamon Press.

Ellis, R. 1985. *Understanding Second Language Acquisition*. Oxford: Oxford University Press.

Ellis, R. 1994. *The Study of Second Language Acquisition*. Oxford: Oxford University Press.

England, E. 1987. 'The design of versatile text materials.' *Open Learning* 2/2:

Fasold, R. 1984. *The Sociolinguistics of Society*. Oxford: Basil Blackwell.

Fox, M. 1975. *Language and Development: a Retrospective Survey of Ford Foundation Language Projects, 1952–1974*. New York: Ford Foundation.

Freeman, D. 1989. 'Teacher training, development, and decision making: a model of teaching and related strategies for language teacher education.' *TESOL Quarterly* 23/1: 27–45.

Freeman, D. 1992. 'Language teacher education, emerging discourse, and change in classroom practice.' In J. Flowerdew (ed.) *Perspectives on Second Language Teacher Education*. Hong Kong: City Polytechnic.

Freire, P. 1972. *Pedagogy of the Oppressed*. Harmondsworth: Penguin Books.

French, F.G. 1948. *The Teaching of English Abroad. Part 1: Aims and Methods*. London: Oxford University Press.

Gorham, J. 1986. 'Assessment classification and implications of learning styles as instructional interactions.' *ERIC Reports* 35/4: 441–17.

Gower, R. and Walters, S. 1983. *Teaching Practice Handbook*. London: Heinemann.

Gramsci, A. 1971. *Selections from the Prison Notebooks*. London: Lawrence & Wishart.

Harmer, J. 1991. *The Practice of English Language Teaching*. (New edn.) Harlow: Longman.

Hawes, H. 1979. *Curriculum and Reality in African Primary Schools*. London: Longman.

Hawkey, R. 1982. *An investigation of inter relationships between personality, cognitive style and language learning strategies: with special reference to a group of adult overseas students using English in their specialist studies in the UK*. University of London: unpublished thesis.

Haycraft, J. 1986. *An Introduction to English Language Teaching*. (Rev. edn.) Harlow: Longman.

Holden, S. (ed.), 1979. *Teacher Training*. London: Modern English Publications.

Holliday, A. 1994. *Appropriate Methodology and Social Context*. Cambridge: Cambridge University Press.

Howatt, A. 1984. *A History of English Language Teaching*. Oxford: Oxford University Press.

Hulmes, E. 1989. *Education and Cultural Diversity*. London & New York: Longman.

Hunt, J. 1986. *Managing People at Work: a Manager's Guide to Behaviour in Organizations*. (Second edn.) Maidenhead: McGraw-Hill.

Hunt, E.K. and Sherman, H.J. 1986. *Economics: an Introduction to Traditional and Radical Views*. (Fifth edn.) New York: Harper & Row.

Hyde, G. 1978. *Education in Modern Egypt: Ideals and Realities*. London: Routledge & Kegan Paul.

Inter-Agency Commission. 1990. *World Declaration on Education for All, and Framework for Action to Meet Basic Learning Needs*. New York: IAC, for the World Conference on Education for All.

Kachru, B. 1976. 'Models of English for the Third World: white man's linguistic burden or language pragmatics?' *TESOL Quarterly* 10: 221–39.

Kachru, B. 1986. 'The power and politics of English'. *World Englishes* 5/2–3: 121–40.

Keegan, D. 1990. *Foundations of Distance Education*. (Second edn.) London: Routledge.

Kennedy, C. 1987. 'Innovating for a change: teacher development and innovation' *English Language Teaching Journal* 41/3: 163–70.

Kennedy, C. 1988. 'Evaluation of the management of change in ELT projects.' *Applied Linguistics* 9/4: 329–42.

Latouche, S. 1989. *L'Occidentalisation du Monde*. Paris: La Découverte.

Lee, R. and Field, M. 1985. 'Stimulating educational innovation: the pragmatics of institutional change.' IHE, 2/1: 12–14.

Maslow, A.H. 1954. *Motivation and Personality*. (2nd edn.) New York: Harper & Row.

Maslow, A.H. 1962. *Towards a Psychology of Being*. Princeton, N.J.: Van Nostrand.

Maw, J. 1984. 'Approaches to curriculum design'. *Dunford Seminar Report: Curriculum and Syllabus Design in ELT*. London: The British Council. Part 1: 13–14.

Max-Neef, M.A. 1982. *From the Outside Looking in: Experiences in 'Barefoot Economics'*. Uppsala: Dag Hammarskjöld Foundation.

Max-Neef, M.A. 1991. *Human Scale Development: Conception, Application and Further Reflections*. London: Zed Books.

McLeod, N. 1989. *What Teachers Cannot Do in Large Classes*. Language Learning in Large Classes Research Project Report 7. Leeds: University of Leeds.

Munby, J. 1978. *Communicative Syllabus Design*. Cambridge: Cambridge University Press.

Murphy, D. 1985. 'Evaluation in language teaching: assessment, accountability, and awareness'. In Alderson, J.C. (ed.) *Lancaster Practical Papers in English Language Education, Vol. 6: Evaluation*. Oxford: Pergamon.

Naidu, B., Neeraja, K., Ramani, E., Shivakumar, J. and Viswanatha, V. 1992. 'Researching heterogeneity: an account of teacher-initiated research into large classes.' *English Language Teaching Journal* 46/3: 252–63.

Ngũgĩ wa Thiong'o. 1986. *Decolonising the Mind: the Politics of Language in African Literature*. Nairobi: Heinemann Kenya.

Nicholls, A. 1983. *Managing Educational Innovations*. London: Unwin Educational.

Nisbet, J.D. 1972. In Entwistle, N.J. and J.D. Nisbet, *Educational Research in Action*. London: University of London Press.

Nolasco, R. and Arthur, L. 1988. *Large Classes*. London: Macmillan.

ODA 1983. *Planning Development Projects*.

Olsen, J. Winn-Bell and Gosak, A. 1978. 'Initiating communication in the classroom' *English Language Teaching Journal* 32/4: 265–70.

Papert, S. 1980. *Mindstorms: children, computers and powerful ideas.* Brighton, UK: The Harvester Press.

Parrott, M. 1991. 'Factors relating to programme design.' In Bowers, R. and Brumfit, C. (eds) *Applied Linguistics and Language Teaching.* Basingstoke: Modern English Publications/Macmillan in association with The British Council.

Pask, G. 1976. 'Styles and strategies of learning.' *British Journal of Educational Psychology* 46: 128–48.

Pattison, B. 1965. 'English as a foreign language over the world today.' *English Language Teaching* 20/1: 2–10.

Paul, R. 1990. *Open Learning and Open Management: Leadership and Integrity in Distance Education.* London: Kogan Page.

Peters, R.S. 1959. *Authority, Responsibility and Education.* London: George Allen and Unwin.

Phillipson, R. 1990. *English Language Teaching and Imperialism.* Tronninge, Denmark: Transcultura.

Phillipson, R. 1992. *Linguistic Imperialism.* Oxford: Oxford University Press.

Prabhu, N.S. 1983. 'Procedural syllabuses'. Paper presented at the eighteenth regional seminar of the SEAMEO Regional Language Centre, Singapore.

Psacharopoulos, G. 1985. 'Returns to education: a further international update and implications.' *Journal of Human Resources* 20/4: 583–684.

Rahnema, M. 1992. 'Poverty'. In W. Sachs (ed.) 1992.

Ramani, E. 1987. 'Theorising from the classroom.' *English Language Teaching Journal* 41/1: 3–11.

Rea, P. 1983. 'Evaluation of educational projects with special reference to English language instruction'. In British Council *ELT Documents* 116 85–98.

Reid, W.A. 1990. 'Strange curricula: origins and development of the institutional categories of schooling.' *Journal of Curriculum Studies* 22/3: 203–16.

Richards, J. and Nunan, D. (eds) 1990. *Second Language Teacher Education.* Cambridge & New York: Cambridge University Press.

Richards, K. 1991. 'Professional development and distance learning: a natural partnership?' In British Council (ed.) *Information Update Issue 7: Distance Learning.* London: The British Council.

Richterich, R. 1973. 'Definition of language needs and types of adults'. In Trim *et al.* 1980.

Riding, R. 1991. *Cognitive Styles Analysis.* Birmingham: Learning and Training Technology.

Riding, R. and Ashmore, J. 1980. 'Verbaliser-imager learning style and children's recall of information in pictorial versus written form.' *Educational Studies* 6/2: 141–5.

Riding, R., Buckle, C., Thompson, S. and Haggar, E. 1989. 'The computer determination of learning styles as an aid to individualised computer based training.' *Educational and Training Technology International* 26: 393–8.

Riding, R. and Cheemai, I. 1992. 'Cognitive styles – an overview and integration.' *Educational Psychology* 11/3 & 4: 193–215.

Riding, R. and Douglas, G. 1993. 'The effect of learning style and mode of presentation on learning performance.' *British Journal of Educational Psychology* 63: 273–9.

Riding, R. and Sadler-Smith, E. 1992. 'Type of instructional material, cognitive style and learning performance.' *Educational Studies* 18: 323–40.

Rivers, W. and Temperley, M. 1978. *A Practical Guide to the Teaching of English as a Second or Foreign Language*. New York: Oxford University Press.

Rixon, S. 1979. '"The Information Gap" and "The Opinion Gap"' *English Language Teaching Journal* 33/2: 104–6.

Roberts, 1993. *History of the World*. London & New York: Helicon Publishing.

Robinson, C. 1991. 'Language use and language attitudes.' In P. Meara and A. Ryan (eds) *Language and Nation*. London: BAAL in association with CILT.

Rodney, W. 1972. *How Europe Underdeveloped Africa*. Dar es Salaam: Tanzanian Publishing House.

Rogers, J. 1982. 'The world for sick proper'. *English Language Teaching Journal* 36/3: 144–51.

Sachs, W. (ed.) 1992. *The Development Dictionary*. London: Zed Books.

Serageldin, I. (ed.) 1993. *Development Partners: Aid and Cooperation in the 1990s*. Stockholm: Swedish International Development Authority (SIDA).

Shaw, A. 1977. 'Foreign language syllabus development: some recent approaches'. *Language Teaching and Linguistics Abstracts* 10: 217–33.

Shiva, V. 1989. *Staying Alive: Women, Ecology and Development*. London: Zed Books.

Simon, R. 1987. 'Empowerment as a pedagogy of possibility.' *Language Arts* 64: 370–83.

Skutnabb-Kangas, T. and Cummins, J. (eds) 1988. *Minority Education: from Shame to Struggle*. Clevedon: Multilingual Matters.

Skutnabb-Kangas, T and Phillipson, R. 1994. *Linguistic Human Rights: Overcoming Linguistic Discrimination*. Berlin: Mouton de Gruyter.

Smyth, J. 1989. 'When teachers theorise in their practice: a reflexive approach to a distance education course.' In T. Evans and D. Nation (eds) *Critical Reflections on Distance Education*. Lewes: The Falmer Press.

Snell, R. *et al.* 1987. 'Beyond distance teaching towards open learning.' In V.E. Hodgson, S.J. Mann and R. Snell (eds) *Beyond Distance Teaching, Towards Open Learning*. Milton Keynes: Society for Research into Higher Education/Open University Press.

Soper, K. 1993. Review of L. Doyal and I. Gough (1991) *A Theory of Human Need* (London: Macmillan) In *New Left Review* 197.

Soyinka, W. 1994. 'Bloodsoaked quilt of Africa.' Interview in *The Guardian*, 17 May, p.20.

Stenhouse, L. 1975. *An Introduction to Curriculum Research and Development*. London: Heinemann.

Strevens, P. 1981. 'Training the teacher of foreign languages: new responsibilities require new patterns of training.' *Canadian Modern Language Review* 37/3.

Swales, J. 1971. *Writing Scientific English*. London: Nelson.

Thomas, F. 1891. *The History and Prospects of British Education in India*. Cambridge: Deighton Bell.

Tickoo, M.L. 1992. 'Realistic goals and manageable means: a phenomenon examined.' *English – a World Language* 1/1: 51–9.

Trim, L.J.M. 1973. 'Draft outline of a European unit/credit system for modern language learning by adults'. In Trim *et al.* 1980.

Trim, L.J.M., Richterich, R., van Ek, J.A., and Wilkins, D.A. 1980. *Systems Development in Adult Language Learning.* Oxford: Pergamon.

Unesco, 1953. *The Use of the Vernacular Languages in Education.* Paris: Unesco.

Unesco, 1989. *Qualities Required of Education Today to Meet Foreseeable Demands in the Twenty-First Century. (Final Report of International Symposium and Round Table, Beijing. 22 November–2 December, 1989.)* Paris: Unesco.

Unesco, 1991. *World Education Report.* Paris: Unesco.

Underhill, A. 1989. 'Process in humanistic education' *English Language Teaching Journal* 43/4: 250–60.

van Ek, J.A. 1973. 'The "Threshold Level" in a unit/credit system'. In Trim *et al.* 1980.

van Ek, J.A. 1976. *The Threshold Level for Modern Language Learning in Schools.* London: Longman/Council of Europe.

Verhelst, T.G. 1990. *No Life without Roots: Culture and Development.* London: Zed Books.

Wallace, M. 1991. *Training Foreign Language Teachers.* Cambridge: Cambridge University Press.

West, R. 1994. State of the art article: 'Needs analysis in language teaching.' *Language Teaching* 27/1:1–19.

Widdowson, H. 1978. *Teaching Language as Communication.* Oxford: Oxford University Press.

Widdowson, H. 1983. *Learning Purpose and Language Use.* Oxford: Oxford University Press.

Wilkins, D.A. 1973. 'The linguistic and situational content of the common core in a unit/credit system'. In Trim *et al.* 1980.

Wilkins, D.A. 1976. *Notional Syllabuses.* Oxford: Oxford University Press.

Willis, J. 1981. 'The training of non-native-speaker teachers of English: a new approach'. In British Council *ELT Documents* 110: 41–53.

Wilson, P. and Harrison, I. 1983. 'Materials design in Africa with particular reference to the Francophone Primary School Project, Cameroon'. In British Council *ELT Documents* 116: 29–49.

Wiseman, S. and Pidgeon, D. 1970. *Curriculum Evaluation.* Slough: The National Foundation for Education Research in England and Wales.

Woodward, T. 1991. *Models and Metaphors in Language Teacher Training.* Cambridge: Cambridge University Press.

Woodward, T. 1996. 'Paradigm shift and the language teaching profession'. In Willis, J. and Willis, D. (eds) *Challenge and Change in Language Teaching.* Oxford: Heinemann 4–9.

World Bank, 1991. *The Challenge of Development (World Development Report).* Oxford & New York: Oxford University Press for World Bank.

Zwingmann, C. and Gunn, A. 1983. *Uprooting and Health: Psycho-social Problems of Students from Abroad.* Geneva: World Health Organisation (Division of Mental Health).